Crime Stories

50 More Crime Stories

Selected By
Robert Weinberg,
Stefan R. Dziemianowicz,
& Martin H. Greenberg

GOODWILL PUBLISHING HOUSE™
B-3, RATTAN JYOTI, 18, RAJENDRA PLACE, NEW DELHI-110008 (INDIA)
TEL.: 25750801, 25755519, 25820556 FAX : 91-11-25763428

© by Robert Weinberg

All Rights Reserved.

This special low priced Indian reprint is published by arrangement with Sterling Publishing Company, Inc. New York, U.S.A.

No part of this publication may be reproduced; stored in a retrieval system or transmitted in any form or by any means, mechanical, photocopying or otherwise without prior written permission of the publisher.

Published in India by
GOODWILL PUBLISHING HOUSE™
B-3 Rattan Jyoti,18 Rajendra Place
New Delhi-110008 (INDIA)
Tel. : 25750801, 25755519, 25820556
Fax : 91-11-25763428
E-mail : goodwillpub@vsnl.net
website : www.goodwillpublishinghouse.com

Printed at :-
Sanjeev Offset Press

CONTENTS

Introduction ix

Last Laugh 1
Lix Agrabee

Let Nature Take Its Corpse 5
C. William Harrison

The Letters of Halpin Chalmers 12
Peter Cannon

The Man of The Knife 17
Alexandre Dumas

Many Happy Returns 24
Justin Case

Marked in Red 30
Ralph Powers

A Matter of Proof 38
Grover Brinkman

Mind Over Mayhem 41
Mack Reynolds

Mine Host-The Ghost 45
Costa Carousso

Motive 53
August Derleth

Murder in Bronze 57
Herbert L. McNary

Mushrooms   62
Chet Williamson

New Blood   72
Gary Lovisi

Nimble Fingers   75
W. Ryerson Johnson

No Flowers for Henry   79
Carl Hughes

Nobody, That's Who   87
William F. Nolan

Numb   91
Wayne A. Harold

On a Dark October   95
Joe R. Lansdale

One Man's Poison   99
Curt Hamlin

The Pigeon Drop   104
Michael A. Black

A Quarter for Crazy Eddie   110
Will Murray

The Raffle   116
Wayne D. Dundee

A Real Nice Guy   127
William F. Nolan

Red Runs The Tide   137
John P. Foran

The Red Sail   142
Lester Dent

A Retrieved Reformation   146
O. Henry

Sacrifice   153
C. J. Henderson

The Sapient Monkey   156
Headon Hill

Side Door To Hell   164
Cyril Plunkett

The Silver Protector   171
Ellis Parker Butler

The Slave-Maker   177
Edgar Wallace

Some Jobs Are Simple   187
Chet Williamson

Strictly Accidental   191
Morgan Talbot

Sudden Violence   199
Robert Petyo

Switch   205
Gerald Tollesfrud

The Tell - Tale Heart   210
Edgar Allan Poe

Terror's Night   215
I. R. Austin

Thaxton's Call   221
Jack Dolphin

They Tell No Tales   226
Francis Chase, Jr.

Till Death Do Us Part   229
Dana McGuire

The Time Is Now!   238
Dorothy Dunn

To The Point 243
Hugh B. Cave

Turnabout 246
Colby Quinn

Two Must Die! 251
Ric Hasse

Untimely Visitor 258
John Bender

A Valentine from Teacher 263
Jim Knapp

The White Square 273
Everett M. Webber

Whitemail 280
Joyce Kilmer

Whose Turn Is It? 287
C. J. Henderson

The Witch's Way 293
Joseph Shallit

Introduction

How long does it take to plot and commit a serious crime? According to the stories collected in *50 More Crime stories*, no more than ten minutes. Celebrating the fascination with a subject that has grown into one of the most popular genres in contemporary fiction, we present the reader with 50 tales of crime and suspense in the short-short-story form, the type of tale conducive to clever crimes and cleverer solutions.

The selections span more than 200 years and encompass virtually every story type known in the genre: the puzzle tale in Alexandre Dumas's "The Man of the Knife," the classic detective story in Headon Hill's "The Sapient Monkey," the modern hard-boiled story in Joe R. Lansdale's "The Job," the police procedural in Gerald Tollesfrud's "Switch," and the *noir* thriller in Ernest Leong's "Incense Sticks." The police blotter of crimes investigated includes fratricide in Allen Beck's "Always Together," embezzlement in Ferenc Molnár's "The Best Policy," serial murder in Gary Lovisi's "New Blood," swindling in Michael A. Black's "The Pigeon Drop," kidnapping in Edgar Wallace's "The Slave-Maker," bigamy in Joyce Kilmer's "Whitemail," drive-by shootings in Dane Gregory's "Jackie Won't Be Home," the ever-reliable homicide in Chet Williamson's "First Kill," and a crime so bizarre in Geoffrey Vace's "The Hard-Luck Kid" that it hasn't yet got a name by which it can be described.

Readers who enjoy their crimes "straight" will find that the lion's share of these stories take a hard-nosed approach to their subjects. For those who enjoy a respite from the often-grim chore of seeing criminals brought to bay, several stories offer laughter as the only possible solution to their predicaments. In all, the contents of *50 More Crime Stories* show that petty crooks are not the only criminals dealt with in the short-short crime story.

—*Stefan Dziemianowicz*
New York

LAST LAUGH

LIX AGRABEE

It's the damnedest joke. I'm going to die laughing. . . .
Ella is little and soft and plump, and her mouth was crushed velvet under mine. I was crazy about her, and I couldn't believe my luck when she actually consented to keep house for me. Funny thing—even as I watch her leaning there against the table, blowing perfumed cigarette smoke into my perspiring face, I can't say I'm really sorry for any of it. It was worth it while it lasted. After a lifetime of Emily, Ella was worth it. It's like trying to live with a gaunt, spitting old alley cat, then having a silky, purring Persian to pet.

You don't see women like Ella in hayseed towns like this one very often. Usually they marry young, enchanted by a haystack, a full moon and some young farmer. Or they go off to the big city. Or run off with a traveling salesman who eventually runs out on them.

I could hardly sleep nights for thinking about her after she came to spend a vacation at old lady Harkinson's boarding house, though I did wonder why in the world she had picked Orrinville. It's not even one of those picturesque post-card villages one reads about in travel books and such.

I know now why she came here, but I didn't then.

I don't think anyone in town was surprised when they heard that Emily had picked up and walked to Blorr Junction, caught the train and left me, as she'd always threatened to do. I think, too, that they were secretly pleased when they found out she'd gone. Don't get me wrong. They all liked me, but there wasn't a soul who could deny the hatred they had for Emily. She caused more trouble with her tongue than you could believe possible, created eternal friction with her spiteful gossip and general vindictiveness, and broke up at least two homes that I know of. So that I think there was a sigh of relief, and perhaps a prayer of thanksgiving for my sake.

"Don't know how you ever stood her," Tom McCracken said to me on Main Street. "Beggin' your pardon, but she were a mean, cantankerous person, weren't she?"

"Oh, well, it takes all kinds, you know Tom," I said feebly. It didn't seem right to say anything against her.

"Hear tell that Widder Stone at the boarding house has her eye on you." He grinned, smirking just a trifle to show his man-of-the-world status and his complete understanding.

"Well, I can't very well think of getting married again, can I? I'm not free."

"Who said anything about getting married?" Tom cackled, spewing a stream of tobacco juice to the side of the boardwalk. "Maybe she'd like to come keep house for you." He winked with pleasure. "Gus Larsen gets away with it, even if the Ladies Aid don't like it. After all, they can't prove nothin', can they? Man's got a right to keep a housekeeper, ain't he?"

So after a while Ella Stone came to keep house. Everybody in town took a sort of sneaking joy out of it, remembering nosy Emily and her spiced tongue and the years of nagging misery she'd put me through.

I'm not kicking about the way things turned out. As I say, it was worth it while it lasted. Even at the beginning I couldn't understand why Ella with the gleaming hair—though after a while I noticed it was dark at the roots—and the dimpled satin hands, saw anything in me, taciturn, hardbitten Lute Brown. She wasn't extravagant. Even when she discovered the box where years of savings had accumulated, she didn't beg for pretty things and such stuff. Of course, there was method in her madness. But I never guessed, never dreamed.

I thought my breakfast coffee tasted a mite bitter, but Ella curled up on my knee, nuzzling my neck like a playful kitten, running her hands through my sparse gray hair and—well, I'd have swallowed hemlock without noticing anything much out of the ordinary about it.

Then the pains began. I dismissed them for a while, but when they got so bad I couldn't get off the living room couch, I told Ella she'd better get old Doc Bradley to come up and see me.

Her eyes went wide. "Honey-pet—is it really that bad? Here, darling, perhaps a massage will make the nasty old pains go away."

But I was in agony. Soon I moved away from the smooth little hand that was caressing my body so gently. "Afraid I'll have to have the doctor, Ella. Go see if he's around."

She went out, and the minutes ticked away. I staggered to the window to see if they were coming, fell in a crumpled heap on the floor, then managed to pull myself up again. For a second I didn't know what to think. There she was, sitting in the frayed old hammock between the oak trees, a cigarette going at intervals in her full, pouting mouth, a dull curl of smoke twisting around a scarlet-tipped finger, a sandaled foot swinging free and accentuating the curve of a silken leg.

I hung there, doubled up. It was impossible for me to go for help. It was too late for that. It was too late for a lot of things. I saw everything, understood everything. I saw why a woman of her sort would come to a little town, where it is comparatively easy to become friendly enough to pick up a good thing when you see it. She'd be very comfortable with me out of the way. But—how did she expect to get away with it?

I guess she saw me there, for she came to her feet with a satisfied smile, ground the cigarette out beneath her toe, and sauntered in. She was safe. It was too late for me to do anything for myself, or to her. She knew it, and she knew I knew it.

"How you feeling now, Lute?" Perfectly relaxed, I thought wonderingly. She sounded as though this were old stuff to her, to get mixed up with an old fellow, then get rid of him for what she could get out of it.

And so it was I found out. Sitting on the edge of the table she told me about herself, smoking, watching me with waiting eyes, just as though we were simply trying to pass the time away. She had lived on a farm in an isolated area within a hundred and fifty miles of Orrinville. . . .

"I got damn sick of having nothing—no nice clothes, no fun, no nothing. . . ." So she had conceived the idea that she had so successfully carried into execution. "You're the third old gaffer I've done business with—after all, these are extended business trips and nothing more," she said, laughing in indulgent amusement at herself. "This is the last time though. I've enough now to keep myself in all the luxuries I want for the rest of my life. Thanks, Lute, for how you've helped me."

How did she get away with it? Simple. "I took them—I'll take you—back with me. You'll just disappear, and so will I, as far as Orrinville is concerned."

How would she take me back? "I'm not so foolish as not to have that all planned out," she gurgled, delighted at her own cleverness. "I'll do what I've done before—it's a cinch I couldn't leave you here. If there's no body, no evidence of foul play, and, most important, no suspicion of it, everyone will take it for granted we left town, and no one will wonder over much."

"But—but how," I gasped. I was in a tortured agony, but that iron will of mine kept me going until I could straighten this fantastic maze out. Ella! Silly, giggling, delicious Ella—a professional murderess! "Bury me?"

She seemed irritated by my thick-headedness. "Don't be foolish—how could I do that? There isn't a minute when some nosy busybody isn't watching this house, titillated by what they all suspect is true, but can't prove! Bury you? How could I here? Back home, there's any number of places for that, where you could never be found. But here? Hah! And it's a sure thing that there's no place in this house for me to get rid of you."

Her satisfied smile grew until it was a genuine laugh. She was inflated by her own ego. Are all murderers like that? Do they think they can get away with it? Because, of course, I see now, it simply can't be done.

"I'm going to put you in that huge iron-bound trunk up there at the back of that smelly attic of yours. I discovered it one day when I was hunting around to see if I could avoid buying a trunk—that's a dangerous thing to have to do. I'll take no other luggage, so there'll be no suspicion aroused, and in an hour Tom can take me to Blodd Junction—he's already promised. By tonight you'll be sleeping in a permanent bed—far away from Orrinville. There'll be nothing here to show—"

She was gabbling away with the details, but I wasn't listening. Her eyes widened as I started to laugh. Even with the wracking pains, it still sounded like a laugh—a groaning, horrible caricature of a laugh.

I can't help it. It's the damnedest joke I ever heard. And I am, I really am, going to die laughing. You see, she's not going to be able to get me in the trunk. Emily's in there now.

LET NATURE TAKE ITS CORPSE

C. WILLIAM HARRISON

Eph knew a stranger was coming to camp half an hour before the man made his appearance. Knowing this required no great amount of intellectual discernment. As a matter of fact there were many times when you could ask Eph what state he lived in, and he would have been at a loss to give the correct answer. Some of the local wags have replied that Eph lived in a state of constant confusion. Which was not entirely wrong, at that.

In the hazy recesses of Eph's brain there was no room for complicated problems. When he needed food he prepared it as simply and easily as possible. When he needed sleep, he slept.

And when the crows clamored over around Turkey ridge, as they just had a few minutes ago, it meant a stranger was at the edge of the swamp. It had always been so, and Eph never questioned it—or worried about it. It had to be a stranger because Professor Carthage was too woods-wise to cause such a disturbance among the crows. It was as simple as that.

He paused briefly to listen to the crows, and then returned stolidly to his work of pulling a few of the weeds out of his small garden patch.

His crude shack and scrubby garden were on a low knoll that thrust up from the swamp, and all round him down below were murky waters and treacherous stretches of marsh. He worked thoughtlessly at his weeding. He had never bothered to do this before, but the Professor had said his cabbage and turnips and tomatoes would grow better if the weeds were removed. So Eph unquestioningly pulled weeds.

A chicken hawk rose suddenly out of the underbrush near the lightning-scarred beech tree, and so Eph knew the stranger was coming into the swamp. The trail, as thin and uncertain as a shadow, passed near the foot of the beech, and no stranger to the swamp could have found or followed that crooked path without help. Therefore Eph knew Professor Carthage was with the stranger, guiding him to Eph's camp.

The two men came out of the marsh and approached the knoll on which was Eph's shack. Eph watched them indifferently. In his vague way he liked the little professor, and equally vaguely he resented the intrusion of the stranger.

Professor Carthage was a small thin man with thick white hair and a surprisingly deep voice. He slipped the bulging pack-sack from his narrow shoulders.

"Forage for the human animal, Eph. Bacon, flour, beans—manna from Morganville, and enough to last us a week." But he wasn't a man to give more than fragmentary interest to food. He waved his ever-present butterfly net.

"Caught this fellow on that hummock east of Bear Wallow. A beauty, Eph, an exceptionally fine specimen of the *Euproctis chrysorrhoea.*"

Eph squinted through the close-meshed netting. "Ha?"

"Browntail Moth, to you," Professor Carthage said.

A thought struggled through the placid waters of Eph's mind. "You write Miz Carthage in town, Professor?"

The little man said with amused severity, "I told you to remind me to write my wife *before* I left for town, not after I got back."

Eph shook his big head uncertainly. "I guess I must've forgot."

Professor Carthage smiled. "But I didn't. I wrote the letter, and now Mrs. Carthage will feel confident I'm in my hotel room writing a profound paper on the caterpillars native to the north-central states. She'd have a hemorrhage if she knew where I really am. She thinks my health can't stand hunting specimens in a swamp."

He seemed to remember for the first time the stranger he had brought into the swamp with him.

He said, "Eph, this is Mr. Johnson. I met him in town, and he asked me to bring him here. He wants to hire you to dig some peat moss for him."

Johnson was not tall, but there was a suggestion of toughness and leashed energy in his compact shape. He stood somewhat back from Professor Carthage, and he didn't smile when he was introduced. He had quick dark eyes that were strangely humid in their restlessness; his mouth was thin and long.

Eph thrust out his hand. "H'lo."

Johnson didn't seem to see his hand. Eph let it sag uncertainly to his side.

Johnson said, "Quite a place you've got here. I don't imagine you have many visitors."

Eph considered this dully. Professor Carthage said with a chuckle, "Not in this swamp. I imagine I'm the first visitor Eph ever had out here. With the exception of you, of course."

A shadowy thought suggested to Eph that Johnson seemed oddly pleased with this information. But it was a thought that slid into Eph's mind and out again without leaving a mark.

He said, "You want to buy peat moss, ha?"

"Yeah." But the man's eyes were on the thin strand of wire stretching across the shingle roof of Eph's shack. "You got a radio here?"

"Ha?"

"A radio?"

"Uh-huh." Eph thought the man seemed displeased by this information. "But the batteries are dead, and it ain't much good."

A faint smile traced the stranger's thin mouth. "That's too bad." But he didn't seem to think it was too bad.

"The batteries went dead last night," Eph said. "You like radios, Mr. Johnson?"

"Sure."

"I like radios too. I like to hear music on them."

Mr. Johnson looked at Professor Carthage, and winked. "I like music, too." He seemed to think something was funny, and Eph couldn't understand it.

Eph said, "Last night the music was pretty. Then the music stopped and some feller said something about a bank or postoffice being robbed up around—I don't rightly remember what town it was."

"Greenfield," Professor Carthage said.

Eph was unaccountably disturbed by some quality in Johnson's dry question. "You know about that holdup?"

"Just what I read in the papers while I was in town this morning."

Eph wished the stranger would go away. He felt more at ease when he was alone or with Professor Carthage. There was something about this stranger that made Eph feel as he did when he sensed the danger of quicksand out in the swamp. He didn't know what made him feel that way. He just wished the stranger was gone.

Johnson's softness asked, "What did you read about that holdup?"

Professor Carthage was bent, rummaging in the sack. "The usual newspaper account. A bandit held up the Greenfield bank yesterday afternoon. He killed the teller, and got away with an undetermined amount of cash. Before the teller died, he described the crook as medium tall, well dressed, and using a gun with a broken butt plate. The killer was believed to have fled in this direction."

The Professor found what he was looking for, a greasy brown-paper sack. He looked at Eph. "Where's Skipper? I brought him some bones."

Eph grinned broadly. "Skip like bones." He waved his big hand vaguely in the direction of the swamp. "Skip's out there someplace. Huntin', I guess." He pursed his lips, and sent a whistle echoing through the marshes.

It was just a little terrier with muddy feet and burr-tangled hair. The dog came bounding up the knoll, saw the stranger, and began barking challengingly. Johnson put his hand in his coat pocket.

Eph said, "Skip's all right. He ain't never bit nobody, and he don't see no strangers out here. Just let him sniff you, Mr. Johnson, and he'll be all right."

Johnson swore gratingly. "I don't like dogs. Keep him away."

Eph said, "He likes to play big, Skip does. But he won't bite, mister."

The dog walked stiff-legged toward the stranger, hackles raised, growling out his challenge. Johnson's hand came out of his pocket, gripping a blued automatic by its barrel. He bent and lunged toward the dog with sudden violence. His hand raised, and whipped down. The terrier yelped only once. The gun butt clubbed down again.

The stranger straightened and spun, holding his gun level. "I told you to call him off," he said harshly. "I don't like dogs."

Professor Carthage was looking at the broken butt plate on the automatic. He raised his eyes. "Why—why, you're that murderer!"

The killer's laugh was a raw thing. "That makes you know too much, pop." His dark eyes were humid with mockery. "It ain't good to know too much about a guy the cops are hunting, pop. I suppose you're going to turn me in now."

Professor Carthage was a mild little man whose world of science had not prepared him for the cruel realities of the civilization he lived in. To him crime was a thing to be read about and deplored but which never came into his personal life.

He should have been afraid, but he wasn't. He was a harmless little man who didn't know enough about the realities of life to be afraid. He should have known the futility of trying to get away. But he didn't.

"Indeed I shall report you, sir!"

He went down the weedy slope of the knoll, a small man hurrying to bring justice to a wanted murderer. He didn't once glance back over his shoulder. It didn't occur to him that such things as violence and murder could ever touch him.

He started along the narrow path that bridged the swamp waters, and it was there that the bullet struck him between his shoulders. He fell face down in the stagnant water and didn't move.

What had happened was slow sinking into the hazy depths of Eph's brain. When realization finally came full and strong into him, he could show only a simple man's childlike resentment.

"You killed my Skip, and he never hurt anybody in his life." He put his dull eyes on the murderer. "You killed Professor Carthage, and he was good to Eph. You shouldn't ought to have done that, mister."

He brought up his huge hands. He said heavily, "Now Eph will kill you. Eph never hurt anybody before, but Eph is going to make you dead."

The killer said with brittle harshness. "You big ox, I've got the gun, see! You try anything with me, I'll put a slug in your guts. You're big, but you're not bigger than a bullet. Get that into your thick head, and don't forget it."

Slow-dawning realization of danger halted Eph's advance. But fear never got to him. He looked at his big hands, and he looked at the killer, and a crafty light stirred sluggishly in his resenting eyes.

Johnson said corrosively, "We're going to stay here in this camp, just you and me. You're going to cook meals, if you know enough to cook, and if you ever try to slip away I'm going to put a bullet in your stomach. No one will ever look for me here, and I'm staying until the pressure is off."

Eph said heavily, "Sometime Eph is going to make you dead like Skip and Professor Carthage. You just wait and see, mister."

Eph made his break the next morning. There was no great cunning in what he did. He walked out of his shack, the killer following him warily. He paused at the crest of the knoll where he had dug the graves for Skipper and Professor Carthage. He paused to gaze down at the fresh-turned earth, the dim recesses of his mind awed by the swiftness with which death can replace life. He wished he could hear Skip's excited barking again when he treed a 'possum. He wished he could again see Professor Carthage's slight shape prowling through the swamp trails after an elusive butterfly for his collection.

Behind him the killer said, "The same thing can happen to you, pal-o. Keep that tucked away in whatever you use for a brain."
Eph turned heavily. "You wouldn't kill Eph. You say you would, but you wouldn't."
"Just try me and see, pal-o."
"Only big Eph knows the trail out of the swamp. You make Eph dead and you can't get out alone."
Johnson said malevolently, "I'd rather rot in here than let you bring the cops in after me." He showed his gun, and the tawny glint of danger was in his dark eyes. "Get back to the shack, dumbo."
"Eph wants to walk."
The big man turned his back on the gun. He went down the knoll's slope, and moved onto the path that bridged dark stagnant water. The killer followed, silently watchful.
The sun rays had been bitter on the shadeless knoll, but here beneath the green roof of the swamp trees it was quite cool. The air was stale and clogged with the heavy wetness of the marshes, and the dank smell of decay was everywhere. Turtles, disturbed by the passing of the two men, slid down muddy banks into the stagnant waters, and somewhere not far away a bird ribboned the silence with its raucous cry.
"Any snakes in here?"
"Copperheads and moccasins."
Johnson's eyes narrowed. "So that's your pitch! You're hoping you can walk me around in here until I get snake bit. It won't work, dumbo. We're going back."
Eph kept walking.
Johnson said harshly, "I said we're going back, damn you!"
Eph's walking had carried a low-hanging limb with him, and suddenly he released it. The branch lashed Johnson's face, and he heard the sound of the big man's heavy running. He cursed savagely, broke clear of the limbs, and jerked up his gun.

He fired, and saw Eph stumble. But the big man kept running. Johnson broke into a run. Limbs clawed at him, and he fought through tangles of brush, goaded on by the red lust to kill.
He fired again, and knew his bullet had found its mark in Eph's leg, but he couldn't stop the big man. Eph's direction changed sharply, turning his flight across a low grassy knoll. Johnson fired again, but he hurried his shot and missed. He sprinted on to the knoll.
"You damn fool, you can't get away!"

Even the dim working of Eph's mind must have told the big man that. But he kept running heavily, limping and weakened by hurt. The knoll ended on a cutbank, and there was water beyond, broken a short distance out by a narrow spit of sand. Another island lay past that.

Ephs' leap overshot the sand spit, and he splashed heavily in the muddy water. He slogged on toward the island.

The killer ran to the edge of the cutbank. He shouted harshly, "I've got one more bullet left in this gun, but I've got plenty more back at camp. Come back here, damn you. You ain't got a chance to get away now."

Eph kept moving on.

"Then I'll come after you," Johnson swore.

The sand spit curled like a bent finger jutting out from the island. Johnson leaped for the sand, and his judgment of the distance was good. It was too good.

The killer struck the sand, but there was nothing dry and solid to it. It seemed to melt away as he touched it, and he plunged to his hips in loose, heavy wetness. He cursed and struggled with swift panic plunging through his brain.

"For God's sake, man, do something! Pull me out of here."

"You made my Skip dead, Mister Johnson. You shouldn't ought to have done that."

"I'll give you enough money to buy a dozen dogs. Get something and pull me out."

"You made Professor Carthage dead, Mister Johnson."

The offer of money could not argue against big Eph's simple condemnation. The gritty wetness was rising across the killer's chest, swiftly and inexorably toward his shoulders, his neck, his face.

He leveled his gun on big Eph. "Damn you, I'll kill you! I've got one more bullet in this gun. I'll put it through your guts if you don't help me!"

But Eph did not move. And the killer did not shoot. He had only one more bullet in his gun, and he could not wait until the quicksand locked all air from his lungs.

Only one more bullet, and the killer could not wait. . . .

THE LETTERS OF HALPIN CHALMERS

PETER CANNON

"I'm glad you've come," said Ida Carstairs. She was sitting by the window beneath the pagoda-shaped bird cage, her face nuzzled by Max, her pet conure. Little had changed in the three years since I had last stopped in, to pick them up for the drive to the Halpin Chalmers centennial conference. About the cluttered living room, displayed on walls or tables, were the dusty souvenirs and tattered testimonials I had come to know over countless visits, the tokens of a long career that had brought its share of recognition but limited financial gain. If anything the place looked tidier and neater than in the past, thanks to the current services of a series of home attendants—and of course emptier. When earlier in the month I had seen the obituary in the *Partridgeville Gazette*, I had decided that it was time to put aside our differences, that I should pay my respects to the widow.

And then there were the letters, the letters of Halpin Chalmers to his best friend, Fred Carstairs, to whom he wrote almost daily during his prolific Brooklyn period. Having recently received the contract for the first critical biography (provisionally titled *Secret Watcher: The Life and Strange Death of Halpin Chalmers*), I was determined at long last to lay my hands on these priceless epistles from the pen of America's foremost author of the occult.

"I knew you'd come, Peter," said Ida Carstairs. "Please sit down." She gestured at Fred's old wheelchair.

For a woman in her late eighties Ida was in remarkably good shape, as strong in body as her husband had been frail. With no sign of strain she rose and lifted Max off her shoulder and into his cage.

"Fred's last months were very difficult," she said. "After he got out of the hospital he wouldn't let anyone touch him. And his language! Such words I had never heard out of his mouth before. He was no longer my sweet little Fredela."

I had known that Fred had been hospitalized, that for a time he had even been placed in the psycho ward.

"His pain wasn't just physical, Peter. 'Why doesn't anyone come see me?' he'd cry. 'I'm so lonely.' "

Why indeed? Why didn't the fans—and certainly Fred had his own followers, apart from those who cared only about his connection with his more illustrious friend—line up at his bedside to comfort him in his final days? Partridgeville may be off the beaten track, but I believed it when she said no one came. The sad truth is they stayed away, we all stayed away, because of her.

"He was so unworldly, my beloved," she said, mercifully not mentioning my own neglect of Fred, "like Prince Myshkin in Dostoyevsky's *The Idiot*."

As fond as she genuinely was of her late husband, in my experience she could never stand him getting all the attention, even if that attention was motivated out of a regard more for the occult tales of Halpin Chalmers than for the occult tales of Fred Carstairs. I alone of the Chalmersians recognized that the key to Fred lay through Ida. I alone knew of the existence of the Chalmers letters, secreted in a musty old trunk I had managed to inspect in Fred's bedroom while pretending to go to the bathroom during one of my earlier visits. So over the years I listened for hours to her wild and fantastic stories of her glamorous youth on the stage and to her grandiose dreams of future travels and triumphs, if only to gain a few minutes with Fred—who might if I was lucky drop a fresh, precious nugget or two concerning Halpin Chalmers all those decades ago.

But I could take only so much. My patience ran out in 1991, the year of the Chalmers centennial. I had written Ida a letter politely suggesting that she stay home while I drove Fred to Brooklyn to be the guest of honor at the 100th-birthday celebration weekend. But she didn't take the hint. She had insisted on going too—with her parrot. Those who attended need not be reminded how her antics (and those of her bird) on more than one occasion disrupted the proceedings. She defied me. She had to pay the price. As a consequence I ceased my visits to Fred. I refused to return her phone calls.

"You know, Peter, Fred and I were not all that well matched. My friends, people in the theatre, wondered what I saw in him. He was so shy. At parties he hardly said anything."

As a matter of fact, he hadn't said a whole lot at the centenary either, apart from parroting the same tired anecdotes about Chalmers he'd been repeating for more than sixty years, ever since his fellow author's premature death in 1928. His semi-senile performance there should have been Fred's last bow. No one had expected the venerable occultist to reach his own century or beyond. (While the obituary had reported he died at 100, he was really 101, having shaved a year off his age at some point in his career. To one correspondent Chalmers clearly states that his boyhood pal was born in 1893, not 1894.) But he astonished everyone by surviving another three years. In the meantime, I concentrated on producing shorter critical works for *Chalmers Studies* and other learned journals, knowing that sooner or later I would get my chance at the letters in Fred Carstairs' trunk.

The Chalmers letters to Carstairs! What a trove! A few teasing extracts, a mere fraction of the total, had been published in the *Collected Letters of Halpin Chalmers*. Literally hundreds of virgin pages had yet to meet the feasting eyes of the Chalmers scholar. Why hadn't their recipient sold them? In his declining years, before he fell and couldn't leave their Central Square apartment, Fred had consigned other items in his occult collection to a local secondhand bookdealer, including his copy of *The Secret Watcher*, inscribed by Chalmers himself. I know; I was the one who had picked up this treasure at a price so enviable I forbear from citing the figure. Had he tried to sell off the letters, whether piecemeal or as a lot, my informant, the proprietor of the Angell Hill Bookshop, would have alerted me immediately.

As much as he could have used the money, did Fred deliberately keep the Chalmers letters to himself out of spite? Whenever I hinted at their existence, he pretended not to understand. In face of such coyness I decided early on not to push the matter, instead to adopt a waiting policy, hoping to gain his confidence and eventually the prize that would secure my own name as the world's leading authority on Halpin Chalmers.

"Nobody knew he was a writer. He certainly didn't dress like one. Let me tell you, Peter, before he broke his hip he used to go out in that shabby coat of his and do the shopping. When he sat down to rest, strangers would put a dollar in his hand, thinking he was a homeless person! Can you imagine, Fred Carstairs, the great occult author, mistaken for a homeless person!"

If it can be said that Chalmers died before his time, then Carstairs lived beyond his time—long after his time. At his death Chalmers was at the peak of his powers. His posthumously published work established his reputation as the supreme practitioner of the genre. His heirs are rich today from the royalties generated by the millions of copies of his books still in print. On the other hand, Carstairs in his prime never achieved more than a workmanlike competence. In his old age he was honored more for his longevity than for any lasting contributions to the field. During the occult resurgence of the late 1960s and 1970s he enjoyed a revival of sorts, but by the 1980s and early 1990s he could expect only the rare anthology appearance, or possibly a foreign rights sale, to supplement the monthly social security checks that supported him and his wife and their bird in their golden years.

To be fair to Fred, he could be perfectly candid about his own lack of genius relative to his best friend's. One has only to read that sketchy, rambling, error-riddled, if often charming memoir of his, written in his dotage, *Halpin Chalmers: Voyager of Other and Many Dimensions,* to appreciate the man's modesty. And yet, and yet, there must have been times when he deeply resented his old friend—when the interviewers, their indifference to Fred Carstairs only too evident, asked him just one question too many about Halpin Chalmers.

"He lived in this dump of a town all his life and they completely ignored him. But Fred's big-shot celebrity-author friend, that turd, they named for him that fancy housing development in Mulligan Wood!"

Both writers had grown up in Partridgeville, but Chalmers had left that provincial New England city and settled in Brooklyn, to compose the masterpieces on which his fame rests today. As for Carstairs, he had remained in Partridgeville, where nothing newsworthy had occurred since the death of Halpin Chalmers, brutally and mysteriously murdered at age thirty-seven during a short homecoming sojourn. Fred, in fact, had been the last person to see him alive, though he had apparently been no more illuminating when questioned by the police at the time than in 1976 when I first queried him on the subject. (To another correspondent Chalmers records his frustration over his friend's tendency to mix things up— a tendency that did not improve with age.) This was soon after I moved to Partridgeville, where I had been quite fortunate to find a one-bedroom condo in the then newly erected Halpin Chalmers Estates.

"Occult writers, bah! Such people—no class, no culture," Ida continued. "But what did I know? It was only a month after we met that we decided to elope."

Fred and Ida had married late in life, after a brief courtship in New York, he for the first time, she for the fourth or fifth (she was always vague about how many husbands she'd had). Fred had brought his bride back to Partridgeville, a place that she grew to despise and that she loved to abuse almost as much as occult writers. But I had heard the story of their tragicomic marriage a thousand times before. I could care less, especially now. All that mattered was obtaining the letters. At the next pause in the monologue I excused myself and headed down the hall.

Proceeding past the bathroom door I entered Fred's dank, curtained bedroom, hoping to find it unchanged since my last snooping expedition. It was in one essential: the ancient trunk still rested at the foot of the bed. While feigning to listen to Ida, I had conceived a plan—to remove the letters a bundle at a time, to slip them into my jacket or the bookbag I habitually carried. In the coming weeks and months I would visit Ida regularly. I was forgiven; we were, after all, friends again. I wished I had thought of this expedient long before, and wondered at my past scruples. But time had not seemed of the essence, until I received permission from the Chalmers estate for the biography—which would be a lesser thing without ample quotations from the Chalmers letters to Carstairs. I didn't want to disappoint the heirs.

From the living room I could hear Ida conferring heatedly, in French, with the Haitian home attendant. The moment had come to act. As before, no lock secured the rusty clasp of the trunk. My heart in my mouth, I raised the lid. There was the same stale, musty odor I remembered, though somewhat less pungent than previously. I could dimly see—I could see nothing! Or rather, almost nothing. On the bottom lay a few scattered sheets. I seized an envelope, and as I peered closely at the familiar handwritten scrawl, behind me I heard a squawk.

I turned and saw Ida in the doorway, her pet parrot on her shoulder.

"We knew you wanted those letters, Peter. Fred and I often talked about it. It was so obvious. My little 'idiot' said he was going to reward you for your kindness by leaving you the letters after he died. It was to be a surprise. But then, for no good reason, after that horrible trip to Brooklyn, you stopped coming. Then Fredela got ill and I tried to call you and you still wouldn't come. You, the most faithful and loyal of all the Chal*merde*sians!"

I made no apologies. All I could do was stammer something about the letters and their value.

"Oh, yes, I knew we could sell for a pretty penny such drek. Fools! But at our age, what did we need for cash? Because Fred was a fighter he protested at first when I said I had a better use for them. From his wheelchair, though, he couldn't really go against my will. In the end he went along."

I followed her back into the living room, hoping against hope that she had simply removed the letters of Halpin Chalmers to elsewhere in the apartment.

"The supply has nearly run out, so I'll have to go back to using old newspapers." She placed the conure inside the pagoda-shaped cage and shut the door. "There, I bet you didn't realize Max was also a critic!"

The Man of the Knife

Alexandre Dumas

There dwells in Ferdj' Ouah a Sheik named Bou Akas ben Achour. It is one of the most ancient names in the country, so we find it in the history of the dynasties of the Arabs and Berbers of Ibu Khaldoun.

Bou Akas is 49 years of age. He dresses like the Kabyles; that is, in a gandoura of wool girt with a leathern belt, and fastened around the head with a slender cord. He carries a pair of pistols in his shoulder-belt, at his left side the Kabyle flissa, and, hanging from his neck, a little black knife. Before him walks a Negro, carrying his gun, and at his side bounds a large greyhound.

When a tribe in the vicinity of the twelve tribes over which he rules occasions him any loss, he deigns not to march against it, but is satisfied with sending his Negro to the principal village, where the Negro shows the gun of Bou Akas, and the injury is repaired.

There are in his pay two or three tolbas who read the Koran to the people. Every person passing by his dwelling on a pilgrimage to Mecca receives three francs and at the Sheik's expense remains in Ferdj' Ouah as long as he pleases. But should Bou Akas learn that he has had to do with a false pilgrim, he sends emissaries to overtake the man wherever he may be, and they, on the spot, turn him over on his face, and give him twenty blows of the bastinado on the soles of his feet.

Bou Akas sometimes dines 300 persons, but instead of partaking of the repast, he walks around among his guests with a stick in his hand, marshalling his domestics; then, if there is anything left, he eats, but the very last.

When the Governor of Constantina, the only man whose supremacy he acknowledges, sends him a traveler, according to whether the traveler is a man of note, or the recommendation is pressing, Bou Akas presents him with his gun, his dog, or his knife. If he presents his gun, the traveler shoulders it; if his dog, the traveler holds it in leash; if his knife, the traveler suspends it from his neck. With one or another of these talismans, each of which bears with it the degree of honor to be rendered, the traveler passes through the twelve tribes without incurring the slightest danger. Everywhere he is fed and lodged for nothing, for he is the guest of Bou Akas. When he leaves Ferdj' Ouah, it is sufficient for him to deliver the knife, the dog, or the gun to the first Arab that he meets. The Arab, if hunting, stops; if tilling the ground, he quits his plough; if in the bosom of his family, he departs; and taking the knife, the dog, or the gun, returns it to Bou Akas.

In fact, the little black-handled knife is very well known; so well known, that it has given its name to Bou Akas—Bou d'Jenoui, or The Man of the Knife. It is with this knife that Bou Akas cuts off people's heads when, for the sake of prompt justice, he thinks fit to decapitate with his own hand.

When Bou Akas succeeded to his possessions, there were a great number of thieves in the country. He found means to exterminate them. He dressed himself like a simple merchant, then dropped a douro, taking care not to lose sight of it. A lost douro does not remain long on the ground. If he who picked it up pocketed it, Bou Akas made a sign to his chiaous, disguised like himself, to arrest the culprit. The chiaous, knowing the Sheik's intention in regard to the culprit, beheaded him without more ado. The effect of this rigor is such that there is a saying among the Arabs that a child of twelve years of age wearing a golden crown could pass through the tribes of Bou Akas without a finger's being raised to steal it.

One day Bou Akas heard mentioned that the Cadi of one of his twelve tribes rendered judgments worthy of King Solomon. Like another Haroun al Raschid, he wished to decide for himself the truth of the stories which were told him. Consequently, he set out in the guise of an ordinary horseman, without the arms which usually distinguished him, without any emblem of rank, nor any followers, and mounted on a blood-horse about which nothing betrayed that it belonged to so great a Chief.

It so chanced that, on the day of his arrival at the thrice-happy city where the Cadi sat in judgment, there was a Fair, and, in consequence of that, the Court was in session. It so chanced also—Mahomet watches over his servants in all things—that at the gate of the city Bou Akas met a cripple, who, hanging upon his burnoose, as the poor man hung upon the cloak of St. Martin, asked him for alms. Bou Akas gave the alms, as behooves an honest Musselman to do, but the cripple continued to cling to him.

"What do you want?" asked Bou Akas. "You have solicited alms, and I bestowed them on you."

"Yes," replied the cripple; "but the Law does not say only, 'Thou shalt bestow alms on thy brother,' but, in addition, 'Thou shalt do for thy brother all in thy power.'"

"Well, what can I do for you?" inquired Bou Akas.

"You can save me, poor wretch that I am, from being crushed under the feet of the men, the mules, and the camels, which will not fail to happen if I risk myself in the city."

"And how can I prevent that?"

"By taking me up behind you, and carrying me to the marketplace, where I have business."

"Be it so," said Bou Akas, and lifting up the cripple, he helped him to mount behind. The operation was accomplished with some difficulty, but it was at last done. The two men on the single horse traversed the city, not without exciting general curiosity. They arrived at the market-place.

"Is it here that you wished to go?" inquired Bou Akas of the cripple.

"Yes."

"Then dismount," said the Sheik.

"Dismount yourself."

"To help you down, very well!"

"No, to let me have the horse."

"Why? Wherefore should I let you have the horse?" said the astonished Sheik.

"Because the horse is mine."

"Ah, indeed! We shall soon see about that!"

"Listen, and consider," said the cripple.

"I am listening, and I will consider afterward."

"We are in the city of the just Cadi."

"I know it," assented the Sheik.

"You intend to prosecute me before him?"

"It is extremely probable."

"Now, do you think that when he sees us two—you with your sturdy legs, which God has destined for walking and fatigue, me with my broken legs—think you, I say, that he will not decide that the horse belongs to the one of the two travelers who has the greater need of it?"

"If he say so," replied Bou Akas, "he will no longer be the just Cadi, for his decision will be wrong."

"They call him the just Cadi," rejoined the cripple, laughing, "but they do not call him the infallible Cadi."

"Upon my word!" said Bou Akas to himself, "here is a fine chance for me to judge the Judge." Then he said aloud, "Come on, let us go before the Cadi."

Bou Akas made his way through the throng, leading his horse, on whose back the cripple clung like an ape; and presented himself before the tribunal where the Judge, according to the custom in the East, publicly dispensed justice.

Two cases were before the Court, and of course took precedence. Bou Akas obtained a place among the audience, and listened. The first case was a suit between a taleb and a peasant—that is to say, a savant and a laborer. The point in question was in reference to the savant's wife, with whom the peasant had eloped, and whom he maintained to be his, in opposition to the savant, who claimed her. The woman would not acknowledge either of the men to be her husband, or rather she acknowledged both; which circumstance rendered the affair embarrassing to the last degree. The Judge heard both parties, reflected an instant, and said:

"Leave the woman with me, and return tomorrow."

The savant and the laborer each bowed and withdrew.

The second case now came on. This was a suit between a butcher and an oil merchant. The oil merchant was covered with oil, and the butcher was besmeared with blood. The following was the butcher's story:

"I went to buy oil at this man's house. In paying for the oil, with which he had filled my bottle, I took from my purse a handful of money. This money tempted him. He seized me by the wrist. I cried thief, but he would not let go of me, and we came together before you—I clasping my money in my hand, he grasping my wrist. Now, I swear by Mahomet that this man is a liar when he says that I stole his money, for in truth the money is mine."

The following was the oil merchant's story:

"This man came to buy a bottle of oil at my house. When the bottle was full, he said to me, 'Have you change for a gold piece?' I then felt in my pocket, drew out my hand full of money, and put the money down on the sill of my shop. He snatched it up, and was about to go with both it and my oil, when I caught him by the wrist, and cried thief. In spite of my cries, he would not return my money, and I have brought him here, that you may decide between us. Now, I swear by Mahomet that this man is a liar when he says that I stole his money, for in truth the money is mine."

The Judge made each of the men, complainant and defendant, repeat his charge. Neither varied. Then the Judge pondered a moment and said:

"Leave the money with me and return tomorrow."

The butcher deposited in a fold of the Judge's robe the money of which he had never relinquished his hold; whereupon the two men bowed, and each went his way.

It was now the turn of Bou Akas and the cripple.

"My lord Cadi," said Bou Akas, "I have just come from a distant city, with the intention of buying goods at this mart. At the gate of the city I met this cripple, who at first asked me for alms, and finally begged me to allow him to mount behind me; telling me that, if he risked himself in the streets, he, poor wretch, feared he should be crushed under the feet of the men, the mules, and the camels. Thereupon, I gave him alms, and mounted him behind me. Having arrived at the market-place, he would not alight, saying that the horse which I rode belonged to him; and when I threatened him with the law, 'Bah!' he replied. 'The Cadi is too sensible a man not to know that the horse is the property of that one of us who cannot travel without a horse!' This is the affair, in all sincerity, my lord Cadi, I swear it by Mahomet."

"My Lord Cadi," responded the cripple, "I was going on business to the market of the city, and mounted on this horse, which is mine, when I saw, seated by the wayside, this man, who seemed about to expire. I approached him, and inquired whether he had met with any accident. 'No accident has befallen me,' he replied, 'but I am overcome with fatigue, and if you are charitable, you will convey me to the city, where I have business. After reaching the market-place, I will dismount, praying Mahomet to bestow upon him who aided me all that he could desire.' I did as this man requested, but my astonishment was great, when, having arrived at the market-place, he bade me dismount, telling me that the horse was his. At this strange threat, I brought him before you, that you might judge between us. This is the matter, in all sincerity, I swear by Mahomet."

The Cadi made each repeat his deposition, then having reflected an instant, he said:

"Leave the horse with me, and return tomorrow."

The horse was delivered to the Cadi, and Bou Akas and the cripple retired.

The next day, not only the parties immediately interested, but also a great number of the curious, were present in Court.

The Cadi followed the order of precedence observed the first day. The taleb and the peasant were summoned.

"Here," said the Cadi to the taleb, "here is your wife; take her away, she is really yours." Then turning toward his chiaouses, and pointing out the peasant, he said: "Give that man fifty strokes of the bastinado on the soles of his feet."

The case of the oil merchant and the butcher was then called up.

"Here," said the Cadi to the butcher, "here is your money; you did really take it out of your pocket, and it never belonged to that man." Then turning toward his chiaouses, and pointing out the oil merchant, he said: "Give that man fifty strokes of the bastinado on the soles of his feet."

The third case was now called, and Bou Akas and the cripple approached.

"Could you recognize your horse among twenty horses?" inquired the Judge of Bou Akas.

"Yes, my lord Judge," replied Bou Akas and the cripple with one accord.

"Then come with me," said the Judge to Bou Akas, and they went out.

Bou Akas recognized his horse among twenty horses.

"Very well!" said the Judge. "Go and wait in Court, and send me your opponent."

Bou Akas returned to the Court, and awaited the Cadi's return.

The cripple repaired to the stable as quickly as his bad legs would allow him to go. As his eyes were good, he went straight up to the horse, and pointed it out.

"Very well!" said the Judge. "Rejoin me in Court."

The Cadi resumed his seat on his mat, and everyone waited impatiently for the cripple, who in the course of five minutes returned out of breath.

"The horse is yours," said the Cadi to Bou Akas. "Go take it from the stable." Then addressing his chiaouses and pointing out the cripple, he said: "Give that man fifty strokes of the bastinado on the back."

On returning home, the Cadi found Bou Akas waiting for him.

"Are you dissatisfied?" he inquired.

"No, the very reverse," answered the Sheik; "but I wished to see you, to ask by what inspiration you render justice, for I doubt not that your two other decisions were as correct as the one in my case."

"It is very simple, my lord," said the Judge. "You observed that I kept for one night the woman, the money, and the horse. At midnight I had the woman awakened and brought to me, and I said to her, 'Replenish my inkstand.' Then she, like a woman who had performed the same office a hundred times in her life, took my inkglass, washed it, replaced it in the stand, and poured fresh ink into it. I said to myself immediately, 'If you were the wife of the peasant, you would not know how to clean an inkstand; therefore you are the taleb's wife.' "

"Be it so," said Bou Akas. "So much for the woman, but what about the money?"

"The money; that is another thing," replied the Judge. "Did you notice that the merchant was covered with oil, and his hands were greasy?"

"Yes, certainly."

"Very well! I took the money and placed it in a vase full of water. This morning I looked at the water. Not a particle of oil had risen to the surface. I therefore said to myself, 'This money is the butcher's, not the oil merchant's. If it had been the oil merchant's, it would have been greasy, and the oil would have risen to the surface of the water.' "

Bou Akas again inclined his head. "Good," said he; "so much for the money, but what about my horse?"

"Ah! that is another thing, and until this morning, I was puzzled."

"Then the cripple was not able to recognize the horse?" suggested Bou Akas.

"Oh, yes indeed, he recognized it."

"Well?"

"By conducting each of you in turn to the stable, I did not wish to ascertain which one would recognize the horse, but *which one the horse would recognize!* Now, when you approached the horse, it neighed; when the cripple approached the horse, it kicked. Then I said to myself, 'The horse belongs to him who has the good legs, and not to the cripple.' And I delivered it to you."

Bou Akas pondered for a moment, and then said: "The Lord is with you; it is you who should be in my place. I am sure, at least, that you are worthy to be Sheik, but I am not so sure that I am fit to be Cadi."

MANY HAPPY RETURNS

JUSTIN CASE

The house was an old one on an old road, miles from anywhere, but the freshly painted sign by its driveway—TOURISTS' REST—was as reassuring as a cleric's smile of welcome.

"Let's," Grace Martin said, squeezing her husband's hand. "There's no telling what we might find!"

Their car was already bulging with antiques collected in six states, but Tom Martin didn't care. He had just acquired his M.A., a teaching job at a highly regarded prep school, and a beautiful bride. "Done," he agreed without hesitation.

The warped and weathered door creaked open as they wriggled from the car. A man as old as they had expected, with a crown of white hair glowing in the dusk, limped down the rickety steps to greet them. An equally old woman, doll-dainty, smiled and nodded in the doorway.

It was the woman who escorted the newlyweds to their upstairs room. "Our name is Wiggin," she said, "but please call me Anna. And when you've freshened up, do come down for tea."

Grace Martin became enthusiastic about the massive four-poster bed while her husband irreverently bounced on it and pronounced it comfortable. They "freshened up" by lamplight and went downstairs to a dim parlor filled with antiques and the smell of age.

Anna Wiggin poured tea into fine old cups, and her husband Jasper, in reply to Grace Martin's question, said in a cracked voice, "No, we do not collect antiques. Not really. We have just acquired these things as we needed them."

"You are only just married, you two," Anna said with her smile. "I can always tell."

"Five days," Grace admitted.

"You are very young," Jasper said.

"Not so young. I'm twenty-two. Tom is twenty-four."

The old man moved his head up and down as if to say he had made a guess and the guess was correct. He did not say how old he and Anna were. He did remark, "I am a little older than my wife, also," then sipped his tea and added, "You must tell Anna your birthdays. She will read your futures."

"By our birthdays?" Grace Martin said.

"Oh, yes."

"How can you do that, Mrs. Wiggin?"

"I can do it." The doll-woman leaned closer, nodding and nodding. "When were you born, my dear?"

"May eleventh."

"It won't work, you know," Tom Martin said with a grin. "She—" Then puzzled by the old woman's expression, he was silent.

Jasper rose from his chair and placed his hands on his wife's frail shoulders. Though all but transparent in the lamplight, the hands were strong and long-fingered. "Now, Anna," he said softly, "do not be excited."

Grace Martin sent a half-frightened glance at her husband and said, "Is there something special about that date?"

"It is Anna's birthday also."

"Oh, how nice! We *are* special, then, aren't we?"

"Don't go putting on airs," Tom Martin chided. "You're forgetting—"

"Now, darling, don't spoil it."

"I will get some more tea," the old man said. "Fresh cups, too. We must have a toast."

The others were joking about the birthday when he returned from the kitchen with a tray. Placing four full cups on the table, he sat down again. The lamplight splashed his shadow on a wall as he raised a hand and said, "To the day that gave us two such lovely ladies."

They laughed and drank.

"You see, my dear," the old man said to his wife, "it never fails."

"What never fails?" Tom Martin asked.

"Only yesterday Anna was saying we would have to leave this house and find another. So few travelers use this old road any more. And even with many guests we sometimes wait years, of course."

"Wait for what?" Tom said.

"They have to have the same birthday, you see."

Tom nodded solemnly. It was past the old folks' bedtime, he supposed. When you were that old, a break with custom could make the mind a bit fuzzy. "Well, of course—" He started to rise. Grace and he had had a long day too, more than three hundred miles of driving.

"Wait, please," Jasper Wiggin said. "It is only fair that you understand."

With a tolerant smile Tom sank down again.

"There is a mathematical master plan, you see," the old man said. "Each day so many people are born, so many die. The plan insures a balance."

"Really?" Tom suppressed a yawn.

"I can simplify it for you, I think, if you will pay close attention. Each date—that is to say, each eleventh of May or ninth of June or sixth of December and so forth—is a compartment in time. Now suppose a thousand people are born today, to take their place with all the thousands born on this date in previous years. If the plan were perfect, all those born today would live exactly a year longer than those born one year ago, and so on. You follow me?"

"Uh-huh," Tom said sleepily.

"But the plan is not perfect. There is a thinning out through sickness and accidents—there has been from the beginning—and as a consequence, some of those born today will die before the expiration date, and others will live beyond it to maintain the balance."

"Sure," Tom mumbled.

"Each time compartment in each of the time zones is controlled this way. Life moves according to mathematics, just as the stars do."

"Remarkable," Tom said. Across the table his wife Grace was practically asleep. "What about the normal increase in population?"

"Oh, that's accounted for. So are wars, plagues, and things of that sort. If we had more time, I could make it all quite clear."

"You discovered this yourself, Mr. Wiggin?"

"Oh, no. There was a man from Europe staying with us one summer—a mathematical genius named Marek Dziok. Not in this house, of course; we have moved many times since then. Dziok had an accident—he was very old, and one night he fell down the stairs, poor man—but before he died, he took us into his confidence."

"I see."

"You don't believe me?" Jasper Wiggin said. "Dziok was writing a book—a philosophy based on his mathematics. He never finished it. But I have the manuscript . . ." He left his chair and limped to a bookcase, from which he lifted out a thin, paper-bound sheaf of papers. "Perhaps you would like—but no, you won't have time." Shaking his head, he put the sheaf of pages back.

"I guess I'd better take my wife to bed," Tom Martin said. "She's asleep."

"Yes, it works faster on women."

"What works faster?"

"The powder."

"You mean you put something—" Staring at his wife, Tom placed his hands flat on the table and pushed himself erect. It required enormous effort. "You mean—"

"You haven't been listening, have you?" the old man complained sadly. "And I've tried so hard to explain. Your wife and mine share the same time compartment, don't you see? You know yourself by now that Anna and I are much older than people get to be *naturally*. There's only the one way to do it."

"By—by killing off—"

"Precisely."

"And you think you're going to kill *Grace?*"

"It's been nineteen years since the last one for Anna," the old man sighed. "Hasn't it, dear?"

The doll-woman nodded, "Jasper has been luckier. He had one eight years ago."

"You're crazy!" Tom Martin shouted. "Both of you, you're crazy! Grace, wake up! We're getting out of here!" But when he leaned across the table to shake his wife awake, his legs went limp. He collapsed onto his chair. His head fell on his hands.

After a moment he was able with terrible concentration to bring the faces of Jasper and Anna Wiggin into focus again. There was something he had to remember—something he or they had said earlier, or he should have said but hadn't . . .

"It won't hurt, you know," the old man was saying sympathetically. "You'll both be asleep."

"Both . . . both . . ."

"Oh, yes. We'll have to kill you too, of course. Otherwise, you'd tell."

"Wait," Tom whispered. The room was filling with shadows now. "Wait . . ."

"But it won't be a waste, your dying. Somebody in *your* compartment will benefit, you know. Somebody with your birthday."

"Birthday," Tom repeated. That was it—birthday. "You're wrong about Grace—about—her—birthday." He made a supreme effort to get the words out before it was too late. "I tried—to tell you. She wasn't born May eleventh—"

"Oh, come now, Mr. Martin," the old man said sadly.

"No, no, it's true! She was born May eleventh in *Manila*. The Philippines. Her father taught—taught college there. Different—time—zone. Don't you see? A whole—day—different—"

The room went dark. In the darkness, though, he thought he heard the old woman begin to weep, and was sure he heard the old man saying, "Now, now, Anna, don't do that. There will be another one before too long."

Then nothing . . .

He was in the big four-poster bed when a shaft of sunlight wakened him. His wife lay asleep at his side. Their clothes were neatly folded on chairs.

Tom yawned and sat up. His wife opened her eyes and said, "Hi."

"You know something? I don't remember going to bed last night," Tom said.

"Neither do I."

"I don't remember getting undressed or folding my clothes like that. Grace"—he was frowning now—"I *never* fold my clothes. You know that."

"All I remember," she said with a yawn, "is getting sleepy at the table." She looked at her watch. "Anyway, we'd better be moving. It's after nine."

When they were ready to go they walked downstairs together, Tom carrying their suitcases. Anna Wiggin came from the parlor to greet them. "Did you sleep well?" she asked, peering into their faces.

"I'll say we did," Tom said.

"You were both so tired," Anna said, nodding. "Won't you have breakfast before you go?"

They said no, thanks, they were late as it was, and Tom took out his wallet to pay for their night's lodging. Anna said wait, please, she would get her husband, he was out in the field. So Tom and Grace Martin went to their car with the suitcases and Tom went back into the house alone.

It came back to him when he walked into the parlor and saw the table and the tea service and the extra cups. The extra cups! At first it was fuzzy and confused; then it sharpened and he remembered everything—just as Grace had remembered everything up to the time of *her* falling asleep.

He snatched the sheaf of papers from the bookcase. It was indeed a manuscript, handwritten and yellowed with age. Its title was *The Mathematics of Life* and its author was Marek Dziok.

Under the author's name, in a different hand, was written: *Born 1613. Died (by accident) 1802.*

There was a sound of footsteps in the kitchen. Tom thrust the manuscript inside his shirt and quickly stepped away from the bookcase.

"You know, I'm still sleepy," his wife said later as their car purred along a parkway. "It must have been that house. They were nice old people, though, weren't they?"

"Remarkable," Tom said.

"I wonder how old they really are."

Tom did not answer. He had already finished his figuring and now he was thinking of the pilfered manuscript inside his shirt. That, too, was remarkable. With the information it contained, a man could live a long time.

Of course, it was all pretty weird and sinister. Nevertheless . . .

In spite of himself, he began to think about birthdays—his wife's and his own.

Marked in Red

Ralph Powers

The back room of Retti's grew dangerously quiet as Tip Marbury entered. It was a long room cluttered with tables and chairs and with the slouched figures of men and women. Cigarette smoke eddied in shifting layers and through it two pasty-faced waiters in dirty jackets moved like fish in a milky aquarium.

A girl at a corner table spoke nasally, breathing the silence.

"There's that hot-foot dick again! Why don't somebody throw him out on his ear?"

Marbury grinned and nodded his head and grinned again. But he could feel hard bright eyes stabbing through the smoke, hostile and curious.

He crossed the room quickly on the balls of his feet and stopped in front of the man who stood propped against the farthermost door with a cigarette hung on his lower lip. The man stared at him with silent disapproval.

"Hello, Retti," said Marbury.

Retti, the speakeasy proprietor, spoke softly without taking the cigarette from his lips.

"Are you gonna spend every night wit' us, chief?"

"I told you I had a steer, Retti. I said there was a guy comes here I wanted to meet."

"Who?"

Marbury stared at Retti's sloe-black eyes, his thin lips and his slicked-down hair.

"Duke Hadden," he said. "He got out of stir yesterday. I thought he might show up in your place. You haven't seen him have you?"

For a moment Retti looked sidewise across the room. Then he shook his head.

"No, he ain't showed up."

Marbury glanced where Retti's eyes had swiveled and his lips spread in a sudden pleased smile.

"I see his moll's here though," he said. "Stella Rusano! He used to pal around with her in the old days."

"Yeah, they were both sent up. She got out first."

"And she's been waiting ever since," said Marbury. "I think I'll have a little chin with her, Retti. Maybe Hadden will drop in later."

He walked across the floor again to the table where the girl was sitting alone and as he did so he studied her face intently.

It was a hard little face, chalk-white under the overhead lamp, with a painted red slit of a mouth. But it wasn't all bad. There were hints of softness in the eyes. Hints of strength in the small, pointed chin.

Marbury nodded and grinned at her, and eased himself into a seat at her side. Her lips hardly moved. She was staring straight down at her whisky glass, fingering the edge of it.

"You've got a hell of a nerve," she said.

"So have you, coming here—with the Beckerman case not cleaned up. Where's Hadden?"

"I'd like to know!"

There was something in her voice that made his head jerk around, made him look at her with sharp intentness. All the softness had left her eyes now. Her mouth was a straight, bitter line.

"Tell me some more," he said. But she only shook her head.

"Waitin' for the split, eh? And Hadden hasn't shown up."

"You know everything," the girl sneered.

Her tone gave her away. He knew he was on the right track. Burke Hadden and she had both done time for the same job—the Beckerman jewel robbery. They'd been caught red-handed with some of the small stuff, pins and things—but the big grab, the blue-white rocks, had never been located.

"Listen, kid," he said. "Why don't you stay away from that guy? You was pretty straight till you started playing around with him."

The girl shrugged her slim shoulders. Her mouth grew hard and ugly.

"He can't—double-cross—me."

She bit the words out slowly and Marbury, looking down at her, saw that she was shaking. She opened the small, bright-colored handbag she carried and began fumbling for a package of butts. Marbury started to offer her one of his, then suddenly he made a grab for her wrist.

"Hold on, sister! What you got there?"

* * *

He was looking down at her lap, looking into the handbag that the girl tried to snap shut. Then his hand dived in and his fingers came out holding a small, gleaming revolver.

"So—you've started going around heeled?"

She tried to snatch the gun from him, but he held her off.

"Gimme that, you big, pussy-footing shamus. You ain't gonna run me in for—"

He shook his head.

"I could, but I won't. It's you I'm thinking of, kid. You just got out of stir a month ago. Why don't you try goin' straight for a while?"

"I will after—"

"After what?"

"Never mind—but lemme have my gun, Marbury. I ain't gonna shoot anybody—it's only for protection."

"Yeah?"

"Yeah!"

His eyes were shrewd and kindly as he stared down at her sullen face. The same face he remembered when she was just one of Rusano's kids, roller skating in front of her dad's grocery store down on Sullivan Street. The same kid who'd swiped apples to give to him, back when he was a rookie cop, and who'd tripped him up on the sidewalk a couple of times and made him sweat and swear.

Then she'd disappeared for years and he hadn't seen her again till she'd turned up as Burke Hadden's moll, tough and hard as they made 'em.

But somehow, looking at her now, he still saw that knock-kneed, funny-faced little kid who'd handed him apples.

"I'm getting sentimental," he said huskily, "but you know I won't run you in. How are you on dough?"

"I spent my last five bucks for that cannon. Retti's givin' me credit till Burke comes."

"Till he comes," said Marbury slowly and saw the girl's eyelids flicker. He fished in his pocket then, drew out a thin wallet and peeled off five one-dollar bills.

"Here's a loan," he said. "It ain't much, but it will help till you get a job."

She shook her head first, then took the bills. But her hand came back with the fingers open.

"Gimme that gun. Be a sport. You wasn't so bad when you was a cop, Marbury."

"You win," he said, and stuck the gun back into her sweaty little hand.

He ordered himself a glass of beer, drank it and eased out of his seat.

"I'll be seein' you," he said. "Be a good kid, and don't do anything I wouldn't."

He left the iron-grated door of the speakeasy, walked down the block, then turned and came back on the other side where the shadows were thicker. He ducked into the doorway of an empty house and waited, eyes slanted on Retti's place.

Patience was one of Tip Marbury's strong points.

It was nearly two hours before Stella Rusano came out. She was still alone and when the light from a street lamp fell on her pale little face there was a look there that he didn't like.

She teetered down the block on her high-heeled shoes. A couple of prowling youths made catcalls at her, but she didn't seem to hear. She signaled a taxi at the corner and got in.

"There goes one of my bucks. She's getting high-toned for a dame who's broke."

He came out of his doorway at a run and loped down the block toward the corner. Headlights of another cab goggled up the street. He raised a big paw and signaled, waiting till the taxi slid in to the curb.

"Keep that other bus in sight," he said to the driver.

Then he settled back and lit a cigarette. It might be a bum steer he was on, but it was worth trying. The cab eased into Seventh Avenue and headed uptown.

At Twentieth Street the taxi ahead swung left and headed for the river. Marbury's cab followed, past garages, cheap apartments, a theological seminary, and on into a block of run-down rooming houses.

"Slow down," said Marbury suddenly. He saw that the cab ahead was doing the same. Stella Rusano was bending forward in her seat, looking out of the side window, staring at the house numbers.

"She's a bad kid to welch on," he muttered. "I think this guy Burke Hadden has made a mistake."

If he could locate the Beckerman diamonds he knew his own stock would go up at headquarters. But he was going to see that Stella Rusano wasn't implicated.

The cab ahead stopped and the girl got out. She paid her fare and started walking. Marbury got out, too, and followed her.

He kept well behind, but not too far. He saw her turn into a gate halfway down the block and go up the front stoop of a house. He saw her press a bell button, and then disappear. And he crossed the street and slouched along, getting the number of the house.

It was hard to figure what to do next. Hadden might be inside, or he might not. It wasn't her own place or she wouldn't have spent so much time looking at the numbers. She might be just nosing around; or she might have followed a hot tip.

Marbury waited on the corner, puffing a cigarette, eyes slanted back. A half hour passed and he began to get restless. Another fifteen minutes and he was uneasy. Then he snapped into sudden alertness.

An old woman with stringy hair and a wrinkled face was running down the steps of the house Stella Rusano had gone in. She turned on her flat heels and started shuffling up the block where the light of a cigar store showed. She was walking faster, Marbury figured, than a dame of her age should.

He crossed the street at a quick angle and stepped in front of her.

"What's your hurry, mother?"

The old woman started and looked up at him with suspicion in her watery eyes, and he saw that she was breathing hard.

"None of your business, mister. Get out of my way—I gotta find a phone."

He opened the edge of his coat and let the light of the arc lamp gleam on his first-grade detective's badge. The old woman stared at it, stepped back and spoke in a croaking voice.

"There's been a shooting in my house. I heard a girl scream. The door was locked and I couldn't get in. I was gonna call the cops—but you'll do."

"Come on, mother."

He took her arm and began pulling her back, making her heels flap and her breath come in gasps. Then he snatched the key from her hand and ran up the stoop ahead of her.

"First floor rear," she panted.

He walked down a dark, stuffy hallway, came to a door and palmed the knob; but it was locked as she had said. The old woman came hobbling up to him and he jerked a question at her.

"Ain't you got a key?"

She made sweeping motions with her calloused hands.

"It won't go in, mister. The fella left his key on the inside."

"The fella?"

"Yeah—Burney Hampden—the gent that had the room."

"Burney Hampden—that's what he calls himself now is it? He was always dumb about his monikers."

Marbury stepped back then, turned a muscular shoulder to the door and lunged forward. The old woman made complaining cluckings with her tongue. The door cracked and Marbury lunged again. Wood snapped this time and he pitched into the room.

His gun was out, in his hand; but he didn't need to use it. One light was burning and Stella Rusano lay on the floor. Beyond her he saw an open window, and he ran to that. Then he saw that it was only a six-foot drop to the yard. There was a fence with a door in it and that was open, too, and the night was dark and silent.

He turned back into the room and stared down at the girl. Her face was even whiter than it had been and the front of her dress was discolored and soggy. He didn't need to look twice to see that she was dead. A man's necktie hung over the back of a chair, and the three drawers in the bureau were open, showing that somebody had made a quick getaway.

"The louse," said Marbury harshly. "The dirty louse!"

He stared at Stella Rusano. She didn't look much now like the little knock-kneed kid he remembered. She looked like what she was—a moll who had got hers. But there were runs in the stockings that covered her thin legs, and there were coppery lights in her dark, wavy hair, and Marbury swallowed hard. He wasn't as tough as he liked to appear.

Then he bent forward and swore under his breath.

"What the hell?" he said.

Stella Rusano's handbag was open. The gun was still in it. Burke Hadden hadn't given her a chance to use it. But a dollar bill, one of those that Marbury had given her, was lying on the floor, and the girl's white, still fingers near it held her lip-stick. She'd used the lipstick—drawn a red, irregular line down the back of the bill, until the bullet lodged close to her heart had stopped her. She'd been trying to tell somebody something.

With his face screwed into a puzzled knot Marbury picked up the bill and studied it.

"She knew she was getting ready to croak," he muttered. "She knew I'd turn up when the call went in to headquarters. What did she want?"

He slid a big hand across his forehead and rubbed the end of his nose. Then he drew a cigarette from the package in his pocket and squeezed the tobacco out of it slowly, letting it dribble on the floor.

"What did you want, kid?" he muttered again. "What were you tryin' to tell me?"

He shook his head, staring at the bill, angry with himself. Then suddenly he jumped and turned on the old landlady.

"Stay here, mother. I'll put that call in to the cops for you—and when they come tell them that Tip Marbury's working on the case. Tell them he's got a hot steer."

His eyes were bright now and his face was hard. He went out of the room, through the hall and down the steps at a lope, and headed for the corner cigar store. He snapped into a telephone booth, took down the receiver and put in a call to headquarters.

"Marbury speaking. Stella Rusano, Hadden's moll, has just been bumped off. I'm going after Hadden now—the guy that did it."

He gave the street and house number and heard the desk sergeant's excited query.

"Where is Hadden?"

"Where I'm going to get him—and the Beckerman rocks."

Marbury grinned humorlessly then and hung up. He spent a minute thumbing through a telephone directory, found what he was after, and went out into the street. He signalled another cab and gave the driver an address in Jersey City.

"Make it snappy," he said, "there's a boat sailing and a guy on it I want to see."

He fumed as they crossed on the ferry, but the driver made up for lost time when they reached the other side. He turned left, sped along the river front and came to a screeching stop in front of a dock with a long shed on it.

Marbury dived into the shed, ran up a covered gangplank and on board a twin-funneled steamer that was tied up alongside the pier. He went to the purser's office and flashed his badge.

"Lemme see the passenger list."

When the startled young man behind the window shoved it to him he ran a thick finger down the long columns of names. Then he clicked his tongue.

"It wouldn't be Hampden this time. No—Horner Burkley—the dumb egg!"

He turned and crooked his finger at a steward.

"Take me to Horner Burkley's cabin—nine twenty-two."

The steward started off and Marbury followed, fingering the gun in his right coat pocket. When the steward stopped at a stateroom door he took the gun out and thrust its blunt nose forward purposely. The steward started to knock, but Marbury pushed the door open and jumped inside.

A big man with sharp features whirled around, glaring. His hand started to move toward his pocket.

"Don't do it, Mr. Burkley-Hampden-Hadden—it wouldn't do you any good. Stick 'em up—you lousy murderer!"

The big man's face went white and his hands up.

"Now," said Marbury, "I'm gonna give you some new jewelry to play with—since you like it so much."

He took a pair of jingling handcuffs from his pocket and snapped them on the big man's wrists. Then he snapped open the suitcase that rested on the lower berth and searched through it till he came to a small, flat package wrapped in soft leather. He undid it and stared at the glistening heap of sparklers, diamond necklaces, rings and bracelets worth a quarter of a million—the Beckerman jewels. Hadden spoke between clenched teeth, his eyes dark with fury.

"Who tipped you off—how did you know?"

"That girl-friend of yours. She was dead, but she left a message for me." Marbury shook his head slowly. "You're dumb about two things, Hadden—those tricky names you pick and the frails you pal around with—and try to double-cross. You ought to of known that you couldn't welch on a kid like Stella Rusano and get away with it. Here's the note she left."

Marbury reached into his pocket and pulled out the dollar bill with the red line on it that Stella Rusano had drawn with her dying fingers. He held it close to Hadden's uncomprehending eyes.

"I don't get you, Marbury," the big man grated. "What kind of a gag—"

"She outwitted you, Hadden—made you look like the dumb, murdering, double-crossing cluck you are. You taunted her, didn't you—told her you were sailing tonight, even showed her your passport? Then when she asked for her share of the split you gave her lead instead. And the game kid stayed alive long enough to tell me where to find you."

Marbury raised his hand then and pointed to the side of the suitcase that rested on the bunk. There was a big label on it, put there by the steamship company, and it proclaimed to the world at large what Stella Rusano's dying message had meant. Hadden's jaw sagged as he read the words:

"Dollar Steamship Line, Inc."

Marbury was nodding slowly.

"Yeah, she drew a line right through the middle of the bill—get it? 'Dollar Line'—and told me where to find you just as though she'd written it on a board fence in letters six feet high."

A Matter of Proof

Grover Brinkman

Something was moving far up the dusty St. Croix Road. Old Jim Fargo laboriously tied a second knot in the bandage on his throbbing, badly infected finger, and shuffled inside his peeled-log shack to get his telescope. Presently he came out to the porch again, poured some antiseptic solution on the crude bandage, then carefully focused the ancient glass. He stared long and earnestly, until he was quite sure the black dot, now rapidly growing larger, was an automobile. When he put down the glass he seemed suddenly weary, and dejected in spirit.

However, when the low-slung sedan finally jolted to a stop in front of his disreputable abode, Old Jim had again assumed a nonchalant attitude. He hummed an old Creole chant as he awkwardly pared potatoes, trying valiantly to keep his sore finger out of the way.

Three strangers slid out of the car and came up to the porch. They were dark-skinned and shifty-eyed. They acted nervous and ill at ease.

The taller of the three flipped back his coat for an instant, just long enough to flash a badge. Old Jim noted the bulge of shoulder holsters.

"We're looking for a guy," the tall man said bluntly. "We're officers from upstate. They told us back at St. Croix that you were the only old-time hermit in this area who knew the Okefenokee. We was wondering if you happened to see anyone come down the bayou."

Old Jim stopped his paring, spat derisively over the broken porch rail.

"I ain't paid much attention to the bayou, or anything else," he said evasively, waving a fly off his bandage. "Been too busy tryin' to save this blamed finger from gangrene."

"We trailed this guy to St. Croix. We're certain he was heading for the swamp. If he was, wouldn't he go in by way of the bayou?"

"Mebbe. And then agin, mebbe not. What kind of a guy was this feller?"

"He's a big man—must weigh all of 225. A surgeon by profession, red-headed, and his eyes are blue like robins' eggs—"

Something clattered to the porch floor. Old Jim tried mightily to steady his good hand as he picked up his paring knife. When he looked up, however, his weatherbeaten old face had the immobility of a faro dealer.

"Big guy, you say? Hell, if he's thet heavy, the bog's got 'im by now." He sent tobacco juice over the railing again. "Nobody can go into this part of the Okefenok' less'n you're a pint-sized runt like me. Know thet, don't you?"

The tall man was scowling. "They told us as much in St. Croix. That's why we came all the way out here. You're the only guy who can go in and get this fellow."

Old Jim perked up his head. "I ain't no man-catcher, mister. Besides, if this guy is a hard egg, I'm liable to stop a bullet—"

"There isn't much danger," the tall man returned. "Doctors don't carry guns. Besides, if your theory is right, he's liable to be a mile down in the bog by now."

Old Jim nodded. There was no way out, evidently. Laboriously he slipped into hipboots, donned a dirty old hat. "I'll go," he said wearily, "but it's liable to take hours. Better come up an' cook some grub. There's sweet potatoes ready, an' a squirrel—"

The tall man peeled off a bill from an overly fat roll. Old Jim was scowling, rubbing an imaginary bite on the top of his cranium, as the tall man crammed the bill inside a pocket of his dirty vest.

"We've got to get this guy, see?" the tall man persisted. The statement undeniably was an order.

"Scared I'll bring 'im out dead," Old Jim argued. "If he don't know the swamp, some varmint'll git 'im, even if the bog don't."

"Just so we have some proof," the tall man concluded. "Some positive proof."

* * *

Minutes later, Old Jim was poling his scarred pirogue down the bayou, following the black waterlane that led into the heart of the swamp. There was a hard, steely light in his watery old eyes as he poled deeper into the treacherous bog. From time to time he spat derisively into the brackish water, as if ridding his mouth of some extremely bitter taste. . . .

The scorching July sun was well past the meridian when he finally came out of the swamp. He was alone. The trio shuffled down to the muddy bayou edge to meet him.

"I found 'im," Old Jim began, wiping his brow, "but I can't git 'im out. He's in the bog. Must have floundered right onto a big cottonmouth. Can't move 'im, for the bog won't hold me up thet long, and my one hand's no good. Was wonderin'—"

"Nix on that!" the tall man interrupted. "Not on your life! If the bog won't hold you, how could any of us go in? We're all heavier than you."

The tall man scowled as he pondered, tossed a pebble idly into the tepid stream. "All we need is some evidence that this guy is actually dead—some positive, undisputable proof."

"Proof?" echoed Old Jim, "you mean—"

He left the sentence unfinished, turned back to his boat, grimacing at the pain in his puffed finger.

Without further parley he started poling his battered pirogue back into the Okefenokee. But now a whimsical smile lingered on his leathery face despite his pain.

Finally he grounded the pirogue on a low mud bank, whistled softly. A giant of a young man came splashing through the slush and bramble toward the boat. He was mud-spattered, dirty, haggard, but his blue eyes burned with an intense light that changed and softened as the older man approached.

"They want some proof you're dead, Nat," Old Jim said.

A film of fear suddenly veiled the eyes of the younger man. "Take them my class ring, clothing—anything," he began feverishly.

"That wouldn't do. The tall one would catch on."

"He's too damned smart." Nat Fargo wiped clammy sweat off his freckled brow. "Watch him like a hawk, Dad. Don't even hint we're kin. He thinks I come from the Everglades instead of the Okefenokee. He's a snake, and he'll try to get me if it takes a lifetime. All his mob are behind bars, excepting these three. My evidence put them there."

"Calm down!" Old Jim said, scratching his seedy old head in bafflement. "We'll figure out somethin'. You're safe here. Nobody knows 'bout the cabin on the island but me an' you. You can stay here till the law catches up with these birds, and that shouldn't be long. Let's see. . . ."

A pair of whippoorwills was circling high above the mirror-like surface of the bayou, cutting mad capers in the cobalt sky, when Old Jim came out of the swamp for the second time.

"Here's your proof," he told the tall man. "Positive proof."

As the trio gathered around the oil-cloth-covered table in his kitchen, he unwrapped his red handkerchief. The tall man took one look, prodded gingerly with the tip of a pencil until he was certain of the insignia on that gold band. Then he turned away without a word. His two henchmen made wry faces and hurried outside.

When the last exhausts of the big car dimmed into the distance, Old Jim smiled.

"Thet son o' mine'll be the greatest doc in the world some day," he soliloquized, as he studied his bandaged hand. "Takin' off thet old rotten finger didn't hurt a bit!"

Mind Over Mayhem

Mack Reynolds

The others had straggled out one by one and I was the only remaining customer. The bartender drifted down and wiped the bar in front of me listlessly, and yawned.

"Why the hell don't you go home, Jerry?" he asked conversationally.

I put the tabloid I'd been glancing at to one side and grinned at him. "Haven't got a home, Sam; just a hotel room with four walls and a bed and a chair or two and a couple hundred pocket books. I'd rather sit here and look at you."

He leaned on the bar before me and said, "You oughta get married, Jerry. Why don't you ask that girl . . . what was her name? The blonde, pretty little girl."

"Frances."

"Yeah, that's right. Frances. Why don't you ask her to marry you?"

I twisted my glass on the bar, lifted it over to a new spot, twisted it again and then again, making small wet circles.

"I did," I said. "A couple of months ago I asked her, 'Why don't we get married, Frances?'"

"Well, what'd she say?" Sam asked, yawning again.

"She just laughed and said, 'Who'd have either of us, Jerry?'"

Sam snorted. "I've heard that one before."

"It's almost two o'clock. You can't expect me to be original this time of the night."

A guy came in and took a stool two down from me and Sam walked over to him.

"Only fifteen minutes to go," Sam said. "What'll it be?"

"Bourbon," the stranger told him. "You gents like to have one with me?"

Usually the guy who comes into a bar the last few minutes before closing has already been drinking pretty heavy; he's been put out of a place that shuts up early and he's looking for that last drink that's suddenly become so important. This guy was an exception; he was cold sober. About thirty, which makes him a few years younger than me and maybe twenty years younger than Sam, he was neatly dressed and had an air of sharpness that seemed out of place this time of night.

"Thanks," I told him. "I could use another beer."

Sam poured the stranger's whiskey, drew my beer and then got himself a glass of vermouth, which is the only stuff I've ever seen Sam drink.

Sam said, *"Prosit."*

The stranger said, *"Skoal."*

I said, "Here's how," and we all started working on our drinks.

I said something about the weather and they both agreed and

everybody lapsed into silence. After a minute or two, the stranger started looking at the tabloid I'd discarded.

Finally he laughed and said, "Did you see this item about the old lady that socked some punk who was trying to hold up her liquor store? She slugged him with a bottle of Scotch."

Sam said, "Did it break the bottle? She would've saved money if she'd used something cheaper."

"Every once in a while you read something like that," I said. "That old doll must be a terror. I'd hate to be her old man."

The stranger finished off his drink and ordered another. Sam glanced up at the clock, saw we had time, and said this one was on him. I had another beer.

"The guy was an amateur," the stranger said. "If he'd had any sense, he wouldn't have tried anything on the old lady."

"Hell," I said, "How'd he know, when he pulled the gun on her, that she was going to haul off and conk him with a bottle? It was just one of life's little surprises."

"He should've sized her up before pulling the caper. If he'd taken his time, he could've seen she was the type that'd blow her top and start screaming, or throwing things or some such. Five minutes of analyzing her character and he would've seen he'd better go somewhere else."

"Maybe you're right," Sam said argumentatively, "but how would he go about analyzing her character in just the few minutes time he'd have? He couldn't hang around the store very long or it'd look suspicious and she'd be calling for the cops."

"You wouldn't need very long," the stranger told him. "You can size a person up in just a few minutes by the way they walk and talk and by their gestures—that sort of stuff."

I grinned. "Okay. Size me up. If you were analyzing my character, would you go ahead and stick me up or not?"

He smiled back. "Sure I would. You're the easy-going type. Even if you had much money on you, and you probably never have, you wouldn't think it was worth taking a chance on getting yourself killed."

Sam grunted, "That sounds like Jerry, all right. How about me?"

The stranger flicked his hand almost disdainfully. "You're easy. I'd take a chance on you right off the bat. You'd be scared stiff at the first sight of a gun."

The old boy was irritated. "Where'd you get that idea?"

"It's the little things I watch," the stranger said. "Like the fact that you crook your little finger when you pick up your glass. A thing like that tells a lot."

Sam had been just about ready to take a sip from his vermouth. Sure enough, the little finger was crooked. It looked sort of ridiculous on the part of a big burly guy like Sam.

Sam snorted.

The easy-going smile left the stranger's face. He put his right hand in a pocket and brought out a snub-nosed revolver.

His voice was chilly now. "Let's try the experiment out," he said. "This is it. Fork it over, gents."

I said, "I'll be damned," and got my hands up in a hurry. "Take it easy, buddy—sometimes those things go off," I told him nervously.

He smiled a little, contemptuous smile at me and waggled the gun at Sam. "You too, big boy," he snapped. "Put 'em up."

Sam stood there, his two beefy red hands on the bar, and stared blankly at the gunman for a long moment. Finally he gave a deep sigh, and began to make his way around the end of the bar.

"Hold it," the stranger said sharply. "Get back to that cash register and—"

"In your hat," Sam said, coming toward him.

"Take it easy, Sam!" I warned him shrilly, expecting to hear the gun's roar at any split second.

But he kept advancing.

A muscle was twitching in the gunman's neck; his finger began to tighten on the trigger. "You're asking for it," he snarled.

"And over your ears," Sam said, and reached out suddenly and hit the guy sharply across the wrist with the edge of his hand. The gun dropped to the floor, and Sam stooped quickly and scooped it up with his left hand.

"Call a cop, Jerry," Sam told me softly, keeping the gunman covered. He made his way around the end of the bar again, and took his old place.

I went down to the other end of the room, where Sam has a pay phone booth, and shakily made the call.

By the time I came back I was boiling, I was so mad. "You conceited crackpot," I snapped at Sam. "Just because he said you'd be yellow in an emergency, you didn't have to show off like that."

The gunman had slumped back onto a stool, perspiration standing out heavily on his forehead. He started to say something, but then shut up.

Sam shrugged. "There wasn't any danger of his shooting. Any guy with enough brains to figure out that character analysis stunt before pulling his stickups has too much sense to kill a man. He wouldn't want to risk a murder rap. As it is, he'll only get sent up for a year or so."

He picked up his vermouth glass and finished his drink. I noticed that he still crooked his little finger. He saw my eyes on it and grinned wryly. He held it out so that I could see a small white scar running along the knuckle.

"Piece of shell fragment creased it back during the first war. Haven't been able to bend that finger since," he said.

Mine Host— The Ghost

Costa Carousso

The heat had been unbearable all day. But now, a breath of air was stirring. Pedestrians looked hopefully at masses of clouds forming on the horizon. Presently, thunderheads swelled toward the zenith, cutting off the sun. Yellow squares of light began to show against the black walls of the office buildings. Muted rumblings sounded. The clouds merged overhead and sank downward.

"Like the first dawn of creation," I said to myself, looking through the window.

"Or the first dawn of doom!"

I wheeled sharply. I hadn't heard the man arrive at my side. I wasn't aware that I had spoken aloud. He was a gnarled little gnome of a man. His hair was white and his little eyes were black and bright.

"You'll forgive me," he said politely, "for presuming to read your mind?"

I nodded, still puzzled.

"It was not difficult," he said. "I have learned that a young writer invariably thinks in trite phrases at first. It occurred to me that you were comparing the scene before us to the popular conception of the first dawn of creation, so I hazarded an alternative."

"How did you know I was a writer?" I said, nettled.

A mischievous smile tugged at the old man's lips, but his voice was bland. "I asked our esteemed bartender," he said, nodding toward George. "Would you join me in a drink?"

At that moment the storm broke. Thunder crashed through the room. Rain streaked down the windows till it was impossible to distinguish anything outside. Pitiless lightning blasted the sky apart.

It would be hours before I'd want to go out, and besides, I felt that a writer could pick up something useful from one of these old timers. I agreed to join him and we sat down.

"I haven't seen a storm like this for eight or nine years," I said. "Since the summer lightning struck the old Hollingway mansion and killed the three Hollingway cousins."

My host sipped his Scotch-and-soda appreciatively. "Lightning didn't strike the Hollingway place," he said.

Now everyone knew that lightning had struck the Hollingway place and burned it to cinders along with the three cousins who were inside. So if this ancient little man believed in a different version, I wanted to hear it.

"What did happen?" I asked.

"It was set afire deliberately," the old man said. He stirred his drink carefully, then raised it to his lips. "By a ghost." He looked at me, obviously enjoying my impatience.

"Come now," I said. "Surely you don't expect me to believe in ghosts."

"No," said the old man. "The point is—the Hollingways did."

My curiosity was itching, but at the same time I was detached enough to realize that the old man had a superb gift for story telling. "You should have been a writer," I said.

"I was," he answered. Thunder crashed outside. The old man smiled.

"Go on," I prompted. "The Hollingway house wasn't struck by lightning; it was set afire by a ghost. The Hollingways weren't killed accidentally; they were murdered."

"That," said the old man, "is something that you'll have to decide for yourself." He looked at his glass, which was empty, so I told George to bring the bottle. I sat back to listen to his story. He told it well—so well that I could see the rain glistening down the walls of the Hollingway mansion; see the headlights of Eric Hollingway's car as it wound up the half-mile bluestone driveway bordered by dark trees. . . .

Eric slammed shut the door of his car and turned up the collar of his coat. Flashes of lightning grotesquely illuminated the empty house. In another moment it was lost in the darkness and rain. Eric ran toward the steps, cursed when he stumbled. Then his huge fist was turning the key, pushing the heavy door inward. He snapped on the switch and brilliance flooded the room. He went from one room to another, turning on the lights, looking into the closets, searching beneath the beds and behind the furniture. Finally he went downstairs and paced the floor.

Half an hour later he ground out his fourth cigarette and looked at the telegram again. COME TO THE COUNTRY HOUSE TONIGHT, it said.

A noise sounded on the porch. A moment later his cousin Jim was standing before the door. Water streamed from his clothes and made a puddle at his feet.

"Well, here I am," he said. "What do you want?"

"What do I want! What do you want?"

"Nothing," said Jim. "I got your telegram and I came." He held the pale yellow slip to Eric.

Eric read it. It was the same as his. "What made you think I sent it?"

"Well," said Jim. "The whole thing was your idea in the first place, so I figured—"

"My idea!" Eric roared. "Cut that stuff. All of us were in on it. And you know it!"

"Of course we were," said Jim. "Don't get excited. If you didn't send that telegram, Perce must have."

"Yeah," said Eric. "But why doesn't he show up?"

Jim lit a cigarette and tossed the match into the fireplace. "I wish I had a drink," he said.

"Take it easy on the drinks," growled Eric. "Someday you'll shoot your mouth off and then we'll all be sunk."

Jim's lips tightened, then he opened them to speak. "Some day—" he began. The door creaked open and Perce stood dripping on the threshold.

"What happened?" he asked. "What's up?"

"Didn't you send those wires?" Jim asked.

"No," said Perce. "I thought that—" He took a telegram from his pocket and handed it to Jim. "I got one, too. I didn't—"

47

"I'll be damned!" snarled Eric.

Thunder crashed against the house. Lightning stabbed at the windows. The rain beat an incessant tattoo upon the roof. The room was silent save for the breathing of the three men.

"Maybe Kelston sent them," suggested Jim. "Maybe he wanted to talk to us about the will."

"Why wouldn't he sign his name, then?" asked Perce. "And why come all the way out here?"

"You've got me," said Eric. "Do you think that shyster suspects anything?"

"For God's sake, watch what you're saying," warned Perce.

"It's all right," said Eric. "I searched this place from top to bottom when I came in. Nobody's here."

"I don't like it," said Perce. "I'm getting out." He moved toward the door.

"Wait a minute," said Eric. "Kelston will probably show up."

Perce's hand was on the doornob. He turned, his face colorless. "It's locked!"

Jim and Eric sprang forward. Eric seized the knob, turned it one way and then the other. Then he grasped it with both hands and heaved with all his body. The door didn't budge.

Jim sprang to the window and threw it open. Wind lashed the curtains, rain splashed on the floor. Jim said, "Good Lord!"

"What!" shouted Perce.

"Bars," said Jim. "Inch-thick bars."

"The devil you say!" bellowed Eric, shouldering Perce aside and leaping forward. Fear was in his face when he turned.

"You and Perce take the upstairs rooms," ordered Eric. "I'll take the downstairs and the cellar."

"Let's all go together," said Jim.

"What's the matter," sneered Eric. "Scared?"

"No, I'm not scared," said Jim. "And lay off me. Someday you're going to push things too far and I'll—"

"You'll what?" asked Eric.

"Cut it out, you two," said Perce.

"What I meant," said Jim, "was that we all ought to search this place carefully. Maybe someone planted a dictaphone. This looks like a sly police trick."

"Oh," said Eric. "Yeah, that sounds like a good idea. I never thought of that."

"No brains and all brawn," said Jim.

"Shut up, you guys," said Perce. "And be careful what you say. I don't like this."

"Come on," said Eric, moving toward the cellar stairs.

The storm receded with rumbling growls, then awakened with even greater fury. Branches lashed the house; lightning threw eerie shadows against the windows.

"Well," said Eric. "There's no dictaphone."

"There's no way out, either," said Jim.

"The phone!" said Perce. "Why didn't I think of the phone!" He leaped forward and snatched up the receiver. He jiggled the hook. The other two men pressed in close. Finally Perce let the phone slip from his fingers. "Dead," he whispered.

"All right, Eric," said Jim. "What's next?" His voice was hard.

Eric looked up, bewilderment on his heavy face. "I don't get it," he said. "What do you mean?"

"I mean how much of our cut do you want—to let us out of here alive? Or is Perce with you on this?"

The bewilderment on Eric's face slowly changed to understanding; the understanding exploded into rage. "Why, you dirty little—" he bellowed, lunging forward. "I'll break every—"

Jim ducked beneath Eric's flailing arms and grabbed his legs. They crashed to the floor together. "Hold him, Perce!" he shouted. "Hold him before he gets his gun!"

Perce waited uncertainly for a moment. Then he dived in. One of Eric's thrashing heels caught him in the chest and sent him reeling across the room. Eric's hands closed on Jim's throat.

"Perce! He'll kill us both! Quick!"

Perce got unsteadily to his feet, then jumped at Eric's back. He got a strangle hold and twisted. Jim struggled free and pinned back Eric's arms. Perce kept squeezing till Eric began to choke. "No!" he coughed. "Stop. Haven't any gun!"

Perce stopped choking him and searched him while Jim held down his arms. Finally he stood up. "Let him go," he said. "He hasn't got a gun."

"Well, don't try anything like that again," warned Jim. "Perce and I can finish you."

Eric struggled to his feet and sank into a chair. His lips were bleeding and he wiped away the blood with the back of his hand. "You damn fools," he said. "I didn't have anything to do with this."

Neither of the two men met his eyes. He looked at Perce and then at Jim. "Don't you believe me?"

"I don't believe anyone when that much money is concerned,"

said Jim. "You were here first. How do we know you didn't fix up this place and send those telegrams?"

"And then lock the door from the outside?" jeered Eric. "Don't be ridiculous. You're supposed to be the brilliant Hollingway."

Jim was silent for a moment, then he turned to Perce. "You were the last one in here," he said. "You made this trap. You—"

Perce stepped back slowly. He watched Jim advance toward him and looked to see what Eric would do. "No! I swear I didn't. Eric, you've got to believe me!"

Thunder crashed against the house. The lights went out. Silence held the room.

"I suppose he cut the wires, too," said Eric. "Don't be so damn suspicious, Jim. We're not trying to double-cross you."

"The lights don't prove a thing," said Jim. "The storm did that. I'm not trusting anybody."

"Cut the jaw," said Eric, "and let's see if we can find some candles."

Hurried footsteps sounded on the rug. Then Perce screamed "Look! Lights! Anderson's place has lights, and it's on the same line!"

"Someone cut the wires," whispered Eric. "Someone . . ."

Perce slammed himself against the door and pounded on it with his fists. "Let me out of here," he screamed. "Let me out of here! Let me out!"

"That's no good," said Eric. "I'm going to see if I can find a candle." He stumbled against a chair and cursed. He lit a match and walked into the hall. Perce fell into a chair and covered his face with his hands. Jim stood nearby, motionless.

"Find anything?" Perce asked, when Eric came back.

"I got a candle," Eric said. "But it won't last very long." He came in holding the candle in front of him. The spasmodic light deepened the lines on his drawn face, outlined his eyes with cavernous shadows. His face was like a mask of fear. He set the candle on the mantle and then drew back.

The three men were seated far apart. They didn't speak. Their eyes darted from the flickering flame to one another. Their hands were clenched. A wrist watch inexorably counted the tickings of eternity. Eric was the first to move. "Got to see a man," he said, rising to his feet. His words were strained.

Jim watched him out of the corner of his eyes and glared back at Perce. The sound of Eric's feet faded into silence. The silence was shattered by a gasping scream. Eric came pounding back.

"I saw him," he said. There was no expression in his words. "I saw him."

"Saw whom?" snarled Jim.

"I saw Uncle John!"

"No!" screamed Perce. "No!"

"I saw him. Upstairs in the hall. He was standing there looking at me."

"Don't be a damn fool," said Jim. "He's dead."

"I know," said Eric. "This thing was dead, too. It didn't move. It didn't speak. It just stood there."

"It's your imagination," said Jim.

Eric shook his head. "No. I saw it."

"I'm going to see it," said Jim. He began moving toward the stairs. Then he stopped and turned. "Come on, Perce," he said. "We'll both go. Just to prove Eric's wrong."

"I don't want to see it," said Perce. But he rose slowly to his feet and went to Jim. "I don't want to see it. I want to prove to myself that there's nothing there." They walked off together.

Eric covered his face with his hands. His hands tightened convulsively when he heard Perce scream. He got up and met Perce and Jim in the hall.

"You saw it," said Eric.

"Yes," said Jim. "It just stood there."

"But he's dead," said Perce. "He's dead."

"I know," said Eric. "I gave him enough to kill ten like him."

"I saw him in his coffin," said Jim. "I saw him in his grave. I saw him buried under six feet of ground, and the dead don't walk again."

The candle guttered and went out.

Finally the rain stopped and there was no sound at all. Then there was the soft rustling of cloth and the sound of feet moving across the carpet; a gasp and a groan.

"He's dead," said Jim. "Eric's dead."

"You killed him," said Perce.

"Yes," said Jim. "Because he killed Uncle John. Now maybe the thing is satisfied. Now maybe it will go away."

"Light a match," said Perce.

Jim lit a match. It showed Eric sitting in his chair, leaning slightly forward. The light of the match reflected from the knife blade in his throat, just below the ear. Then the match went out.

"You killed him because you want all the money," said Perce. "You're going to kill me, too."

51

"No," said Jim. "I left the knife there. I killed him so the thing would go away. I don't want the money."

"Light another match," said Perce.

Jim lit another match. His face was haggard and his eyes were wild. His features wore the slackness of an idiot's.

Perce lifted the gun and aimed between Jim's eyes. Then he pulled the trigger.

"You wanted all the money," he said. "You were going to kill me, too. Now I'll get all the money." The echoes quieted and died.

Footsteps sounded upstairs in the hall. Then on the stairs.

"It's coming down," said Perce. "It's coming down to get me." He laughed. "It won't get me," he said. He lifted the gun to his head. "It won't get me." The gun roared. . . .

I poured a stiff drink from the bottle and drank it straight. The old man was looking at me, waiting for me to speak.

"That makes a hell of a good story," I said, searching in my mind for what name he used to write under.

"But of course you refuse to accept it as the truth," he said.

"Naturally, I don't believe in ghosts," I shrugged.

The old man smiled tolerantly. "At first Eric and Jim and Perce didn't believe in them either. But when tension developed in their minds, they finally did—and went mad."

"But you said this Uncle John was dead," I protested.

"No," he corrected me. "*They* said he was dead. What actually happened was that the heart medicine he was taking acted as an antidote to the poison they gave him, and he only became very sick.

"With all his money it was easy to have a sculptor make a wax effigy of him to be buried. The rest was relatively simple."

It still made a good story, but all I had seen in the Hollingway tragedy was the bare fact that a house had been struck by lightning and burned to the ground, with three unfortunate men trapped inside.

"What about the fire?" I asked. "You forgot to explain about the fire."

"Oh, that! Well, the whole mess was pretty sickening, and if the newspapers got hold of it, it would have been nauseating, so I punctured the oil tank down in the cellar and attached a long fuse to it."

"*You!*"

"I? Did I say *I*? Pardon me. A slip of the tongue. I meant Uncle

John." He smiled at me benevolently. "Fancy me doing a thing like that."

But suddenly it struck me that there was only one writer whose mind was capable of thinking up a situation like that. His name had been J. J. Drake. And J. J. Drake was the pen-name used by a mild little man called John Hollingway.

MOTIVE

AUGUST DERLETH

Eliphas Jackson could have been summed up in a few words: middle-aged, timid, going bald. He wore glasses over mild, watery blue eyes, and had blond hair around his bald spot. He dressed neatly, whether following his profession or not, and was surprised when people took an interest in him. But he appreciated it very much. He did not have much companionship and was always somewhat lonely.

So when the elderly traveler who had come to the hotel only a little while after he himself had come invited him to his room for a little talk, he accepted readily enough and eyed his acquaintance anew: a bluff, red-faced man, with twinkling eyes and graying moustache. Probably in clothes. There was nothing distinctive about him.

Jackson was talked at effusively, waved expansively to a chair, and had the slightly disagreeable sensation of having a newspaper fanned under his nose.

"Murch is the name, sir," his red-faced host said jovially. "Just plain Murch. It's not much of a name, but it'll do."

Jackson smiled. "It's not as common as Jackson," he said almost apologetically.

"Perhaps not," conceded Murch. "But I don't know that I'd a lot rather have a common name like that. It's a good sound name, whatever you say."

He bustled about and got out a siphon and some glasses, explaining that he had been experimenting with some Sauterne—"Gassing it a bit," he said, but it tasted good enough. Of course, if Jackson were a connoisseur, or something like that, he wouldn't care for it. Jackson tried it gingerly and admitted that it was good.

Murch settled himself into a chair which fitted him too snugly and waved the paper at him again. "Been reading about these queer murders," he said. "Awful stuff, I call it."

"You mean those people dying in the small towns around here?" Jackson asked.

Murch nodded. "One in almost every town so far, right up the line to here. Seems to be working along this route, and it wouldn't surprise me if one hit this town, too—but I hope not until I get out of it." He giggled.

Jackson reflected briefly that he had a vaguely disgusting giggle.

Murch leaned confidentially over the table. "You know, Jackson, I've got a theory—a great theory about those crimes," he said. "I'll bet I could tell you just how they were done."

Jackson looked polite. "Could you?" he asked.

"I could," affirmed Murch gravely.

"The papers said the police didn't have any clues," mused Jackson thoughtfully.

"Well, it's true they hadn't much to go on. Take that first murder now—an old woman. Like a bolt out of the blue, it was. She'd no relatives, no money to leave, nothing; there was absolutely no motive. Nothing to be gained by her death. I can well imagine the police were baffled on that one especially. It was the lack of motive —that always gets them, you know. They go looking for it right off, and when they can't find it, most of the time they're lost right at the start. At that, I don't know that the second didn't puzzle them still more. Young man that time, remember? They couldn't find a shred of motive that time, either. And no connection among the six who died."

"Have they found a motive in any?" inquired Jackson.

"Not one," replied Murch proudly, and then leaned forward again to add, "But *I* have. I've found a motive for every one of them!"

Jackson looked at him a little more closely. The twinkling quality seemed to have left Murch's eyes, and a light seemed to glow from behind them. There was something hard and glittering about them. It was uncanny and disturbing. A breath of uneasiness fanned up in Jackson.

"Really," he said.

"I have," repeated Murch.

Jackson waited.

"Going around the way I do," continued Murch, "I found out that every town where a murder was committed was visited by a medicine show. A one-man show on a one-night stand. The fellow sold some kind of laxative pills by the box, cheap, too. Well, sir, in one of those boxes in each town, that man put a poison pill. Cyanide—that's what the autopsies showed on these bodies, remember? He didn't know who'd get that poison pill, but he didn't care. He'd be safely out of there before anything happened, and in that way, no one would ever suspect, because he never sold more than one poison pill in a town."

"But there's no sense to it," protested Jackson.

"Of course not," agreed Murch instantly. "But that's the way it was done. I'll bet on it. I'll bet the police have been making inquiries and traced some of the cyanide. Fellow wasn't shrewd enough, but they'll find him, they'll find him, all right, you mark my words!"

"They will?"

"They most certainly will. It's only a matter of time. But I'll bet they won't guess at the motive until the last, and then if they'll look up that fellow's ancestry, they'll find proof and trace of it." He leaned over and tapped Jackson's knee, and his voice dropped to a harsh whisper. "You see, the fellow's a murderer of the worst kind, and it's very likely he doesn't know it."

Jackson was fascinated against his will. He stared at the remarkable hardness of his companion's eyes until he felt his mouth go dry. Unaccountably, he felt himself loathing this sinister fellow-traveler, he felt a revulsion rising within him, and he wanted desperately to escape. But he did not move. He licked his lips tentatively and asked in a whisper as low as Murch's,

"How so? How so he doesn't know it?"

"It's the motive," said Murch triumphantly. "That's the secret!"

"And what—what is the motive?"

"You'd never guess, not in a hundred years," said Murch. "I'll tell you how I've got it figured out. The man's a homicidal maniac, that's what. Every little while he has to kill someone. It's a strange kind of mania—he might know what's the matter with him, and he might not. Ten to one, he doesn't. It works like this—Every little while a sort of spell comes over him, he becomes someone else for that time and he has to kill someone. Do you understand that, Jackson? He simply must kill someone, or he must put into operation a plan to kill someone. Most of the time when they're like that, they get violent; they take up a knife or pistol and go after the first person they see. But sometimes it's different; sometimes they work secretly. Like this man now, this fellow who's done all these murders and got away with it. Take him, now—can you guess what happens to him?"

Jackson shook his head mutely, his eyes almost afraid to leave Murch's face. He saw that his companion was perspiring.

"Well, he gets a spell like that, and he likely gets it when he's making his pills. He makes them all, you know, and when he gets such a spell, he's a dangerous maniac, the worst kind. And he makes one pill up with deadly poison in it, only one; and he puts it in one of the boxes to be sold in the next town—or if he makes them up for several towns, he puts one poison pill in each batch. If he expects to sell twenty boxes, he puts a pill in one of them. That's the way he does it. Once he's done that, he'll be satisfied; he doesn't know who'll get that pill, but he knows that somebody will die by his hand. And very likely, once it's done, he forgets all about it. He comes out of his spell, and he never knows what happened. He sees his pills done, but he doesn't know that somewhere among those boxes are scattered deadly poison pills. He's had his spell, you see, and like as not he's imagined all the suffering and agony those poor people are going through before they die. But after he's done the pills, he forgets; he's as sane as you and I."

The theory held Jackson almost as strongly as Murch's hypnotic eyes. His uneasiness had congealed into terror, but no sign of it passed his lips.

"If he doesn't know it," he began, "how can they prove it to him? What can they do to him?"

"They'll lock him up in an asylum—keep him in solitary, most likely, dark all the time. It'll be hell on him, being sane most of the time, sane as you and I, but it's the only thing to do."

Jackson caught what seemed to him a rising light in Murch's eyes; Murch was looking at him so strangely that his uneasiness and terror thrust sharply up within him, and he got up suddenly, mumbling that he had to go to his own room, that he had some letters to answer and had to get at them.

Murch waved the paper after him jovially enough but made no move to stop him.

Once in his own room again, Jackson shuddered. He sat down as if still under the influence of Murch's baleful eyes, and picked up a letter he had already read once that day—from the board chairman of the next village.

Dear Mr. Jackson:
We enclose herewith our permit as per your payment of the seventeenth for a one-night stand of your medicine show in our village on the night of the twenty-third . . .

What was it Murch had said? *Homicidal mania.*

He got up quite calmly and drew himself a glass of water. Then he brought his stack of pills to the table and began methodically going over them, going over the small boxes, one by one.

In the seventh one he found a pill somewhat different from the others—a little darker where the sugar coating had begun to crack and peel slightly.

He looked at it, took it out, and held it in his palm.

Then he pushed the box away, got up and pulled over the glass of water.

He took the pill and sat down to wait.

Murder in Bronze

Herbert L. McNary

Mr. Brickley walked into the office of Mr. Jennings. If there is any foundation for the adage that successful business partnerships are built upon contrast the firm of Jennings & Brickley, dental supplies, should be flourishing, even in these times. Oliver Jennings knew the dental supply business from the roots up and Bert Brickley knew how to get customers.

Mr. Brickley, short and rotund, and garbed in an eye-catching gray mixture, entered by the corridor door. The partners maintained separate offices in the same suite and there was a connecting door between the two offices, but Brickley had misplaced the key.

He undoubtedly could find it if he put his mind to the task, but such minor details annoyed him.

Jennings, crossing towards the filing cabinets with papers in hand, looked up over his spectacles. He, too, was short, about the same height as Brickley, but not nearly so plump. He was mild, meek, a typical business drudge with pale eyes and thinning gray hair.

"Did you want something Bert?"

"No, nothing particular," answered the partner, toying with a cigar, his small dark eyes squinting through the smoke, "just having my office floor oiled."

The senior partner frowned. "Have that done every week, don't you?"

"Well, I got stuck with that oil. Might as well use it. Besides I like to have my place looking—impressive."

Jennings surveyed the unpretentious furnishings of his office defensively. Despite the fact the funds came from the same account the two offices contrasted just as severely as the two partners.

"Hmm, as long as it's serviceable, that's all that counts."

"Well, you know how it is. The people who come into my office—well, we have to make a show." It was an old argument, but the senior partner recognized the fundamental truth. Money had to be spent to make money, only Bert had extravagant habits he should curtail in times like these. Jennings tugged at one of the drawers in the tall wooden file case and grumbled in exasperation as it stuck. He almost pulled the case over before he yanked the drawer open.

"You ought to get a new one of those," suggested Brickley. "It's out of date—"

"Can't afford it," snapped Jennings testily. He inserted the papers in the file and turned around.

"And while on the subject, Bert, we've got to put a little more pressure on our accounts."

Brickley waved the expensive cigar. "Oh, we can't be too hard on the dentists. People owe them money and take their time paying. We've got to be indulgent."

"Still, we ought to be getting more than we have." Jennings went to the closet for his coat and hat. He lunched between twelve and one while his junior partner, who arrived later in the morning and presumably had a later breakfast, went to lunch from one to two.

"I met Dr. Wynant yesterday," continued Jennings, pulling on his coat carefully because of torn sleeve lining and not observing that his partner stiffened tensely. "I mentioned our account with him casually, and he said he felt certain he had settled with you."

"Well, you know Wynant," protested Brickley with a short laugh. "No head for business. He probably *thinks* he made payment. Not that he isn't good. I'll drop around and see him this afternoon."

"He is going up to Maine on a two weeks' hunting trip," said Jennings curtly. "That is what gets under my skin. If they can afford hunting trips they can afford to pay their bills."

"Right," agreed Brickley and seemed anxious to change the subject. He knew how to do so. He crossed to Jennings' desk and picked up a book.

"New one? And on Caesar, too."

Jennings frowned uneasily. "Why—it's a first edition. A real bargain."

"How much?" challenged the junior partner.

"Er—three hundred—but you don't understand."

"Sure I do. We all have our weaknesses. With me it's clothes and showy things. With you it's anything connected with Caesar."

"After all, it affords me enjoyment," said Jennings a bit tartly. "Are you coming?"

The senior partner locked the door behind them and stepped into the outer office. It was his custom to lock his door when leaving. Any phone calls would come through the switchboard and could be transferred to Brickley.

Bert Brickley went into his office, richly furnished in mahogany, and sat down to think, rolling his cigar thoughtfully in his mouth and occasionally doing some figuring on a pad.

When the senior partner returned from lunch, Bert Brickley departed immediately. He did not go directly to his favorite dining place but crossed to the Avenue where he liked to stroll leisurely as though very much a part of this atmosphere of luxury; smiling and bowing at the least provocation and gazing into the art shops with all the appearance of a connoisseur. But today he hurried rather than strolled; and he did little bowing and smiling. But he did, however, gaze in a shop window displaying antiques and pieces of art. If his memory served him right—yes, there it was!

The junior partner of Jennings & Brickley stepped inside and made a purchase.

Bert Brickley's phone buzzed. Jennings was on the other end of an inside call.

"Bert, come in here at once. There's—well, come in here."

Brickley went into the senior partner's office, passing through the outer office as usual to do so. He found, in addition to the perplexed senior partner, two deliverymen and a large crate.

"Bert, do you know anything about this? What did we ever order from Bentino's? That's an art shop."

"It's a little surprise from me," smiled the junior partner, rubbing spatulate fingers. "A real bargain I knew you would appreciate. Open it, boys. I'll need your help."

The two deliverymen went to work on the box and soon had the top removed. Carefully they separated the packing and then with difficulty lifted out a heavy bronze bust.

"Julius Caesar—almost in the flesh," exclaimed the junior partner, spreading his hands. Jennings said nothing immediately. His sagging lips denoted mingled emotions. Of course the younger partner could not distinguish the enormous gulf between rare editions and manuscripts on Caesar and this grotesque monstrosity in bronze; yet, Bert meant well, and Jennings was too gentle to offend.

"It's—it's very thoughtful of you, Bert. You shouldn't have spent your money this way. Er—I was wondering what I would do with it—"

"Put it right up here," suggested the junior partner, indicating the filing cabinet. "Come on, boys, give me a lift."

The senior partner was about to protest. To have that with him all day long forecasted torture; but on second thought he realized that if he did not keep it here he would have to bring it home and keep it exposed where Bert could see it any time he dropped in. No, better to have it here where he would be engrossed in work and able to forget about it; and with it reposing on the file cabinet his back would be to it most of the day. Even when he went to the cabinet he would have to look up almost deliberately to see it. After a time he could devise some excuse to get rid of the gift.

About a week following this exposition of generosity on the part of Bert Brickley, the junior partner returned from luncheon to find the office force in a state of confusion.

"Oh, Mr. Brickley—Mr. Brickley," moaned Miss Stevens, the old maidish secretary, "something dreadful has happened. There has been an accident."

"An accident?"

"Yes. Mr. Jennings. He's been killed. I phoned the police. Perhaps I shouldn't. Maybe I should have waited."

"You did exactly right, Miss Stevens. We'll let them take entire charge when they come."

"They are here."

"Here?" exclaimed Brickley. "Er—they must have been very prompt."

The junior partner stepped into Jennings' office. A tall, somewhat gawky young chap in blue uniform stood at the door; probably the policeman picked up at the corner. At Jennings' desk sat a middle-aged man in drab civilians. His round face denoted curiosity rather than shrewdness as Brickley entered.

"I'm the junior partner," announced Brickley. "Miss Stevens told me there had been an accident. Is it—serious?"

"Yeah, pretty serious," said the headquarters man. "He's dead. That ain't official, of course. I have to wait for the coroner. But if he ain't dead I never saw a stiff."

Brickley peered past the desk. There on the floor near the filing cabinet lay the huddled form of the senior partner with matted blood in the thin gray hair. Near by on the floor reposed the up-ended bronze statue of Caesar.

"When did it happen?" asked Brickley.

"About quarter past one, if the dame outside phoned immediately like she said. She heard the crash and rushed in."

"I was to lunch. My office is next to this—"

"Yeah. I was there. Sit down, Mr. Brickley. I want some facts. We gotta turn in a report."

The junior partner took the other chair near the desk, careful to turn his back to the gruesome sight. There wasn't much to tell about Jennings. His age. Lived alone. No near relatives—

The headquarters man's feet went up on the desk as he tilted back in his chair. He saw Brickley frown.

"Seems natural to put my feet on the desk. It helps to think. Blood rushes to the head, or maybe it's the brains. Try it." The gray, level eyes seemed suddenly impelling. Brickley felt confused. "Try it," repeated the detective, "an' see if I ain't right."

Almost as if hypnotized Brickley obeyed. His feet lifted to desk in a fashion similar to the detective's. If Jennings could see this lack of dignity. . . .

"Think any better?"

"I—I can't say that I do."

"Well, just think back over the last couple of hours. Say between 12 and 1. Maybe I can help. Jennings, here, goes to lunch. You come in that door. Yeah, I know it ain't used much. You lost the key. But it was used recent. There's fingerprints. Too blurred to be read, but damp enough to show they were placed there recent. Fat fingers have a way of sweating.

"Then the last page of this report on the desk is missing. Jennings comes in; wonders where it can be, and finally goes to the file. Maybe he's mad. He don't look up and notice that the statue is balanced on the edge, havin' been shifted that way while he was out to lunch. He jerks open the drawer. It sticks anyway. I tried it. Down comes—who is it? Napoleon? Well, it don't matter. He did a complete job."

Brickley had been staring open-mouthed. Now he recovered his composure.

"Why—why, this is preposterous! Just because there are a few fingerprints on the door—"

"Fingerprints—hell! *Heel prints!* You're kind of short, Brickley, and you had to stand on a chair to fix that statue. You left your mark. Yours is the only office that was oiled recently; and besides these heels that you're so kindly showin' me are peculiar. Must be expensive. Well, there's an impression of one of them on the chair. No wonder I asked Miss Stevens if you bought that statue.

"Don't know the motive; but I've a hunch that if I impound the books I'll find it. I'm impoundin' them shoes, too. You'll have to come along in your stocking feet."

But just then Brickley looked as if he would have to go on a stretcher.

Mushrooms

Chet Williamson

When 3-Ball and X-Too got on the train, they walked immediately to the last car, X-Too in the lead. 3-Ball was glad, since it gave him a chance to watch X-Too move, and X-Too moved about as def as any brother he'd ever seen, even with a piece on his hip. The piece made X-Too move even cleaner than usual, thrusting out his hip to the left as if to make up for the uneven balance the pistol caused.

They didn't pass any cops on the way, and there was nobody in the last car except a tall and stringy blind kid with shades and one of those long white canes with the red tip. He was sitting near the center of the car, his head back, blind eyes looking up. Looked a little like Stevie Wonder, 3-Ball thought, wondering if the blind brother could be a musician.

"Think he's a musician?" he asked X-Too.

X-Too gave him The Look. "Whatta fuck you talkin'?" he said.

"Blind homeboy. Look like Stevie Wonder."

"Well, I look like fuckin' Ice Cube, only badder, and I don't rap. Now stop talkin' shit."

They sat down at the very back of the car, which ran across a section of dead track, throwing the train into total darkness and stopping the noisy fans for five seconds. "Wonder if that home know when that happens," said 3-Ball when the lights and fans came on again.

"What?"

"When it gets dark in here."

"How he know? Homeboy's blind."

"Well, y'know, sometimes they can tell between light 'n dark."

X-Too didn't say anything, just kept looking at the door at the front of the car. Finally he spoke. "We ice that motherfucker soon's he come in. Don't give him no chance to grab his own piece."

"Yeah. Smoke 'im in the fuckin' feet."

"Not the feet *first*, asshole. Fuckin' *head* first, or chest. *Then* his feet." X-Too nodded. "Right in his goddam Air Jordans, home. Nail his feet to the cross with bullets."

Lord Jake-Ay was the man they were about to kill. Jake-Ay had been the one who had shot Luther JD dead, then shit in his suede Fila hightops and jammed them back on Luther JD's feet, leaving him lying in an alley with shoes full of crap. On top of that, Jake-Ay had pissed on Luther JD's colors. It had been stupid of Jake-Ay, but everybody knew that Jake-Ay was stupid, even Jeango, the Blews' main man, but he kept Jake-Ay around anyway, since Jake-Ay would smoke anyone anytime.

Well, now X-Too and 3-Ball would smoke Jake-Ay.

They knew that he got on every night at the third stop past where they got on, always at the same time, after he got done pushing rock in the Van Norris Street arcade, got on and headed uptown to chill with Jeango. 3-Ball thought they'd grab his take, but maybe not. It would be some def gesture, leaving the money on him, just banging his feet until they were bloody stumps of dirty white leather and muscle and bone. The Blews would get the message all right. All the boys in the hood would know it was The Chillin Crew. And no shit and no piss. That kind of jive was for animals like Jake-Ay.

David heard the voices at the end of the car. Two young black men. They spoke seldom, and although they made no attempt to talk quietly, the sound of the train prevented his picking out more than the occasional word.

He felt the train begin to stop, and knew they must be just below the theatre district, although he could not see the walls of the tunnel pass by more slowly until the individual bricks and the name of the station were discernible. When he felt the train stop and heard the doors slide open, he started to loudly whistle, "Stop in the Name of Love."

"What the motherfuck . . ." he heard one of the young men say, but kept whistling, thinking about Nancy and how hard it was going to be for her. He had been blind from birth, but to learn what it was like when you were in your twenties—damn, that was tough.

He kept whistling, heard the door at the front of the car rasp open, heard the scrape of a cane on the floor, heard her call his name, tentatively, and with no little fear. "David?"

"Here, Nancy," he said. "Fifth seat back on the right."

The cane stuttered along, and he felt the vibration as she grasped the edge of each seat, counting. "That's right, here," he said when he heard her beside him.

Just as she sat, the train lurched and started, as she fell against him. He felt something strike his thigh and clatter to the floor. Unerringly he leaned forward and skimmed his fingers just above the linoleum, immediately contacting her sunglasses. As he lifted them, he could feel that they were the type with side panels, allowing no one to peer in. He took her hand and placed the left stem into it.

"Thanks," she said.

"Get down okay from your apartment?"

"Yeah. But God, it was rough. Getting down the street to the station was scary, but once I was down here, finding the right platform . . ." She sighed with a shudder. "I must have asked half a dozen people. I feel so much at the mercy of just anybody."

"You'll get over it," he told her. "It's rough at the start."
"I don't know how it could get any rougher," she said.

"Fuck, man," X-Too said.
"What?"
"Thought that blind fuck be off by now. 'Stead he meet some bitch."
"She fly, though," 3-Ball said, then added, " 'Cept she blind."
"Wouldn't stop me. Fly's fly. Head down, butt up, don't matter they see or not. Bust her butt."
"We do that?" asked 3-Ball, trying not to sound anxious.
"Shit, no. We bangin' Lord Jake-Ay tonight, not pussy. Wish they get off, though."
"Got another stop. Maybe they will."
"They don't, we tromp 'em down we have to. They just mushrooms."
"Yeah." 3-Ball chuckled. "Mushrooms." He thought it would be a pity, though, to burn a bitch that good looking. "You know, I seen her somewhere," he said after a moment's thought. "Ain't she that bitch inna commercial—for that, what the fuck, secretary school or somethin'?"
"What trash you talkin'? Blind secretaries?"
"Nah . . ."
"How them bitches type? Got Braille typewriters?"
"Nah, nah, they ain't *blind* secretaries."
"Then what that bitch be sellin' for 'em? Motherfucker, but you dumb."
"She fly enough to do commercials," 3-Ball insisted.
"Yeah, fuck, sellin' canes." X-Too glared at the couple. "They don't get off the next stop, they need more than canes. Fuckin' mushrooms. Smash 'em. Cold smoke 'em."
The lights and the fans went off, started again. The train began to slow.

"You hear those guys?" David asked Nancy.
"What guys?"
"Two homeboys in the back of the car. Left side."
"How do you know that?"
"Heard them talking. You'll hear when we stop now."
The train shivered to a halt. The doors slid open, but David heard no one get on or off. The men in the back were silent, and

David thought he sensed a tension in them. When the doors closed, he heard only a few words, one of which was "mushrooms."

Mushrooms. They were hardly talking about fungi, David thought, so it must have been innocent bystanders they were referring to. But what the hell, it was probably just gang talk, bravado. He had heard enough of it growing up in the projects. If the two had been planning to do anything to him and Nancy they probably would have done it by now.

David had little fear of the trains. He'd been robbed before, but he had always been cooperative and never been hurt. He always carried twenty dollars with him. It was no more than he could afford to lose, and just enough to satisfy a mugger.

"I hear them now," Nancy whispered.

David heard them too. Their voices were pitched lower now, and from their tone he knew he had been right about the tension he had sensed. But he had heard it all before, and if he had left a subway car every time he heard those tight, choppy tones, he would have had to cab everywhere. Maybe they were on their way to a drug deal, or, hell, maybe just a date. People could get edgy about a lot of little things.

"I hear them," Nancy repeated, "but I can't tell exactly where they are. How do you know?"

"Same way I knew where to get your sunglasses. Get a sense from the sound of things. I know—aurally—what a subway car's like, how the sounds bounce off the walls, how many rows, how many seats. And something close, like your glasses, well, that's easy. Most sighted people could do it, they put their mind to it. They drop things in the dark, they poke around for a while. But if they'd just listen to it hit, even something little, they could reach right for it."

"Um. That's neat. I really appreciate you helping me like this, David."

"No problem." David smiled, and hoped she could sense it. He had helped a lot of people like Nancy who came to the Blind Association. He always enjoyed it, showing people the ropes, fascinating them with his abilities and teaching them to do the same kind of thing. He just hoped it would do her some good.

The train jerked, and began to move.

"Shoulda told 'em to get off, maybe," said 3-Ball.

X-Too frowned even deeper than before. "Hell, we make 'em get off, they's a cop at the next stop. They don't get off in time, fuck 'em. Maybe we bust caps on 'em, they don't get smoked before."

3-Ball sat back and tried to relax, but it was hard. He heard that Lord Jake-Ay had an Uzi, though Luther JD had been smoked with a .38. X-Too had an Uzi too, but only used it to cap homes from cars. It was too big to carry around. What X-Too had tonight was a .44 magnum, its six and a half inch barrel jammed down his pants leg next to his dick. It was still a big gun, big enough to tear off Jake-Ay's feet once they smoked him dead.

'Course maybe they could shoot him so that he didn't die right away, but could feel his toes being blown off. 3-Ball grinned at the thought, and his hand went inside his bright red jacket, to his waistband and his own pistol, a sweet little Colt Cobra that X-Too called a pussy gun. That hadn't stopped 3-Ball from capping three Blews with it in as many months. And tonight, Jake-Ay.

Then he looked at the man and woman sitting halfway up the car, and thought he should tell them, tell them now before the train stopped, so that they could get off right away, before Jake-Ay got on and the shooting started. He knew mushrooms were mushrooms, but damn, there was no point in blind people being hurt. After all, they hadn't seen him or X-Too, couldn't make any I.D.

He stood up and started to walk toward them, but X-Too's shout stopped him. "3-Ball! Whatta fuck you doin'?"

"I'm just—"

"Get yo' ass back here. *Sid*down!"

3-Ball shambled the few feet back to where X-Too sat. When he looked behind him, he saw that the man and woman were cocking their heads as if listening to the rebuke. 3-Ball sat down and said softly, "Man, don't dis me in front of them people, okay?"

"Fuck, they can't see, they don't know I dissed you."

"Still, man . . . I just wanted to tell them to get off fast, the train stop. You know, 'fore Jake-Ay get on."

"Well, that was dumbfuck. What you care? They start walkin' off, Jake-Ay use 'em for cover comin' in, now that's fuckin' brighta you. Just leave 'em where they sittin'." X-Too looked out the window at the dark rushing past. " 'Sides, we gotta cap 'em anyway."

"What? Why?"

"They heard your name. I call it."

3-Ball could only see X-Too's reflection in the dirty glass, but thought that the dark line of X-Too's mouth was smiling. Maybe X-Too called his name on purpose. Sometimes 3-Ball thought that X-Too just liked smoking people, it didn't matter who. Yeah, maybe he did it on purpose.

"Damn," 3-Ball said. "Thassa shame, have to waste a fly piece of pussy like that."

"Accidents happen," said X-Too, still looking out the window.

When the train started to slow, X-Too and 3-Ball didn't wait until it stopped to take out their pistols. X-Too slid his .44 from his pants slow, a smooth smile on his face, like he was slipping out his dick to show a bitch. 3-Ball just tugged his Cobra from his waistband, and out it came, the grips getting wet fast from the sweat on his palms. "Watch the side," X-Too said. "I take the front."

Finally the train stopped, and the doors opened, but no one came in. After half a minute the doors closed again, the train started rolling. "Ain't comin' in the side," said 3-Ball.

"Shut up," X-Too said, his yellow glare fixed on the window of the door at the front of the car. "I see 'im."

Now 3-Ball saw him too, and they both slouched down so that only the tops of their capped heads were visible over the seat in front of them. Jake-Ay slammed a fist against the door, smashing it open, and came into their car. He was wearing a heavy leather coat and a Kangol whose brim hid his eyes.

X-Too's first shot took him by surprise, giving him no time to draw his gun. It hit him in the left shoulder, slamming him back against the edge of the door.

The sudden motion made 3-Ball's shot miss, and he saw blood and more splatter from the rip in Jake-Ay's leather coat. Then Jake-Ay dove into the corner, flipped back his coat with his good arm, and 3-Ball knew why Jake-Ay's coat was so huge. It had to be to keep an Uzi under it.

X-Too stood up to get off a second shot just as Jake-Ay let loose with the Uzi. It spat a trail of bullets across the width of the car, and 3-Ball ducked down behind the seat. The last thing he saw had been the blind man and woman dropping, and he wondered if they had been hit, then decided they hadn't, because he would have seen their heads pop.

Then he heard X-Too's .44 roar again, and X-Too's voice screaming, and the Uzi stop chattering, and when he looked he saw X-Too falling down on top of him like a big black tree, and he caught him, one Crew catching another, and felt a hot wetness in X-Too's belly, and heard X-Too moan, "Fuck, fuck, *motherfuck*," over and over like some dumb, simple rap.

3-Ball staggered to his feet, his Cobra up and pointing toward the end of the car, but Lord Jake-Ay's face beneath the Kangol looked like grape jelly, and he wasn't moving. The Uzi lay silent across his lap.

Now X-Too was saying something that 3-Ball couldn't make out, something that sounded like X-Too was trying to whistle through his teeth. 3-Ball leaned across, and X-Too grabbed him with the hand that wasn't holding his insides.

"*Feet,*" X-Too said. "Feet . . . shoot his . . . motherfuck . . . feet. Use the Uzi . . ."

3-Ball nodded, climbed over X-Too, and ran down to the end of the car, his Cobra trained on Jake-Ay just in case. As he passed their seat, he saw the man and woman crouched behind the seat, probably wondering what the hell was happening.

He grabbed the Uzi, stuck the Cobra in his belt, stood over Jake-Ay's body, and fired into the dead man's feet. The bullets went through the floor of the car, and blood, ripped muscle, and bone shards spattered his own clean hightops, but he kept smoking until the Uzi was empty, and Jake-Ay's right foot was only pink pulp. There wasn't even that much left of the severed right foot, most of which had been smashed down through the floor onto the tracks.

Then 3-Ball put the empty weapon under his arm, and trotted back to X-Too. X-Too's face was ashy, and blood and something yellow was seeping through his fingers where he held them against his stomach.

"Now . . . cap the mushrooms," he rasped. ". . . then get me out . . ."

The train was starting to slow for the next stop, and 3-Ball knew he'd have to be quick. He set the Uzi next to X-Too, yanked the Cobra from his belt, walked up to the seat, and lifted the gun to fire.

But when he saw the girl's face, so pretty even though masked by sunglasses, he hesitated for just a moment, just long enough for the train to cross a rough switch and lurch savagely, so that he nearly fell, and the pistol slipped from his sweating, trembling hand. He saw it spinning down into the dark space between the man and the woman, and the image locked in his sight as they hit dead track, and all the lights in the car went out.

David had heard the shots, the running footsteps, then the same coming back, had heard them stop beside him and Nancy, had heard the gun hit the floor and slide across it.

He reached down, to the right, and grasped it with his right hand, took Nancy's hand with his left, pressed it against her palm, said, "Do it," praying that she would.

Then he felt the gun wrenched away from him, and heard her sunglasses clatter again on the floor. This time he didn't reach down to pick them up.

In three seconds, when the lights came back on, 3-Ball found himself unarmed, and the bitch with the gun in her hands, swinging it in his direction. Blind or not, he wasn't taking any chances. If he grabbed it, she'd sure as hell pull the trigger, and the way the damn piece was waggling in his direction, he didn't want to risk it. So he moved back slow, watching the black muzzle like a blind eye.

Then he heard a voice roar, "*Geddown!*" and he hit the floor, scuttling back toward X-Too, thinking that if he got X-Too's .44 he could smoke the bitch. But then he heard his gun go off in the bitch's hand, and saw X-Too's gun come thudding down into the aisle, along with X-Too's shoulders and head, part of which had been blown away by the crosscut bullets with which 3-Ball kept his Cobra loaded. Damn, he thought, not bad cappin' for a blind bitch.

3-Ball kept crawling toward the .44, now only eight feet away, moving as silently as he could so the bitch wouldn't hear him. He had halved the distance between himself and the gun, when he heard footsteps behind him. He turned, looked, and froze when he saw the woman standing, her face and the Cobra pointing in his direction. Her sunglasses had come off, and he could see her eyes now, blue and real pretty for blind eyes.

But it was all right. As long as she didn't hear him, he could grab that gun, take sweet, slow aim, and drop her like a sack of shit. He made himself look away from her, and kept crawling.

"Stop," she said. Her voice was real pretty, even shaking like it was, but he just smiled and kept crawling toward the gun, now nearly within his reach.

"Stop," she said again. "*Stop*, red jacket!"

Red jacket? The words froze him. How'd the bitch know what he had on, unless . . .

He turned and looked up at her, at her bright, blue, pretty eyes that he damn well *knew* he'd seen on the TV, staring at him, seeing him . . .

Yeah. Really *seeing* him.

"Stop," she said again, in the voice he'd heard telling all about that secretarial school.

But he couldn't stop. Not this close. And he turned and reached for the gun, grabbed it, brought it around, and then the bullet smashed into him and he went blind and deaf and dumb for always.

When the police got on at the next stop, they found three dead men and two people alive, one blind man, one sighted woman. One of the cops helped the woman pick up the things that had fallen out of her bag. The last thing he found was a script of a play entitled *Wait Until Dark*.

"Did you get enough of a lesson for tonight?" David asked Nancy when they finally left the hospital.

"Yes," she said, holding his arm in hers, guiding him down the strange steps, over the strange sidewalk, toward a corner where they could catch a cab.

"Sedative helping?" he asked her, thinking that he felt a lot calmer now. But he hadn't killed anyone.

"I think so. I'm still shaky. God, what a nightmare. A bad dream that got worse. Let's sit down. Just for a minute. My knees are still trembling." They sat on a bench, but she still held David's arm.

"I thought I was playing, you know?" said Nancy, almost to herself. "Like a game. Sensually slumming. But now I feel like being blind is . . . as much of a craft as acting. Even an art. How you ever found that gun, just grabbed it so fast . . . I never could have found it in the dark that way."

David turned toward her. "Mushrooms were meant for the dark," he said, and she gave a little laugh, then stopped, as if angry with herself for being flippant after what she had done.

"I found it," David said, then added slowly, softly, "But I couldn't have shot them."

"No. No. You couldn't see them."

Now he was even quieter. "I didn't say that."

She said nothing, then released his arm. When she spoke again, her words were chill and distant. "God. It must be hard to be blind."

"Maybe we should all be blind," David said. "It makes it a lot harder to kill people."

Nancy looked at him for a long time. Though he couldn't see her, he felt her eyes on him. By the time the cab drove by, it had grown colder, and no less dark.

NEW BLOOD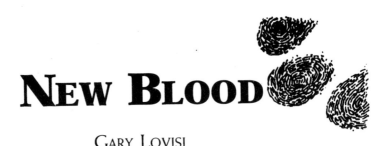

GARY LOVISI

He only had one more to go. One more and he'd be in the record books. One more and he'd be Number One! One more and he'd be the greatest of them all.

But it wasn't easy. With every killing the cops closed in on him more and more. The noose circled and constricted. His scent grew warmer and the chances of getting caught came closer. And he still had so much work to do. So much left unfinished.

It wasn't as easy as all the papers made it look either. No one seemed to understand. The victims, they all had to be just right. They couldn't be just anyone. That was the hard part and it was getting impossible now. There weren't that many accessible nurses in the city hospital system. Everyone was on the lookout. They were all so careful now, and the police were watching. Many of the best prospects didn't even go to work anymore. It made it hard to find out where they lived. Many others were guarded day and night. He knew. He checked. They were not accessible.

He preferred long-haired blondes. He knew he'd have to get at least one more of these to break his record. The papers said it all in big bold headlines:

> NURSE KILLER STILL AT LARGE!
> 12 NURSES SLAIN IN 12 WEEKS!
> TERROR GRIPS THE CITY!
> WHO WILL BE NUMBER 13?

It was not easy. One nurse a week. Twelve long weeks. He'd wanted to give up weeks ago. Stop it all. Maybe turn himself in? He had actually hoped to get caught—but then the record stared him in the face—the newspapers and TV news played it up so big— he was *almost* the greatest mass serial murderer of nurses of all time —it was a challenge he could not ignore. But enough musings. He had work to do. Tonight was the last night of the thirteenth week. He'd have to do it tonight. It must be tonight. He had to stay on schedule.

* * *

He found another nurse. He had this one picked out since yesterday. He'd followed her. Watched her. Found her address where she lived on First Street in Park Slope. It was a short walk from where she worked at the Medical Center. The giant Methodist Hospital had plenty of nurses to choose from. But too many were Puerto Rican, a lot were black or from the islands, too many were Indian or Paki. All not right. Then there was this nice Irish blonde. And she was just right.

He'd noticed her. Her hair so long. So blonde. He'd never seen her before at the hospital. He figured she was new. She was. He liked that. Laughed about it in his twisted mind. New blood. He needed new blood.

He stalked her. She was a harmless young doe. He was the big bad wolf. He felt the sharpness of his knife, as he did so he touched himself, feeling himself grow. He anticipated the time. It would be very soon now.

This was just what he needed. A new girl. She was one of the prettiest he'd ever had this way. He was getting more excited minute by minute. Anticipating.

Moving fast he followed her down the dark and lonely streets.

She looked back now! Thought she saw someone. He ducked behind a stoop, she saw nothing and kept walking. He followed again.

She reached Number 127. He'd cased the apartment building yesterday. There were ten floors. Her place was on the seventh floor, apartment 7A. He moved in quickly and carefully behind her.

She startled, jumped.

"Oh, hi, I'm sorry," he said so cordially, with such a smile, "I know I've got the key here somewhere. . . ."

She turned, she looked at him. Sized him up. Wrong.

She held the door for him. Smiled.

She smiled! He liked that!

"You're the guy from 8C, Mr. . . . ?"

"Sure. Johnson. Can never find my key."

She held the door open for him to enter the building. They walked together to the elevator. They got in the elevator together.

She pressed 7.

He remembered just in time and pressed 8.

She relaxed.

He got that weird feeling. Kept quiet. Watched her without

letting her see him watching her. She turned and smiled. He smiled back.

The doors opened on the seventh floor. She got out and walked across the hall to her door. He watched her put her key into the door. Turn the knob. Saw the door open a crack and before she could open it farther—before the elevator doors closed and took him up to the eighth floor—he was upon her. Pushing her into the apartment. Throwing her down to the floor. Closing the door behind him. Locking it quickly. Tight shut. Like a vault. So she could never escape. Never!

Then he turned to the girl. Blonde. Long hair. Pretty. Very pretty. Laying on the floor at the other end of the room. Motionless. She was all his now.

She was laying there face down. She still didn't move. He came closer to her. The shadows of the dark room making his movements mysterious. Fearsome.

He touched himself in anticipation. Looking at her laying there. Helpless. Touching himself. Imagining.

He drew out the knife. It was long, sharp, the steel called out to him.

And then the lights went on! From out of nowhere a dozen armed men came at him. Knocking the knife from his hand. Grabbing him tightly. Holding him roughly with guns to his head while they frisked him for other weapons. He could not move.

The girl got up from the floor then. She took off the long blonde wig. Her real hair was short and black.

She held out the wig, "Here. Is this what you were after!"

"Liar!" he yelled at her, "You were so pretty. Instead you're just a disappointment like all the others."

"All those others you've killed?" she asked.

He didn't speak.

The girl held his knife so he could see it. "This is what you used to torture them. Such a terrible weapon. Why?"

He was quiet for a second, then smiled, said, "I know my rights. I want to see a lawyer. You can arrest me, but I don't have to tell you anything."

The girl smiled back, "Why darling, what makes you think we're the police?"

NIMBLE FINGERS

W. RYERSON JOHNSON

This much I knew: that Laramie had succeeded in opening the safe at 114 Rue Lovais, Paris, and had disappeared with the famous Voutir ruby.

Beyond that I knew nothing. A newspaper dispatch from Paris had been my source of information. That had been three weeks before. And I had had no word from Laramie since the night he sailed from New York. Frankly, I was worried.

Laramie was a new man in our select little crowd. We knew his record, of course, before ever we admitted him to our circle. That he was a brilliant and successful worker could not be denied. But, though we had the greatest respect for his prowess, we did not entirely approve of his methods, which were erratic, daring, and sensational to an extreme. He was an inveterate gambler—a magnificent bluffer. He would take a dozen chances where there was but need of taking one.

Once for a whole day he accompanied a detective who was out on his trail. He went the entire rounds, reported with him at headquarters, and returned at night with the dick's identification papers as a souvenir. He was as elated over the feat as if he had lifted a string of pearls.

Harwell censured him severely, but what was the use? Laramie only smiled, shrugged his lithe shoulders, went out the next day with the same dick and returned that evening with a new .45 blue-steel automatic. It was his way. He liked the excitement, he said. After that we took his escapades more or less as a matter of course. He *was* devilish clever.

We had planned the Voutir affair together, Laramie and I, the day before he sailed for France. He was to secure the ruby, and get it past the customs officials in whatever manner seemed expedient. I was to be of use only in disposing of the stone for a straight cash payment, after Laramie should get it into my hands. The profits, as always, were to be divided according to our respective risks in the enterprise.

And now it was three weeks, according to the newspapers, since Laramie had secured the well-known ruby. He should have been in New York before this. I stood gazing moodily out of the window. As I have said before, I was worried. The police of two continents were looking for the man. And he was given to taking such useless daredevil chances. Then, too, Laramie was, in a way, untried. True, he had always played square before. But this was his first really big job with us, and—Well, it was three weeks now. He should have been here in two at the most.

A taxi pulled up to the curb in front of the house and stopped with a jerk. A man stepped out.

"Laramie!" I cried, joyously, impulsively, to myself.

But, even as my lips formed the word, some of my old fears returned. It was Laramie, all right. But not the dashing, care-free Laramie of a month before. His old swagger was gone. As he turned toward the house he walked bent over, like an old man. It was with undisguised apprehension that I met him at the door and grasped his hand.

"Right in here, Laramie," I said.

He sank into a chair, wearily, as I looked to him eagerly for some sign. He gave me no satisfaction. I was alarmed. The man looked bad, worn, clearly haggard. White skin, hollow cheeks, dark circles under the eyes, all told of wearing days, sleepless nights, trouble. Or was it worry? My heart seemed to stop beating. Had he failed? Could he be holding out on us?

"Well, how's everything?" I asked, as casually as possible.

He answered, his eyes half closed, gazing at the floor:

"They hounded me from the moment I got the stone. Day and night—I couldn't shake 'em. It was hell."

He spoke jerkily, with apparent effort.

"I couldn't get a ship out of France. Tried on both coasts. Narrow escape both times. Managed to make it through Spain to Lisbon. Got an old tub, the *Queen Ann*, for New York. Young French dick got the ship, too, at the last minute."

He was speaking more evenly now.

"I bought off the wireless operator. It was hide-and-seek between the Frenchman and myself, all the way across. I used a disguise for the first couple days. But he was wise. Night and day we played the game. It just about wore me out.

"I was near all in to start with, you know, from a week's hounding around the continent. I took his gat away from him, though, a couple days out of New York."

Laramie, for the first time raising his eyes from the floor, smiled grimly at the recollection.

"Had a little peace then. Pitched the gat overboard, of course, before we made New York, and his papers too. I couldn't use 'em. They've got me tagged at the custom's office.

"When we docked, I no sooner stepped ashore than a dick and a customs officer grabbed me and rushed me to an inspection office at the end of the pier.

" 'We won't have to hold you here long, Laramie,' the customs guy says, grinning. 'Just long enough to go through your clothes. See you haven't any baggage.'

"I admitted readily enough that I was Laramie; they knew it, anyway. But I pretended to be wholly at a loss as to the reason I was being held. And when they ordered me to strip I protested, naturally; asked them how they got that way; told them to go to the devil.

"They stripped me themselves, then, and stood me in a corner of the room. They looked in my mouth, my ears. They combed carefully through my hair. After a long time in which they finally satisfied themselves that there was no ruby concealed on my body, they started in on my clothes.

"Garment by garment, they scrutinized every square inch of them. They ripped open my belt and necktie and pulled the padding out of the shoulders of my coat. They jerked the sweatband from my hat. Look at my shoes!—heels pulled off and toes cut clear through.

"It was nearly two hours before they tossed me my clothes in disgust and allowed me to dress. Oh, yes, they were good enough to lend me a bathrobe, and they wrote me out a check for my ruined clothes, too.

" 'Well, you're free, Laramie,' the inspector growled. 'That Paris wire was the bunk. The ruby's not on you.'

"So I dressed, and then in a roundabout way came here." He lowered his voice with an air of finality and his weary eyes again sought the floor.

I was disappointed—bitterly disappointed. Why had not Harwell seen through this blunderer? He had insisted that I do this job with him. And the man had failed! Doubtless he had attempted to pull the old plant trick. I turned on him, savagely.

"Why did you do it, man? You've been in the game long enough to know better than that. Why, that's amateur stuff, rank amateur. They've got it now. It doesn't matter where on the boat you hid it, in the stateroom or out of the stateroom—they've got it now."

Laramie spoke sharply, his features hardening, a glow in his dull eyes. "What do you mean, amateur stuff? Who said anything about hiding it on the boat? I'm not quite hopeless, you know."

Then his manner changed. He regarded me, a curious expression on his face. "Did I ever mention to you, Johnson, that I once played in vaudeville? I did, for several years," he went on, not waiting for me to reply. "I used to pull guinea pigs out of my hat, palm coins, do all sorts of sleight of hand, you know."

He smiled.

I was furious.

"Guinea pigs?" I railed. "Guinea pigs be damned! What's that to do with smuggling in the Voutir ruby, you fool?"

"The Voutir ruby, as you know, is perfectly flat on one side, and round—about the size of a quarter," he said, still smiling. "It has nothing to do with guinea pigs, particularly. *But remember what I said about sleight of hand and palming coins?*"

I stared at him, incredulously. "Then," I gasped, "then—you mean—"

He said not a word. Slowly he extended his arm and opened his hand.

The ruby lay in his palm.

NO FLOWERS FOR HENRY

Carl Hughes

The Shaws were in their kitchen, doing the dinner dishes, when the car turned into their driveway between the high mounts of snow. Henry took off his apron. "Here they are," he said, partly to his wife Alice and partly to the nondescript yellow tomcat, Bertie, who sat there on a kitchen chair.

It was only fair, he thought, to warn Bertie that his most voluble critic, Marguerite Bensinger, was arriving. In fact, he had had a little talk with Bertie earlier, about not being too offended by the things Marguerite was likely to say.

Henry knew, of course, that Bertie understood him. From the day the old boy had strolled into the yard to be adopted, the two had been able to communicate.

"You let them in, dear," Henry's wife said. "I don't want Sis to see my kitchen looking like this."

Henry went down the hall and pressed his forehead against the rectangle of glass in the upper third of the front door. He did not open the door at once, knowing the cold would chill him and he might shiver for as long as ten minutes. The cold affected him that way all the time now.

He did not wait for the Bensingers to ring the bell, however. When he saw them through the glass, he drew the door open.

"Welcome back to the frigid north," Henry said. Actually, his sister-in-law and her husband had returned three weeks ago from their Caribbean vacation, but this was the first time he had seen them. They had been too busy to visit, although the two sisters had talked at least once a day, at some length, on the telephone.

Carl Bensinger grinned and shifted his slide-projector case to his left hand so he could grasp Henry's outthrust hand with his right. They were the best of friends. "Frigid is the word," he agreed. "Henry, you lucky old buzzard, wait'll I tell you what—"

"For heaven's sake, go on *in!*" His wife gave him a push. "Do you want them to pay for heating the whole outdoors?" Like a performing bear in her bulky fur coat and high fur hat, she followed Carl over the threshold. "Where's Alice?" she demanded.

"In here, Sis," Alice Shaw called from the kitchen. "Come see my new refrigerator when you get your things off."

Marguerite Bensinger watched Henry hang her coat in the front-hall closet, then handed him her fur hat and went down the hall to the kitchen. Her husband frowned at Henry while shrugging his coat off. "You bought a refrigerator?"

Henry only nodded.

"What for? I thought you were all set to sell this place."

"Well," Henry said, "your wife's been talking to Alice, and we see a lot of problems." He picked up Carl's projector case and steered Carl into the living room. "I'm glad you brought this. Ours isn't working right."

"What do you mean, a lot of problems? What problems?"

"Oh, you know."

Carl backed up to an overstuffed chair and seated himself, still peering at Henry and still frowning. "No, I don't know. When you sold the florist shop you were like a kid getting out of school. You were all steamed up about leaving this lousy climate and going down there to Jamaica and growing flowers. What's wrong?"

Henry sat, too. "Nothing's wrong, Carl. Not *wrong*. Nothing's even decided yet. It's just that—"

"They hike the price on you? Man, if they did, I wouldn't blame them. That's a beautiful place you've got lined up there, Henry. We rented a car in Kingston and drove out for a look, and I want to tell you those Blue Mountains are really something. The house, too. *Did* they up the price?"

"No. It's not that."

"Then what is it, for Pete's sake? You were in seventh heaven about this thing when Marguerite and I went down there on our vacation."

"Well, I'm fifty-five years old, you know."

"What the hell's that got to do with it?"

"Alice, too. She's almost that age, Carl. Marguerite's been reminding her. It would mean starting all over—"

Henry paused to reach down and stroke his cat, who had wandered in from the kitchen. The cat rubbed its face against his hand and went over to Carl, who looked down with a grin and said, "Hi, you old buzzard. How's the world treating you?"

"Meow," said Bertie, strolling on to a favorite spot under the coffee table.

"As I was saying," Henry said, "It would mean starting all over in a strange place, finding new friends and getting used to new things and—well, you know. There'd be a certain amount of risk, too. There's no risk if I just retire."

"You're out of your mind," Carl said. "Look, Henry. I went into some of those flower shops in Kingston and checked on prices. In Montego Bay, too. They get a fortune for flowers there. A man like you, with your know-how, would have it made." He leaned forward to point a finger at Henry's chest. "What will you do if you *retire*, for Pete's sake?"

"Well, Alice thinks I could take up golf."

"You? *Golf?*"

"Or fishing or something. There are lots of things a man can do, Carl. Growing flowers is hard work. I don't believe you realize how hard it is. If you'd spent practically your whole life in the business as I have, you—"

"You should say 'whole entirely life,'" Carl corrected, grinning.

"What?"

"That's how they talk in Jamaica. I asked a higgler in Kingston what something cost, and she said I could have the whole entirely thing for so much."

"Oh." Henry turned his head, thinking his wife had called him. She had not, though. The two women were in a bedroom now, and Alice was only talking to her sister.

"You don't mean it!" Alice said. "Why, that's just what Henry and I have been looking for, to go with this new wallpaper!"

Carl Bensinger frowned at Henry. "You papered the bedroom over?"

"Alice got a good buy at Hallowell's. Marguerite phoned her about it." Henry studied the back of his right hand. "The old paper *was* pretty shabby, I guess."

"And what are you looking for to go with it?"

"Huh?"

"She just said—"

"Oh. Spreads. We need new bedspreads now, Marguerite said."

"You going to do the whole house over?"

"Oh, I don't suppose we—"

The women came into the room then, and Carl Bensinger said how about looking at the slides he had brought over. Carl was an avid photographer. A good one, too.

"We're dying to see them," Alice said. "Aren't we, Henry?"

Henry said they were, and began to set up the screen while Carl arranged the projector and slides on a table. While the men were thus occupied, Henry's cat, Bertie, came out from under the coffee table in front of the divan, where the women had seated themselves. He sat there with his head atilt, studying Marguerite. If he understood what people said—as Henry swore he did—he had no reason to be fond of her.

She did it again now, while gazing down at him with an expression of total dislike. "You are just about the ugliest cat I have ever seen," she said slowly and distinctly. "The very ugliest." Then to Henry she said, "If you must have a cat around the house, Henry, can't you at least get one with some breeding?"

"He's got breeding enough for me," Henry said. "Bertie's a real smart cat."

"He's nothing but an alley cat, and you know it."

"The book I bought says he's a Domestic Short-Hair," Henry countered, fiddling with the screen.

"Good grief," Marguerite snorted. Then as Bertie took a step toward her: "Don't you come near me, you grubby beast! You're just an old flea-bag."

"Not a flea on him," Henry said.

"Well, I don't care. He looks like a worn-out yellow rug."

Henry finished adjusting the screen and moved over to a light switch. With a nod to Carl, he put the lights out and sat down. He did not sit on the divan with the sisters. He sat on a chair in a corner.

The first slides were of the hotel where Marguerite and Carl had stayed in Kingston, and then there were two of a Jamaican policeman with red stripes on his pants directing traffic at a busy downtown intersection. Carl said he never hoped to see a more efficient policeman. Marguerite said it was true, but of course he had to be efficient because the traffic was just ghastly.

There was a picture of a man dragging a block of ice along a sidewalk, on a rope, and Carl said by the time the poor guy got it home it probably would not be big enough to chill a rum punch. Marguerite said that was true because Jamaica was so wickedly hot, but he would be better off without the rum punch because everybody in Jamaica drank too much, all the time.

Then, dramatically, Carl said, "Now watch this, Henry! I don't think you saw anything like this when you were there!" And the screen was full of blue flowers.

"Aren't they something?" Carl said. "Women were selling them on the *sidewalk*, Henry, in some stalls right by the court house. If you ever wondered about growing flowers there, you've got your answer now. What are they, you know?"

Henry leaned forward on his chair. "Agapanthus. Lilies of the Nile."

"They grow them up in the mountains, the woman told us. Right up where you . . . here, this shot shows the stalls and the women. I had to get back a way."

"And he almost got run over," Marguerite said. "They drive on the *left* there and he was looking the wrong way. You wouldn't catch me driving in a crazy country like that, I can tell you."

"You get used to it," Carl said. "Now here's the car we rented: one of those little English jobs. And here's the mountain road to the place you're buying, Henry. I guess I don't have to tell you that, huh?"

"Just looking at it scares me half to death," Marguerite said.

"Oh, it isn't that bad. Just a bit winding is all." Carl showed some more pictures of the road, then paused again. "Now!" he said. "Here's your house, Henry, and what a marvelous old house it is! How old is it, anyway?"

"Ninety-three years," Henry said from his chair in the darkness.

"The plumbing is certainly old enough," Marguerite said. "If you could call it plumbing."

"Here's the view from the porch," Carl said. "Man, look at those mountains! They make you feel—"

"The trouble is, you get tired of just a view," Marguerite said.

"You know, you could actually *hear* those mountains," Carl said. "Everything up there was so still, you could almost hear things *growing*."

"We asked if you could get TV there," Marguerite said, "but nobody seemed to know. They said almost nobody *had* TV because you have to make your own electricity with a generator or something. But I don't suppose the reception would be any good, anyway. Even the radio reception wasn't too good, because of the mountains. I don't know what in the world you'd do for entertainment, Alice. Carl, show the ones of Montego Bay."

"Just a second," Carl said. "Henry, here's a shot of an interesting old guy we met on the property, and a cat he said belonged to him. He said you stopped to look at some flowers in his yard, and the two of you got to talking, and you promised him a job." The slide showed a solemn black man in blue denim shirt and pants standing on the veranda steps of the 93-year-old house, with a cat as yellow as Bertie curled around his left ankle. "He said his name was Manny."

"Yes. Emmanuel. And the cat's name is Emilina." Henry leaned forward and thrust his right hand into the beam of light from the projector. "He gave me this piece of serpentine. Said it came from the property. Just for the fun of it, I had Kartin the jeweler mount it for me."

Glowing eerily in the light, on a plain silver band on Henry's third finger, was a greenish stone the size of a flattened pea.

Carl leaned forward to look at it. "Why'd he do that, Henry?"

"Well, he said he was an obeah man."

"Isn't that a kind of voodoo?" Marguerite asked.

"Not exactly. They both originated in Africa, he told me, but voodoo is a ceremonial thing while an obeah person works alone. In this case, with a cat."

"You mean that's an obeah cat in the picture?" Carl said.

"Well, Emmanuel said he and Emilina were one."

"Just like you and *your* awful cat—is that what you're saying?" Marguerite said. "And you actually wear that ring?"

"Oh, he doesn't wear it all the time," Alice intruded with a little laugh of embarrassment. "He just put it on this evening because you two were coming. You know—a conversation piece."

"He told me," Henry said, "if I ever needed his help, all I had to do was rub the stone. Like that fellow with the lamp in the Arabian Nights."

"I should think you'd be afraid to have a man like that working for you," Marguerite said. "I know *I* wouldn't hire such a person."

"Oh, come on," Henry said. "You know I don't believe in voodoo or obeah or any of that stuff. He was just a nice old guy with a wonderfully green thumb."

"You haven't tried the ring, then?" Carl said.

"Of course not. What do you take me for?"

"Please, Carl," Marguerite said impatiently, "Alice wants to see Montego Bay. She didn't get there. Henry was too wrapped up in his flowers."

Carl glanced at Henry but Henry stayed silent, so with a shrug he put a stack of slides aside and showed pictures of the north-coast tourist town, running through them mechanically while the two women commented on the clothes being worn by the tourists. Then after a pause Carl said, "Well, that's it, I guess. Anything you'd like to see again, anyone?"

Henry said, "Could I see those shots of King Street again, Carl? You suppose?"

"The flower vendors? Sure!"

"He means the policeman," Marguerite said quickly. "He's not really interested in flowers any more. Are you, Henry?"

Henry's voice was a long time coming out of the darkness. When it came, it sounded as though he were shivering as he had at the front door, though the room was warm enough. "I guess it isn't important." Reaching out to put a light on, he stood up. "Shall we have a drink?"

His wife's sigh seemed to be one of relief, and she nodded. Carl said, "Rum for me, please, Henry. I'm a convert now."

Henry turned to his sister-in-law. "And you, Marguerite? The usual?"

"You don't mind, do you, Henry? I know it's a lot of bother, using the blender just for me."

"No bother," Henry said.

Bertie, his yellow cat, silently trailed him into the kitchen.

The blender whirred on the kitchen counter for a while, and then Henry came back with drinks on a tray. It was a lovely, two-toned tray of Jamaica's most beautiful wood, blue mahoe. After serving the two sisters and Carl, he returned to his chair, lifted his own glass, and said in a voice filled with resignation, "Well . . . here's to not growing flowers in Jamaica."

"Now, Henry," his wife protested.

"Henry, you're crazy to give it up," Carl Bensinger said.

Marguerite emptied her glass without comment, then suddenly sucked in a noisy breath and let the glass drop to the carpet while clutching her throat with both hands. Her eyes became the size of half dollars and in trying desperately to speak, she nearly fell off her chair.

Henry and Carl rushed to her and got her to her feet. They led her into a bedroom and made her lie down. But still she struggled to speak as though someone had stuffed a gag into her mouth and she could not get a word out past it.

Henry's wife frantically called a nearby hospital.

An ambulance came. Alice rode in it with her sister, holding Marguerite's hand, while Henry and Carl followed in a car. When Marguerite was released two hours later, she was still unable to talk though otherwise quite all right.

She never did talk again, though a dozen doctors and psychiatrists took turns telling her there was absolutely nothing physically wrong with her.

One day months later, while Henry's wife Alice was visiting her speechless sister at the latter's home, Carl Bensinger and Henry sat in Henry's living room watching football on TV. When a beer commercial came on, Carl suddenly rose and shut the TV off.

"All right, Henry," Carl said. "Before I ask the obvious, just let me say you actually did me a pretty big favor, and I'm grateful. It's been real peaceful around my house since that night we showed the Jamaican slides. Now come clean. Tell me the truth. What did you put in Marguerite's drink that night?"

Henry shook his head. "Nothing."

"Oh, come on now, Henry. Maybe you fooled the medics, but you can't fool me. What—"

"I didn't do a thing, I tell you," Henry said. "I was running the blender to make Marguerite's drink, see? All of a sudden Bertie here" —he nodded toward the yellow cat lying at his feet—"jumped up on the counter and rubbed his head against my hand. Well, not my hand, actually. Against *this*."

Henry tapped the serpentine stone on his ring.

"And when he did it, I heard old Emmanuel's voice in my head, clear as I can hear yours right now, asking me how he could help."

"And?" Carl said, wide-eyed.

"I said, 'Just make her shut up.' That's all. I swear it. 'Just make her shut up.' I only wanted some relief, man. I don't think I meant it to be forever."

Nobody, That's Who

William F. Nolan

Look, Danny, you're my lawyer, aren't you? Can't you get me *out* of this? Hell, it's all crazy, it's a frame. Sure, I can go all over it again for you if that'll help. Sure, right from the beginning outside her apartment.

Well, like I said, I didn't really have anything *definite* to go on. I mean, I had this kind of hunch is all. Just a feeling that she was playing house with some other guy while I footed the bill. When I get a strong hunch on something I usually play it out. So that night I decided to stick around after leaving her apartment. Just in case. I kissed her like nothing was wrong and pretended to leave. But I only took the elevator down one floor, then climbed the stairs back to her apartment. I posted myself down at the end of the hall where it was plenty dark, where I figured I wouldn't be seen. And, by God, I didn't have long to wait, either. Maybe ten, fifteen minutes. Then along comes this guy. Like I told you, I never did get a look at his face. Wore a hat pulled down low and the collar of his topcoat was turned up all the way round, so I couldn't make out any features. Just a tall guy in a dark blue outfit.

Anyway, he tapped on the door, quiet like, two shorts and a long, and she opened it while he slipped inside. Now that was two o'clock on the nose. I checked my wrist watch, because I wanted to see just how long he'd stay in there with her. Hell, I felt like rushing in there and catching the pair of them at it, but I'd have to break the damn door down to do it and by that time he'd be long gone down the fire escape outside her window. So I decided to see just how long he'd stay.

Figured I couldn't hang around in the hall. Too suspicious in case the house dick came along, or maybe another hotel guest or somebody. I knew this guy would have to cross the lobby on his way out, so I took the elevator down and planted myself in a leather chair by the doors and waited. Just waited it out for him. I didn't know, right then, just what the hell I'd do when he finally showed. I was boiling, I'll admit. I hate being played for a sucker. That really ate into me. I mean, after the way I'd set her up and all. I just sat there in that chair and boiled.

Finally, two hours later, the elevator door slides back and he steps out. Same guy. Same dark blue outfit, hat and all. And, damn it, I *still* couldn't make out what he looked like. My chair was too far back and the lobby was pretty dark by then. I would have had to catch him and knock off that hat of his to really get a look, but what the hell, *she* was the one I wanted, not him. So I let him go. That was my first big mistake.

Then I got the idea about scaring her. I mean, I wanted to teach her a lesson. Shake her up good. Not hurt her, understand, just scare her. Sure, I had every right in the world to work her over for two-timing me, but I decided not to lay a hand on her. I figured why play it dumb and get myself in hot water with the law.

So I took the stairs up to her apartment. Four flights, just enough to wind me, get me to breathing hard like I was half nuts, you know. Figured that would help.

I tapped on her door, soft, the same way he had. Two shorts and a long. I knew she'd be plenty surprised to see me—and she sure was. She thought her lover boy had come back until she got a look at me. Then she tried to shut the door in my face, but I just pushed hard and forced my way inside.

"Whatta you want?" she says, and starts backing away from me toward the bed.

I didn't say a damn thing, just stood there looking mean, breathing hard and ragged. She let out a gasp, a kind of little choking sound. Then she dropped on the bed and curled up there, watching me like I was some kind of animal.

I locked the door behind me, then went over to the open window and shut and locked it. Like maybe I was going to do something that I didn't want anyone else to hear.

Oh, she was scared, all right, *plenty* scared. She didn't know what the hell I'd do next. I could see her eyes shining out at me from the bed, wild and wide. She had on a pink and blue shortie nightgown and her legs were all drawn up under it. She looked like a rabbit you catch in the headlights of your car, kind of frozen with fear.

I eased down into a chair by the window, where she could see my face in the reflection of the outside neon. Then I thought of a beautiful touch.

I began to scrape my fingernails. You know, just sitting there quiet in that chair, with the red and yellow neon lighting my face, breathing slow and hard—and scraping each nail with one of those sharp little silver files. Listen, that threw the fear of God into her. She figured I was just waiting till I finished the last nail before I went for her, so she was as still as a cat. Just her eyes moved, watching me.

Well, this went on for maybe ten minutes. Then she began to see I was bluffing, that I wasn't going to try anything. She sat up and dug out her cigarettes. She lit one, with the pillow propped up behind her. Then she tried some bluffing on her own.

"What's the idea?" she said. "Why the big spook routine?"

"I know all about your boy friend," I told her. "I saw him come in and I saw him come out."

"So what?" she snapped. "So a guy spends a couple of hours in my apartment."

The goddam nerve of her! Here I'd set her up in this place of her own, bought her some nice clothes and things and always treated her fine. And this is what she gives me. I'm telling you, it knocked me out. Then I asked her if she denied sleeping with this guy.

"He made a few passes and we wrestled around some, that's all," she told me.

Oh, sure. I believed that was all like I believed there wasn't any moon in the sky.

When she saw I wasn't having any she got sore. Her whole face changed. I mean, she suddenly turned hard, like some two-bit hustler. All the softness went fast and it was like I was seeing her for the first time with the shell off. She knew the game was finished and she didn't give a damn.

Then I got the full treatment. She began to laugh at me like I was a fool.

"You're not very bright," she told me in that new hard voice of hers. "Sure I had some kicks with this guy. Why? Because I'm fed up with playing around with you, that's why."

Then she told me that this other guy was a real *man*—not just a weak excuse for one—and that one like him was worth ten of me.

God, but she had nerve! Wasn't afraid of me at all by then. Not at all.

And I didn't intend to touch her. She wasn't worth it. Maybe I *was* the dumb cluck she made me out to be. Maybe I deserved what I was getting. I was as sore as hell at myself for playing along with her.

"I'm finished," I said. "This is the end of the line for us."

She just kept on laughing. Told me the sooner I got out the happier she'd be.

And here's where the crazy part starts. I was on my way to the door when it opened—and there, outlined against the light from the hall, was this guy of hers in the blue coat. And right away I saw something glint in his hand and I knew he had a gun.

It was all real freaky. He'd done the same thing I'd done. Come back, I mean. He'd probably seen my car parked in the hotel lot and recognized it. Had come back up and heard our voices outside the door. Figured she was playing *him* for the chump. Hell, it was all mixed up ten ways from Sunday.

Well, this guy didn't give either of us a chance to say a damn thing. Just stood there for a split second, long enough to make out the girl good and clear. Then he just pumped two slugs into her, one, two. Just that quick. Slammed the door and he was gone. Only first he tossed in his gun and it landed right at my feet on the rug.

That's when I *really* played it dumb. I actually picked the damn thing up and looked at it. Now, I've seen guys do that in the movies maybe fifty times and I always figured it was phony. No innocent party, I told myself, would ever pick up a murder weapon and get his fingerprints all over it. But I swear that's just what I did. Who knows why? Shock, I guess. The shock was terrible, the kind you get after a real bad auto accident. I was trembling, I remember, and weak all over.

I knew she was dead without even walking over to her. Nobody could miss at that kind of range. So I just stood there holding on to that damn gun and looking down at it while the outside hall filled up with people.

Next thing I know, somebody is pounding like hell on the door and yelling for me to open up. Oh, I dropped the gun quick enough then, all right. I knew I was a goner if they found me in here with her body, so I unlocked the window and took off down the fire escape.

What else is there to tell? The cops were waiting for me when I dropped into the alley—and I guess I sure looked guilty enough. I told them about the other guy in the blue get-up, but they just grinned and treated me like I was already on my way to the chair.

Hell, Danny, can't you find this guy? *He* killed her, not me. I never even touched her that morning. I don't know what this guy looks like, but he's *got* to be found. What chance have I got without him? Who's going to believe my story?

I'll tell you. Nobody, that's who.

Start looking for this guy, will you? He could be almost anybody. A mutual friend maybe. Hell, Danny, *You* knew her—and I've seen *you* wearing a dark blue topcoat. And . . . the guy's about your height, too.

Just do one thing for me, will you? Quit grinning like that. That's the way the damn cops grinned at me.

Will you *quit* it?

NUMB

WAYNE A. HAROLD

Bert Jacobs couldn't believe it when the young black man whipped out the gun, right in front of the library.

The kid was shaking in his dirty jacket, droplets of rain trapped in his unruly hair. The crack rock blazed in his dead eyes.

He waved the gun for emphasis. "Gimme your wallet."

Bert put up his hands. "Look, I don't have my wallet on me. I was just studying. I didn't think that I'd *need* it."

The mugger shook his addled head, seemed confused. Finally, he exhaled a short burst of air from his runny nostrils. "Well, you *did*," he said, then he squeezed the trigger.

There was a hot cloud of gas, a short burst of flame, then the bullet struck Bert in the chest. There was no pain. For a split second, Bert thought that the gun was full of blanks.

Then he looked down at his chest.

His forehead started to sweat and he wanted to vomit. He looked up at the mugger. "You *bastard*."

The young predator's jaw dropped. He threw the gun to the wet pavement, started running.

Bert gazed down at his hands; they were bluish, clammy.

He started after his attacker.

The thug sped across the street. Bert was close behind. He

tramped through a puddle and cold water splashed up on his leg. His head felt fuzzy. Numb.

For a split second he thought that he was five years old again, tearing through the massive puddles that always formed in his Grandma's back yard after a heavy rain.

On the street, in the present, he shook his head, tried to concentrate on running.

The mugger shot toward East 12th Street.

There were a few people out, despite the late hour and the rainy weather. The thug collided into a bag lady, knocked her down to the wet pavement. On her butt, her humble belongings scattered around her, she cursed him. He quickly regained his footing, started fleeing again. He passed through a pair of spike-headed punk kids who were hanging out in front of an alternative music bar.

Down half a block, Bert shouted to them. "Stop him! *Stop* him! He *shot* me!"

The kids looked at the thug (who was rapidly disappearing down the sidewalk), then back at Bert, confusion showing in their bleary eyes.

Bert sped past them.

He suddenly remembered the sick kitten that he found outside once, when he was a young teenager. It was screaming in pain, dying of some unknown ailment. Bert carried it to a clear, grassy area, started to clean the mucous from its eyes. Just as he was ready to wipe it away with his handkerchief, he saw that the mucous was moving. It was maggots. Flies had laid thousands of eggs in the helpless kitten's eyes, ears, and mouth, and now the tiny maggots were burrowing through its head, causing it unbearable pain.

Tears streaming down his face, young Bert found a heavy rock and lifted it high. . . .

He was breathing hard now. Without the numbness, his legs would have long since tired. Just ahead of him, the young mugger looked bushed. Not to mention scared. Bert kept after him, left, right, left, right.

"G-Get away from me!" the mugger shouted back.

The chase continued, now down South Prospect. There were three hookers on a corner up ahead, one of them a thin black girl with a beehive hairdo, the other two dumpy, white, and unattractive. "Whoa," the black girl exclaimed, seeing what was heading their way.

"Stop him!" Bert screamed. "He just *shot* me!"

One of the white girls grabbed the black girl's arm. "Stay out of it, Lee. Might be big trouble."

The black girl frowned.

Frustrated, Bert tapped into his final resources and poured on the speed. He drew closer, ever closer, reached out with his arm, almost able to touch his attacker. . . .

In his mind he saw himself on the high school football field, chasing a running back from the rival team. He knew that Jeannie was in the stands, hating football because she thought that it was pointless and stupid, but getting excited all the same, dry washing her hands as Bert moved in for the kill. . . .

Jeannie. They were engaged to be married. One month away. One month.

Bert was starting to despair. His attacker was getting away from him.

The black hooker was still frowning. "That white boy said that the black boy *shot* him."

The other fat hooker agreed with her peer. "You don't need no more hassles, Lee. Let 'em go by."

Lee sighed. "Hell with that."

She stuck her thin leg out and tripped the young black man. He hit the pavement. Hard.

The other two hookers stepped back.

Bert was on him in no time flat. He beat him with his fists, over and over again. "You bastard! How does *this* feel? You like *this*?" Both of them were screaming, crying. Finally, his fists bloody, Bert quit.

Lee ran over to Bert. "Hey, man. You okay?"

Hunched over his attacker, Bert coughed up blood. "He *shot* me. Wasn't gonna let him get a . . . *away* with it. Call cops. Gun over . . . on Euclid. Right in front of . . . *library.*"

She bent over, took his hand. "Your chest—it's bleeding."

"Yeah," Bert replied. "I was . . . studying." His eyes closed.

He was at the drive-in, making love to Jeannie for the first time. They had both been virgins. In the back of his dad's old Ford, they tried to keep their heads down, out of the line of sight of the other cars. They were giggling, both of them tickled by each other's nervous incompetence.

On the street, Bert laughed out loud.

"What's so funny?" Lee asked.

He grinned stupidly, let out a gurgle, then dropped dead on the spot.

The homicide detective was a tall black man with a totally shaven head. He was questioning Lee. Behind them, the Mobile Crime Unit was burning the midnight oil, sketching, photographing, and tagging away with reckless abandon. The unfortunate object of all their attention was Bert, who lay on the pavement, as dead as the concrete.

The detective forced a grin. "Workin' late tonight, Lee?"

She lifted an eyebrow. "Ain't illegal to step out for a walk, Klohn. I'm free, black, and over twenty-one. . . ."

"*Way* over," Klohn added with a smile.

Lee shook her head, smiled back.

They glanced over at Bert's body. Both of them stopped smiling.

"Chased him down, huh?" Klohn asked.

"Yeah. Said the other kid shot him in front of the library."

"We just sent a patrolman over there. If there's a gun, he'll find it."

"Think it'll have fingerprints on it?"

"Probably," Klohn replied. "But that don't matter much. The kid's in the back of the patrol car, confessin' up a storm. Stupid crackbaby's scared to death."

Lee pulled her green leather jacket tight around her to keep out the chill. "Can't believe it. That white boy runnin' all that way, bein' all shot up an' everything."

"It happens, Lee. Not often, but it happens. Sometimes they don't even *realize* that they've been shot. It's from the *shock*. Turns them numb and they can't even feel the pain. Then, a few minutes later, they just konk out."

Lee wiped a tear from her eye. "That sucks. He was just a kid."

"Yeah," Klohn replied. "But he was stubborn like a man."

ON A DARK OCTOBER

Joe R. Lansdale

The October night was dark and cool. The rain was thick. The moon was hidden behind dark clouds that occasionally flashed with lightning, and the sky rumbled as if it were a big belly that was hungry and needed filling.

A white Chrysler New Yorker came down the street and pulled up next to the curb. The driver killed the engine and the lights, turned to look at the building that sat on the block, an ugly tin thing with a weak light bulb shielded by a tin-hat shade over a fading sign that read BOB'S GARAGE. For a moment the driver sat unmoving, then he reached over, picked up the newspaper-wrapped package on the seat and put it in his lap. He opened it slowly. Inside was a shiny, oily, black-handled, ball peen hammer.

He lifted the hammer, touched the head of it to his free palm. It left a small smudge of grease there. He closed his hand, opened it, rubbed his fingers together. It felt just like . . . but he didn't want to think of that. It would all happen soon enough.

He put the hammer back in the papers, rewrapped it, wiped his fingers on the outside of the package. He pulled a raincoat from the back seat and put it across his lap. Then, with hands resting idly on the wheel, he sat silently.

A late model blue Ford pulled in front of him, left a space at the garage's drive, and parked. No one got out. The man in the Chrysler did not move.

Five minutes passed and another car, a late model Chevy, parked directly behind the Chrysler. Shortly thereafter three more cars arrived, all of them were late models. None of them blocked the drive. No one got out.

Another five minutes skulked by before a white van with MERTZ'S MEATS AND BUTCHER SHOP written on the side pulled around the Chrysler, then backed up the drive, almost to the garage door. A man wearing a hooded raincoat and carrying a package got out of the van, walked to the back and opened it.

The blue Ford's door opened, and a man dressed similarly, carrying a package under his arm, got out and went up the driveway. The two men nodded at one another. The man who had gotten out of the Ford unlocked the garage and slid the door back.

Car doors opened. Men dressed in raincoats, carrying packages, got out and walked to the back of the van. A couple of them had flashlights and they flashed them in the back of the vehicle, gave the others a good view of what was there—a burlap-wrapped, rope-bound bundle that wiggled and groaned.

The man who had been driving the van said, "Get it out."

Two of the men handed their packages to their comrades and climbed inside, picked up the squirming bundle, carried it into the garage. The others followed. The man from the Ford closed the door.

Except for the beams of the two flashlights, they stood close together in the darkness, like strands of flesh that had suddenly been pulled into a knot. The two with the bundle broke away from the others, and with their comrades directing their path with the beams of their flashlights, they carried the bundle to the grease rack and placed it between two wheel ramps. When that was finished, the two who had carried the bundle returned to join the others, to reform that tight knot of flesh.

Outside the rain was pounding the roof like tossed lug bolts. Lightning danced through the half-dozen small, barred windows. Wind shook the tin garage with a sound like a rattlesnake tail quivering for the strike, then passed on.

No one spoke for awhile. They just looked at the bundle. The bundle thrashed about and the moaning from it was louder than ever.

"All right," the man from the van said.

They removed their clothes, hung them on pegs on the wall, pulled their raincoats on.

The man who had been driving the blue Ford—after looking carefully into the darkness—went to the grease rack. There was a paper bag on one of the ramps. Earlier in the day he had placed it there himself. He opened it and took out a handful of candles and a book of matches. Using a match to guide him, he placed the candles down the length of the ramps, lighting them as he went. When he was finished, the garage glowed with a soft amber light. Except for the rear of the building. It was very dark there.

The man with the candles stopped suddenly, a match flame wavering between his fingertips. The hackles on the back of his neck stood up. He could hear movement from the dark part of the garage. He shook the match out quickly and joined the others. Together, the group unwrapped their packages and gripped the contents firmly in their hands—hammers, brake-over handles, crowbars, heavy wrenches. Then all of them stood looking toward the back of the garage, where something heavy and sluggish moved.

The sound of the garage clock—a huge thing with DRINK COCA-COLA emblazoned on its face—was like the ticking of a time bomb. It was one minute to midnight.

Beneath the clock, visible from time to time when the glow of the candles was whipped that way by the draft, was a calendar. It read OCTOBER and had a picture of a smiling boy wearing overalls, standing amidst a field of pumpkins. The 31st was circled in red.

Eyes drifted to the bundle between the ramps now. It had stopped squirming. The sound it was making was not quite a moan. The man from the van nodded at one of the men, the one who had driven the Chrysler. The Chrysler man went to the bundle and worked the ropes loose, folded back the burlap. A frightened black youth, bound by leather straps and gagged with a sock and a bandanna, looked up at him wide-eyed. The man from the Chrysler avoided looking back. The youth started squirming, grunting, and thrashing. Blood beaded around his wrists where the leather was tied, boiled out from around the loop fastened to his neck; when he kicked, it boiled faster because the strand had been drawn around his neck, behind his back and tied off at his ankles.

There came a sound from the rear of the garage again, louder than before. It was followed by a sudden sigh that might have been the wind working its way between the rafters.

The van driver stepped forward, spoke loudly to the back of the garage. "We got something for you, hear me? Just like always we're doing our part. You do yours. I guess that's all I got to say. Things will be the same come next October. In your name, I reckon."

For a moment—just a moment—there was a glimmer of a shape when the candles caught a draft and wafted their bright heads in that direction. The man from the van stepped back quickly. "In your name," he repeated. He turned to the men. "Like always, now. Don't get the head until the very end. Make it last."

The faces of the men took on an expression of grimness, as if they were all playing a part in a theatric production and had been told to look that way. They hoisted their tools and moved toward the youth.

What they did took a long time.

When they finished, the thing that had been the young black man looked like a gigantic hunk of raw liver that had been chewed up and spat out. The raincoats of the men were covered in a spray of blood and brains. They were panting.

"Okay," said the man from the van.

They took off their raincoats, tossed them in a metal bin near the grease rack, wiped the blood from their hands, faces, ankles and feet with shop rags, tossed those in the bin and put on their clothes.

The van driver yelled to the back of the garage. "All yours. Keep the years good, huh?"

They went out of there and the man from the Ford locked the garage door. Tomorrow he would come to work as always. There would be no corpse to worry about, and a quick dose of gasoline and a match would take care of the contents in the bin. Rain ran down his back and made him shiver.

Each of the men went out to their cars without speaking. Tonight they would all go home to their young, attractive wives and tomorrow they would all go to their prosperous businesses and they would not think of this night again. Until next October.

They drove away. Lightning flashed. The wind howled. The rain beat the garage like a cat-o'-nine-tails. And inside there were loud sucking sounds punctuated by grunts of joy.

ONE MAN'S POISON

CURT HAMLIN

The sign rather amused Mr. Petten. He thought it clever. He saw it, of course. His eyes were small, deep-set in his fat cheeks like halved grapes pushed into a bowl of lumpy gruel, but those eyes missed very little. It wasn't the big sign that interested him. That was simply the name—HARITH'S—lettered in tarnished gilt over the door. The other was quite small, a footnote done in black paint at a lower corner of the single display window.

>PRESCRIPTIONS FOR DIFFICULT CASES

Chuckling to himself, he pushed open the door and waddled inside.

The outer room of the place was no more than six-by-eight, empty except for an elderly, straight-backed chair that leaned wearily against one wall. At the back were a grilled window and a narrow doorway with a swinging door. Mr. Petten moved over and peered between the bars of the window. Inside, a dark young man in a white, linen coat was hunched over a table, inking entries into a large ledger. He raised his head as Mr. Petten stared in at him, and nodded pleasantly.

"Yes?"

"I'm George Petten," said Mr. Petten ponderously.

"Petten?" The young man marked his place in the ledger and closed it slowly, his eyes thoughtful. "Petten. Yes. Of course. Petten." He rose and came through the swinging door, blotting ink-stained fingers with a wad of cotton. "What can I do for you?"

"I want to see the manager."

"I'm the manager," said the young man, "and the druggist, and the clerk. In short, I own the place."

Mr. Petten scowled and shuffled his thick, broad feet uncertainly. "I expected someone older."

The young man rolled the cotton into a ball and tucked it neatly away in a trouser pocket. "My dear sir," he said gently, "I studied for years under my father. Since his death I have discovered a good many things even he didn't know. You have nothing to worry about. Absolutely nothing." He grasped Mr. Petten by one arm and urged him through the swinging door. "We can talk more comfortably in here. Also, it's absolutely private."

The inner room was as crowded as the outer had been bare. The walls were tiered by narrow shelves, all of them lined with bottles, jars, and flasks. There was a large sink, the drainboards on either side of it littered with a variety of chemical equipment.

The dark young man brought out a second chair, dusted it lightly with the sleeve of his jacket, and pushed it into place. "I'm interested to know how you heard of me."

Lowering himself, Mr. Petten waved a plump, vague hand. "Somebody told me. I'm not sure who it was. At a party, I think."

"You don't remember?"

"No. Does it make a difference?"

"I hardly think so," said the young man, smiling a soft smile. "No, I hardly think so. Not in this case. Well, now." He folded his hands on the table top and leaned over them. "If you'll please tell me about your problem."

Mr. Petten's eyebrows curled like furry caterpillars. "I'll do no such damned thing. I came here to buy something. You're here to sell it to me. I'll buy it and leave. That's the end of it."

"Don't be an ass," the young man said calmly. "I'm a specialist. A specialist has to know the facts. Cases differ. A member of the family, for example, is quite a different problem from, say, a casual acquaintance. Even you should be able to see that."

Mr. Petten reddened and puffed angry lips. "It's both."

"Two?" asked the young man. "Well! You *have* a tidy little project for yourself, haven't you?" He pulled at one earlobe, regarding Mr. Petten with interest. "Go on."

"The rest of it's none of your damned business."

"If it wasn't my business," snapped the young man sharply, "you wouldn't be here. If you won't be reasonable, get out. I've work to do."

Reopening the ledger, he picked up his pen and set to making entries in a careful, neat hand.

Mr. Petten fumed. He sucked his teeth. He blew out his cheeks.

He tapped the tips of his fingers ominously on his paunchy middle. "All right," he finally muttered. "Have it your way."

"Eh?"

"I said have it your way. I'll tell you. Only this makes you an accessory before the fact. Don't forget that."

The young man smiled a little and closed the ledger again. "I'll take that chance."

"Damned right you will," said Mr. Petten. "Damned right. Now. The first one's my wife. Marion. She's twenty-seven. We've been married three years. I bought her and paid for her. That's the way I do business. Put my money on the line and take delivery. All I expect is a fair return on my investment. Get what I mean?"

The young man murmured smiling agreement.

"Right," said Mr. Petten. "Fair return. Only I'm not getting it. There's another man."

"Ah."

"Get what I mean?"

"Perfectly."

"I was thinking," said Mr. Petten, "of poison. Something that couldn't be traced."

The young man put back his head and gave a short, hard laugh. "My dear sir," he chuckled, "you've been reading these murder books. There's no poison known that can't be found by an expert analyst. Now in my father's day . . ." He broke off to stare reminiscently at the ceiling, then shrugged his shoulders. "However, that's neither here nor there. The fact is, the science of detection has advanced beyond all reasonable bounds. What used to be a simple problem in murder is no longer simple. Quite the contrary."

"Um." Mr. Petten gloomily regarded the floor.

"Don't worry," said the young man. "I'll fix you up with something. Let me see. Does your wife—Marion, I think you said her name was—like any particular kind of food?"

"Food?"

"Yes. Like fish. Or mushrooms. Or—"

"Mushrooms," said Mr. Petten. "She's crazy about mushrooms."

"Excellent."

"Eh?"

"I said that was excellent. Now then. The—er—gentleman in question? Is he also fond of mushrooms?"

"Him? He's the one that got her started on them. Never used to have the blasted things. Now we have them all the time. Having them tonight." Mr. Petten spat. "Never touch them myself."

"Better and better." The young man gave his hands a brisk, cheerful rubbing. "Tell me—does the gentleman come often to dinner?"

"He comes," Mr. Petten said sourly, "every night. Every single, blasted night of the week."

"And tonight you're having mushrooms?"

"I said so, didn't I?"

"Fine," said the young man, rising from his chair. "Tonight, Mr. Petten, you eat mushrooms along with the rest of them. Don't forget. That's important."

He went to the rear of the room, opened a cabinet and fumbled about inside. Coming back, he placed two small vials on the table in front of Mr. Petten. One was red, the other blue, and each contained a liquid of uncertain color. "The red one," he explained, "contains muscarine. And some other things. Muscarine is a mushroom poison."

Mr. Petten poked at the red vial with a suspicious forefinger. "How does it taste?"

"Very pleasant," said the young man. "An old recipe of my father's. And simple to use. You just pour it into the mushroom sauce. It does the rest."

Mr. Petten's face went suddenly pale. "But if I eat—"

The young man chuckled. "You'd better let me finish. Listen. If three people eat a meal, and two of them die while the third remains perfectly all right, the police are going to get suspicious. But if the third one gets sick, even though he doesn't die, there's no particular reason for suspicion. The point is, Mr. Petten, you get sick but you don't die." He indicated the blue vial. "That's where the other stuff comes in."

Mr. Petten prodded the blue vial. "What is it?"

"An antidote," said the young man. "A really remarkable antidote. Different. You take it *before* you take the poison. At least six hours before. That way, no one can ever suspect you've taken it. By the time you eat the mushrooms, all traces of this will have vanished." He pushed the two vials together and stepped back, beaming. "That," he said, "will be five hundred dollars. For both of them."

Mr. Petten reared up in his chair. "What!"

"Very moderate, I think," the young man stated.

"It's outrageous," shouted Mr. Petten. "It's highway robbery. It's—"

"Of course," the young man said gently, "you could always use a gun. The only thing is, the police have such an embarrassing way with guns."

"Look here." Mr. Petten pounded the table with a fat, forceful hand. "I don't believe in buying pigs in a poke. For all I know those damned things may be filled with common tap water."

The soft, wise smile curled on the young man's lips. "You could try one of them," he suggested. "The red one, for example. I'm sure—"

"I'll do no such thing," Mr. Petten snapped. "Now you listen to me. I'm a business man. I'll make you a business proposition. I'll pay you a hundred dollars now. If the stuff works the way you say, I'll pay you the remainder. You can trust me."

The young man hesitated a long moment. Finally he nodded wearily. "All right. It's a deal."

"Cash," said Mr. Petten. He reached for a plump wallet, laid out five twenties, and picked up the two vials. "Fair and square. Cash."

They walked together through the outer room. Mr. Petten went into the street. The young man stood in the doorway. Mr. Petten jerked a thumb at the gold-lettered sign. "Harith. That you?"

The young man shook his head. "He was the original owner," he said. "He—uh—died. My father never would change the name. He always said that Harith kind of started him out in this business. In a way, that is. He was quite sentimental about it." He giggled.

"Oh," said Mr. Petten. "Well. See you again."

The young man raised his hand. "Good-bye, my friend."

Waddling down the street, Mr. Petten was quite pleased with himself. He blew a toneless tune through fat, pursed lips. The vials clinked pleasantly in his pocket. He was thinking he'd turned a nice piece of business. Two murders, and at fifty dollars a throw. "Afterwards," he told himself, "he can whistle for the rest. But he won't whistle loud. Not that one. Not when he's an accessory before the fact." He smiled grimly.

Back in his office, with the door securely locked, he uncorked the blue vial and poured its contents down his throat.

After Mr. Petten left, the dark young man returned slowly to the rear room of his shop. He thought it unlikely that he would ever see Mr. Petten again, certainly not after he swallowed the contents of the vial—poison. He thought that very probably Mr. Petten wasn't entirely honest, anyway. Even alive, he probably wouldn't have paid the remainder of his bill. Shaking his head, the dark young man bent again over the big ledger. A few minutes later he took an empty statement blank from the drawer of the table. In a neat, orderly hand he wrote:

For Services Rendered $500.00

He got out the telephone book, leafed through it, and carefully copied out the address.

>   Mrs. Marion Petten
>   1930 N. Lindenwald Rd.
>   City

THE PIGEON DROP

Michael A. Black

Laura had stationed herself outside, just to the right of the revolving doors. She could look through the big plate-glass windows and study the people inside the bank, sizing them up. Picking the right one—that was the key. The all-important first step. If you got the right pigeon, everything else would fall right into place.

Through the window she saw Andrea, her partner, stand up. She had been sitting inside near the row of lobby chairs, and standing up was the signal if she saw a good prospect making a large deposit or withdrawal. Laura then saw the woman that Andrea had indicated exiting through the revolving glass doors.

The mark was older, and a bit on the plump side, with thick, somewhat old-fashioned glasses perched on her nose. Her flowered dress had a clean but well-worn look to it.

Good, thought Laura. One that's too stingy to buy new clothes. Probably worth a bundle.

She got up and began walking parallel with the woman, just slightly ahead of her.

The older lady stopped when Laura turned and smiled disarmingly.

"Excuse me," Laura said, in her perfectly affected Southern drawl. "Could you help me?"

"Why I'll certainly try, dear," the older woman said, smiling back.

"My name's Laura."

"I'm Mildred. Mildred Castle."

"Oh, my mother's name was Mildred," Laura lied. "Perhaps you knew her. Mildred Stone?"

"No," Mrs. Castle said, shaking her head. "I don't believe so."

"Oh, anyway," said Laura. "I've just moved up here from Tennessee, and I found this envelope with all kinds of money in it, along with this funny note. Can you read it?"

She handed Mildred the note after giving her a quick glimpse of the cash roll. Actually it was a hundred dollar bill wrapped around a large wad of ones, inside a large manila-colored envelope.

"This looks like shorthand, dear," said Mildred looking at the note.

Laura scratched the side of her head, which was the signal for Andrea, who was already walking in their direction, to steer toward them.

Laura looked up and pointed to Andrea, who looked rather prim and proper in a gray business suit.

"Oh, she looks like a secretary," Laura said. "Excuse me. Could you help us?"

Andrea raised her eyebrows demurely as she approached.

"Yes?"

"I'm Laura and this is Mildred. We've found a bunch of money and this note, but it's in shorthand. Can you read it?"

Pausing to take out her glasses, Andrea took the note. Her brow furrowed as she read it, then she looked up at them.

"Where did you get this?" she asked. "This note says the money is proceeds from illegal gambling."

"Goodness," said Laura, feigning surprise. "What should we do?"

Andrea removed her spectacles and put them in her purse. "Well, whatever you decide, it's doubtful the money could, or even should, be returned to its owner."

"That's true," Laura said, giving Mildred's face a quick scan to see if they were drawing her in.

"Have you counted the money?" Andrea asked. "How much is there?"

"Yes I have. It's fifty thousand dollars," Laura said, emphasizing each word.

"Merciful heavens," Mildred said.

"Why don't we all three keep the money?" Laura blurted impetuously. "We can split it three ways. Is that legal?"

"Well," said Andrea. "I'm a legal secretary. My boss is a lawyer in that building." She gestured, indicating one of the tall structures behind them. "I could go call him."

Laura looked anxiously at Mrs. Castle. This was the second hook. If the pigeon went along with this phase, they were usually in for the rest.

"What do you think, Mildred?" she asked.

"Well," Mildred said slowly, "I suppose it wouldn't hurt to ask."

Andrea told them that she'd be right back, and went through the revolving doors of the bank building. She went to the pay phones in the lobby near the elevators. While she was gone Laura sat down with Mildred on one of the stone benches and flipped to the pictures of two small children in her wallet. Their father, she explained, was a fireman who had recently been killed in the line of duty. She took out a picture of an old boyfriend to show Mildred, and even managed to produce a convenient tear drop to roll down her cheek.

"I moved back here so we'd be close to his folks," Laura said. "To give the kids a chance to know their grandparents."

"That's nice, dear. I certainly treasure mine."

"Oh, you're a grandmother," Laura said solicitously. "Do you have their pictures?" Her job at this point was to keep the pigeon talking until Andrea returned for the rest of the set-up.

But Mrs. Castle made it easy for her, pulling out pictures of her grandchildren and telling Laura all those little stories that she really couldn't care less about.

After a few minutes Andrea came back through the revolving doors, walking briskly now, as if eager to share her newly obtained knowledge.

"My boss said it's legal for us to split the money, but we should register the serial numbers and wait thirty days," she said. "That's the legal time limit for claiming lost items."

"Register the serial numbers?" asked Laura quizzically.

Andrea nodded. She was speaking rapidly now, the way somebody does when they're speaking about a complex subject that, to them, is routine."

"My boss can do that for us," she said. "What he does suggest is that he hold onto the money in the mean time."

"Ah, I don't know about that," Laura said hesitantly.

"Well, if you're worried," Andrea continued, "we can each put up a certain percentage of what's in the envelope, as . . . good-faith money. And at the end of the thirty days, we can legally split up the money."

Laura narrowed her eyes slightly and glanced at each of them. "Mildred, I trust you. Why don't you hold the money? Would you have any objections to that?" she said, turning toward Andrea.

Andrea took in a long breath before she answered.

"Maybe the best thing to do is for each of us to put up the good-faith money," she said. "Say like I give you a certain percentage of what's in the envelope. . . ."

"Oh, I see. That way nobody would cash in the money before the thirty days," Laura said. "Sure, I'm willing to do that. Mildred, how about you? I think that's fair, don't you?"

"I would agree with that," Mildred said slowly. Then added, "There's an old saying: Sometimes it takes money to make money."

Oh, this is great, thought Laura. An old saying, my ass. She'd have to remember that one for the next mark.

"So if I put up, say, ten thousand," Andrea said, trying to gauge how much they could make on this one, "could you each match that?"

At this point the pigeons were usually worried at the prospect of the money slipping away. And they were also confused by all the double talk but hesitant to admit it, lest they appear stupid.

"I've got my insurance money," Laura said. "Mildred?"

"Like I said, it takes money. . . ." Mildred said, showing them a denture-perfect smile. "I just need to make a withdrawal."

"This sounds like a wonderful opportunity," Laura said. "Doesn't it, Mildred?"

Mildred flashed her smile again. "Yes, dear, it certainly does."

"Well, like I said, I was just on my way to deposit some insurance settlement money," said Laura. "I can't pass up a chance like this. My kids are gonna be so happy."

"She's a widow," Mildred said, as if she and Laura were old friends. "Her husband was a fireman."

Great, thought Laura, she's so caught up in the story the rest will go like clockwork.

"Well, I bank down the street," Andrea said, smiling with a venal gleam in her eye. "It's agreed then? We each put up ten thousand, and Mildred can hold the envelope for thirty days?"

"Oh, Mildred," said Laura. "Let's all do it. It's like a dream come true."

"It certainly does sound like a great opportunity," said Mildred, smiling back at her. "Let's just step back inside the bank, and I'll be right back with my third," she said.

Andrea and Laura exchanged surreptitious winks. Just like clockwork. The only thing they had to do to complete the scam was switch the envelopes once they had Mildred's "good-faith money" in it. Then, after a quick excuse to disappear for a moment, they'd slip away to their car, which was parked on the other side of the building.

Usually, Laura would go to the car to get her money while Andrea went to telephone her boss again. They'd leave the pigeon sitting there holding what she thought was the envelope with all the money in it, for safekeeping. By the time the mark finally opened it and discovered that it only contained cut-up newspaper, Laura and Andrea would be long gone with the real cash.

Mrs. Castle went to the glass desks that held the bank withdrawal slips as Andrea and Laura watched from the lobby, turning so they'd be out of the range of the surveillance cameras. The old woman wrote out her withdrawal slip and walked to the tellers' window. Laura glanced furtively over her shoulder. The teller moved with a ponderous slowness, but it always seemed that way. The waiting was the hardest when the pigeon drop was almost complete.

Finally, Mildred moved toward them, a well stuffed envelope in her hand. As she approached, she smiled conspiratorially.

"I've got my share," she said.

"Good. Let me put it in this big manila one," Laura said.

Mildred handed over her heavily stuffed envelope, and Laura stuck it inside the large 8 × 10 manila envelope. Stuffing it in her large purse, she turned slightly away from Mrs. Castle for a moment as she looked at Andrea.

"Nothing left to do but see your boss, right?" Laura said.

"Wait, is your money inside?" Andrea asked, pointing to Laura's purse.

"Oh no, it isn't," she said. "I was keeping it in the trunk of my car until I'd decided on a bank." Laura opened her purse, withdrew the dummy manila envelope, and handed it to Mrs. Castle. "Here, Mildred, why don't you hold the money until I run out to my car?"

"All right," Mildred said. The big envelope felt stuffed.

As Laura moved toward the doors Mrs. Castle trailed close behind her. Andrea said she wanted to visit the ladies' room before going to her bank and went toward the washrooms. Laura smiled at Mrs. Castle as she stepped inside the revolving doors.

"I'll be right back, Mildred," she said.

"I doubt it, dear," answered Mrs. Castle.

As the door swished around Mildred bent down and deftly slipped the heavily padded envelope in between the door frame and the edge of the thick glass cylinder in which the doors revolved. Laura jolted to a stop, trapped inside. She pushed forward, but the door wouldn't move with the envelope binding it. Nor could she push the door backwards against the gears.

"Mildred," Laura said, desperation edging into her voice. "Take that out of the door."

Mrs. Castle ignored her and whistled loudly, gesturing for the bank security guard. As he approached, Mildred pointed to the ladies' room.

"I've got this one. The other one's in there, wearing a gray suit. The cops are on the way," she said. "Now move your butt."

The detective watched as both Laura and Andrea were handcuffed and placed into the back of the squad car. Then he turned to Mildred.

"Mrs. Castle, I'd like to thank you for catching another one of these bunco teams for us."

Mildred smiled and patted his arm.

"That's perfectly all right, Detective Meyers," she said. "Just doing my civic duty, as usual. Now, when's the court date?"

The detective told her, then scratched his head.

"You know, ma'am, your note to the teller for her to call us was enough. You didn't need to trap them for us."

"This way I figured it'd be a stronger case," said Mildred. "No way they're gonna beat this one, right?"

"Yes, ma'am," the detective said. "Instructing the teller to record the serial numbers on the bills you gave to her will probably assure a conviction, but, Mrs. Castle, what I mean is, it's kinda dangerous for civilians to get too involved in police business."

"Civilians," Mildred said with a smile. "Just whose collar do you think this *is*, sonny?"

A QUARTER FOR CRAZY EDDIE

WILL MURRAY

They tell me I could make more money robbing banks or holding up liquor stores, especially drifting as much as I do. I know that. I also know that's not for me. I'm a regular guy with old-fashioned ideas about working. It's just that I'm a little unorthodox in the way I go about it.

This time it was Boston. The company's name was the Dyna Corporation. According to their want ad, they manufactured electronic components for the Automatic Testing Industry and needed stock help. Perfect.

The Dyna Corporation was an old twelve-story building on Summer Street. I was waiting outside before they opened for business, and before any other applicants showed up.

The interview was routine. I called myself "Carl Shaner" on the application—keeping my first name as I always do—and claimed my only prior work experience was ten years as a shipper for the mythical Highsound Stereo Component Company in Baltimore. Employers don't expect falsified credentials and they almost never check out-of-state references.

A big jowly guy named Salwak took my application. I answered the usual questions and did my best to create a good impression. I had deliberately undervalued myself on the application. That was the hook.

"According to this," Salwak said, "your last employer went out of business."

"Yes, that's true," I told him. "I couldn't find another job down home—it's that bad there—so I'm trying to make a new start here in Boston." I tried to sound down and out.

Salwak looked at the application again, then proceeded to fill me in on the company.

"We manufacture state of the art circuit boards. These boards are used in automatic testing equipment of all types. They are small, but very delicate and expensive. Your duties will be to help maintain our regular inventory and you will be responsible for shipping hardware to our customers."

"Sounds right up my alley," I said.

Salwak nodded. "The position starts at $3.40 an hour."

The ad had said $3.70 an hour.

"Fine," I said.

"In that case, Mr. Shaner," Salwak beamed, "I think you are exactly the individual we are looking for. You start tomorrow. Report to Mr. Roberts at the dock."

The next day I reported to Shipping and Receiving at eight sharp. Jerry Roberts, a bluff character who reminded me of a Keystone Kop, was in charge. The rest of the crew were a predictable bunch. Tony Cellini was the jokester of the group—there's one in every place. Lance Royston was quiet, black, and smart as a whip. He really should have been in charge, but the smart ones never are. If I ever retire from this game, I might write a book about the people I've worked with. They're part of what I enjoy about this.

I fitted in without any trouble. I always do. The work was easy. We were the low men on the Dyna totem pole, which didn't surprise me. Shipping and Receiving was in the basement, out of sight, and our loading dock was in the rear alley, which was below street level. Finished printed circuit boards—PC boards for short—came down to us in plastic bags for storage or shipping. Whatever went on upstairs, it didn't concern us much. The shipping crew kept apart from what Jerry called the "boy geniuses" upstairs. We didn't even eat in the company cafeteria. Instead, we ate at a neighborhood bar or sent out. That was how I first met Crazy Eddie.

It was on my second day. The buzzer had announced lunch.

"Where are we eating today?" I asked Jerry.

"I sent out for it. Pizza. I hope you like it with onions and peppers."

"I can handle it," I grinned. The pizza arrived almost immediately, brought by a vacant-faced kid who might have been anywhere from 16 to 26. He handed the pizza to Tony and stuck out his hand, palm up.

"Hey, hey," he said. "Gimme a quarter."

"Here you go, Eddie."

The kid's eyes got wide and a sappy grin spread over his face. He scooped up the coin with a pudgy hand. He turned to Lance next and repeated his demand. Lance gave him a quarter. So did Jerry. Then he came up to me.

"Gimme a quarter." His eyes were fish-gray. I hesitated.

"Go ahead, man," Lance said.

I dug into my pocket. The kid was grinning and bouncing on his feet. "C'mon, get it up. Get it up." He gave me the willies.

I pulled out a fifty-cent piece. "Here, take four bits," I said. Anything to get rid of him.

The kid took the coin, looked it over once, and dropped it in the alley dirt. "C'mon, get it up," he said again.

"Give Eddie a *quarter*," Tony told me. "He only takes quarters."

I fumbled out a quarter. He took it and skipped away, grinning and shaking the quarters in his cupped hands like a five-year-old.

"That's Crazy Eddie," Jerry told me as we sat on the dock to eat. "He's been in and out of institutions most of his life, but he's harmless. Goes around begging quarters off people—that's how he makes his living. When he's around, we send him out for food and pay him in quarters. He's sort of a tradition around here, so we try to take care of him."

"The reason he wouldn't take your fifty cents," Lance put in, "was because he doesn't understand money. He just knows that a quarter will buy him a candy bar, and that's all he cares about."

I picked up my half dollar and finished my lunch. "Crazy."

We saw Crazy Eddie about twice a week, and I sort of got used to his idiot grin. He has to be one of the strangest characters I've met in this game. If I ever write that book, I told myself, Crazy Eddie's going to be in it.

Yeah, he sure is.

It was at the end of the first week that I met John Grodin. John worked upstairs in Design, but he was a maverick and welcome in Shipping. He had lunch with us whenever he got fed up with the upstairs crowd. When he did, we would get in a few hands of poker.

I made a point of getting to know John. I liked him and he had the inside track at Dyna.

"Just what do you do up there all day, John?" I asked.

Most people don't show much interest in what others do for a living. Consequently, when someone does, the floodgates open.

John launched into a long explanation of how he mocked up PC board designs with mylar sheets and pressure-sensitive tape to simulate circuitry. The boards were used the way computers are used to test car performance. John designed the custom boards for special equipment, he told me.

"Worth a lot of money?" I asked.

"The regular boards you guys store aren't worth more than a few hundred dollars each, but some of the custom PC boards cost heavy bread, let me tell you. I'm working on a design now that will be worth a cool five grand."

I whistled. "What do you make them out of—platinum?"

"No, the parts are just fiberglass and copper solder." John got a board and took it out of its plastic bag. It was about the size of a ruler, except that it was made out of green plastic.

"See how thin these circuit lines are? The tolerances are unbelievable. This is art."

"Are these things worth anything to anyone outside of the companies you make them for?"

"Sure," John said. "Any number of people would love to get their hands on some of our designs. Some other computer outfit who can't afford our boards. Or our competition. A thief could do well for himself if he had connections in the industry."

I smiled to myself. I had hopes of being that thief.

The weeks slid by and I slipped into the routine. The work was simple. The regular stock boards were kept in a locked storage cage. The custom jobs, when they were being held before shipping, were kept in individual combination lockers in another cage. I knew all the combinations—it was my job.

In the meantime I pumped the others as much as I could. It was Jerry's job to lock up at night, so I learned about the alarm and where the keys were kept. From Lance I found out that the night security guard mainly patrolled the upper floors. The Dyna Corporation was shaping up very nicely.

One night I checked out the place under actual "working" conditions. I entered the alley behind Dyna after eleven on a Saturday night, walking at a quick pace past the dim bulbs glowing over the rows of loading platforms and service doors—as if I had taken a wrong turn and was anxious to find my way back. It looked perfectly deserted. Then a foot kicked a pebble somewhere in front of me and a voice said, "Hey, hey!"

I froze. There was someone there I couldn't make out in the dark. When he said, "Get it up," I recognized Crazy Eddie's voice. Sure enough, he stepped into the dim light.

I let out a pent breath. "Hi, Eddie."

"Gimme a quarter," he grinned. I flipped him a quarter. He caught it and went past me. He didn't say thank you—he never does. I got out of that alley in a hurry, making a mental note to carry a quarter for Crazy Eddie—just in case—when the job became ripe.

I had been there almost seven weeks when the opportunity of a lifetime came. I almost didn't take it. I hadn't set up a fence yet and, worse, I hadn't put in my three months. I always put in at least three months before I make my move. Paying my dues, so to speak.

It happened over lunch. John Grodin came down looking harried.

"Just finished five board designs for a jet-engine test unit," he informed me. "Man, were they *tough*. I figure that by the time they add up all the costs of redesigning and experimentation, those boards will cost the contractor $25,000 each."

I munched on my burger to cover my excitement. Throwing in some of the random stock, I could walk off with more than $150,000 in the trunk of my car. I could worry about a fence later.

"When are they going out?" I asked John. Everything depended on his answer.

"Tomorrow morning. They're being loaded and inspected now. You should have them by three for packing."

The boards came down at 2:30. They didn't look any different from any of the zillion other boards that had passed through my hands, but the amber plastic and copper circuitry might as well have been solid gold. I stored them carefully.

When five o'clock came, I pretended to misplace a shipping form. I told the others to go ahead, that I would lock up. Just like that. Why not? I was a trusted co-worker. They didn't know it was good-bye, not good night.

I disconnected the alarm first. Then I punched out, shut off the lights, and left by the service door, taking the ring of keys that hung beside it with me.

I drove home wearing a grin as big as Crazy Eddie's.

I had dinner, watched the news, and waited. It was going to be a cinch. Only one thing bothered me—I hadn't put in my three months' time. I was superstitious about that, but I put it out of my mind. If I unloaded those boards right, I could be in Las Vegas inside of a month. I always went to Vegas after a job.

At ten o'clock I eased my car into the alley behind Dyna and parked beside the dock. I got in through the service door with the key.

Once inside, it was just a matter of unlocking the storage cages and working the combination lockers. I carried the five special boards out first. Then I got the rest of the custom boards and some of the inventory stock. Everything fitted into the trunk.

I reset the alarm, replaced the keys, and shut the service door behind me. Simple, no? Yes, but I had put in almost two months at Dyna to make it that simple. The whole thing had taken 20 minutes. I made for the car, feeling only a little tightness in my gut.

Then the alley turned white with light. I ducked instinctively. A prowl car had turned the corner, moving slowly with its flashers off.

No time to start the car. I ran. Car doors slammed open and shut behind me. Heavy feet pounded. I heard a shout as I cut around a corner.

Damn the luck! They must have been late on their regular patrol. I ducked into a passage between two buildings, and around a corner. Breathing more from nerves than effort, I stopped to get my bearings.

A voice from the shadows said, "Get it up!" and my heart stopped.

Then I recognized that voice. It was Crazy Eddie, a foolish grin on his loose face and his white hand outstretched. "Hey, hey! Gimme a quarter," he demanded. I couldn't have been more scared if those two cops had jumped out of the shadows.

The heavy feet sounded again. I got an idea. Then I felt sick. I had forgotten to check my change! I dug into my pocket frantically, finally pulled out a quarter by feel.

"Here, Eddie. When those cops come, tell them I went the other way, understand?" Eddie nodded vacantly. Running the opposite way, I turned into a blind alley. I waited, listening, my gut like a drum. Crazy Eddie would steer the cops the other way and I'd be home free—maybe I could get back to the car.

I heard a voice order, "Hold it!"

"Wait, Joe. It's Crazy Eddie. He's okay. Hey, Eddie, did you see a guy run this way? Yeah? Which way did he go?"

Crazy Eddie mumbled something I couldn't hear, but I did hear the cops trot away. It worked. I waited some more, then peered out. Crazy Eddie was still standing there. He looked confused, but he didn't matter any more. I legged down the street and around the corner.

The two cops were waiting for me with guns drawn. "Right there, buddy," one of them ordered. I put my hands up—there was nothing else to do. They frisked me against a wall and read me my rights. Crazy Eddie came to watch. When I saw his face, I knew he'd tipped them off.

"What the hell's the matter with you?" I yelled at him. "I gave you your damn quarter! Why'd you do it?"

One of the cops looked at me funny. The other one told him,

"Crazy Eddie will do almost anything for a quarter, but he has no use for any other kind of money." He walked down the street, and came back with something shiny he'd picked off the pavement.

"Looks like you made a common mistake, pal." He held up a Susan B. Anthony silver dollar to the light.

THE RAFFLE

WAYNE D. DUNDEE

I waited until the operator hung up in disgust, after telling me repeatedly and with growing impatience that no one at the random long distance number I'd given her was willing to accept charges for the call.

"Did you tell them this is urgent—an emergency?" I wailed loudly into the dead pay phone.

I gave it a beat, like I was listening to her say something back, then held the mouthpiece out a little farther and raised my voice a couple more notches, loud enough this time to be heard even above the plinkety-twang of the godawful hillbilly music playing on the juke box. "Yeah, well, thanks a whole fucking heap, operator," I hollered. "You're about as compassionate as that tightwad damn brother of mine. To hell with you and him both, then!"

I returned the phone to its cradle with a loud bang and stormed back toward my stool at the bar. I could feel different sets of eyes following me, exactly the way I wanted them to. I didn't look back at any of them, just set my face in the frustratedly pissed-off expression I wanted them all to see and made for the stool.

Angie sat on the one next to it, waiting.

I dropped onto the seat, grabbed the half-empty glass of beer I'd left behind, tipped it up, and drained it.

"Bad luck, baby?" Angie wanted to know.

"Do I look like I had any *good* luck?" I snapped, keeping the act going.

"That high and mighty brother of yours . . . you should have known he wouldn't lift a finger to help. Let alone spend a dime."

"Lousy tightwad wouldn't even take a collect call to hear what the problem was." I brought the empty glass down heavily on the bartop. "Rotten cheap bastard!"

The fat, sweaty bartender waddled over. "Keep a little tighter lid on it, buddy, whatya say? Everybody in here's got their own share of grief, they ain't interested in hearing you cuss about yours."

Outside, the wind slapped late summer rain against the roof and windows and carried the growl of rolling thunder.

I dragged my palm down over my face, like a guy with the weight of the world grinding him under. I said, "You know the old saying that goes, 'Ever had one of those days?' Well, I've had a whole string of *nothing but* 'one of those days,' mister. A fella gets chafed pretty damn raw after a while, so you'll have to excuse me all to hell and gone if my lousy attitude is spoiling the mood for anybody else."

"Take it easy, baby," Angie said.

"I'm cool," I told her.

"That's the way," the bartender said. "Just keep cool."

Like that's what he was doing, the fat slob. His eyes were dull slits in folds of pasty white blubber and he was unable to stop them from gazing down the front of Angie's dress. Of course, paying attention to the way Angie's curves filled out her rain-soaked dress was exactly what we wanted every guy in the place to be doing, but I didn't need lard-ass there behind the stick to get so overheated by the display he'd have a stroke or something; he was the key to getting the whole gig off on the right foot, making it work or not.

"How about another beer?" he said to me, finally managing to tear his gaze away from Angie's cleavage. But not for long. "And how about you, ma'am—another sloe gin?"

We both told him yeah and he set to work fixing us up.

The tavern was your typical country junction joint, located where a county blacktop crossed a neglected stretch of two-lane highway between a couple jerkwater little towns that were hell and gone away from any decent-sized city. The whole area seemed heavy into pig farming, judging by the barnyard layouts and the billboard advertising, not to mention the smell that had hung in the steamy air ahead of the storm. The gin joint was a place where the blue-collar hicks came to swill beer, shoot a little pool, listen to pathetic cowboy music, talk big, and pretend their lives were right on track. A place ripe for making a quick score but one where I'd damn sure go buggy if I had to spend more than a couple hours.

"On the house," the bartender said, returning to set fresh drinks in front of us. "The spell of bad luck it sounds like you're having, you need to catch a break, even if it's only a small one."

One of the men a ways down the bar, a whiskery old coot who looked to be pushing eighty or so, said, "What's so small about a freebie? I started coming here when you was still crapping yellow, Andy Torple—hell, before that, before you were even a gleam in your old man's eye—and in all the time since you took up behind that bar you never once offered *me* a round on the house."

"No, and I don't intend to," the bartender replied good-naturedly. "I might get you spoiled, Gleason, and before I knew it you'd come to expect a freebie every forty or fifty years."

"I'd know better than to expect anything from a cheapskate like you," the old man groused. "I see now the only way to get any decent treatment around here is to be built like a brick you-know-what."

The bartender—Andy, the old guy had called him—actually blushed a little bit. But that didn't stop him from glomming another eyeful of Angie's swelling breasts as he said, "Don't pay no attention to Gleason. He's so damn old his brain dried up and turned to dust sometime back in the fifties."

"Don't worry about it," Angie said, showing him a microsecond of her full candlepower smile. "Thanks for the drinks, all the same. That was sweet of you."

Andy blushed even more and I made a silent bet with myself that he might actually say something as corny as, "Shucks, it was nothing." But he didn't. Instead, though, he came up with a question almost as lame. "You folks ain't from around here, are you?"

"Not on your life," I said. "Strictly passing through."

"We're on our way to Tulsa," Angie added. Then, after a perfectly timed pause and with just the right dejected tone in her voice, she tacked on, "Well, at least we *were*."

"What do you mean 'were'?" Andy wanted to know.

I knew then she had him hooked. From that point, she could have gone into a spiel about gross bodily functions or a lecture on the mating rituals of the South American pissant and he would have hung on her every word. Him and practically everybody else in the joint. Over the click of pool balls and the blare of the juke box—and in spite of what the bartender had said earlier about nobody wanting to hear our problems—the dozen or so other customers, all men, were straining pretty obviously to catch what was going on. Us being strangers could have accounted for a certain amount of that; one of us looking the way Angie did made it unanimous.

Angie answered the bartender's question with a kind of forlorn sigh. "I don't see how we can make it now. Not in time, anyway. Milo's got this really great job waiting in Tulsa, see—the break we've been needing—but he's got to be able to start right away. We were deadheading straight on through. Then our car broke down. That's why we showed up here all soppy wet and everything, we had to walk in the rain from back up the road. Milo says the car needs a-a . . ." She looked flustered and turned to me. "What did you call it, baby?"

"Transmission," I muttered. "Damn thing's been acting up. Finally went."

Andy looked hopeful. "Hey, there's a really good service station in Cottonville. Only a few miles from here. I bet they could fix your car easy, get at it first thing in the morning and maybe have you going again before noon tomorrow. Wouldn't the start of your job wait that long?"

I gave him a look like you'd give a kid who just handed you a rotten report card. "You don't listen too good, do you? I told you I'm coming off a whole string of shitty luck. I had barely enough money for gas to make Tulsa, and I had to go in hock for that. You know what an automatic transmission—even a rebuilt one—is likely to run? You could line up service stations from hell to breakfast, pal, but it wouldn't do me any good because I'm tapped out and I got nowhere to turn. You heard my luck on the phone—I can't even get anybody to take a call." I let out a raspy laugh. "Let's face it, things just haven't been going my way and they're not ready to change yet. Not in Tulsa, and sure as hell not here."

Angie put her hand on my arm. "Don't be so down, baby. Something will work out. We always got each other."

"Sure," I said. "Sure."

The bartender just stood there looking kind of sad and confused. Sad because he had a soft heart and the chump really wished he could say or do something to help; confused because to his mind having a lady who looked like Angie ought to be enough good luck for any man.

"Look, pal," I said to him. "I appreciate your concern and the free drinks and all, really. But could you . . . well, not crowd us right at the moment. We got some things to work out here, just the two of us. You understand, right?"

119

He held up his hands. "Sure, mister. I didn't mean to pry or anything. You go on and take your time." He started to back away, his eyes unable to keep from lingering on Angie. "Just holler if you need anything."

Outside, lightning split the night and made the windows blink rapid bursts of brilliant silver.

Angie and I sat sort of hunkered over our drinks, our soaked clothes and slumped shoulders showing two people nearly worn to a frazzle by adversity. Her hand was very warm on my arm. We talked low, making sure nobody was close enough to hear.

"The fat sucker bought every damn word of it," Angie was saying, an edge of disdain in her voice.

"They almost always do," I reminded her. "Only difference is, this one seems a little more genuinely concerned about our plight."

"As far as I could tell, the main thing he was concerned about was getting a look at my tits."

"I don't blame him."

She smiled slyly. "It makes you hot, doesn't it? Seeing the suckers get all jazzed up over me, knowing you're the only one getting what they're all wanting so bad."

"That better be the way it is."

"What's that supposed to mean?"

"You figure it out."

I tipped up my beer and used the motion as an opportunity to survey the room once more. Counting the bartender, there were eleven guys present. Eleven marks. I'd figured on more, even for a weeknight, but the storm was probably keeping some of the less dedicated drinkers at home. Twenty was about the right number. Not too many to manage, but enough to assure a decent take.

Too late to do anything about it now, though. We'd put time into this, had it all set up. The only thing left was to play it out and settle for what we got.

Lowering my drink, I said to Angie, "The bartender's made the rounds. Those that didn't already hear what we were telling him, know by now all about our situation. I can see in their eyes that none of the jerks feel a bit sorry for me. They're all wondering the same thing: What does such a knockout chick see in such a loser?"

"When you talk mean to me, I sometimes wonder myself what I see in you."

"Knock that shit off. We're in the middle of a gig here, we got no time for tender feelings." I put my hand over hers. "In about ten

seconds, jerk your arm away and give out a loud *No*. Make them think we're arguing about something, let them wonder what it is."
 "I know the routine. We've been through it enough times."
 "Then do it."
 She jerked her arm away and said sharply, "No!"
 I put my arm around her and pulled her closer, held her tight against me. "Good job. That got their attention."
 "Maybe I wasn't acting."
 "Everybody in the world spends ninety-nine percent of their lives acting. Most of them just never figure it out."
 "That's what you always say."
 I kept track of things in the reflection off the bottle-strewn wall mirror behind the bar. "Okay, they've settled back down. They can see you're not struggling so they figure we made up over whatever caused you to try and jerk away. In a little bit now, it'll be time to make your trip to the juke box."
 "I hate that part. Hate their eyes all over me."
 "Who's kidding who, you little tease. You love it, and we both know it."
 The sly smile again. "You prick."
 "I just tell it like it is."
 "You want me to put on a show for these rubes? Fine. You got it. Just sit back and watch me work." She scooped a handful of quarters from the change scattered in front of me, slid off her stool, walked over to the juke box.
 Well, *walked* doesn't quite say it. With the rain-soaked dress hugging every inch of her like a layer of paint, she sort of slithered and jiggled her way across the floor in a manner that threatened to singe every eyeball in the place. Once at the machine, she leaned slowly over to peer more closely at the song selections, in the process striking a wildly provocative pose with her fine ass jutted out like a highway sign. Even Gleason, the ancient old grump seated down the bar from me, perked up at the display.
 I sipped some of my beer and let them drool over her for a while. Let their minds start to conjure up fantasies that would play right into my hands when I made the next move.
 I waited until Angie's first selection was playing and she'd started to switch her fine ass to the beat while she took her time pondering another choice. By then all the marks were wearing slack-jawed expressions and staring as openly as front-row customers in a grind house.

I had to wave my arms like a windmill to get the bartender's attention. He trudged over to see what I wanted.

"Another beer?"

"In a minute, maybe. What I need first is a word or two with you." I held my voice in a kind of conspiratorial hush.

Andy looked uncertain. "About what?"

"Listen. You own this place, right?"

"Free and clear. My old man left it to me and I take good care of it."

"Good, good. Then you got nobody to answer to if it came to making what you might call, well, a controversial decision."

"I guess not. What do you mean?" He aimed the question at me but he couldn't keep his eyes off Angie over at the juke box.

I dragged my hand down over my face again, laying on the act of somebody struggling with a real dilemma. "This isn't easy to bring up, I want you to understand. But you already know the fix I'm in. . . ."

Andy gave a firm shake of his head. "Come on, mister, if this is about a loan or something you can't expect me to—"

"Hell, I'm not talking about a loan," I cut him off. "I'm talking about nothing more than a little game of chance. A raffle. Held right here, tonight, in your place. A chance for me to raise the money I so desperately need, a chance for you and your customers to win a mighty fine prize."

His piggy little eyes turned skeptical and just a bit smug. "And what would this 'mighty fine prize' be that you've got to raffle?"

I gave him smug right back. "You've been gawking at it ever since I brought it in here. You and every other swinging dick in this place."

It took him about half a minute to get it. When he finally did, his jaw practically dropped onto the bartop. "Sweet Jesus. You mean . . . *her?* You mean the prize is your lady?"

"Winner gets half an hour with Angie. Do whatever he wants. You've got some kind of back room here, don't you? A cot maybe? If not, there are a couple pickups outside with camper shells. I guarantee the setting won't really matter. A half hour with Angie—no matter where—any man will think he's in paradise."

"Are you serious? Jesus, mister. It's hard to believe anybody would . . ."

"It's my only chance to make Tulsa in time. And Tulsa may be my only chance of keeping Angie for much longer at all. I can live with what we got to do. So can she. You and your customers sure haven't minded drooling and staring at her ever since she walked in. But if you're a bunch of Bible-thumpers by day, or goody-goods of some other cut who only sneak peeks and are afraid of a chance to get it on for real, then I guess I read you wrong and we can forget it. We'll find some other way—"

"No. No, no. Nobody said that. Jeez, give me a minute to catch up with all this. Nothing like this has ever happened to me before."

"I'm guessing the guys here are all regulars. You know them all, right? I'd have to have your word that none of them will go running to the law afterward, or that none of them are kinky in some way Angie's got to worry about in case they win."

"You got no worry about any of that. I know all these boys. Well, all but that young fella in the back shooting eight ball. He's some biker passing through, waiting out the storm. Sure don't have to worry about his type running to the law."

"You up for it, then?" I asked him point blank. "I can't afford to offer you a cut, but think what it'll do for business if you let word get around. Not just tonight, but from now on. Guys you never saw before will start stopping in just to hear you tell the story. And they'll keep coming back because they'll be hoping they're lucky enough to have lightning strike again while they're here. You *do* reckon the boys we got on hand tonight are willing to try and get lucky, don't you?"

He grinned wolfishly. "Are you kidding? Look at the way they're all looking at her. Who can blame them? And who in his right mind wouldn't go for a chance at . . . well, something so fine."

I reached across the bar and clapped a hand onto his meaty shoulder. "Good, good. Here's the way we'll work it then. . . ."

I drew twenty squares on a sheet of paper, numbered each one. While I was doing that, Andy, the bartender, went around and explained to the others what was up. Every one of them was eager to participate. It would cost them twenty-five bucks a square. They could pick their number, first come first serve. I'd write their name in the square carrying the number of their choice. When the sheet was full, I'd cut it up, drop the squares into a hat, draw out the winner. Everything in plain sight, everything above board.

The squares went almost faster than I could take money and write in names. Andy alone bought four of them, a hundred bucks' worth, and just shelling out the dough made him as flushed and sweaty as if he'd already had the sex he was gambling on. Old Gleason, who must have had a hell of a lot more steam stored up in him than you'd ever guess, antied up for two chances. Some of the others were also willing to increase their odds by buying two. By the time it was done, I had five hundred bucks and a sheetful of filled-in squares in front of me.

Through it all, Angie remained off by herself at one end of the bar. Calmly smoking a cigarette and sipping sloe gin. Cool and aloof, like a queen bitch in heat waiting for a winner to emerge from the pack of hounds snarling after her scent.

The place went quiet as a tomb while I held the hat at arms' length in one hand, reached in with the other, swirled the bits of paper, then withdrew one. Or so most of them thought. The piece of paper I held up and began to unfold had actually been deftly palmed back when I was cutting up the squares and dropping them into the hat to begin with.

"Number twelve," I read aloud. "Sam Stone."

Everybody started looking at one another. Their expressions were perplexed. They didn't seem to recognize the name.

Then the young biker with the sullen eyes and the mane of wheat-colored hair pushed his way through. "That'd be me."

A general groan of despair and a handful of curses rolled out of the pack of slump-shouldered losers.

"You're a lucky man, son," I said, looking into his eyes. Sam Stone. Stoney, we'd taken to calling him shortly after he joined our crew back in Kansas City. He'd proven himself to be sharp, a fast learner. Lately I'd taken to wondering just *how fast* on the uptake he might be. I wondered exactly what him and Angie did during those half-hour chunks of time they spent alone together whenever we ran this scam, playing out the rigged "win" while I waited somewhere else with the sorry remains of whatever flock we'd just fleeced.

"Yeah, sometimes I do get lucky." Stoney replied now, meeting my gaze evenly.

A deeply disappointed Andy pointed the way to the back room and Stoney and Angie disappeared through the doorway.

The rest of us didn't have much to say while we waited. A couple of the players finished their drinks and left.

Eventually Andy came over by me. "Now that you got yourself some money, you be wanting the name of that service station I told you about?"

I shook my head. "Don't think so. Figure the quickest way is for us to catch a ride to the nearest town with a train or bus station and go on into Tulsa that way."

"What about your car?"

"The junk parts off it probably wouldn't be worth the price of towing. I don't much care what happens to it."

"Guess you won't be needing it where you're going anyway."

"Tulsa, you mean?"

"Uh-uh. Not exactly."

The warning was there in his voice but I wasn't quick enough to catch on. Not before I got grabbed from behind by two of the others, two burly farmer types. My arms were pinned to my sides, my chest slammed hard against the edge of the bar. There was no sense in struggling. I've never been very physical, I get by on my wits.

"What the hell gives?" I demanded.

"The jig is up, you phony fucker—that's what gives," Andy sneered, leaning across the bar and shoving his fat face close to mine.

The two guys holding me jerked me around in time to see Angie and Stoney being shoved from the back room by two other guys—the same two I thought had left. One of the guys was flashing a pistol. Stoney's hands were tied behind his back with a torn and knotted strip of bar towel. Both he and Angie were bare from the waist up. Their two captors might have peeled Angie for a cheap thrill, but that wouldn't explain Stoney being partly undressed. What it meant was that the two of them had started to strip each other before they got interrupted. I felt a sickening anger toward both of them and the guilty look in Angie's eyes when she tried to meet mine only made it worse.

"We had you sharpies spotted from the minute you walked in," Andy was saying, continuing to sneer. "Old Gleason here was off visiting relatives in Missouri last month and heard stories about you three recently pulling this stunt in several rural counties over that way. The folks involved only figured out they'd been scammed after they got to comparing notes. Gleason recognized you from the descriptions they gave, and clued the rest of us in on what you were up to."

"Why'd you go so far along with it, then?" I said.

"Just to make sure, sonny," Gleason answered. "Just to make damn sure."

"So what now? I suppose the cops are on their way."

Andy wagged a scolding finger at me. "Oh, no. You made me promise no one would run to the law, remember?"

"You've obviously got something in mind. You trying to say you've put together some kind of half-assed lynch mob?"

"No!" Angie cried. "Do something, Milo. Offer them money. Pay them whatever it takes."

Andy chuckled. "Don't worry, little lady, we ain't going to lynch nobody. And it ain't money we want in payment . . . but it's something else you got plenty of."

Angie's eyes went big. "No!"

"We're going to take what we already paid for, that's all. You tried to cheat us, so now we remove the risk. Everybody gets to be a winner."

Stoney tried to say something but Andy backhanded him with surprising viciousness. When he was through, breathing hard from the exertion and breaking into a fresh sweat, the bartender turned to old Gleason. "You earned top honors, old man, you and your eagle eyes. Take her in the back again. Then it'll be my turn."

Angie started to tremble, too scared to resist.

"Don't try to fight him, lady, he's a lot stronger than he looks. And if we have to, there's plenty of us willing to come hold you down for him."

Gleason laughed nastily. "That'll be the day, when I need any of you young whelps to hold a girl down *for me.*" He shoved Angie roughly ahead of him and followed her into the back room.

After the door had closed, Andy motioned for Stoney to be dragged over closer to where I was. When that was done, he said, "Now for you two bastards."

He motioned again and a tall, gangly, tow-headed man stepped up to stand next to him. "This here's Homer Dobbins. Homer might not look like much to a couple of sharpies like you two, but it happens he's a successful local businessman. And he's got a real special skill. Almost like fate, him being on hand tonight. Homer runs the local hog market, see, has for years . . . and in that time he's become the champeen hog nutter in all of Caliboros County."

Something icy clutched my insides.

"We ain't going to run to the law," Andy continued. "But we're by-God going to have us some justice. And since you two were fixing to screw every one of us like you already screwed who knows how many other trusting old country boys before this, we decided the only right thing to square all of that is to fix it so you don't screw nothing ever again. . . . Show 'em, Homer."

Grinning, Homer held up two gleaming blades; a straight razor and what looked like a curved linoleum cutter.

I heard somebody start to scream and it took a minute to realize it was me. More hands grabbed me, pulled me down, pressed my shoulders to the floor and began yanking my limbs spread-eagled. I caught a final fleeting glimpse of Homer's grinning face and glittery blades before he knelt down and went out of sight behind the heads and shoulders of the guys pinning my legs.

In the background, fat Andy was cackling. "Spread em wide, Milo baby!"

The only hope I had left was that I could stay conscious long enough for the satisfaction of hearing that bastard Stoney do some screaming too.

A Real Nice Guy

William F. Nolan

Warm sun.
    A summer afternoon.

The sniper emerged from the roof door, walking easily, carrying a custom-leather guncase.

Opened the case.
Assembled the weapon.
Loaded it.
Sighted the street below.
Adjusted the focus.
Waited.
There was no hurry.
No hurry at all.

He was famous, yet no one knew his name. There were portraits of him printed in dozens of newspapers and magazines; he'd even made the cover of *Time*. But no one had really seen his face. The portraits were composites, drawn by frustrated police artists, based on the few misleading descriptions given by witnesses who claimed to have seen him leaving a building or jumping from a roof, or driving from the target area in a stolen automobile. But no two descriptions matched.

One witness described a chunky man of average height with a dark beard and cap. Another described a thin, extremely tall man with a bushy head of hair and a thick mustache. A third description pegged him as balding, paunchy and wearing heavy hornrims. On *Time*'s cover, a large blood-soaked question mark replaced his features—above the words WHO IS HE?

Reporters had given him many names: "The Phantom Sniper" . . . "The Deadly Ghost" . . . "The Silent Slayer" . . . and his personal favorite, "The Master of Whispering Death." This was often shortened to "Deathmaster," but he liked the full title; it was fresh and poetic—and *accurate*.

He *was* a master. He never missed a target, never wasted a shot. He was cool and nerveless and smooth, and totally without conscience. And death indeed whispered from his silenced weapon: a dry snap of the trigger, a muffled pop, and the target dropped as though struck down by the fist of God.

They were *always* targets, never people. Men, women, children. Young, middle-aged, old. Strong ones. Weak ones. Healthy or crippled. Black or white. Rich or poor. Targets—all of them.

He considered himself a successful sharpshooter, demonstrating his unique skill in a world teeming with three billion moving targets placed there for his amusement. Day and night, city by city, state by state, they were always there, ready for his gun, for the sudden whispering death from its barrel. An endless supply just for him.

Each city street was his personal shooting gallery.

But he was careful. Very careful. He never killed twice in the same city. He switched weapons. He never used a car more than once. He never wore the same clothes twice on a shoot. Even the shoes would be discarded; he wore a fresh pair for each target run. And, usually, he was never seen at all.

He thought of it as a sport.

A game.

A run.

A vocation.

A skill.

But never murder.

* * *

His name was Jimmie Prescott and he was thirty-one years of age. Five foot ten. Slight build. Platform shoes could add three inches and body pillows up to fifty pounds. He had thinning brown hair framing a bland, unmemorable face. He shaved twice daily—but the case of wigs, beards and mustaches he always carried easily disguised the shape of his mouth, chin and skull. Sometimes he would wear a skin-colored fleshcap for baldness, or use heavy glasses—though his sight was perfect. Once, for a lark, he had worn a black eye patch. He would walk in a crouch; or stride with a sailor's swagger, or assume a limp. Each disguise amused him, helped make life more challenging. Each was a small work of art, flawlessly executed.

Jimmie was a perfectionist.

And he was clean: no police record. Never arrested. No set of his prints on file, no dossier.

He had a great deal of money (inherited) with no need or inclination to earn more. He had spent his lifetime honing his considerable skills: he was an expert on weaponry, car theft, body-combat, police procedures; he made it a strict rule to memorize the street system of each city he entered before embarking on a shoot. And once his target was down he knew exactly how to leave the area. The proper escape route was essential.

Jimmie was a knowledgeable historian in his field: he had made a thorough study of snipers, and held them all in cold contempt. Not a worthwhile one in the lot. They *deserved* to be caught; they were fools and idiots and blunderers, often acting out of neurotic impulse or psychotic emotion. Even the hired professionals drew Jimmie's ire—since these were men who espoused political causes or who worked for government money. Jimmie had no cause, nor would he ever allow himself to be bought like a pig on the market.

He considered himself quite sane. Lacking moral conscience, he did not suffer from a guilt complex. Nor did he operate from a basic hatred of humankind, as did so many of the warped criminals he had studied.

Basically, Jimmie liked people, got along fine with them on a casual basis. He hated no one. (Except his parents, but they were long dead and something he did not think about anymore.) He was incapable of love or friendship, but felt no need for either. Jimmie depended only on himself; he had learned to do that from childhood. He was, therefore, a loner by choice, and made it a rule (Jimmie had many rules) never to date the same female twice, no matter how sexually appealing she might be. Man-woman relationships were a weakness, a form of dangerous self-indulgence he carefully avoided.

In sum, Jimmie Prescott didn't need anyone. He had himself, his skills, his weapons and his targets. More than enough for a full, rich life. He did not drink or smoke. (Oh, a bit of vintage wine in a good restaurant was always welcome, but he had never been drunk in his life.) He jogged each day, morning and evening, and worked out twice a week in the local gym in whatever city he was visiting. A trim, healthy body was an absolute necessity in his specialized career. Jimmie left nothing to chance. He was not a gambler and took no joy in risk.

A few times things had been close: a roof door that had jammed shut in Detroit after a kill, forcing him to make a perilous between-buildings leap . . . an engine that died during a police chase in Portland, causing him to abandon his car . . . an intense struggle with an off-duty patrolman in Indianapolis who'd witnessed a shot. The fellow had been tough, and dispatching him was physically difficult; Jimmie finally snapped his neck—but it had been close.

He kept a neat, handwritten record of each shoot in his tooled-leather notebook: state, city, name of street, weather, time of day, sex, age and skin color of target. Under "Comments," he would add pertinent facts, including the make and year of the stolen car he had driven, and the type of disguise he had utilized. Each item of clothing worn was listed. And if he experienced any problem in exiting the target area this would also be noted. Thus, each shoot was critically analyzed upon completion—as a football coach might dissect a game after it had been played.

The only random factor was the target. Pre-selection spoiled the freshness, the *purity* of the act. Jimmie liked to surprise himself. Which shall it be: that young girl in red, laughing up at her boyfriend? The old newsman on the corner? The school kid skipping homeward with books under his arm? Or, perhaps, the beefy, bored truckdriver, sitting idly in his cab, waiting for the light to change?

Selection was always a big part of the challenge.

And *this* time . . .

A male. Strong looking. Well dressed. Businessman with a briefcase, in his late forties. Hair beginning to silver at the temples. He'd just left the drugstore; probably stopped there to pick up something for his wife. Maybe she'd called to remind him at lunch.

Moving toward the corner. Walking briskly.

Yes, *this* one. By all means, this one.

Range: three hundred yards.
Adjust sight focus.
Rifle stock tight against right shoulder.
Finger inside guard, poised at trigger.
Cheek firm against wooden gunstock; eye to rubber scopepiece.
Line crosshairs on target.
Steady breathing.
Tighten trigger finger slowly.
Fire!
The man dropped forward to the walk like a clubbed animal, dead before he struck the pavement. Someone screamed. A child began to cry. A man shouted.

Pleasant, familiar sounds to Jimmie Prescott.

Calmly, he took apart his weapon, cased it, then carefully dusted his trousers. (Rooftops were often grimy, and although he would soon discard the trousers he liked to present a neat, well-tailored appearance—but only when the disguise called for it. What a marvelous, ill-smelling bum he had become in New Orleans; he smiled thinly, thinking about how truly offensive he was on that occasion.)

He walked through the roof exit to the elevator.

Within ten minutes he had cleared central Baltimore—and booked the next flight to the West Coast.

Aboard the jet, he relaxed. In the soft, warm, humming interior of the airliner, he grew drowsy . . . closed his eyes.

And had The Dream again.

The Dream was the only disturbing element in Jimmie Prescott's life. He invariably thought of it that way: The Dream. Never as *a* dream. Always about a large metropolitan city where chaos reigned —with buses running over babies in the street, and people falling down sewer holes and through plate glass store windows. Violent and disturbing. He was never threatened in The Dream, never personally involved in the chaos around him. Merely a mute witness to it.

He would tell himself, this was only *fantasy*, a thing deep inside his sleeping mind; it would go away once he awakened and then he could ignore it, put it out of his thoughts, bury it as he had buried the hatred for his father and mother.

Perhaps he had *other* dreams. Surely he did. But The Dream was the one he woke to, again and again, emerging from the chaos of the city with sweat on his cheeks and forehead, his breath tight and shallow in his chest, his heart thudding wildly.

"Are you all right?" a passenger across the aisle was asking him. "Shall I call somebody?"

"I'm fine," said Jimmie, sitting up straight. "No problem."

"You look kinda shaky."

"No, I'm fine. But thank you for your concern."

And he put The Dream away once again, as a gun is put away in its case.

In Los Angeles, having studied the city quite thoroughly, Jimmie took a cab directly into Hollywood. The fare was steep, but money was never an issue in Jimmie's life; he paid well for services rendered, with no regrets.

He got off at Highland, on Hollywood Boulevard, and walked toward the Chinese Theater.

He wanted two things: food and sexual satisfaction.

First, he would select an attractive female, take her to dinner and then to his motel room (he'd booked one from the airport) where he would have sex. Jimmie never called it lovemaking, a *silly* word. It was always just sex, plain and simple and quickly over. He was capable of arousing a woman if he chose to do so, of bringing her to full passion and release, but he seldom bothered. His performance was always an act; the ritual bored him. Only the result counted.

He disliked prostitutes and seldom selected one. Too jaded. Too worldly. And never to be trusted. Given time, and his natural charm, he was usually able to pick up an out-of-town girl, impress her with an excellent and very expensive meal at a posh restaurant, and guide her firmly into bed.

This night, in Hollywood, the seduction was easily accomplished.

Jimmie spotted a supple, soft-faced girl in the forecourt of the Chinese. She was wandering from one celebrity footprint to another, leaning to examine a particular signature in the cement.

As she bent forward, her breasts flowed full, pressing against the soft linen dress she wore—and Jimmie told himself, she's the one for tonight. A young, awestruck out-of-towner. Perfect.

He moved toward her.

"I just *love* European food," said Janet.

"That's good," said Jimmie Prescott. "I rather fancy it myself."

She smiled at him across the table, a glowing all-American girl from Ohio named Janet Louise Lakeley. They were sitting in a small, very chic French restaurant off La Cienega, with soft lighting and open-country decor.

"I can't read a word of this," Janet said when the menu was handed to her. "I thought they always had the food listed in English, too, like movie subtitles."

"Some places don't," said Jimmie quietly. "I'll order for us both. You'll be pleased. The sole is excellent here."

"Oh, I love fish," she said. "I could eat a ton of fish."

He pressed her hand. "That's nice."

"My head is swimming. I shouldn't have had that Scotch on an empty stomach," she said. "Are we having wine with dinner?"

"Of course," said Jimmie.

"I don't know anything about wine," she told him, "but I love champagne. That's wine, isn't it?"

He smiled with a faint upcurve of his thin lips.

"Trust me," he said. "You'll enjoy what I select."

"I'm sure I will."

The food was ordered and served—and Jimmie was pleased to see that his tastes had, once again, proven sound. The meal was superb, the wine was bracing and the girl was sexually stimulating. Essentially brainless, but that didn't really matter to Jimmie. She was what he wanted.

Then she began to talk about the sniper killings.

"Forty people in just a year and two months," she said. "And all gunned down by the same madman. Aren't they *ever* going to catch him?"

"The actual target total is forty-one," he corrected her. "And what makes you so sure the sniper is a male? Could be a woman."

She shook her head. "Whoever heard of a woman sniper?"

"There have been many," said Jimmie. "In Russia today there are several hundred trained female snipers. Some European governments have traditionally utilized females in this capacity."

"I don't mean women *soldiers*," she said. "I mean your nutso shoot-'em-in-the-street sniper. Always guys. Every time. Like that kid in Texas that shot all the people from the tower."

"Apparently you've never heard of Francine Stearn."

"Nope. Who was she?"

"Probably the most famous female sniper. Killed a dozen schoolchildren in Pittsburgh one weekend in late July, 1970. One shot each. To the head. She was a very accurate shootist."

"Never heard of her."

"After she was captured, *Esquire* did a rather probing psychological profile on her."

"Well, I really don't read a lot," she admitted. "Except Gothic romances. I just can't get *enough* of those." She giggled. "Guess you could say I'm addicted."

"I'm not familiar with the genre."

"Anyway," she continued, "I know this sniper is a guy."

"*How* do you know?"

"Female intuition. I trust it. It never fails me. And it tells me that the Phantom Sniper is a man."

He was amused. "What else does it tell you?"

"That he's probably messed up in the head. Maybe beaten as a kid. Something like that. He's *got* to be a nutcase."

"You could be wrong there, too," Jimmie told her. "Not all lawbreakers are mentally unbalanced."

"This 'Deathmaster' guy is, and I'm convinced of it."

"You're a strongly opinionated young woman."

"Mom always said that." She sipped her wine, nodded. "Yeah, I guess I am." She frowned, turning the glass slowly in her long-fingered hand. "Do you think they'll ever catch him?"

"I somehow doubt it," Jimmie declared. "No one seems to have a clear description of him. And he always manages to elude the police. Leaves no clues. Apparently selects his subjects at random. No motive to tie him to. No consistent M.O."

"What's that?"

"Method of operation. Most criminals tend to repeat the same basic pattern in their crimes. But not this fellow. He keeps surprising people. Never know where he'll pop up next, or who his target will be. Difficult to catch a man like that."

"You call them 'subjects' and 'targets'—but they're *people!* Innocent men and women and children. You make them sound like . . . like cutouts in a shooting gallery!"

"Perhaps I do," he admitted, smiling. "It's simply that we have different modes of expression."

"I say they'll get him eventually. He can't go on just butchering innocent people forever."

"No one goes on forever," said Jimmie Prescott.

She put down her wineglass, leaned toward him. "Know what bothers me most about the sniper?"

"What?"

"The fact that his kind of act attracts copycats. Other sickos with a screw loose who read about him and want to imitate him. Arson is like that. One big fire in the papers and suddenly all the other wacko firebugs start their *own* fires. It gets 'em going. The sniper is like that."

"If some mentally disturbed individual is motivated to kill stupidly and without thought or preparation by something he or she reads in the newspaper then the sniper himself cannot be blamed for such abnormal behavior."

"You call what *he* does normal?"

"I . . . uh . . . didn't say that. I was simply refuting your theory."

She frowned. "Then who *is* to blame? I think that guy should be caught and—"

"And what?" Jimmie fixed his cool gray eyes on her. "What would you do if you suddenly discovered who he was . . . where to find him?"

"Call the police, naturally. Like anybody."

"Wouldn't you be curious about him, about the kind of person he is? Wouldn't you *question* him first, try to understand him?"

"You don't question an animal who kills! Which is what he is. I'd like to see him gassed or hanged. . . . You don't *talk* to a twisted creep like that!"

She had made him angry. His lips tightened. He was no longer amused with this conversation; the word game had turned sour. This girl was gross and stupid and insensitive. Take her to bed and be done with it. Use her body—but no words. No more words. He'd had quite enough of those from her.

"Check, please," he said to the waiter.

It was at his motel, after sex, that Jimmie decided to kill her. Her insulting tirade echoed and re-echoed in his mind. She must be punished for it.

In this special case he felt justified in breaking one of his rules: never pre-select a target. She told him that she worked the afternoon shift at a clothing store on Vine. And he knew where she lived, a few blocks from work. She walked to the store each afternoon.

He would take her home and return the next day. When she left her apartment building he would dispatch her from a roof across the street. Once this plan had settled into place in the mind of Jimmie Prescott he relaxed, allowing the tension of the evening to drain away.

By tomorrow night he'd be in Tucson, and Janet Lakeley would be dead.

Warm sun.
A summer afternoon.
The sniper emerged from the roof door, walking easily, carrying a custom-leather guncase.
Opened the case.
Assembled the weapon.
Loaded it.
Sighted the street below.
Adjusted the focus.
Waited.
Target now exiting.
Walking along street toward corner.
Adjust sight focus.
Finger on trigger.
Cheek against stock.
Eye to scope.
Crosshairs direct on target.
Fire!

Jimmie felt something like a fist strike his stomach. A sudden, shocking blow. Winded, he looked down in amazement at the blood pulsing steadily from his shirtfront.

I'm hit! Someone has actually—

Another blow—but this one stopped all thought, taking his head apart. No more shock. No more amazement.

No more Jimmie.

She put away the weapon, annoyed at herself. *Two* shots! The Phantom Sniper, whoever he was, never fired more than once. But *he* was exceptional. She got goosebumps, just thinking about him.

Well, maybe next time she could drop her target in one. Anybody can miscalculate a shot. Nobody's perfect.

She left the roof area, walking calmly, took the elevator down to the garage, stowed her guncase in the trunk of the stolen Mustang and drove away from the motel.

Poor Jimmie, she thought. It was just his bad luck to meet *me*. But that's the way it goes.

Janet Lakeley had a rule, and she never broke it: when you bed down a guy in a new town you always target him the next day. She sighed. Usually it didn't bother her. Most of them were bastards. But not Jimmie. She'd enjoyed talking to him, playing her word games with him . . . bedding him. She was sorry he had to go.

He seemed like a real nice guy.

RED RUNS THE TIDE

JOHN P. FORAN

The yacht basin nestled peacefully at the foot of green hills dotted with white, where fresh-water streams foamed over rocky ledges and flowed down to join the river's march to the salty sea. About thirty yachts, ranging in size from the river cruiser, *Judy-Ann*, to the ocean-going *Corsair*, were tied to buoys in the basin.

The tide pinned a police launch against the dock that was used as a landing and fueling station. A cop stood on the dock, guarding what was left of David Salisbury after nine days under the rotted wooden hulk that lifted out of the water south of the basin. A weathered tarpaulin protected the body from the heat of the sun.

Sergeant Eaton, of the marine division, sat in a wicker chair on the clubhouse porch. Despite the heat, his ruddy face was placid and his pale blue eyes were deceptively tranquil.

"Pretty," he murmured. "Like a marine toyland."

"Some toys," said Syd Bohm, his engineer. "A hundred grand—and you own the *Corsair*; or, if you don't have that kind of dough, you murder Salisbury and marry his widow." He was younger and leaner than Eaton. The heat of the sun and the waiting kept him mopping nervously at his thin face. "What's keeping them?" Irritably he pushed away from the porch rail. "This sun is murder—"

He stopped as two cars, a big black limousine and a small and somewhat battered sedan, came through the basin's gate and drove

137

over to the dock. A big, florid man got out of the limousine and helped a dark-haired woman alight. A slender man carrying a small, black bag got out of the sedan.

"Well, at least Phil's on time for once," growled Syd. "Now if he can forget he's a deck hand and make like a medical examiner—"

"Don't worry about Phil," said Eaton placidly. "Did you turn the wire recorder on?"

"Yeah." Syd checked his watch. "Got 'bout twenty-five minutes to run. I shifted it. It's under the couch in the commodore's office. Ran the wires out the window and around to the beam right over your head. You can hear a whisper on the porch."

Eaton watched what was going on down on the dock. Phil stood to one side while the cop knelt down and lifted a corner of the tarpaulin. The woman took a look at the body. A thin scream floated up to the porch as she recoiled and buried her face in the florid man's shoulder. He held her close for a moment, then turned toward the clubhouse. Phil set his bag on the dock, knelt down and went to work.

"Sarge, are you sure this is going to work?" Syd wiped his thin neck with quick, nervous gestures. "I mean, testing a ship's boiler water is one thing, but river water—hell, why not leave it to the shoreside detectives? It's their job anyway."

"It's a job for men who know the river and its ways," Eaton commented quietly.

"Yes, but—" Syd frowned and went on uneasily: "Remember it was La Salle who kicked up such a fuss last winter when brass fittings were stolen from the basin—like he owned a dozen yachts. And he knows the chief personally."

"Easy, now." Eaton got up as La Salle led Mrs. Salisbury up the porch steps. "Sorry to put you through such a grisly ordeal," he said, sounding very solicitous. "A body bloated by the river is a sickening sight."

Mrs. Salisbury shuddered violently. Her heavy-boned face was white and the skin was taut about a full, sensuous mouth. Her dark eyes were tortured.

La Salle glared at Eaton as he helped her into one of the wicker chairs. "I remember you now," he rasped. "The sergeant who couldn't catch those petty thieves last winter. You're much more effective at torturing women, aren't you?"

Behind La Salle, Syd winced.

Eaton took it calmly. "Just a few questions," he said, and before La Salle could interrupt. "I know, you've answered so many questions already. But now we want to know just how friendly you and Mrs. Salisbury were before her husband was drowned."

Mrs. Salisbury gasped.

"That's a damnable insinuation!" La Salle leaned toward Eaton, his full face livid. "Everybody, including the chief of police, knew that Grace and David and I were friends, close friends. David took many business trips for weeks at a time. He *wanted* me to entertain Grace." He stopped abruptly, staring past Eaton and down to the dock where Phil was working a hand pump. "What's that man doing?"

Without taking his eyes from Mrs. Salisbury, Eaton said, "The medical examiner is making a test for us. When did you last see your husband, Mrs. Salisbury?"

"It isn't possible to test a body that's been in the water over a week," snapped La Salle. "The chief's own personal physician discussed that with us last night."

"It's possible," said Eaton negligently, "to test the salt content of the water that went into Salisbury's lungs."

"And what'll that prove?"

"The exact hour he was drowned."

Eaton turned his attention back to Mrs. Salisbury. She was sitting stiffly erect, her hands white on the arms of the wicker chair. She glanced nervously at La Salle before speaking.

"David got home about eleven that night—a few minutes after. He'd been on the *Corsair* with Harold making up a list of pilot charts for a trip down the coast and across the Gulf of Mexico. I promised to stop off at the hydrographic office and pick them up for him the first thing in the morning."

"You three were taking the trip?"

"No. David owned a refinery down in Texas City and he was arranging the trip for a group of prospective buyers. He was almost asleep when he remembered the list on the *Corsair*. Despite my protests he insisted upon getting dressed and going back for it."

"What time was that?"

"Almost two in the morning."

Eaton turned to La Salle, who said angrily, "We've been over all this with the chief of police. The watchman admitted he was out cold in the clubhouse locker room. He'd found a bottle of whiskey—"

"A very convenient bottle," murmured Eaton.

La Salle's eyes narrowed. "So David took the launch out to the *Corsair*," he went on. "He fell overboard and drowned. That's obvious because the launch was found adrift the next morning, and the tide carried his body down to the old wreck and trapped it under the rotting beams where you grappled for it." His voice was like a whip flaying Eaton, while he kept glancing down to the dock where Phil was packing his bag. "And I've already testified that I left here with David about twenty minutes before eleven and went straight to my hotel. The doorman and elevator operator have corroborated that."

"And they also admitted that you—or anyone else in the hotel—could have slipped out the back way." Without giving La Salle a chance to answer, he turned and watched Phil come toward the clubhouse.

There was a tense silence as Phil came up the steps. Looking at Eaton, he asked, "Would you like me to complete the test right here?"

Eaton nodded. Syd picked up a wicker table and set it in front of Phil. They watched in silence as Phil opened the black bag and took out a wooden rack holding three glass tubes half filled with transparent liquid.

Uncorking the tubes, Phil explained, "This first tube contains a sample of high tide water. You see, when the tide sweeps in from the ocean the river has a maximum salt content, but at ebb tide—this middle sample—the fresh-water streams flowing down out of the hills reduce the salt content. This third tube contains fluid taken from the dead man's lungs."

He took a bottle out of the bag. "This is potassium chromate. I'm going to put an equal amount into each tube and the water in each will turn yellow. Now, a solution of silver nitrate. The resultant color will tell us the salt content of each sample."

They watched him squeeze drops of nitrate into the first test tube. The yellow changed to orange, then to pink, which deepened to a bloody red. He shifted the dropper to the low tide sample, and this time the yellow changed to pink.

Eaton held up a hand as Phil poised the dropper over the fluid taken from Salisbury's lungs. "High tide was at nine the evening Salisbury drowned." He took a newspaper clipping out of his pocket and handed it to La Salle. "You can check the tide with that. If Salisbury was drowned after two in the morning," he went on, "the sample taken from his lungs will match the low tide sample."

He sat back, and nodded to Phil. Syd held his handkerchief against a damp cheek, not daring to breathe.

"Here goes," said Phil. He squeezed drops of nitrate into the third tube and the fluid changed slowly from yellow to orange. More nitrate and the orange merged into pink, then deepened to red.

"Sergeant!" Syd's voice smashed the silence. "It matches the high tide water. Salisbury couldn't have drowned at two in the morning!"

Grace Salisbury's dark eyes were fastened in horror upon the bloody test tube. La Salle held the clipping clenched in one hand, his florid face set hard. Eaton's eyes flicked to Phil, then to Grace.

"You look ill, Mrs. Salisbury," said Phil. "Better come inside and rest a while." Syd pushed against the back of the wicker chair and Mrs. Salisbury jerked forward. Phil took her arm, and urged her to her feet. Syd moved swiftly between the chairs, cutting La Salle out of it. He took Mrs. Salisbury's other arm and they led her inside.

Eaton leaned forward. "This must be quite a shock, Mr. La Salle." His voice was low and sympathetic. "But we figured it from the beginning."

La Salle turned back to Eaton, anger pushing shock out of his eyes.

"We were pretty certain Salisbury discovered he'd left the chart list on board the moment he got home and saw his wife. She was going to take the list to the hydrographic office, wasn't she?"

"What the hell does that have to do with it?"

"When Salisbury insisted upon coming back for it," Eaton continued, "his wife decided to come along. The watchman was drunk, so they took the launch out themselves. We figure Salisbury slipped and fell in the river as he was tying up to the *Corsair*. Then Mrs. Salisbury saw her chance—"

"That's ridiculous!" La Salle's voice was blustery, but lacking anger. "Mrs. Salisbury wouldn't have the physical strength—"

"She's an expert swimmer."

"Yes, but—"

"How much does a body weigh in water?" Eaton spread his hands. "There's no way out. Salisbury was drowned at high tide. It has to be Mrs. Salisbury."

"But high tide was at nine, not at eleven-twenty, the earliest they could have come back here."

Eaton shrugged. "Have you forgotten that the tide takes a couple of hours to turn? Face it, Mr. La Salle. When Salisbury fell in the river, he wasn't the husband she'd loved, but a hateful business executive who kept depriving her of the love and affection she craved."

La Salle licked his lower lip. Speculation moved in his eyes, then in his voice. "Naturally, it wasn't premeditated. The sudden temptation, all the loneliness and frustration sweeping over her—temporary insanity—"

"A jury would understand," said Eaton softly. "Perhaps forgive."

Mrs. Salisbury suddenly appeared on the porch. Eaton didn't look up. La Salle's first warning was an angry blast. "You miserable coward! I heard every word over the wire recorder in the commodore's office. You'd sell me out—"

"Shut up, Grace!" La Salle was on his feet, dismayed. "They're trying to trap us!"

"They can't trap me!" she shot back. "You drowned my husband. You took his body over to the sunken wreck and pushed him under it. Then you forced me to alibi for you."

"That's a lie! David was still alive when we left here. He went home to you. You've admitted it in front of dozens of witnesses."

"Liar!" screamed Mrs. Salisbury. "Liar! Liar!"

"Take them away," said Eaton wearily.

Syd flipped the wheel hard over as Phil hopped on board with the bowline in his hands. When the launch was headed for the basin entrance, he glanced over his shoulder. Eaton was in the stern, his legs braced, a placid look on his ruddy face.

"Old poker face." Syd grinned. "I'd have bet two to one La Salle would have guessed we were using two high tide samples."

"Anyone but a murderer," said Eaton, "who was worried about the salt content of the water he'd forced his victim to swallow."

THE RED SAIL

LESTER DENT

He came out on the dock with long steps, putting his feet down hard. Two women tourists had just smiled at him, but he had not noticed, although it was unusual for him to be unaware when a woman noticed him. Some perspiration, the result of excitement, stood on his face.

The sloop was tied to the dock. She was a grandma among boats, but not a very large grandma. The boat was about thirty-six feet long, and a little on the shabby side.

He jumped on the old sloop.

"Ahoy, Charlie," he called.

The young man who put his head out of the cabin companionway was thin, stooped. He wore glasses that magnified his eyes. His chin was small. He was very young, a boy. Twenty, perhaps.

"Say, I don't know you," he said nervously.

The bigger, browner man walked toward him, saying "Better get down in the cabin, Charlie, where we can talk."

Charlie stumbled back into the cabin, alarmed.

The big man took a pair of handcuffs out of his hip pocket. He sat on one of the two bunks in the tiny boat cabin. He swung the handcuffs from one hand and said, "Edna didn't come back, did she, Charlie?"

Charlie swallowed. He couldn't seem to take his eyes off the handcuffs.

"Well, Edna won't be back, Charlie. You might as well know that right off," the big man said.

The blood began to leave Charlie's face.

The handcuffs clinked as the big man tossed them from one hard brown hand to the other. It was the only sound in the cabin.

"Tough on you, at that," the big man said dryly. "You must have loved her. I guess nothing but love would take a hotel clerk and change him around the way you've been changed."

"Who—who are you?" Charlie gasped.

The big man ignored the question and asked, "Ever go to the Indian Village and watch the Seminole wrestle the alligator, Charlie?"

"Huh?" said Charlie. "What?"

"You should go sometime and watch the show. The guy throws the alligator, then rubs it with his hand, kind of soothing like, until he calms it down. Then he gets right out of the pen and away from that alligator. You should have done that with Edna."

Charlie's eyes filled with misery.

"Take Lee Wanuck," the big man said. "That Lee—you don't know Lee Wanuck, Edna's ex-husband, do you?"

"No," said Charlie. "He was—"

"He was in the penitentiary before you met Edna, I know."

"Who are you?" Charlie said bitterly. "And what right have you—"

"Edna was pretty sick of it all when you met her. She was full of crime doesn't pay and all of that stuff. You felt sorry for the kid at first, eh Charlie? And the sorry feeling hatched out and was love. That the way it happened, wasn't it? That was the line she gave you, wasn't it?"

"What right—"

The big man interrupted, "Edna said she wanted a home, kids, peace, comfort, security, so on and so on. You were the guy to give 'em to her. So she married you."

A kind of inner light flashed over Charlie's face. "She wanted them!"

The big man showed his teeth unpleasantly.

"Sure, kid," he said. "Sure—in a pig's eye."

"Damn you!" Charlie cried. "I don't know who you are, but you're as wrong as can be."

"Take Lee Wanuck. Now Edna is Lee Wanuck's kind. The girl of a thief, a cheap crook. She can't settle down. Her feet began to itch, didn't they, right after you were married? She wanted to go to Kansas City. So you went to Kansas City to humor her. And then you went to Arizona, to New Mexico, then down to Florida. You know what she was doing, Charlie? She was tearing you loose from your roots. She was working on you—trying to make you a no-good like Lee Wanuck. She's clever, isn't she?"

"No!" Charlie said hoarsely. "You're wrong!"

The big man laughed suddenly. The laugh was so humorless it could have been bones rattling.

"Oh, stop it! What kind of fool are you, anyway?" he said violently.

Charlie was shaking. "You liar!" Charlie said. "You awful liar! We went to Arizona for my health. New Mexico, too. I was rejected for the army. I was rejected for the army, the navy, everything. We were trying to build up my health, that's why we went to Arizona."

Charlie had clenched his fists with vehemence. "My health is why we came here, too."

The big man jangled his handcuffs. "You poor, blind stupe," he said.

Charlie shuddered and stared at the man.

The big man said, "Last night there was a guy down here wanting you to smuggle refugees in from Cuba."

Charlie froze.

"Friend of Edna's, wasn't he?" the big man said.

"No," Charlie said hoarsely. "No, he only knew her when she was married to Lee Wanuck, was all."

The big man snorted and said, "Charlie, you can be thrown in jail right now. Just that guy being on your boat and propositioning you is enough. Enough to jail you."

There was no sound in the boat now, no sound at all, except the little waves slapping the side of the boat hull, making tiny licking noises.

"You poor sucker," the big man said.

Charlie buried his face in his hands.

The big man stared at him, and shook his head slowly, and said, 'They teach us something in the F.B.I. training course, something that goes about like this: The law is primarily interested in reforming men. We want to prevent men from becoming criminals." He was silent. He cleared his throat a time or two.

He put the handcuffs back in his pocket.

"Beat it, Charlie," he said.

Charlie took his face out of his hands. "What?"

"Vamoose," the big man said. "I don't think you're a crook at heart."

"You—you've arrested Edna?" Charlie asked hoarsely.

"Vamoose," the big man said.

Charlie left. He got out of the boat and fled down the dock. He even forgot his hat.

When Charlie was out of sight, the big man walked around looking over the old boat. He was grinning thinly.

A woman came down the dock. She was slender, about twenty, and radiant. She didn't look radiant when she saw the big man.

"Hello, Edna," the man said. "Charlie is gone. Charlie won't be back. Charlie has scrammed."

"Lee!" The girl's eyes were frightened. "Lee Wanuck."

The big man started at her, and suddenly the evil of the man was all over him.

"Charlie won't be back," he said. "I owed you a paying-off for being too damned good for me—and so Charlie won't be back."

The girl turned white. "You—you—"

"I paid you off," the big man said, and began laughing his ugly, bone-rattling laugh. But that stopped when he saw Charlie again.

Charlie was coming. He had a cop with him. Charlie pointed and said, "That's Lee Wanuck, an ex-convict, officer. I think he knows something about an alien-smuggling plan, or anyway one of his pals tried to hire our boat for some such thing yesterday." The cop arrested Wanuck.

Then Charlie grinned at Edna, and put his arm around her tenderly. "I knew he was Wanuck," he explained. "Nobody else could be so wrong about you, darling."

A Retrieved Reformation

O. Henry

A guard came to the prison shoe-shop, where Jimmy Valentine was assiduously stitching uppers, and escorted him to the front office. There the warden handed Jimmy his pardon, which had been signed that morning by the governor. Jimmy took it in a tired kind of way. He had served nearly ten months of a four-year sentence. He had expected to stay only about three months, at the longest. When a man with as many friends on the outside as Jimmy Valentine had is received in the "stir" it is hardly worth while to cut his hair.

"Now, Valentine," said the warden, "you'll go out in the morning. Brace up, and make a man of yourself. You're not a bad fellow at heart. Stop cracking safes, and live straight."

"Me?" said Jimmy, in surprise. "Why, I never cracked a safe in my life."

"Oh, no," laughed the warden. "Of course not. Let's see, now. How was it you happened to get sent up on that Springfield job? Was it because you wouldn't prove an alibi for fear of compromising somebody in extremely high-toned society? Or was it simply a case of a mean old jury that had it in for you? It's always one or the other with you innocent victims."

"Me?" said Jimmy, still blankly virtuous. "Why, warden, I never was in Springfield in my life!"

"Take him back, Cronin," smiled the warden, "and fix him up with outgoing clothes. Unlock him at seven in the morning, and let him come to the bull-pen. Better think over my advice, Valentine."

At a quarter past seven on the next morning Jimmy stood in the warden's outer office. He had on a suit of the villainously fitting, ready-made clothes and a pair of the stiff, squeaky shoes that the state furnishes to its discharged compulsory guests.

The clerk handed him a railroad ticket and the five-dollar bill with which the law expected him to rehabilitate himself into good citizenship and prosperity. The warden gave him a cigar, and shook hands. Valentine, 9762, was chronicled on the books "Pardoned by Governor," and Mr. James Valentine walked out into the sunshine.

Disregarding the song of the birds, the waving green trees, and the smell of the flowers, Jimmy headed straight for a restaurant. There he tasted the first sweet joys of liberty in the shape of a broiled chicken and a bottle of white wine—followed by a cigar a grade better than the one the warden had given him. From there he proceeded leisurely to the depot. He tossed a quarter into the hat of a blind man sitting by the door, and boarded his train. Three hours set him down in a little town near the state line. He went to the café of one Mike Dolan and shook hands with Mike, who was alone behind the bar.

"Sorry we couldn't make it sooner, Jimmy, me boy," said Mike. "But we had that protest from Springfield to buck against, and the governor nearly balked. Feeling all right?"

"Fine," said Jimmy. "Got my key?"

He got his key and went upstairs, unlocking the door of a room at the rear. Everything was just as he had left it. There on the floor was still Ben Price's collar-button that had been torn from that eminent detective's shirt-band when they had overpowered Jimmy to arrest him.

Pulling out from the wall a folding-bed, Jimmy slid back a panel in the wall and dragged out a dust-covered suitcase. He opened this and gazed fondly at the finest set of burglar's tools in the East. It was a complete set, made of specially tempered steel, the latest designs in drills, punches, braces and bits, jimmies, clamps, and augers, with two or three novelties invented by Jimmy himself, in which he took pride. Over nine hundred dollars they had cost him to have made at ———, a place where they make such things for the profession.

In half an hour Jimmy went downstairs and through the café. He was now dressed in tasteful and well-fitting clothes, and carried his dusted and cleaned suitcase in his hand.

"Got anything on?" asked Mike Dolan, genially.

"Me?" said Jimmy, in a puzzled tone. "I don't understand. I'm representing the New York Amalgamated Short Snap Biscuit Cracker and Frazzled Wheat Company."

This statement delighted Mike to such an extent that Jimmy had to take a seltzer-and-milk on the spot. He never touched "hard" drinks.

A week after the release of Valentine, 9762, there was a neat job of safe-burglary done in Richmond, Indiana, with no clue to the author. A scant eight hundred dollars was all that was secured. Two weeks after that a patented, improved, burglar-proof safe in Logansport was opened like a cheese to the tune of fifteen hundred dollars, currency; securities and silver untouched. That began to interest the rogue-catchers. Then an old-fashioned bank-safe in Jefferson City became active and threw out of its crater an eruption of banknotes amounting to five thousand dollars. The losses were now high enough to bring the matter up into Ben Price's class of work. By comparing notes, a remarkable similarity in the methods of the burglaries was noticed. Ben Price investigated the scenes of the robberies, and was heard to remark:

"That's Dandy Jim Valentine's autograph. He's resumed business. Look at that combination knob—jerked out as easy as pulling up a radish in wet weather. He's got the only clamps that can do it. And look how clean those tumblers were punched out! Jimmy never has to drill but one hole. Yes, I guess I want Mr. Valentine. He'll do his bit next time without any short-time or clemency foolishness."

Ben Price knew Jimmy's habits. He had learned them while working up the Springfield case. Long jumps, quick get-aways, no confederates, and a taste for good society—these ways had helped Mr. Valentine to become noted as a successful dodger of retribution. It was given out that Ben Price had taken up the trail of the elusive cracksman, and other people with burglar-proof safes felt more at ease.

One afternoon Jimmy Valentine and his suitcase climbed out of the mail-hack in Elmore, a little town five miles off the railroad down in the black-jack country of Arkansas. Jimmy, looking like an athletic young senior just home from college, went down the board sidewalk toward the hotel.

A young lady crossed the street, passed him at the corner and entered a door over which was the sign "The Elmore Bank." Jimmy Valentine looked into her eyes, forgot what he was, and became another man. She lowered her eyes and colored slightly. Young men of Jimmy's style and looks were scarce in Elmore.

Jimmy collared a boy that was loafing on the steps of the bank as if he were one of the stock-holders, and began to ask him questions about the town, feeding him dimes at intervals. By and by the young lady came out, looking royally unconscious of the young man with the suitcase, and went her way.

"Isn't that young lady Miss Polly Simpson?" asked Jimmy, with specious guile.

"Naw," said the boy. "She's Annabel Adams. Her pa owns this bank. What'd you come to Elmore for? Is that a good watch-chain? I'm going to get a bulldog. Got any more dimes?"

Jimmy went to the Palmer Hotel, registered as Ralph D. Spencer, and engaged a room. He leaned on the desk and declared his platform to the clerk. He said he had come to Elmore to look for a location to go into business. How was the shoe business, now, in the town? He had thought of the shoe business. Was there an opening?

The clerk was impressed by the clothes and manner of Jimmy. He, himself, was something of a pattern of fashion to the thinly gilded youth of Elmore, but he now perceived his shortcomings. While trying to figure out Jimmy's manner of tying his four-in-hand he cordially gave information.

Yes, there ought to be a good opening in the shoe line. There wasn't an exclusive shoe-store in the place. The dry-goods and general stores handled them. Business in all lines was fairly good. Hoped Mr. Spencer would decide to locate in Elmore. He would find it a pleasant town to live in, and the people very sociable.

Mr. Spencer thought he would stop over in the town a few days and look over the situation. No, the clerk needn't call the boy. He would carry up his suitcase, himself; it was rather heavy.

Mr. Ralph Spencer, the phoenix that arose from Jimmy Valentine's ashes—ashes left by the flame of a sudden and alternative attack of love—remained in Elmore, and prospered. He opened a shoe-store and secured a good run of trade.

Socially he was also a success, and made many friends. And he accomplished the wish of his heart. He met Miss Annabel Adams, and became more and more captivated by her charms.

At the end of a year the situation of Mr. Ralph Spencer was this: he had won the respect of the community, his shoe-store was flourishing, and he and Annabel were engaged to be married in two weeks. Mr. Adams, the typical, plodding, country banker, approved of Spencer. Annabel's pride in him almost equalled her affection. He was as much at home in the family of Mr. Adams and that of Annabel's married sister as if he were already a member.

One day Jimmy sat down in his room and wrote this letter, which he mailed to the safe address of one of his old friends in St. Louis:

Dear Old Pal:

I want you to be at Sullivan's place, in Little Rock, next Wednesday night at nine o'clock. I want you to wind up some little matters for me. And, also, I want to make you a present of my kit of tools. I know you'll be glad to get them—you couldn't duplicate the lot for a thousand dollars. Say, Billy, I've quit the old business—a year ago. I've got a nice store. I'm making an honest living, and I'm going to marry the finest girl on earth two weeks from now. It's the only life, Billy—the straight one. I wouldn't touch a dollar of another man's money now for a million. After I get married I'm going to sell out and go West, where there won't be so much danger of having old scores brought up against me. I tell you, Billy, she's an angel. She believes in me; and I wouldn't do another crooked thing for the whole world. Be sure to be at Sully's, for I must see you. I'll bring along the tools with me.

Your old friend,
Jimmy

On the Monday night after Jimmy wrote this letter, Ben Price jogged unobtrusively into Elmore in a livery buggy. He lounged about town in his quiet way until he found out what he wanted to know. From the drug-store across the street from Spencer's shoe-store he got a good look at Ralph D. Spencer.

"Going to marry the banker's daughter are you, Jimmy?" said Ben to himself, softly. "Well, I don't know!"

The next morning Jimmy took breakfast at the Adamses. He was going to Little Rock that day to order his wedding-suit and buy something nice for Annabel. That would be the first time he had left town since he came to Elmore. It had been more than a year now since those last professional "jobs," and he thought he could safely venture out.

After breakfast quite a family party went down town together— Mr. Adams, Annabel, Jimmy, and Annabel's married sister with her two little girls, aged five and nine. They came by the hotel where Jimmy still boarded, and he ran up to his room and brought along his suitcase. Then they went on to the bank. There stood Jimmy's horse and buggy and Dolph Gibson, who was going to drive him over to the railroad station.

All went inside the high, carved oak railings into the banking-room—Jimmy included, for Mr. Adams's future son-in-law was welcome anywhere. The clerks were pleased to be greeted by the good-looking, agreeable young man who was going to marry Miss Annabel. Jimmy set his suitcase down. Annabel, whose heart was bubbling with happiness and lively youth, put on Jimmy's hat and picked up the suitcase. "Wouldn't I make a nice drummer?" said Annabel. "My! Ralph, how heavy it is. Feels like it was full of gold bricks."

"Lot of nickel-plated shoe-horns in there," said Jimmy, cooly, "that I'm going to return. Thought I'd save express charges by taking them up. I'm getting awfully economical."

The Elmore Bank had just put in a new safe and vault. Mr. Adams was very proud of it, and insisted on an inspection by every one. The vault was a small one, but it had a new patented door. It fastened with three solid steel bolts thrown simultaneously with a single handle, and had a time-lock. Mr. Adams beamingly explained its workings to Mr. Spencer, who showed a courteous but not too intelligent interest. The two children, May and Agatha, were delighted by the shining metal and funny clock and knobs.

While they were thus engaged Ben Price sauntered in and leaned on his elbow, looking casually inside between the railings. He told the teller that he didn't want anything; he was just waiting for a man he knew.

Suddenly there was a scream or two from the women, and a commotion. Unperceived by the elders, May, the nine-year-old girl, in a spirit of play, had shut Agatha in the vault. She had then shot the bolts and turned the knob of the combination as she had seen Mr. Adams do.

The old banker sprang to the handle and tugged at it for a moment. "The door can't be opened," he groaned. "The clock hasn't been wound nor the combination set."

Agatha's mother screamed again, hysterically.

"Hush!" said Mr. Adams, raising his trembling hand. "All be quiet for a moment. Agatha!" he called as loudly as he could: "Listen to me." During the following silence they could just hear the faint sound of the child wildly shrieking in the dark vault in a panic of terror.

"My precious darling!" wailed the mother. "She will die of fright! Open the door! Oh, break it open! Can't you men do something?"

"There isn't a man nearer than Little Rock who can open that door," said Mr. Adams, in a shaky voice. "My God! Spencer, what shall we do? That child—she can't stand it long in there. There isn't enough air, and, besides, she'll go into convulsions from fright."

Agatha's mother, frantic now, beat the door of the vault with her hands. Somebody wildly suggested dynamite. Annabel turned to Jimmy, her large eyes full of anguish, but not yet despairing. To a woman nothing seems quite impossible to the powers of the man she worships.

"Can't you do something, Ralph—*try*, won't you?"

He looked at her with a queer, soft smile on his lips and in his keen eyes.

"Annabel," he said, "give me that rose you are wearing, will you?"

Hardly believing that she heard him aright, she unpinned the bud from the bosom of her dress, and placed it in his hand. Jimmy stuffed it into his vest-pocket, threw off his coat and pulled up his shirtsleeves. With that act Ralph D. Spencer passed away and Jimmy Valentine took his place.

"Get away from the door, all of you," he commanded, shortly.

He set his suitcase on the table, and opened it out flat. From that time on he seemed to be unconscious of the presence of any one else. He laid out the shining, queer implements swiftly and orderly, whistling softly to himself as he always did when at work. In a deep silence and immovable, the others watched him as if under a spell.

In a minute Jimmy's pet drill was biting smoothly into the steel door. In ten minutes—breaking his own burglarious record—he threw back the bolts and opened the door.

Agatha, almost collapsed, but safe, was gathered into her mother's arms.

Jimmy Valentine put on his coat, and walked outside the railings toward the front door. As he went he thought he heard a far-away voice that he once knew call "Ralph!" But he never hesitated.

At the door a big man stood somewhat in his way.

"Hello, Ben!" said Jimmy, still with his strange smile. "Got around at last, have you? Well, let's go. I don't know that it makes much difference, now."

And then Ben Price acted rather strangely.

"Guess you're mistaken, Mr. Spencer," he said. "Don't believe I recognize you. Your buggy's waiting for you, ain't it?"

And Ben Price turned and strolled down the street.

SACRIFICE

C. J. Henderson

Herbert sat at the kitchen table, unable to eat. The television before him blared on and on—its icy glow ruining his digestion, stealing appetite from his empty stomach. He had turned it on, hoping the scheduled comedy might take his mind away from the world around him. Herbert had forgotten the news briefs which started off every hour. He pulled at a hangnail while the screen assailed him.

CHOC-O-CAKES INJECTED WITH CYANIDE—TEN DEAD IN JERSEY NURSERY SCHOOL . . .

The television sat at the end of the metal table, its cord trailing off somewhere into the books on the shelf behind it. Beaming out at Herbert, it offended him daily, taunting him with ever-increasing numbers of blandly different unthinkables, daring him to turn it off —to even turn away.

"I won't," he thought. "No matter what it makes up. I won't give in."

Herbert unfolded his arms and pushed his rapidly cooling Kraft Macaroni & Cheese Deluxe Dinner away from himself, down the table—out of reach.

NO CLUES IN THE WILMERDING REST HOME ARSON CASE . . .

Somehow, he just did not feel like eating.

"There's no avoiding it," he admitted. "I just haven't done enough."

Herbert shuddered at the thought. He wondered if enough could be done—if *anyone* could do enough. He had tried. God—how he had tried. At least, he thought he had. Each time the world had escalated its attempts to cave in on itself, so had his efforts to put things aright. More sacrifices—a greater effort . . .

MORE AT ELEVEN ON THE . . .

Reaching out, straining to reach to the end of the table, he clicked the set off in mid-tragedy, chewing at his nails as he wondered at it all.

Mary had decided to cut her hair again, shorter than the last time. She snipped at it randomly—without any thought set aside for style or appearance. Although she had not left much the last time, she did manage to find some loose bits to clip—shears pressed into the sides of her head, angling after this fast-growing follicle or that one. Looking at herself in the mirror, staring at her handiwork, she wished she had not thrown out every last cigarette—was glad that she did.

In the end, it had been such a little thing to give up. Anything to get back at the radio.

> FOUR MORE WINTER WAR CASUALTIES WERE DISCOVERED TODAY, FROZEN TO DEATH IN THEIR HOMES, VICTIMS NOT ONLY OF THE COLD, BUT OF THE CITY'S MERCILESS UTILITY BARONS . . .

Anything to keep her mind off the world locked outside her door. She had passed on going to the play with Frank, even though she did like him and he had seemed very secure about the whole thing. Something had warned her, however. Something had let her know that the streets just were not the place for her to be. Something made with Japanese technology and German plastic bought on Canal Street for ten dollars that nightly turned the key in the lock of her warm, secure cell.

> . . . TAKING HIS OWN LIFE AFTER KILLING HIS WIFE AND THREE GIRLS . . .

She had not noticed over the last months—not really—how her hair had started getting shorter, and then shorter, and her nails, shorter, and her meals, smaller, and well, who really needs cigarettes, anyway—I mean, the way the world is—

Joe had heard enough. The nightly news had only been a rehash of the slop that had poured out over him from his paper on the way home—more details dripping off the pages and out of the set like broiling fat falling into a fire. It was bad enough that everyone in the office had been talking about it. *Talking.* There was a euphemism for it—

"You mean those people in El Paso?"
"Yeah. They stuffed the drugs inside ketchup bottles."
"Four dead—right?"
"Yeah. Pretty spicy stuff, huh?"

And then the laughter. Four dead in the morning. By the train ride home, and the evening paper, two more had died, making all the jokes funnier by fifty percent.

Turning the TV off with the fingers remaining on his right hand, Joe left the den, heading for his bedroom. No wife waited anymore. Even his dog had deserted him, frightened by the morose, continually cynical atmosphere that had settled around his master and then spread outward through his home and all the things in and around it.

"Maybe Lucky didn't run away. Maybe he was only stolen," Joe whispered to himself. "Or killed."

Forsaking his bed, Joe pulled a blanket from it and then curled on the floor in the black, shivering in his chilly darkness. Duty now for the future, he thought, smiling weakly, trying to fit the edges of his blanket around and under his rear end and his feet.

Herbert sat in the kitchen, still at the table. Tears ran down his face—slow but unstoppable. Nothing he ever did was enough. Maybe the axe would help—maybe. But, if he was wrong, said the little voice in the back of his head, there would be no second chance.

"No second chance?" he asked the air in a small, confused voice. What could he be thinking? There was always a second chance. Clicking his set back on, he watched the small white dot in the center grow in size.

MORE BOMBINGS IN THE CENTRAL LOWLANDS FORCE UN TROOPS TO . . .

The picture faded away as he clicked the screen back to blackness.

"There's no reason for all of this," he thought. "I've just got to make a bigger sacrifice. Something they'll all notice. Something worth the effort."

Lifting himself from his chair, he went to the drawer in his desk where the tools were. He considered the chisel and several of the planes for a long moment before shutting the drawer again. Then, turning to the umbrella stand next to him, Herbert pulled free the saw standing in it, bracing his leg against the chair next to his dresser.

After the eye-crushing pain of the first few strokes, he suddenly found he could not move the saw. Forcing his eyes open, he spotted the problem immediately. Pulling the blade upward, he untangled the pant threads caught in its teeth. Then, with a path cleared, he set back to work, grimly clamping his jaws and bubbling lips together, gamely sawing stroke after stroke, ignoring the swooshing sound and the bone powder and the blood until he had finished his work and had toppled to the floor.

"Maybe that," he thought. "Maybe they'll notice that."

But, even as he fell off into unconsciousness, Mary's radio kept reporting its grim fascinations, and Herbert just kept wondering, as did Joe and the army of their fellows—all sawing away—just how much grist the mill demanded.

The Sapient Monkey

Headon Hill

I would advise every person whose duties take him into the field of "private enquiry" to go steadily through the daily papers the first thing every morning. Personally I have found the practice most useful, for there are not many *causes célebres* in which my services are not enlisted on one side or the other, and by this method I am always up in my main facts before I am summoned to assist. When I read the account of the proceedings at Bow Street against Franklin Gale in connection with the Tudways' bank robbery, I remember thinking that on the face of it there never was a clearer case against a misguided young man.

Condensed for the sake of brevity, the police-court report disclosed the following state of things:

Franklin Gale, clerk, aged twenty-three, in the employment of Messrs. Tudways, the well-known private bankers of the Strand, was brought up on a warrant charged with stealing the sum of £500—being the moneys of his employers. Mr. James Spruce, assistant cashier at the bank, gave evidence to the effect that he missed the money from his till on the afternoon of July 22. On making up his cash for the day he discovered that he was short of £300 worth of notes and £200 in gold. He had no idea how the amount had been abstracted. The prisoner was an assistant bookkeeper at the bank, and had access behind the counter. Detective-sergeant Simmons said that the case had been placed in his hands for the purpose of tracing the stolen notes. He had ascertained that one of them—of the value of £5—had been paid to Messrs. Crosthwaite & Co., tailors, of New Bond Street, on July 27th, by Franklin Gale. As a result, he had applied for a warrant, and had arrested the prisoner. The latter was remanded for a week, at the end of which period it was expected that further evidence would be forthcoming.

I had hardly finished reading the report when a telegram was put into my hands demanding my immediate presence at "Rosemount," Twickenham. From the address given, and from the name of "Gale" appended to the despatch, I concluded that the affair at Tudways' Bank was the cause of the summons. I had little doubt that I was to be retained in the interests of the prisoner, and my surmise proved correct.

"Rosemount" was by no means the usual kind of abode from which the ordinary run of bank clerks come gaily trooping into the great City in shoals by the early trains. There was nothing of cheap gentility about the "pleasant suburban residence standing in its own grounds of an acre," as the house-agent would say—with its lawns sloping down to the river, shaded by mulberry and chestnut trees, and plentifully garnished with the noble flower which gave it half its name. "Rosemount" was assuredly the home either of some prosperous merchant or of a private gentleman, and when I crossed its threshold I did so quite prepared for the fuller enlightenment which was to follow. Mr. Franklin Gale was evidently not one of the struggling genus bank clerk, but must be the son of well-to-do people, and not yet flown from the parent nest. When I left my office I had thought that I was bound on a forlorn hope, but at the sight of "Rosemount"—my first real "touch" of the case—my spirits revived. Why should a young man living amid such signs of wealth want to rob his employers? Of course I recognized that the youth of the prisoner precluded the probability of the place being his own. Had he been older, I should have reversed the argument. "Rosemount" in the actual occupation of a middle-aged bank clerk would have been prima-facie evidence of a tendency to outrun the constable.

I was shown into a well-appointed library, where I was received by a tall, silver-haired old gentleman of ruddy complexion, who had apparently been pacing the floor in a state of agitation. His warm greeting towards me—a perfect stranger—had the air of one who clutches at a straw.

"I have sent for you to prove my son's innocence, Mr. Zambra," he said. "Franklin no more stole that money than I did. In the first place, he didn't want it; and, secondly, if he had been ever so pushed for cash, he would rather have cut off his right hand than put it into his employer's till. Besides, if these thick-headed policemen were bound to lock one of us up, it ought to have been me. The five-pound note with which Franklin paid his tailor was one—so he assures me, and I believe him—which I gave him myself."

"Perhaps you would give me the facts in detail?" I replied.

"As to the robbery, both my son and I are as much in the dark as old Tudway himself," Mr. Gale proceeded. "Franklin tells me that Spruce, the cashier, is accredited to be a most careful man, and the very last to leave his till to take care of itself. The facts that came out in evidence are perfectly true. Franklin's desk is close to the counter, and the note identified as one of the missing ones was certainly paid by him to Crosthwaite & Co., of New Bond Street, a few days after the robbery. It bears his endorsement, so there can be no doubt about that.

"So much for their side of the case. Ours is, I must confess, from a legal point of view, much weaker, and lies in my son's assertion of innocence, coupled with the knowledge of myself and his mother and his sisters that he is incapable of such a crime. Franklin insists that the note he paid to Crosthwaite & Co., the tailors, was one that I gave him on the morning of the 22nd. I remember perfectly well giving him a five-pound note at breakfast on that day, just before he left for town, so that he must have had it several hours before the robbery was committed. Franklin says that he had no other banknotes between the 22nd and 27th, and that he cannot, therefore, be mistaken. The note which I gave him I got fresh from my own bankers a day or two before, together with some others; and here is the most unfortunate point in the case. The solicitor whom I have engaged to defend Franklin has made the necessary enquiries at my bankers, and finds that the note paid to the tailors is *not* one of those which I drew from the bank."

"Did not your son take notice of the number of the note you gave him?" I asked.

"Unfortunately, no. He is too much worried about the numbers of notes at his business, he says, to note those which are his own property. He simply sticks to it that he knows it must be the same note because he had no other."

In the slang of the day, Mr. Franklin Gale's story seemed a little too thin. There was the evidence of Tudways that the note paid to the tailor was one of those stolen from them, and there was the evidence of Mr. Gale, senior's, bankers that it was not one of those handed to their client. What was the use of the prisoner protesting in the face of this that he had paid his tailor with his father's present? The notes stolen from Tudways were, I remembered reading, consecutive ones of a series, so that the possibility of young Gale having at the bank changed his father's gift for another note, which was subsequently stolen, was knocked on the head. Besides, he maintained that it was the *same* note.

"I should like to know something of your son's circumstances and position," I said, trying to divest the question of any air of suspicion it might have implied.

"I am glad you asked me that," returned Mr. Gale, "for it touches the very essence of the whole case. My son's circumstances and position are such that were he the most unprincipled scoundrel in creation he would have been nothing less than an idiot to have done this thing. Franklin is not on the footing of an ordinary bank clerk, Mr. Zambra. I am a rich man, and can afford to give him anything in reason, though he is too good a lad ever to have taken advantage of me. Tudway is an old friend of mine, and I got him to take Franklin into the bank with a view to a partnership. Everything was going on swimmingly towards that end: the boy had perfected himself in his duties, and made himself valuable; I was prepared to invest a certain amount of capital on his behalf; and, lastly, Tudway, who lives next door to me here, got so fond of him that he allowed Franklin to become engaged to his daughter Maud. Would any young man in his senses go and steal a paltry £500 under such circumstances as that?"

I thought not, but I did not say so yet.

"What are Mr. Tudway's views about the robbery?" I asked.

"Tudway is an old fool," replied Mr. Gale. "He believes what the police tell him, and the police tell him that Franklin is guilty. I have no patience with him. I ordered him out of this house last night. He had the audacity to come and offer not to press the charge if the boy would confess."

"And Miss Tudway?"

"Ah! she's a brick. Maud sticks to him like a true woman. But what is the use of our sticking to him against such evidence?" broke down poor Mr. Gale, impotently. "Can you, Mr. Zambra, give us a crumb of hope?"

Before I could reply there was a knock at the library door, and a tall, graceful girl entered the room. Her face bore traces of weeping, and she looked anxious and dejected; but I could see that she was naturally quick and intelligent.

"I have just run over to see if there is any fresh news this morning," she said, with an enquiring glance at me.

"This is Mr. Zambra, my dear, come to help us," said Mr. Gale; "and this," he continued, turning to me, "is Miss Maud Tudway. We are all enlisted in the same cause."

"You will be able to prove Mr. Franklin Gale's innocence, sir?" she exclaimed.

"I hope so," I said; "and the best way to do it will be to trace the robbery to its real author. Has Mr. Franklin any suspicions on that head?"

"He is as much puzzled as we are," said Miss Tudway. "I went with Mr. Gale here to see him in that horrible place yesterday, and he said there was absolutely no one in the bank he cared to suspect. But he *must* get off the next time he appears. My evidence ought to do that. I saw with my own eyes that he had only one £5 note in his purse on the 25th—that is two days before he paid the tailor, and three days after the robbery."

"I am afraid that won't help us much," I said. "You see, he might easily have had the missing notes elsewhere. But tell me, under what circumstances did you see the £5 note?"

"There was a garden party at our house," replied Miss Tudway, "and Franklin was there. During the afternoon a man came to the gate with an accordion and a performing monkey, and asked permission to show the monkey's tricks. We had the man in, and after the monkey had done a lot of clever things the man said that the animal could tell a good banknote from a 'flash' one. He was provided with spurious notes for the purpose; would any gentlemen lend him a good note for a minute, just to show the trick? The man was quite close to Franklin, who was sitting next to me. Franklin, seeing the man's hand held out towards him, took out his purse and handed him a note, at the same time calling my attention to the fact that it was his only one, and laughingly saying that he hoped the man was honest. The sham note and the good one were placed before the monkey, who at once tore up the bad note and handed the good one back to Franklin."

"This is more important than it seems," I said, after a moment's review of the whole case. "I must find that man with the monkey, but it bids fair to be difficult. There are so many of them in that line of business."

Miss Tudway smiled for the first time during the interview.

"It is possible that I may be of use to you there," she said. "I go in for amateur photography, and I thought that the man and his monkey made so good a 'subject' that I insisted on taking him before he left. Shall I fetch the photograph?"

"By all means," I said. "Photography is of the greatest use to me in my work. I generally arrange it myself, but if you have chanced to take the right picture for me in this case so much the better."

Miss Tudway hurried across to her father's house and quickly returned with the photograph. It was a fair effort for an amateur, and portrayed an individual of the usual seedy stamp, equipped with a huge accordion and a small monkey secured by a string. With this in my hand it would only be a matter of time before I found the itinerant juggler who had presented himself at the Tudways' garden party, and I took my leave of old Mr. Gale and Miss Maud in a much more hopeful frame of mind. Every circumstance outside the terrible array of actual evidence pointed to my client's innocence, and if this evidence had been manufactured for the purpose, I felt certain that the "monkey man" had had a hand in it.

On arriving at my office I summoned one of my assistants—a veteran of doubtful antecedents—who owns to no other name than "Old Jemmy." Old Jemmy's particular line of business is a thorough knowledge of the slums and the folk who dwell there; and I knew that after an hour or two on Saffron Hill my ferret, armed with the photograph, would bring me the information I wanted. Towards evening Old Jemmy came in with his report, to the effect that the "party" I was after was to be found in the top attic of 7 Little Didman's Fields, Hatton Garden, just recovering from the effects of a prolonged spree.

"He's been drunk for three or four days, the landlord told me," Old Jemmy said. "Had a stroke of luck, it seems, but he is expected to go on tramp tomorrow, now his coin has given out. His name is Pietro Schilizzi."

I knew I was on the right scent now, and that the "monkey man" had been made the instrument of *changing* the note which Franklin Gale had lent him for one of the stolen ones. A quick cab took me to Little Didman's Fields in a quarter of an hour, and I was soon standing inside the doorway of a pestilential apartment on the top floor of No. 7, which had been pointed out to me as the abode of Pietro Schilizzi. A succession of snores from a heap of rags in a corner told me the whereabouts of the occupier. I went over, and shaking him roughly by the shoulder, said in Italian:

"Pietro, I want you to tell me about that little juggle with a banknote at Twickenham the other day. You will be well rewarded."

The fellow rubbed his eyes in half-drunken astonishment, but there certainly was no guilty fear about him as he replied:

"Certainly, signor; anything for money. There was nothing wrong about the note, was there? Anyhow, I acted innocently in the matter."

"No one finds fault with you," I said; "but see, here is a five-pound note. It shall be yours if you will tell me exactly what happened."

"I was with my monkey up at Highgate the other evening," Mr. Schilizzi began, "and was showing Jacko's trick of telling a good note from a bad one. It was a small house in the Napier Road. After I had finished, the gentleman took me into a public house and stood me a drink. He wanted me to do something for him, he said. He had a young friend who was careless, and never took the number of notes, and he wanted to teach him a lesson. He had a bet about the number of a note, he said. Would I go down to Twickenham next day to a house he described, where there was to be a party, and do my trick with the monkey? I was to borrow a note from the young gentleman, and then, instead of giving him back his own note after the performance, I was to substitute one which the Highgate gentleman gave me for the purpose. He met me at Twickenham next day, and came behind the garden wall to point out the young gentleman to me. I managed it just as the Highgate gentleman wanted, and he gave me a couple of pounds for my pains. I have done no wrong; the note I gave back was a good one."

"Yes," I said, "but it happens to have been stolen. Put on your hat and show me where this man lives in Highgate."

The Napier Road was a shabby street of dingy houses, with a public house at the corner. Pietro stopped about half-way down the row and pointed out No. 21.

"That is where the gentleman lives," he said.

We retraced our steps to the corner public house.

"Can you tell me who lives at No. 21?" I asked of the landlord, who happened to be in the bar.

"Certainly," was the answer; "it is Mr. James Spruce—a good customer of mine, and the best billiard player hereabouts. He is a cashier at Messrs. Tudways' bank, in the Strand, I believe."

It all came out at the trial—not of Franklin Gale, but of James Spruce, the fraudulent cashier. Spruce had himself abstracted the notes and gold entrusted to him, and his guilty conscience telling him that he might be suspected, he had cast about for a means of throwing suspicion on some other person. Chancing to witness the performance of Pietro's monkey, he had grasped the opportunity for foisting one of the stolen notes on Franklin Gale, knowing that sooner or later it would be traced to him. The other notes he had intended to hold over till it was safe to send them out of the country; but the gold was the principal object of his theft.

Mr. Tudway, the banker, was, I hear, so cut up about the false accusation that he had made against his favourite that he insisted on Franklin joining him as a partner at once, and the marriage is to take place before very long. I am also told that the photograph of the "monkey man," handsomely enlarged and mounted, will form one of the mural decorations of the young couple.

SIDE DOOR TO HELL

CYRIL PLUNKETT

The medical examiner paused to talk a moment, despite the rain. "A shot through the heart, Nelson," the M. E. said. "I've placed the time of death two hours ago, at eight or thereabouts."

Jan Nelson's throat was tight and aching. "Any clues?"

"Well," the M. E. said, "one or two things that look promising. Inspector Cray has all the dope. He's waiting for you, Nelson."

"Thanks, I'll go right in." Nelson turned away.

There was a terraced lawn, and deep within it a massive stone building, gray and shapeless in the darkness. The lights on either side of the doorway seemed strangely dim.

"Be very sure," he'd said. *"Cris, don't gamble with our lives, our happiness."* Nelson's mind was filled with Cris, the wonder of her—and the doubt he'd known for months.

He walked stiffly, like a fighter after listening to the count of ten. Tall, with the leanness of a man high-strung, he was stooped a very little, as though the weighty problems of his office—District Attorney—were, indeed, pounds upon his back.

He went inside, then, into the tension of official business, past uniformed police, and reporters pressing for a statement. Naturally, Sordell's murder was big. Sordell had been big-time, an artist whose cover girls were internationally known.

Inspector Cray was in the studio living room, a broadly built man, massive. He was busy with dictation. He waved and said, "Hello, Mr. Nelson. Be with you in a minute." And then, to the patrolman taking notes: "According to the statement of employees, Sordell furnished keys to the side street door, at the bottom of the stairway, allegedly that certain people, female, could come and go at any time, unseen." He turned back to Nelson. "We're good till morning on this one. You know Sordell?"

"By reputation," Nelson said.

Cray's stare was long and irritating. "Well, I can take that word either way and still be right. That's the pattern. Too many girls. Anyway, one of them was here tonight. The switchboard operator and elevator boy both tagged her."

"They know her? They know her name?" Nelson interrupted, queerly.

"That's right," said Cray. "It's Shaw. Catherine Shaw—we've found her address scrawled in Sordell's phone book. Here's the way we reconstruct it: Sordell was seated at his desk, being threatened, maybe. He got up fast, because the chair legs made deep scars in the carpet. He came around the desk, and that's when the bullet got him."

Cray pointed to the chalked outline on the floor, marking where the body had fallen. And then Jan Nelson saw beyond the outline. Nelson saw the drawing, and his heart started thumping in his breast. The pastel upon the desk was a mauve monochrome on illustration board, and recently finished, for no fixative had been applied. The study was of a girl, and her hair was partly smudged, as though the artist's hand had smeared it. And the girl wore a mask, but little else. Behind the mask her eyes smiled archly, invitingly.

"Worries me, that picture." Cray slowly thumbed up and down his jaw. "I've a hunch it's important. Maybe the smear—I don't know. Maybe those erased particles lying on the floor. An artist wouldn't smear his own work, brushing it off. An artist wouldn't do a thing like *that*."

The muscles tightened in Nelson's jaw. "About this girl, Inspector?"

For a moment Cray didn't answer. Then he said, "She was up here about five minutes. She left in a hurry—looking scared, according to the witnesses. I've already sent a man to watch her address. Care to run out there with me?"

"Yes," Nelson said. "I'll be glad to."

They rode a police car, in the back seat, with a detective named Simms at the wheel. Cray and Simms got to talking of the war, but Nelson was silent and frowning. He was thinking of a curious thing, a lipstick. He was thinking of Cris. . . .

They'd met at a party, a year back, in midsummer. She was like someone da Vinci might have painted, or like the girl you dream of. You looked at her and it was like listening to Wagnerian opera. She was the girl millions saw on billboards and the pages of the magazines.

Looking back, the amazing thing was that she had found him at all worthy of her interest. He was thirty-eight, and the war had passed him by; but he was a man whose name was repeatedly appearing in the newspapers—and so. . . .

"Cris, be sure," he'd said, that night, weeks later. "Be so very sure first. I can't be intense tonight, a month—and then casual afterward. I'm not that way. It's all or nothing, Cris. I won't share you. You can't go on with your career. I won't pick up a magazine and see you there. It's got to be the way I want it, Cris—for life."

The police car made a sudden turn and Cray's voice broke into Nelson's thoughts abruptly. "By the way," Cray said, "how is Mrs. Nelson?"

Nelson stiffened. "Thanks, she's fine."

A moment passed. Cray seemed to be considering. "Model, wasn't she?"

They were passing beneath a street lamp, and Nelson saw Cray's eyes. Cray was looking at him, and he felt helpless, very small like a mouse in a dusty corner. From the distance a bell tolled, deep toned and dismal.

They left Simms outside. They talked to the buxom landlady at Catherine Shaw's address. The landlady said, "Miss Shaw? I don't believe she's in. Is it—business?"

"Police business," said Cray.

"Not—not Cathy!"

Cray said, "We'll take a little look at her room."

So they saw Cathy Shaw's room, and it was cretonne and white linen; not at all the velvet that had been Sordell's. The note was crumpled in a wastebasket. Cray found it and handed it to Nelson.

"Dear Mr. Sordell," Nelson read. "I've argued with myself whether to see or write you, but in either case the answer is the same. I hate you—" That was all that had been written.

Cray reclaimed the note, put it in his pocket and began questioning the landlady. Nelson went into the hall, went downstairs. There was a phone just below the stairs. He stood before it, one hand in his coat pocket; and then he removed the hand and the small bright object clasped in it—a lipstick, gold and initialed with tiny jewels. For a moment he stared at the lipstick blankly. He sighed as he dialed Erie-7700.

The whispered ringing on the other end seemed within his brain. He counted with the rings, and with the breathless spaces. But Cris didn't answer. A footfall sounded behind him suddenly. Nelson put the receiver back on its hook, shoved his clenched hand in his pocket.

Cray said from the stairs, "We're going two blocks up the street. To see a lad named Farraday."

They drove the two blocks, and the bell was tolling dismally again, the quarter hour, fifteen after eleven. The door to Farraday's room cracked open slowly at Cray's knock.

He was young, thin. Nineteen, perhaps. He wore slacks and a polo shirt, and he was smoking a cigarette. The room was blue with smoke. Farraday, all right. He looked frightened.

Cray said, "You'd better let us in."

"Police?"

"That's right."

Cray pushed the door, and there *she* was, behind it. Cretonne and white linen. She wasn't wearing that, but she was in her teens, with eyes that were great blue pools, and she was blonde, her slender body beautiful. Catherine Shaw.

Nelson closed the door and sat down as Cray crossed the room. Cray stood facing into the room.

"Let's put the cards down," Cray said. "Just what happened tonight, Miss Shaw?"

She looked at Farraday, and then at Nelson, and her whole body trembled. Cray sighed and swung around a little. "Well, how about you, Farraday? Been here all evening?"

Farraday flung himself into a chair. He was watching Cray warily, but the overflowing ash tray on the end table occupied him a moment. He brushed the loose ash to the floor. "Yes, of course," he said. "Why?"

"Nothing to hide, either of you?"

Farraday laughed shortly. "That's a good one."

Cray didn't smile. He said, "We've found the letter Miss Shaw began to Sordell."

She gasped and put both hands to her face. Farraday's cheeks were chalk-white and he seemed scarcely to be breathing. He shot out of the chair. Cray made a motion to check him, but Farraday straight-armed Cray, spun away from him and darted for the door. He reached the door ahead of Nelson, slammed it in Nelson's face. They heard him running down the stairs.

Cathy Shaw moaned. Cray said, "Get your coat, girlie, and come along with us."

"But—" she began. Cray had turned his back to her. He was saying reproachfully, "You might have been a little quicker, Mr. Nelson. Won't matter though. Won't matter. I expected something like this. Simms will nab him." He turned around again. "Ready, girlie?"

When they reached the front door the detective, Simms, was sitting on the steps with Farraday, handcuffed to him.

"We'll take 'em both in for questioning," Cray said. Simms walked with Miss Shaw and Farraday, between them, down the walk to the squad car.

"Coming, Mr. Nelson?" Cray said.

Nelson shrugged off his preoccupation, shook his head. "I'll catch a cab," he said.

But he walked, to compromise with time, in fear of time. Twice he stopped to phone, at a drugstore, at a restaurant. *Erie-7700* . . . *Erie-7700.* There was no answer either time, and therefore Cris was not at home. Nelson sat a long while in the restaurant, thinking, staring into the past.

At first he hadn't believed there could be such happiness, in the plans he made with Cris, in their marriage, in living with her afterward. Their suite had a broad, revealing view of the rivers meeting to conceive the sea, it was a very special suite, high above the city and well beyond Nelson's means, but one always set a jewel in gold and that's the way he felt about it. He'd awaken each day and look at her—her eyes closed still, in sleep; or at her photograph in the double frame with his, smiling at his own stern expression, her dark head tilted back in a pose altogether glamorous. And he'd sigh and think: *Jan, boy, you've won her.*

But the job, he knew from the beginning, was going to be to *keep* her.

It had been purely accidental that his cab arrived home one night as hers was ready to depart. She was wearing black, something very slim and modish. This was back a few weeks, in cool September, the anniversary month of their marriage. His first thought had been to try to head her off—she'd expected him to return quite late that night—but within a block or two his mind had clouded. He'd followed her uptown. Presently her cab stopped before an imposing building; a side entrance—and she had a key.

"Drive around the block," Nelson told the cabbie.

He'd stared, unseeing. Numb and cold, yet burning, knowing now the ugly, moving plan of things. "Keep driving," he'd said to the cabbie. Anywhere—"

Nelson looked up, now, at the counterman standing before him, and he took a deep breath. He ordered coffee—and drank it black, and then he rose from the counter stool. He left the restaurant. The time was nearing two A.M. when he reached home.

The door was unlocked, and his heart quickened. He opened the door—to stop short and stiffen. Inspector Cray sat there in the living room. Alone. Cray's eyes were very keen. Nelson saw this keenness and momentarily hated it.

"I thought you'd be along soon," Cray said. He was opening a fresh pack of cigarettes. "You know how it is with homicide. A good officer must have an answer for everything. Well, an answer's been missing."

"Indeed?" said Nelson.

Cray offered the pack. "Smoke?"

Nelson shook his head. He sat down.

"I had a talk with your wife tonight," Cray said. "At headquarters."

The smoke was drifting past Cray's watchful eyes. Nelson saw the smoke apart. He wet his lips but didn't speak.

"I've got a photographic mind," Cray said. "That drawing on Sordell's desk worried me. I had a feeling I knew who the model was, and it wasn't Catherine Shaw. It wasn't naive—you know?"

Still Nelson did not answer and Cray smiled a very little.

"Funny thing. I thought you'd say, 'Hello Inspector. How about a drink?' . . ."

"Skip the small talk, Inspector."

Cray shrugged. "All right. You followed your wife to Sordell's tonight?"

"You raise your voice. Is that a question?"

Cray dropped ash in the tray. "Question mark or period—does it matter? We're not getting anywhere, Nelson. And it's late. I'm tired. I never intended to waste time in small talk. But you're in a black mood, and—"

"We can skip my mood too, Inspector."

Cray sighed and shook his head. "No, we can't. A cop can't overlook even a thing like that. But I will pass it by a minute and go on to the missing lipstick."

Nelson's gaze shot up. "Lipstick?" He met Cray's cold stare, and a moment passed, and then he said, "I see." His shoulders sagged, and he looked down at his hands. "Yes, Inspector, as a matter of fact, I did follow my wife tonight. I've followed her many nights, recently. But tonight—I smoked a cigarette, outside, after she went in. I was going in. I'd got an impression of the key she carried. I'd made a decision—but nevermind that, it's unimportant. Cris reappeared very soon, three or four minutes. She went away, and I went in, and Sordell—"

Nelson paused and came out of his chair and suddenly began pacing. "You're a cute one, Inspector. Suppose I say I found Sordell dead?"

"Did you?" Cray cut in softly.

Nelson ignored the interruption. "Suppose I do say that—the case against me switches to my wife. Well, damn you, Cray, I *could* confess to killing Sordell. I could do that and make it stick—to shield my wife. But I won't. You understand that Cray, I won't! I've gone through a hell of doubt tonight. I admit it. I found my wife's lipstick lying near Sordell's body. I picked up the lipstick. No question about it being hers; I'd bought it myself. Her initials were on it. But I picked up the lipstick, and the inference, finding it there, was —but to hell with the inference! I know Cris. I believe in her. I didn't kill Sordell, and Cris didn't, and I'll fight you all the way, Cray, to prove that—"

Nelson stopped, puzzled and wary, for Cray was chuckling.

"It's all right," Cray said. "That's all I wanted to know. Mrs. Nelson says she lost a lipstick; we found no lipstick. Did Farraday take it? Or someone else we hadn't tied into the case yet? You see how I had to know. Anyway, Farraday's our boy."

Cray put out his cigarette and rose. "He didn't like Sordell's propositions, or what he figured Sordell had demanded of his girl friend. He lifted her key to get in, and she chose the same time— and without her key, necessarily the front entrance—to see Sordell and tell him where to get off at. Remember me pointing out that pastel crayon dust, and the smudge on Sordell's drawing? Maybe you saw Farraday brush ash from the end table up there in his room? Well, it looked like a nervous habit; you know, brushing things like lint and such to the floor. So I played the hunch and had Farraday's room searched. We picked up a pair of beige gloves and the left glove showed a crayon smear."

"Cris—?" Nelson prompted, unsteadily.

There was a small sound behind him. He turned. Cris was standing in the bedroom doorway. Her eyes were very bright, glistening.

She began speaking swiftly, as though his silence frightened her. "Jan, my first fear was for you. I—I guessed that you'd found out I was seeing Sordell, and—but I knew Inspector Cray would help us. I went to him. I didn't fear him." A knuckle cracked; the skin above her knuckles showed white. "I—I'd dropped my purse, at the shock of finding Sordell dead, and I didn't miss the lipstick until later. Then I went right down to see Inspector Cray—"

She seemed suddenly surprised to find that she was back where she had started from. Her pause was awkward, pleading. "But Jan, you—you believed in me—"

There were tears and she was in his arms, warm and wonderful. His lips were buried in her hair. The hall door had closed on Cray, but they hadn't noticed.

"Jan," came her muffled voice, "it's just that I was lonely. I've been working again. I've been modeling for Sordell, and nothing else—"

He said, "Don't worry. I suppose every man who marries beauty has to fight it out with doubt. But I'm glad I won, Cris."

THE SILVER PROTECTOR

ELLIS PARKER BUTLER

When our new suburban house was completed, I took Sarah out to see it, and she liked it all but the stairs.

"Edgar," she said, when she had ascended to the second floor, "I don't know whether it is imagination or not, but it seems to me that these stairs are funny, some way. I can't understand it. They are not a long flight, and they are not unusually steep, but they seem to be unusually wearying. I never knew a short flight to tire me so, and I have climbed many flights in the six years we have lived in apartments."

"Perhaps, Sarah," I said, with mild dissimulation, "you are unusually tired today."

The fact was that I had planned those stairs myself, and for a particular reason I had made the rise of each step three inches more than the customary height, and in this way I had saved two steps. I had also made the tread of the steps unusually narrow; and the reason was that I had found, from long experience, that stair carpet wears first on the tread of the steps, where the foot falls. By making the steps tall enough to save two, and by making the tread narrow, I reduced the wear on the carpet to a minimum. I believe in economy where it is possible. For the same reason I had the stair banisters made wide, with a saddle-like top to the newel post, to tempt my son and daughter to slide downstairs. The less they used the stairs, the longer the carpet would last.

I need hardly say that Sarah has a fear of burglars; most women have. As for myself, I prefer not to meet a burglar. It is all very well to get up in the night and prowl about with a pistol in one hand, seeking to eliminate the life of a burglar, and some men may like it; but I am of a very excitable nature, and I am sure that if I did find a burglar and succeeded in shooting him, I should be in such an excited state that I could not sleep again that night—and no man can afford to lose his night's rest.

There are other objections to shooting a burglar in the house, and these objections apply with double force when the house and its furnishings are entirely new. Although some of the rugs in our house were red, not all of them were; and I had no guarantee that if I shot a burglar he would lie down on a red rug and bleed to death. A burglar does not consider one's feelings, and would be quite as apt to bleed on a green rug, and spoil it, as not. Until burglarizing is properly regulated and burglars are educated, as they should be, in technical burglary schools, we cannot hope that a shot burglar will staunch his wound until he can find a red rug to lie down on.

And there are still other objections to shooting a burglar. If all burglars were fat, one of these would be removed; but perhaps a thin burglar might get in front of my revolver, and in that case the bullet would be likely to go right through him and continue on its way, and perhaps break a mirror or a cut-glass dish. I am a thin man myself, and if a burglar shot at me he might damage some of our things in the same way.

I thought all these things over when we decided to build in the suburbs, for Sarah is very nervous about burglars, and makes me get up at the slightest noise and go poking about. Only the fact that no burglar had ever entered our apartment at night had prevented what might have been a serious accident to a burglar, for I made it a rule, when Sarah wakened me on such occasions, to waste no time, but to go through the rooms as hastily as possible and get back to bed; and at the speed I traveled I might have bumped into a burglar in the dark and knocked him over, and his head might have struck some hard object, causing concussion of the brain; and as a burglar has a small brain, a small amount of concussion might have ruined it entirely. But as I am a slight man it might have been my brain that got concussed. A father of a family has to think of these things.

The nervousness of Sarah regarding burglars had led me in this way to study the subject carefully, and my adoption of jet-black pajamas as nightwear was not due to cowardice on my part. I properly reasoned that if a burglar tried to shoot me while I was rushing around the house after him in the darkness, a suit of black pajamas would somewhat spoil his aim, and, not being able to see me, he would not shoot at all. In this way I should save Sarah the nerve shock that would follow the explosion of a pistol in the house. For Sarah was very much more afraid of pistols than of burglars. I am sure there were only two reasons why I had never killed a burglar with a pistol: one was that no burglar had ever entered our apartment, and the other was that I never had a pistol.

But I knew that one is much less protected in a suburb than in the city, and when I decided to build I studied the burglar protection matter most carefully. I said nothing to Sarah about it, for fear it would upset her nerves, but for months I considered every method that seemed to have any merit, and that would avoid getting a burglar's blood—or mine—spattered around on our new furnishings. I desired some method by which I could finish up a burglar properly without having to leave my bed, for although Sarah is brave enough in sending me out of bed to catch a burglar, I knew she must suffer severe nerve strain during the time I was wandering about in the dark. Her objection to explosives had also to be considered, and I really had to exercise my brain more than common before I hit upon what I may now consider the only perfect method of handling burglars.

Several things coincided to suggest my method. One of these was Sarah's foolish notion that our silver must, every night, be brought from the dining-room and deposited under our bed. This I considered a most foolhardy tempting of fate. It coaxed any burglar who ordinarily would have quietly taken the silver from the dining-room, and have then gone away peacefully, to enter our room. The knowledge that I lay in bed ready at any time to spring out upon him would make him prepare his revolver, and his nervousness might make him shoot me, which would quite upset Sarah's nerves. I told Sarah so, but she had a hereditary instinct for bringing the silver to the bedroom, and insisted. I saw that in the suburban house this would be continued as "bringing the silver upstairs," and a trial of my carpet-saving stairs suggested to me my burglar-defeating plan. I had the apparatus built into the house, and I had the house planned to accommodate the apparatus.

For several months after we moved into the house I had no burglars, but I felt no fear of them in any event. I was prepared for them.

In order not to make Sarah nervous, I explained to her that my invention of a silver-elevator was merely a time-saving device. From the top of the dining-room sideboard I ran upright tracks through the ceiling to the back of the hall above, and in these I placed a glass case which could be run up and down the tracks like a dumb-waiter. All our servant had to do when she had washed the silver was to put it in the glass case, and I had attached to the top of the case a stout steel cable which ran to the ceiling of the hall above, over a pulley, and so to our bedroom, which was at the front of the hall upstairs. By this means I could, when I was in bed, pull the cable, and the glass case of silver would rise to the second floor. Our bedroom door opened upon the hall, and from the bed I could see the glass case; but in order that I might be sure that the silver was there I put a small electric light in the case and kept it burning all night.

Sarah was delighted with this arrangement, for in the morning all I had to do was to play out the steel cable and the silver would descend to the dining-room, and the maid could have the table all set by the time breakfast was ready. Not once did Sarah have a suspicion that all this was not merely a household economy, but my burglar trap.

On the sixth of August, at 2 o'clock in the morning, Sarah awakened me, and I immediately sat straight up in bed. There was an undoubtable noise of sawing, and I knew at once that a burglar was entering our home. Sarah was trembling, and I knew she was getting nervous.

"Sarah," I said, in a whisper, "be calm! There is not the least danger. I have been expecting this for some time, and I only hope the burglar has no dependent family or poor old mother to support. Whatever happens, be calm and keep perfectly quiet."

With that I released the steel cable from the head of my bed and let the glass case full of silver slide noiselessly to the sideboard.

"Edgar!" whispered Sarah in agonized tones, "are you *giving* him our silver?"

"Sarah!" I whispered sternly, "remember what I have just said. Be calm and keep perfectly quiet." And I would say no more.

In a very short time I heard the window below us open softly, and I knew the burglar was entering the parlor from the side porch. I counted twenty, which I had figured would be the time required for him to reach the dining-room, and then, when I was sure he must have seen the silver shining in the glass case, I slowly pulled on the steel cable and raised case and silver to the hall above. Sarah began to whisper to me, but I silenced her.

What I had expected happened. The burglar, seeing the silver rise through the ceiling, left the dining-room and went into the hall. There, from the foot of the stairs, he could see the case glowing in the hall above, and without hesitation he mounted the stairs. As he reached the top I had a good view of him, for he was silhouetted against the light that glowed from the silver case. He was a most brutal looking fellow of the prizefighting type, but I almost laughed aloud when I saw his build. He was short and chunky. As he stepped forward to grasp the silver case, I let the steel cable run through my fingers, and the case and its precious contents slid noiselessly down to the dining-room. For only one instant the burglar seemed disconcerted, then he turned and ran downstairs again.

This time I did not wait so long to draw up the silver. I hardly gave him time to reach the dining-room door before I jerked the cable, and the case was glowing in the upper hall. The burglar immediately stopped, turned, and mounted the stairs, but just as he reached the top I let the silver slide down again, and he had to turn and descend. Hardly had he reached the bottom step before I had the silver once more in the upper hall.

The burglar was a gritty fellow and was not to be so easily defeated. With some word which I could not catch, but which I have no doubt was profane, or at least vulgar, he dashed up the stairs, and just as his hand touched the case I let the silver drop to the dining-room. I smiled as I saw his next move. He carefully removed his coat and vest, rolled up his sleeves, and took off his collar. This evidently meant that he intended to get the silver if it took the whole night, and nothing could have pleased me more. I lay in my comfortable bed fairly shaking with suppressed laughter, and had to stuff a corner of a pillow in my mouth to smother the sound of my mirth. I did not allow the least pity for the fellow to weaken my nerve.

A low, long screech from the hall told me that I had a man of uncommon brain to contend with, for I knew the sound came from his hands drawing along the banister, and that to husband his strength and to save time, he was now sliding down. But this did not disconcert me. It pleased me. *The quicker he went down, the oftener he would have to walk up.*

For half an hour I played with him, giving him just time to get down to the foot of the stairs before I raised the silver, and just time to reach the top before I lowered it, and then I grew tired of the sport—for it was nothing else to me—and decided to finish him off. I was getting sleepy, but it was evident that the burglar was not, and I was a little afraid I might fall asleep and thus defeat myself. The burglar had that advantage because he was used to night work. So I quickened my movements a little. When the burglar slid down I gave him just time to see the silver rise through the ceiling, and when he climbed the stairs I only allowed him to see it descend through the floor. In this way I made him double his pace, and as I quickened my movements I soon had him dashing up the stairs and sliding down again as if for a wager. I did not give him a moment for rest, and he was soon panting terribly and beginning to stumble; but with almost superhuman nerve he kept up the chase. He was an unusually tough burglar.

But quick as he was I was always quicker, and a glimpse of the glowing case was all I let him have at either end of his climb or slide. No sooner was he down than it was up, and no sooner was the case up than he was after it. In this way I kept increasing his speed until it was something terrific, and the whole house shook. But still his speed increased. I saw then that I had brought him to the place I had prepared for, where he had but one object in life, and that was to beat the case up or downstairs; and as I was now so sleepy I could hardly keep my eyes open, I did what I had intended to do from the first. I lowered the case until it was exactly *halfway* between the ceiling of the dining-room and the floor of the hall above—and turned out the electric light. I then tied the steel cable securely to the head of my bed, turned over, and went to sleep, lulled by the shaking of the house as the burglar dashed up and down the stairs.

Just how long this continued I do not know, for my sleep was deep and dreamless, but I should judge that the burglar ran himself to death sometime between half-past 3 and a quarter after 4. So great had been his efforts that when I went to remove him I did not recognize him at all. When I had last seen him in the glow of the glass silver case he had been a stout, chunky fellow, and now his remains were those of an emaciated man. He must have run off one hundred and twenty pounds of flesh before he gave out.

Only one thing clouded my triumph. Our silver consisted of but half a dozen each of knives, forks, and spoons, a butter knife, and a sugar spoon, all plated, and worth probably ten dollars, and to save this I had made the burglar wear to rags a Wilton stair carpet worth fifty-nine dollars. But I have now corrected this. I have bought one hundred and fifty dollars' worth of silver.

THE SLAVE-MAKER

EDGAR WALLACE

Once upon a time, in those absurd days of war, when the laws governing the sanctity of human life were temporarily suspended, Captain Henry Arthur Milton, making a reconnaissance to the northwest of Baghdad, saw the solitary figure of a man lying in the desert land. By his side was a dead camel.

Dipping his ship down to take a closer view, the flying officer saw the man's hand raised feebly as though signaling for help.

Captain Milton shut off his engines and five minutes later had landed and was examining the wounded man—a person of some importance, to judge by the trappings of his camel and his own raiment.

He had been shot in the shoulder, was half delirious with thirst, and proved to be one Ibn el Masjik. He had been wounded in a skirmish with British troops, and after his rescuer had made him comfortable El Masjik had a request to make.

"I am the chief of a fighting clan and I could not survive the disgrace of being taken prisoner. Therefore I ask you as a favor that you take me to the city of my father, and I will give you my parole that I will not fight against your people, nor shall any of my tribe fight."

Milton spoke Arabic as though it were his mother-tongue. He was also a man of unconventional habits, and although he had no more authority to carry out the wishes of his prisoner than he had to take upon himself the command of the British Army in Mesopotamia, he did not hesitate.

His airplane made a journey of a hundred and seventy miles, landed within half a mile of the walled city of Khor. And at some risk to himself—for the local inhabitants were unaware of his errand of mercy—delivered the wounded man to the care of his friends.

"Come to me when this war is ended," said Ibn el Masjik, "and, though all the world be against you, I shall be for you. If you are poor, I will make you rich. My father's city is for your asking."

This time he spoke in English, for he had in his youth been educated at a preparatory school in Bournemouth.

Henry Arthur Milton remembered this promise some years later, when he was hard pressed, and for six months was the guest of Ibn el Masjik.

The white-walled city of Khor stood on the edge of the wilderness, and time had passed it by. Raiding parties went out unashamed and returned laden with booty and slaves. Milton saw men and women sold in the market-place, saw life unchanged from what it had been in the days when Mahomet's uncle was guardian of the Kaaba, and the Prophet's disciples were praying in Medina.

One night Henry Arthur expostulated about certain practices, and the thin, ascetic face of Ibn el Masjik lit up in a smile. He tossed a half-smoked cigarette into a silver vase, lit another, and settled himself more comfortably on the cushions.

"My friend," he said, "it is a far cry to Bournemouth, Hampshire. Slavery is merely a name for service, and it is a matter of form whether it takes the shape you see here in Khor, or in some dingy northern town where men and women have to leave their beds at the sound of a whistle and hurry through rain and sleet to the prison-houses you call factories. My slaves are more pleasantly treated: they have the sunshine; they are well fed; they sleep in their own houses."

He was perfectly frank about the traffic. There was a little port on the Red Sea where one could buy, under the very noses of a British administration, this kind of artisan—at a price.

"Not always can I buy what I desire," he explained. "My women ask me all the time for such a man, and where may he be found?" He sighed heavily. "Yes, the West is creeping upon us, and Kemal's new law concerning women has reached even here."

He shrugged his shoulders, smoothed his white silken robe more decorously about his knees, and smiled reminiscently.

"I do not object. There is a piquancy in the new custom which is very amusing. And we differ from most other tribes in that our women are never veiled, and have rights of choice."

After Milton came back to Western Europe he frequently corresponded with his blood brother, and at the back of his mind he always had Khor as a final sanctuary in case things went wrong.

The police might suspect that Henry Arthur Milton, whom they called The Ringer, had many homes, but they did not know where. Certainly they did not know about the place in Norbury where he spent a great part of his time.

There was a small garden at the back of the house which he cultivated, and across the dividing wall it often happened that he discussed with his neighbor such mundane matters as the depredations of cats.

He had few opportunities, for Captain Oring, that gray-bearded man who had dreamed for forty years of a shore life, was captain of a small tramp vessel which traded between London and Suez. He was not only captain but part proprietor, he and his sons holding three-quarters of the shares in his little vessel.

One of the "boys" was his chief officer, another his chief engineer, a third attended to the business end in London. He had, also, a daughter, a floridly pretty girl, who kept the home for her brother and did an immense amount of housework in such time as she could spare from the cinemas.

On an occasion when The Ringer was absent from London the girl disappeared. Her father was at sea, and it was from him, months later, that The Ringer heard the story.

Captain Oring did not tell him coherently—it was not the sort of story that a father could tell straightforwardly—and Henry Arthur Milton listened to the broken narrative with a cold-bloodedness which was his chief characteristic.

"My boy found her after a lot of trouble . . . she's with my sister now, in the country. Naturally, I've tried to find the people. But what chance have I got in London? I can't go to the police. . . . I don't want her name in the papers, do I? If I ever meet this man . . ."

"You won't," said The Ringer. "But perhaps I shall—I travel about a lot."

(In the neighborhood Henry Arthur Milton was registered as Mr. Ernest Oppenton, and his profession was described as "commercial traveler.")

Captain Oring went away to sea, with his sons and his grief and his patched-up little steamer; and Henry Arthur Milton had certain urgent business which took him to Berlin—so urgent that you might imagine that the matter of Lucy Oring had entirely slipped from his mind.

But nothing ever escaped him, and on his return to London he became a great frequenter of that type of West End club which appears on, and is struck from, the register so very rapidly that you might not know it had ever existed.

He overheard a little; waiters told him some things. It is extraordinary how confidential an Italian waiter will become to a man who speaks his language. Women told him most of all, for he paid for drinks with great munificence.

On a certain afternoon a scene was enacted at one of the great London terminals which was so commonplace that only very keen observation would have noted it as being out of the ordinary.

The nice-looking old lady with the white hair and the cameo brooch saw the train come slowly along the platform of Victoria Station, and moved nearer to the barrier.

Presently, the passengers began to trickle past the ticket-collector, not in the hurried way of suburban season-ticket holders, but with the leisure which is peculiar to travellers from a distance. She watched carefully, and after a while she saw the pretty girl with the black suitcase. She was dressed in dark brown and carried in her other hand a bunch of autumnal flowers.

The nice old lady intercepted her.

"My dear, are you Miss Clayford? I thought so! I am Mrs. Graddle. I thought I would come along and see you safely across London."

The girl nodded gratefully.

"I was wondering what I should do. Are you from the agency?"

The nice old lady smiled.

"Oh, dear no! But a friend of mine at the agency keeps me informed about the engagements. I like to do what I can for young people. Now, you must come along and have tea with me. I understand it is a perfectly awful place you are going to! Forty pounds a year for a nursery governess is scandalous! And in a little country village where there is nothing to see and nothing to do . . . !"

She rattled on as she accompanied the girl through the booking-hall to the station yard, and Elsie Clayford listened dismally. Forty pounds a year was a small sum, but she understood that her new employers were very nice people, and that the home was comfortable. It was her first engagement.

"I'd like you to stay a few days with me," said Mrs. Graddle, as she signalled a cab. "I've got a lovely little house in St. John's Wood, and we have young society. I have already telephoned to Lady Shene, and she agrees. You might do a theatre or two. . . ."

Elsie had not the vaguest idea who Mrs. Graddle was. She guessed that the old lady was a member of one of those organizations which undertake the care of young girls. It was a matter for satisfaction that such societies existed.

For instance, as she had met her white-haired guardian she had noticed a lank-looking man with long black hair and large horn-rimmed spectacles; and this sinister-looking individual had looked at her so oddly that she felt a queer little thrill of fear. And now he was standing at her elbow as the cab drew up at the curb.

"Get in, my dear," said Mrs. Graddle, as Elsie pushed in her suitcase. The girl obeyed, and the old lady was following when the man with the spectacles caught her arm, and, drawing her gently aside, shut the cab door.

"King's Cross," he said to the driver, and, still holding Mrs. Graddle's arm, he pushed his head through the open window space. "Your train leaves at 5:32. Lady Shene will probably meet you at Welwyn Station. Have you money for the cab fare?"

"Ye-es," said the panic-stricken Elsie.

"Good. Don't talk to people unless you know them; especially angelic old birds like this one."

He waved the cab on.

"What's the idea?" demanded Mrs. Graddle, breathlessly.

The man had already called another cab.

"Get in," he said. She obeyed tremblingly. The man followed.

"I've told him to drive through the park. I'll drop you at the end of Birdcage Walk."

"I've a good mind to give you in charge!" There was a whimper in the old woman's voice. "Who do you think you are?" He did not answer this question.

"You've been convicted twice—once in Leeds and Manchester,"

he said, "and for a number of offences. You get acquainted with somebody in a registry office who keeps you supplied with information regarding the movement of servants. I understand that you're not above touting and using the cinemas to discover stage-struck girls."

"You can't prove anything," she interrupted. "And even if you arrest me—but you're not going to do a thing like that."

She opened her bag with trembling fingers, groped in the interior and took out a wad of banknotes.

"Be a good man and don't make any trouble," she pleaded.

The Ringer took the notes from her hand, counted them deliberately.

"Sixty-five pounds doesn't seem a very adequate bribe," he remarked.

She opened an inner purse, and sorted out two notes, each for a hundred pounds.

"That's all I've got." Old Mrs. Graddle was inclined to be hysterical. "You 'busies' can't keep your noses out of anything!"

The Ringer tapped at the window and the cab stopped. It was now raining heavily, and there were few pedestrians about.

"Have you any children?" he asked.

"No," she said quickly.

"Apart from the beastliness of your job, do you ever realize what it feels like to be a father or a mother, to be waiting and hoping for somebody to come back . . . to be uncertain about their fate?"

"I don't want any argument with you," she said, with surprising savagery for so picturesque an old lady. "You've got your money, and that's all you care about! I've got no children."

"I think you're right," he said, cryptically, and opened the door for her.

"Let him drive on to the Tube station," she demanded; but he shook his head.

"You can get out and walk. You'll be wet through, probably, and die—and if you do I shan't stop laughing!"

She said something which no angelic old lady should have said. The Ringer smiled. As she moved quickly toward Parliament Square, he paid the cabman.

"Turn round and go back," he said.

And he slipped on a mackintosh which he carried over his arm, took off his glasses, and wiped away his small mustache before the cabman had turned the nose of his machine in the other direction.

He was taking no risks—the more so since he was well aware for what destination Mrs. Graddle was bound.

In the circumstances she went to a lot of unnecessary trouble in taking an Underground train to South Kensington and doubling back by taxi. Eventually she reached her pleasant home in St. John's Wood in a condition of semi-exhaustion.

It was a very nice house, with a beautiful dancing floor; this was necessary, for Mrs. Graddle gave select parties. The peculiar servants she employed were decorating the ballroom when she arrived, but she was not interested in the coming festivities of the evening.

She went upstairs to the small study, where her son was eating greasy toast and reading the evening newspaper.

"Hullo! Did you get her?" he asked pleasantly.

He was a lethargic man of thirty, heavy-featured, heavy-eyed, and decidedly plump. On one finger he wore a diamond ring of great value; stones sparkled from his ornate cravat. He listened while she told her breathless story, stroking his small mustache.

"That's pretty bad," he said. "Who was he? Do you know him? A 'busy?' It's awkward—damned awkward! They know about the Leeds and the Manchester affair too; that's rotten!"

He had reason for his perturbation. Only by the skin of his teeth had he succeeded in keeping clear of the Manchester charge, and it would have been much more serious for him than for his mother.

"What are you scared about—I paid the feller, didn't I?" She rang the bell viciously, and when the servant came: "We shan't want the room for that girl; she's not coming," she snapped, and when the servant had closed the door: "For God's sake don't sit there shaking like a jelly, Julian! There's nothing to be afraid of!"

But Julian thought there were many things to be afraid of, and enumerated a few.

"I've been dreading this," he quavered, "ever since that Oring girl was found. Let's go down into the country, mother—what about Margate? We could stay there for a month or two till this affair blew over?—"

"It has blown over," she interrupted, and went upstairs to change from her street clothes, which were most uncomfortably damp.

Julian Graddle never felt less like following his legitimate profession. He had to go into the West End to attend to two clients, for he was a ladies' hairdresser—an extremely useful trade to his mother: for women gossip to one another. They talk of servants who are leaving them, of girls who have got into scrapes. Some of

183

his mother's best "finds" had been located by Julian in the course of his working day.

He was certainly not at his best after a series of sharp admonitions from his best client—a lady whose temper was by no means equable. And he went to his second call more rattled than ever. The next day he had to attend at the shop which employed him, and he lived on tenterhooks, growing bolder, however, as the day progressed without a sign of a policeman.

In the evening, as he was leaving, the clerk at the desk handed him a slip of paper.

"Miss Smith, 34, Grine Mews, telephoned for you specially."

He frowned at the paper, but the time was convenient. "Six-thirty," said the note. "Miss Smith, very urgent. Pay on completion of work."

He was not at all surprised to be called to a mews. So many fashionable people had converted garages into artistic flats.

The occupant of 34, Grine Mews, was obviously terminating her occupation. There was a board displayed, informing the world that "this handsome and commodious flat" was to let. He knocked at the narrow door, which was immediately opened.

"Come in," said a man's voice pleasantly. "Are you the hairdresser? Miss Smith has been waiting for you."

Julian stumped wheezily up the steep stairs. They were uncarpeted, and so was the landing above. There was also the queer smell which attaches to houses that have been long unfurnished. Possibly Miss Smith was only just moving in.

His conductor opened a door.

"This way. It is rather dark, but I'll get a light."

Julian entered unsuspectingly. The door slammed behind him—then there was a click, and a bare lamp hanging from the ceiling glowed dimly. The room was empty of furniture; the floor and mantelpiece were covered with dust. Over the little window a heavy horse-rug had been fastened with forks.

"Don't move," said the stranger.

His face was covered with a half-mask: a habit of The Ringer's when he was not wearing disguise.

"If you raise a bleat I shall shoot you through the stomach, and you will die in great agony," he said, calmly; and Julian's face went green at the sight of the pistol in the man's hand. .

"What—what—?" he began.

"Don't ask questions. Go through that doorway."

Like a man in a dream, the prisoner obeyed. The inner room had a rickety table and a dark-colored sofa, evidently left by a former tenant. On the table was a glass of red wine, and to this The Ringer pointed.

"Drink," he said curtly.

The man turned an agonized face to him.

"Is it poisoned?" he whimpered.

"No, but I will tell you very frankly it is drugged. I'm not going to kill you—I promise you."

Julian gulped down the draught.

"Who are you?" he asked, hollowly.

"People call me The Ringer," said Henry Arthur Milton.

It was the last word Julian Graddle remembered.

That night The Ringer had a long consultation with Captain Oring.

"He is the man all right, so we need not distress your daughter by bringing her up to identify him. Where is your ship lying?"

"She's lying at Keeney's Wharf, Rotherhithe," said Captain Oring, pondering the problem before him. "If I thought this was the man—"

"He is the man; but you're to do nothing drastic. He is to be kept alive and in good health. You will arrive at El Sass on the 23rd as I reckon the time—a day or two more or less doesn't matter, because you will be expected. You will arrange to hand him over at night to a crew of Arabs who will come out in a boat for him. Here is the money for his passage—two hundred and sixty-five pounds. His mother is paying the fare."

His two sons were with Captain Oring, and one of them spoke.

"If this is the man, Mr. Oppenton, we don't want any payment. I'd like to take the swine and beat his head off, but if you say no—well, your word goes."

In the middle of the night, the "boys" and Captain Oring went down to the little garage at the end of the garden, where Mr. Julian Graddle was sleeping soundly, and bundled him into an old car. He was taken to Keeney's Wharf when the night watchman was dozing, and laid in a bumpy berth in a very uncomfortable little cabin. . . .

To Ibn el Masjik The Ringer wrote a letter, and sent it overland by air mail. It began:

From his friend Arthur, to Ibn el Masjik, the servant of God, on whom be peace!
I have thought much over the trouble which you confided to me, and of Certain Ones in your house who desire to follow the Western custom, making their hair short like men. Also, that you can find none in your city who may do this service for you.
Now, El Masjik, I am sending to you a man very skillful in such things: a slave who has no protection of the law, and you shall keep him in your house all the days of his life, and I ask only that he be a servant to women, such an one as they may beat with their slippers.
On the fourteenth day of the Month of the Pilgrimage a little steamer shall come to the port of El Sass and you shall send . . .

He gave the most minute instructions for the disposal of Mr. Julian Graddle—instructions that he knew would be obeyed to the letter.

A fortnight later he saw an advertisement in the agony columns of three daily newspapers:

> Will Julian Graddle, who disappeared from London, please communicate with his anxious and sorrowing mother?

And when he read this The Ringer laughed. He had read such appeals before, addressed by parents who sought daughters. And where those daughters had gone, and why they did not answer, the angelic Mrs. Graddle knew best.

Some Jobs Are Simple

Chet Williamson

"It took me a long time to find you," she said, looking across the beer-wet table at him. She was a hassled-looking woman, he thought as he looked back and sipped his drink. Young, but not so young that she could hide those bags under her eyes with makeup.

"You sure I'm who you're looking for?"

"If your name's Joe, you are."

He nodded. "Joe."

"I need a . . . something done."

"A job."

"Yes. A job."

"Who told you about me?"

"An acquaintance. He owns . . . owned a fur-storage place."

"Uh-huh." Abrams, he thought. He'd torched the building six months before.

"Not him really. His wife."

"What's the job?"

She looked around nervously. "Can we talk here?"

"See any cops?"

She started to answer before she realized he was joking.

"Don't be so nervous," he said with a thin smile. "You, uh . . ." He glanced down, then up. "You want me to *do* somebody for you?"

"No!" Her eyelids flew up. "Oh no, nothing like that."

"What then?"

"A burglary." She had trouble with the word. It seemed to stick in her throat. He gestured to the half pitcher of beer, but she shook her head. "I want you to burglarize my house. Steal some jewelry of mine."

"Steal your own jewelry. That means insurance."

"Yes. I need money."

"And I give you back the jewels afterwards."

"Well, yes."

"And you pay me."
"Yes."
"You pay me a thousand dollars."
"A . . . that's more than I had thought."
"I'm taking a risk. You see? Any less and it's not worth it."
"A thousand dollars."
"I generally ask for more. Things are slow right now."
"You'd want cash."
He chuckled softly. "Yes indeed."
"Oh!" She looked embarrassed. "Yes. Yes, of course."
"Where do you live?"
"Marion Court. 1636 Marion Court."

He licked the beer from his lip. Marion Court was an upper-class section on the city's outskirts. The houses were widely spaced. "Who else lives there?"

"Just my husband."
"He in on this?"
"He . . . no, he's not. I don't want him to know about it."
"He'll know when the jewels are gone."
"I mean about my meeting you."
"Why not?"
"I need the money for something I don't want him to know about."
"Uh-huh."
"And that's all I want to say about it."

He poured himself more beer and took a swallow. "Once I steal the jewels, how do you know I'll give them back?"

"I would have to trust you."
"I'm a thief."
"If you kept them," she frowned, "I could tell the police you took them."
"Then I'd tell that you hired me to take them."
"You couldn't prove that."
"Then how else would you know that I took them?" A cloud passed over her face, and she moved back, as if trying to decide whether or not to rise from the table. "Don't worry," he said. "You'll get them back. I didn't get my reputation by double-crossing clients. I just want you to know that if you change your mind and get religion, I can take you with me, okay?"

"I won't change my mind."
"Good. When do you want this done?"
"Tomorrow night?"

"That's pretty soon." She didn't respond. "Okay. What time?"

"Two A.M.? You can come in through the kitchen door. I'll have it unlocked. I'll put the jewelry on the desk in the den. It's just off the kitchen."

"Won't your husband think that's odd?"

"He never goes into the den after dinner. When you leave, break the window in the kitchen door."

"Why?"

She beamed as if she were proud of her idea. "That way it won't look as though it was unlocked to begin with."

"Clever. Won't your husband hear it?"

"He's a sound sleeper, and our bedroom's upstairs on the other side of the house."

"Does he have a gun?"

"A gun? Yes. Why?"

"There's always a chance he'll wake up. A chance he'll hear me. Which means I've got to bring a gun."

"No! You won't need it—he'll never hear you, and if he does I'll keep him in the bedroom."

"I'm sorry, but . . ."

"Please, I promise you, you won't need a gun. I'll . . . I'll unload his."

"Bringing it doesn't mean I have to use it."

"I . . ."

"Insurance, that's all. If you know I've got a gun, you'll be doubly sure I won't be bothered."

She sat for a moment, looking worried. "All right. But please, no shooting."

"No shooting. Any pets?"

"No. How can I reach you afterward?"

He scribbled a number on a corner of the paper place mat, tore it off, and handed it to her. "Call this number. If I'm not there, there'll be someone who'll tell you how to reach me. Memorize it and throw it away."

She nodded and stuck the note in her purse. "1636 Marion Court. Two A.M. You won't forget?"

"I won't forget."

The following night he parked his car, a dark blue midsized sedan, four blocks from 1636 Marion and walked to the house. He was relieved to see that it was a good fifty yards between houses and relieved to hear no bayings of dogs as he walked up the driveway and around to the kitchen door. He slipped on his gloves and tried the knob. It was unlocked, as she'd promised, and opened smoothly and quietly. He listened, but the house was still. Closing the door behind him, he took a penlight from his pocket and flashed it low around the room, quickly spotting the entrance to the den. The door was open, and on the desk was a brown leather box. He opened the lid and smiled as the jewelry danced in the light. It was always tempting, but he'd never yet succumbed. With this batch, though, it would be hard, very hard.

His head shot up as he heard the noise, a low squeak, as of a settling floorboard. But he knew the difference between a settling sound and one made by someone's foot. He flicked off the penlight and reached for the .38 Special in his armpit.

"Hello?" The voice was a whisper, high and near. "Is that you . . . Joe?" She said the name as though she knew it was false.

He held the light out at his side and turned it on. She was standing empty-handed in the doorway, a cranberry-colored robe wrapped around her. She blinked as the light hit her eyes. "Jesus," he said. "What are you doing here?"

"I was nervous. I couldn't stay in bed. I wanted to make sure you got in all right."

"Of course I did. I thought you were going to stay with your husband."

"Oh, he's sleeping, don't worry." She pointed to the box. "Those are the jewels."

"I figured."

"And there was another piece I wore today that I forgot to put in the box . . ." Her hand went into the pocket of her robe and came out with a small pistol that fired twice, throwing bullets sharply into his chest so that he staggered back and hit the wall of bookcases, dropping his own pistol he'd been loosely, confidently holding. He slumped to the floor, books plopping on either side of him like giant raindrops. He didn't have to see the blood to know he was dying.

With the same surprising speed with which she'd drawn the gun, she crossed to him from the doorway, knelt, and picked up his .38. He tried to make a grab for it, but only his fingers would move, and those too slowly. "Why?" he asked, tasting blood.

"You'll see. You deserve that much." She crossed to the doorway, turned on the room light, and shouted. "Tom!" There was silence. "*Tom!*" She wrapped a handkerchief around the hand that held the gun.

A muffled cry answered her from somewhere in the house.

"Come here! I'm in the den!"

"What is it? For crissake, it's after two. . . ."

"Just come in here! Something's not right. . . ." She walked over to where he'd been standing when she'd shot him and looked at him. "Now you get it?"

A few seconds later Tom walked through the doorway, and she shot him in the forehead with the .38. Then she wiped the other pistol and put it in her husband's dead hand. "You'll get yours back in a minute," she said to the man dying against the bookcase. "I've got a couple of things to do first."

He listened to her call the police on the kitchen phone, thinking how frenzied and horrified she seemed. The last sound he heard was the sharp clatter of glass as she broke the window in the kitchen door. From the outside, of course.

Strictly Accidental

Morgan Talbot

On practically every fence there was a sign that said in big black letters, NO HUNTING OR TRESPASSING—THIS MEANS YOU! Dolliver looked at the signs and then his two pink chins shook with laughter in the collar of his flossy red hunting jacket. "You suppose that really means us, Benny?"

He was pretty well oiled. There had been a quart of Vat 69 in the side-pocket of the car when we left Seattle that morning, and there was just one good-sized drink left by the time we reached pheasant territory. Dolliver downed that one, too. I wasn't anybody to share liquor with—I was just the guy that drove his car, and carried his gun, and told him when and where to shoot.

I looked at the NO HUNTING signs and then I looked down at a big mud-puddle on this side of the fence. I said, "Hell, Mr. Dolliver, they don't mean us. They must mean two fellows from Syracuse."

He laughed and laughed, his little round nose twinkling like a traffic light in the frosty morning air. "Then let us negotiate yon fence, my good man. Let us tackle the grackle and make the pheasant quail. Ha! Get it, Benny?"

I'm not kidding. That was the way he always talked when he was drunk, and he was drunk at least nine-tenths of the time. We didn't even take a bird-dog along on these hunting expeditions any more, because Dolliver had shot the last two by accident and then had bawled around like a heart-broken kid. Some guy. Maybe you can understand why his wife wasn't in love with him, even though he did wrap her up in Flato necklaces and Russian sables.

I put down the shotgun and held the strands of barb-wire apart so Dolliver could squirm through. He made heavy weather of it, snagging the seat of his pants on the wire and chuckling away as if that were just about the funniest joke in the world. I had the shotgun ready for him by the time he got untangled. I gave the muddy barrels a once-over lightly with the end of my woollen scarf and then I eased through the fence behind Dolliver.

The spot was a three-acre cornfield hemmed in by ash trees, and it was a hell of a good place for Dolliver to die. I guess the other hunters had taken those signs seriously, because there wasn't a single gun popping. Dolliver had fun. He began to scoot from corn-shock to corn-shock, pretending they were Indian teepees and saying loudly, "Hist, Deerslayer! My scattergun, pard!"

Money or no money, could any woman learn to love a guy like that?

A couple of fat Hungarian pheasants slipped out from behind a corn-shock just ahead, hustling along very close to the ground and gathering speed for a quick take-off. I shoved the shotgun into Dolliver's hooks and yelled, "It's a cinch! Let 'em have both barrels!"

Then I turned around and hurried off through the stubble, running the same way the pheasants had run—very fast, very close to the ground. I'd run about the length of a night-club dance floor when I heard the blast, and the instant I heard it my feet quit moving. I stood there like John Farmer's scarecrow and felt my heart chunking away at my ribs and the skin gathering in tight little pleats on the back of my neck. Even when it's something you've been expecting and hoping for, a thing like that puts the fear of the Lord into you.

The blast had sounded like a howitzer shell tearing through a cast-iron roof, and then I heard the whir of pheasant wings just over my head, and then there was silence thick enough to chop up and sell by the pound to public libraries. Dolliver wasn't laughing any more. He wasn't having fun.

He wasn't saying boo.

I turned around and went back and looked down at him, liking him a little better now that he was worth a couple of million dollars to me.

I'd caught detective story writers in a lot of whoppers—one being the old wheeze about how nobody ever gets away with murder—and I'd often wondered if you really *could* kill a man by putting bamboo splinters in his chow mein, or sulphur in his gasoline tank, or good rich mud in the barrels of his shotgun. Well, I knew one thing for certain now: that shotgun gag was the pure quill. Dolliver knew it too, though he wasn't likely to lodge complaints about it.

The blast had thrown him backward into the side of a cornshock, and he was sitting there with his legs spread out and his face turned up to the sky and his fingers locked on what was left of the scattergun. There wasn't much of it left. The explosion had ripped it apart just above the breech, twisting the barrels into a choice piece of scrap-iron. Dolliver's face had taken most of the punishment.

I began to think about Vee Dolliver, who was a widow now and a rich one at that. A beautiful one, too. . . . And I thought about the dead-end cell at double Walla, and how a lot of guys had found themselves rooming there simply because they'd insisted on doing things the hard way. They'd had everything worked out in the blue-prints—they'd had their split-second timing and their tricky alibis and their million-dollar tongues—but they wound up on Gooseneck Avenue just the same.

And why? Because when something looks like murder, the blues are going to find a topsy in spite of hell. When it looks like an accident, they're glad enough to let it go at that. Well, this looked like an accident, and nobody in God's world could prove it wasn't.

I thought about all this and I began to feel pretty good again. I wiped the mud off my scarf and then I doubled back and smeared up my footprints so that they didn't tell any kind of story at all. A pint-sized farmer in a gallon-sized mackinaw came loping through the ash trees just as I knelt down beside the late millionaire's corpse.

"You city guys think you own the world, don't you?" he raved. "Posted land don't mean a thing to you, does it? You come down here and you shoot our cows and you— Get that drunk off my land! Get him out, damn you!"

I said, "He isn't drunk. He's dead. You got a telephone?"

He had a telephone, all right, but it was at least three minutes before he could say so.

They held a coroner's inquest down there in the bird country. I was the star witness, of course, and I spoke my piece just the way I'd rehearsed it.

"Mr. Dolliver looked at those NO HUNTING signs and then he sent me into the field ahead of him to see if the farmer was hiding around anywhere," I said. "I left the shotgun with him, and I guess he must have leaned it up against a fence post with the barrels sticking in that mud puddle. The average hunter would know better than that, but Mr. Dolliver was—well, he'd been drinking all morning and he was always pretty careless with guns, anyhow. I tried to watch him, but a man can't be everywhere and see everything at once. It wasn't until he followed me through the fence and blazed away at those two pheasants that I had any idea what had happened."

Things went my way from beginning to end. Two of Dolliver's country-club pals had come over from the Coast with Vee, and they testified that Dolliver had been dangerous company on a hunting trip because of his eccentric ways with firearms. Vee herself was the only other witness.

She didn't look at me. She didn't look at anybody or anything— just sat there twisting her gloved hands together and staring into space as if she saw something nobody else could see. Her little heart-shaped face was whiter than a Kodiak Christmas, and there were soft blue shadows under her dark blue eyes, and her lips trembled so that she could hardly get the words through them. Can you tie it? Anybody would almost have thought that Dolliver had been the shining light of her life.

She told about his accidentally shooting the two bird dogs. And about him feeling so bad afterwards that he cried like a kid. "You see," she said, "he—he was *kind*. He trusted everybody and everything, and that's why he was always so reckless with guns. He just couldn't believe that—that anything was going to hurt him. Or anybody else. He—well, he had *faith* in things. . . ."

The coroner's jury decided that a double-barreled shotgun was a poor thing to have faith in, and that was that. I wasn't surprised at the verdict. Not even Vee had suspected the truth, though Vee knew that I wasn't likely to spill many tears on Dolliver's cedar nightgown. The cops were satisfied, and I was satisfied, and I guess everybody was satisfied except Dolliver.

So you can't get away with murder, huh? It is to laugh. The next time some weisenheimer pulls that one on you, tell him for me that I got away with it clean as soap. And all because there's a right way and a wrong way of doing things.

They planted Dolliver in Seattle. I drove Vee to the funeral, but she was sandwiched between a couple of Dolliver's nephews and so I didn't have a chance to talk things over with her. Not that that bothered me very much. I was pretty sure of my ground, and I could wait.

There had been those long, lazy drives through the suburbs of Seattle. There had been the little roadside inn east of Vancouver, and there had been Vee's soft, shaky voice telling me all the things I'd been waiting to hear. "I love you, Ben. I'm in love with my husband's chauffeur . . . just like—like somebody in a cheap novel. Oh, darling, darling, what are we going to do?"

"You can't stay married to that clown," I told her. "Ask him for a divorce and a good-sized cash settlement."

"Ben! Please don't talk that way about him, dear. He—he isn't a clown. He's kind, and sweet, and sort of helpless, and—Ben, I couldn't hurt him. I just couldn't. It would be like hurting a baby."

So this had been the only way to do it. It had been the best way, too, from everybody's point of view except maybe Dolliver's. There'd be a bigger block of cash, for one thing.

After the funeral, I sat around in my headquarters above the garage and thought about all this and waited day after day for a word from Vee. She never seemed to go out any more, and I didn't even catch a glimpse of her in all that time. The waiting began to sandpaper my nerves before long. It was a whole lot too early to send out the wedding invitations, of course; but still and all, a guy likes to keep his fences in good repair.

After a couple more weeks of this, I made up my mind I was going to have another squint at my hole-card. The big trouble was, old Aiken seemed to have made up *his* mind that I wasn't. He met me at the service entrance the first time I tried to crash through, and his thin, stiff face was about as inviting as the business side of a straight-edge razor.

Aiken stared at me out of his moss-agate eyes and said coldly, "I don't believe you were summoned, Daly. The madam is not making any appointments at present, and I'm sure she has no intention of using the car today."

I thought, *Have your fun while you can, Stoneface. It'll be just too bad for you when I'm doing the hiring and the firing around here.* "The name is Mr. Daly, Aiken," I told him out loud, "and I have reasons for wanting to see Mrs. Dolliver."

You could have split kindling with his face. "The madam is not seeing anybody," he said, "and I'm sure she would resent any such intrusion. If you will state your business—"

"The Packard needs a couple new rear tires," I ad-libbed, "but I don't want to order them without her say-so. It'll just take a minute to—"

Aiken turned stiffly and plodded away. He came back looking like a cagy old tomcat full of goldfish. "The madam says you may use your own judgment, Daly. She does not care to discuss inconsequential matters at such a time."

I didn't like that.

I waited another couple of days and then I tried it again. If the Cord was in need of an overhaul job, Aiken told me, I was to go ahead and give it an overhaul job without bothering the madam about it. Then he sharpened his face at me and said starchily, "I have no idea why you are annoying her with these trivialities, but if you persist in it I shall most certainly recommend your early discharge."

I didn't like that, either. The more I thought about this whole situation, the less I liked it. I'd got away with murder, sure—Dolliver was pushing grass-roots and the case was closed—but the stake I had banked on was beginning to look a little too much like *if* money. I couldn't chew that. Aiken or no Aiken, I was going to compare notes with Vee Dolliver.

I waited two more days, and then I got my chance.

Aiken was out of the way. I'd been using my upstairs window for a sort of conning tower, and I saw him open his rusty old umbrella and head north along the tree-lined street just beyond the house. He probably wasn't going any farther than the nearest grocery store, but that would give me time for a few chummy words with Vee. It was as good a break as any beggar could choose.

I did a One-Eye Connolly through the service entrance and began to case the house. It took me a good five minutes to find Vee. She was busy writing letters in the upstairs study, and she didn't even know I was around until I said softly, "Vee."

She turned from the writing desk. Her chin jerked up and her face went pale and she looked at me as if I were Lon Chaney. "Daly! What—"

"I didn't mean to scare you, Vee. I had to see you, and this was the only way I could do it. I—I guess it's a little early to be talking about—well, about the future, but I want you to know that I still—"

Vee said, "I can't talk to you, Daly. I haven't been seeing anybody since—since Richard's death, and I gave Aiken orders not to admit you."

I didn't like that. I liked it so little that I could feel the blood heating my cheeks and the muscles tightening along my jawbones. "So it's Daly now, huh?" I said. "It was Benny darling less than a month ago."

Her fingers began to play nervously with a long bronze letter-opener. She dropped her eyes and said in half a voice, "I—I know. I guess I haven't been very fair to you . . . Ben. I guess I should have had enough courage to see you at once and tell you that—that—"

I said, "Well?"

"Oh, Ben, don't make this hard for me! Please! Can't you see that Richard's death has—has changed everything?"

"Hell," I said, "of course it's changed everything. You don't have to worry about hurting him now, Vee. We can—"

She shook her head.

"So it's the brush-off, is it?" I said through my teeth. "It's the old runaround."

Vee began to inch away from me. "Don't, Ben—*please!* Try to understand. After Richard died, I just felt . . . different. I thought of his kindness, and his gentleness, and—and everything, and I realized then that it was Richard I'd loved all the time. I was infatuated with you, Ben, but that was all. We—we've got to forget it ever happened. I wasn't faithful to him in life, but I can—can at least be faithful to him now. . . ."

I said, "I love you. I'm not giving you up. Get that? You think I'm the kind of guy a woman can turn on and off like—"

"Ben!"

I kept on moving toward her. Her fingers curled tight around the handle of the letter-opener, but I don't think she even knew it was there. "Ben!" she whispered in a dry-leaf voice. "Your—your face. . . ."

I tried to hang onto myself. But I couldn't do it. The blood was making high, thin music in my ears, and I could feel my lips pulling back from my teeth and freezing that way. "Damn you," I said, "what's the matter with my face? You liked it well enough a month ago!"

Vee stared at me out of eyes that were like pooled ink. Her voice lifted and went thin. "It's the face of a man who would—who'd commit—" She quit talking then, and her lips turned gray, and I could see the idea building in those wide blue eyes. She screamed, "You killed him! You killed him! You murdered Richard because you thought I'd—"

That scared the sense back into my head. "Stop it, Vee! You don't know what you're saying."

She spun toward the door. "Don't come near me! You murdered Richard, and now you're planning to murder me!"

I said, "Vee! For God's sake!"

She bolted out into the hallway, her fingers still clenched on the letter-knife. I threw the door open and went after her, but I wasn't going to do any arguing about that two million dollars now. The only thing in God's world I wanted was to get her quieted down before Aiken or somebody else barged in. "Vee. . . ."

She reached the mouth of the stairwell. Her face whipped back toward me, whiter than white. *"Don't kill me!"* she screamed. *"Oh, God, don't kill me!"*

That was when the thing happened.

Vee's foot missed the top step of the stairs. She made one frantic effort to catch the bannister, and then I could hear the quick *thud-thud* of her body as it toppled down the carpeted steps. There was one last *thud*, heavier than any of the others, and after that the hush came down.

I found her lying in a motionless huddle at the bottom of the stairs, her hair spread out and her face hidden in the carpet. "Vee!" I said, and then I turned her over and stopped thinking for a minute or two.

That sharp bronze letter-knife had been in her right hand when she went down, but it wasn't there now. It was in her left breast.

I pulled it out and tried to dam the flow of blood with my fingers. "Vee!" I said again. "Vee. . . ."

And that was when Aiken got back from the grocery store.

Can you tie it? I mean, can you? Aiken told about seeing me there with the letter-opener in my fist, and the cops found my fingerprints on the handle, and a neighbor woman testified that she heard Vee screaming, "Don't kill me! Oh, God, don't kill me!" The state prosecutor called me a "fiendish harpy who tried to take advantage of a helpless woman in the hour of her darkest sorrow." Then he put his face close to mine and roared, "You killed her, didn't you? When she scorned your advances, you murdered her like the black-hearted beast you are!"

But nobody even so much as suggested that I'd had anything to do with Dolliver's death. So cops are smart, are they? It is to laugh.

I got away with it, didn't I?

I got away clean as soap with the murder that looked like an accident, and you couldn't really call it my fault that they're going to stretch my neck for the accident that looked like a murder!

SUDDEN VIOLENCE

ROBERT PETYO

Myron didn't know who she was. The blonde hair that glistened in the lights as she left the Riverfront Restaurant was all that mattered to him. She was young, maybe twenty-five, and was the kind of woman Myron used to fantasize about. Soft. Full of life. The kind of woman he might fall in love with and marry, so they could move into a nice country house with a big yard, and play with their children.

But Myron had given up those fantasies long ago.

He followed the woman as she circled behind the restaurant toward the parking lot, and in the murkiness between the streetlights along the riverbank and the glowing lamps of the parking lot, he pounced. When he slammed the butcher's knife into her belly she uttered a soft gasp, more of surprise than of horror or pain, and she doubled over as she tried to hold her guts in place. Myron slipped behind her and wrapped his left arm around her shoulders.

He drove his knee into the small of her back and pulled her upright. With the blade he sliced open her throat.

As she crumpled he leapt back, waving his arms to shake off the blood. He hid the knife under his sweatshirt and strode into the darkness beyond the parking lot.

Now, alone on the twisted city streets, Myron was scared. He had lived on these streets for fifteen years ever since he ended a childhood of orphanages and foster homes by running away from the alcoholic couple who tried to save their marriage by focusing their rage on him. He dropped out of life, drank cheap whiskey like water, and tried to survive on the streets. Those streets now terrified him. He wanted to escape the uncertainty of where his next meal would come from, the taunts from hateful people, the hardship of a steam grate as his only warmth on a bitter night, and the danger of sudden violence lurking around the next dark corner.

While he had stalked his victim his mind had been occupied, but now fear quickened his breath and poked his skin. The streets were not safe.

Soon, though, he would escape. There would be no more uncertainties, no more taunts, no more hardships, no more danger.

He had to get rid of the bloody clothes. He had thought there would be a lot of blood, so he had worn a sweatsuit he had found in a garbage can on 82nd Street. The pants were shredded and the sweatshirt stank, but they were enough to shield his regular clothes underneath. However, to be seen in the bloody sweatsuit was too risky. He had to reach his friends at the 13th Precinct, the only people he trusted. Anyone else who might stop him would be an unknown quantity. Anything might happen. There were too many crazy people in this world. Even on the police force. He had heard about what happened to old Mr. Crane, badly beaten by some thugs who found him sleeping under Fulton's Bridge. And one of those thugs had been an off-duty policeman.

Myron shuddered. No, he would not end up like old Mr. Crane.

He put the knife on the ground and tore off the sweatsuit, revealing grubby slacks and a long-sleeved wool sweater with holes in the elbows. He threw the suit into a dumpster behind the Fish House on Morris Avenue. He retrieved the knife and stuck the handle in the band of his pants then pulled his sweater up and over the blade. When he hunched forward as he usually did it was unnoticeable. He hurried to the 13th Precinct.

"Hiya, Myron." The desk sergeant didn't look up from the papers he scribbled on. "What's shakin' tonight?"

"I'm the one you're looking for." Myron's scratchy voice had been scarred by too many cigarettes, and often people made him repeat himself. "The Blade. The one in the papers. The one who's been killing all those women."

He leaned over his papers and peered out from under craggy eyebrows.

"I am," Myron insisted proudly.

Shrugging, he leaned back. "Why don't you sit down?" He gestured toward a row of chairs against the wall. "I'll get one of the detectives to come out to talk to you." Shaking his head he bent to an intercom.

"Thank you," Myron said as he sat and crossed his legs. The 13th Precinct was like home. He liked the soft yellow lights that left the corners shadowy. He liked the thick scent of the deodorizer that never completely covered the stale men's room smell. Though they rarely let him stay long, they were nice to him here. And once in a while he got to spend the night in "The Tank."

"Hi, Myron."

He smiled as he stood. It was Tom Peterson. The knot of his tie hung to his chest and his shirt was wet and wrinkled. "C'mon back. I'll get you a coffee. But you can only stay a little bit." He trudged away.

Ten desks were cramped in the small windowless squadroom. A bulletin board blanketed with papers held on by red pushpins filled one wall. Myron smiled at each detective they passed. Some nodded, some ignored him. Beyond Peterson's desk was the holding cell, "The Tank."

"We're really busy," Peterson said as he collapsed into a chair that groaned under his bulk. "We're working overtime on this Blade thing. The papers are hitting the mayor, the mayor's hitting the captain, and the captain's hitting us."

"That's why I'm here. I want to help you."

Fatigue melted from his face as he straightened. "You saw something?"

"I'm the one you want."

"What?"

"I'm the Blade."

"Oh, Jesus, Myron!"

"I am. I just killed another one tonight."

"This isn't funny, Myron."

"I'm not funny. I killed her behind the Riverfront Restaurant. Less than a hour ago. Somebody musta found the body by now."

He rocked back on the chair. "Who was she?"

"I don't know. A woman with blonde hair."

"And why are you killing blondes, Myron?"

"I don't know. I can't help myself. You have to stop me. You have to lock me away before I kill anyone else."

"Sit down, Myron!"

He stumbled to the side and clambered into the chair beside the metal desk.

"Why are you doing this?"

"I'm trying to help."

"Do you know that I've had four confessions in the last twenty-four hours?"

"You have?"

"Whenever there's a gruesome murder, or worse, a series of murders, everybody and his sister comes out of the woodwork to confess. It's this twisted society of ours. Crazy. We know they're loonies, but we gotta go through the motions. We gotta quiz 'em. I hate it. We gotta waste time with those sickos while the real sicko's still out there. But why you, Myron? Why would a guy who we never picked up for anything worse than vagrancy or drunkenness try to pull a stunt like this? We know you got problems, but are you a real sicko like the rest of the nuts I been talking to?"

"Don't be mad. I didn't—"

"Get outta here!" he shouted. Heads swivelled.

"I'm sorry, Tom. I just want to help." He struggled out of the chair and straightened. "I'm not nuts. The doctors would keep me locked up if I was nuts."

"They do lock you up. But budget cuts put you back on the streets."

"I like the hospital," he whispered.

"Get outta here before I throw you out. I got no time for this."

"No. Please. You gotta lock me up. For the rest of my life."

Peterson cocked his head to one side and rocked in the chair. "Is that what this is about? You want to go to prison?"

"I have to."

"Why?"

Trembling hands found the back of his chair. "I'm tired. And I'm scared. I been living on the streets a long time. It's not safe."

"You think prison's any better?"

"A bed each night. Food. You know what kind of people hang out in the shelters in this city. It's not safe. Phil got mugged the other night. Almost died. Right there in the shelter. At least prisons have guards."

"It doesn't work that way, Myron."

"I can't go on like this. I gotta do something."

"I don't believe this." Peterson wiped the heels of his palms down his face.

"I thought you guys would understand. That's why I came here." He shook his head. "You're nuts."

Head hanging, he turned to leave.

Then he stopped. He had almost forgot.

"Listen," Peterson sighed, his features softening. "How about if we put you in 'The Tank' for the night?"

"Look." Myron struggled to get his sweater up over the blade.

"What are you doing?" Peterson stood. "Jesus!" He jumped a step back, knocking his chair back to the wall. "What is that?"

Myron took the blade by the handle and yanked it from his pants.

All the fatigue of endless hours of drudging spadework hooded Peterson's eyes as he focused on the knife. Slowly he looked at Myron and twisted his lips as if sucking on a sour fruit. "Drop it!" he suddenly shouted.

"What? I—" Myron heard scrambling noises of other detectives moving toward him.

"Drop it, Myron!"

He opened his fist and the blade jumped to the floor, clattering once on the hard linoleum and slapping to its side. Peterson, Myron, and three detectives who had surrounded him stared at the blood-encrusted blade like it was a wounded creature that might lash out at any moment.

"Jesus, Myron! Is that blood?" Peterson was leaning over the desk, his fists digging into the battered blotter as he studied the blade. "Where did you find that knife?"

"I told you. I told you. I killed her."

He looked up at Myron. "You did see something, didn't you?" The eyes widened with anger. "You saw the guy!"

"I told you, I—"

"You shouldn't've touched it." Peterson circled around the desk. "You got your prints—"

"No! No!" Myron screamed.

Peterson reeled back.

Suddenly Myron dropped to a crouch and snatched the blade. As he did, one of the detectives lunged for it but ended up sprawled on the floor.

Myron scrambled back until he banged into another desk. "Stay back!"

"Don't do this, Myron."

The blade swivelled in a semicircle as Myron looked at the tense faces hemming him in. "I already did it." His voice shook with tears. "I killed her. It's what I've been trying to tell you."

"Put the knife down, Myron."

He turned and saw that one of the detectives had drawn his gun.

"I'm not going to hurt you guys," Myron said. "You guys are my friends. That's why I'm here. I'm helping you with your big case. You arrest me and put me in prison."

"Stop it," Peterson said. "You're not a killer."

"Yes, I am. *I'm the Blade!*" His arms spread out like wings.

There was a commotion to the front of the squadroom and Myron turned. "We got another dead blonde," he heard someone shout from the doorway.

He started to turn back toward Peterson when someone crashed into him from the side. There was shouting and screeching as a jumble of limbs and torsos hit the floor. Myron tried to stand, but he was hurt. His head ached where he had crashed into the desk. And his left hand was burning like a hot wire had been slashed across the palm. He tried to look at it but was contorted on the floor. Someone was holding him down. Someone was on top of him, hurting him. For an instant he saw old Mr. Crane's gnarled face, and he tried to break free.

But he wasn't strong enough. . . .

The blade. He still had the blade.

He twisted, trying to slash free.

"Hold him!"

Another weight crashed onto him, forcing him down. He tried to turn. Someone had his wrist. He saw the blade flash in front of his eyes. There was a sudden pain in his arm as his body was twisted again. A fiery volcano seared his gut. His face squished into the cold metal desk. He couldn't breathe.

"I got it!" The blade clattered across the floor. "Shit! Where'd it go?"

"Look at that blood."

"What's going on here?"

"It's all right. We got it under control."

"Then let's hit the streets. We got another dead blonde."

"Where?"

"The parking lot at the Riverfront Restaurant."

Yes! Myron tried to shout but he was out of breath. He struggled to all fours, but his left arm collapsed when he put pressure on his hand, and he hit the floor. Then somebody helped him up.

"Myron, what did you see at the Riverfront?"

"Are you going to lock me up now?" Myron bobbed his head to the side and saw that the squadroom was almost empty. "No. They're out looking for the Blade," he whispered sadly. "I tried to help you guys." He looked at his left hand and saw blood seeping from a gash just under the knuckles. "Lock me up. I'll be safe." The volcano in his gut erupted again and he gasped. He looked down and saw that his sweater was soaked with blood.

"I got an emergency here!" Peterson shouted as he saw the gaping wound. He helped Myron to a chair. "I need a paramedic. I . . ."

But Myron no longer heard him.

SWITCH

GERALD TOLLESFRUD

Nikki looked like a hooker. And she was. It had been one of the first things she told me, saying, "Sure, Mr. Danzer, that's what I do. I ball guys for money, fifty dollars for either way or seventy-five for both." Then she uncrossed her legs, stood, and moved forward to bend over my desk, her tawny hair cascading from her shoulders to cradle her breasts. "But I'm a person, I have feelings, real ones. And friends. And Angie is my friend." She had reached into her purse and produced cash and a folded newspaper clipping and dropped them on my desk.

I leaned forward and picked up the clipping, my eyes on hers. "And I'm a P.I. and I do a pretty good job. I like honest people, people who can hurt like you hurt. And I don't care if you're a hooker or a saint." Then I added, "And it's Joe."

She had smiled grimly, hopefully, and returned to her chair while I read what she had given me. Woman murdered in her own bedroom. Beaten, then strangled with a pair of pantyhose while in other parts of the city people were sleeping or working night jobs or taking in a late movie or making love. No sexual assault. Still wearing a bathrobe over a nightgown. Money and jewels missing. A pried window in the middle-class, brick ranch in a nice neighborhood until the night before last, now changed forever, the house where something terrible had happened.

Nikki described how her roommate Angie, also in the play-for-pay business, had accepted an all-night "date," describing the house, the man; it would be safe because she had played night games there before.

Then she hadn't returned in the morning.

"And you think . . . what?"

She stared at an invisible point in the air, chewing her full lips for a moment. "I don't know, Joe. I only know she didn't come back from there. We take care of each other. Maybe . . . maybe she got caught there by the dude's wife. Maybe there was a fight and he went freako. She . . . I don't know!" I didn't usually take cases like this one. I preferred cleaner stuff. Insurance fraud, missing persons who usually wanted to stay missing, company security consulting. But sometimes the boredom made me restless. Besides, one of my best friends had been an out-call lady before quitting the life and moving west to a clean world.

Don Ching, guy I had carried a badge with at the Mid-North station before I switched to a private ticket, told me there were no promising leads. The husband of the murdered woman, owner of a chemical-processing plant in the burbs west of Chicago, was the first to be scrutinized. Standard procedure. Look at the spouse first. Love or money, the motives in most crimes. But the trifecta—means, motive, opportunity—didn't wash; he had been in St. Louis as one of the speakers at a seminar and had an alibi as solid as the vault at Citibank. He had driven back immediately and, in semi-shock, tears streaming, had identified the brutalized body of his wife.

The hooker's concern for her roommate had brought me here, at a spot down the street from the death house in my car with its heavily tinted windows, a cup of luke-warm coffee in my hand. There had been no activity at the house except for the removal of the yellow crime-scene tape by two blues in a patrol car. Until now.

The garage door moved upward and a white, middle-aged Buick

rolled down the drive, paused in the street while the man inside twisted about to scope all directions, then sped toward Palatine Road. I moved into traffic three cars behind in my plain-vanilla Chevy Beretta. We traveled eastward through Arlington Heights, then hung a left through Northbrook and as far as Deerfield. The Buick swung into a small shopping-center parking lot, slowly followed its edge to the far corner, and pulled close alongside a black car with government plates, drivers' windows aligned. An arm extended with an envelope. The arm from the Buick stretched across minutes later with a thicker package. Deal. Arrangement.

As the cars parted I noted the black car's plate number and kept my tail on the Buick. Less than four blocks away it pulled into a Motel Six and nosed in to room 110 on the ground floor. The man must have some Strange stashed; wife's body barely cold. Interesting. After one knock the drapes shifted slightly and the door opened about a foot as the bereaved husband glanced about quickly, then slipped inside. Minutes later he left. There went my first theory; minutes would hardly be enough.

Four hours. Time enough for the brightness of day to fade into early-evening half-light, the sky turning from red to dull purple in the west. Time enough to slip across the street for a greasy hamburger and an urgently needed kidney drain; the jar in my car was already full of used coffee. Finally, as the legs making up half of my six-four threatened terminal cramping, a slender brunette woman in an orange raincoat and sunglasses not needed in the dimming light emerged and walked quickly to the corner. Fifteen minutes later she left the Yen Ching restaurant with a large, white carry-out sack and squirreled herself back in the room. I'd had plenty of time to place myself outside the restaurant and get a good look at her. Dark hair under a scarf. Slightly long nose. No hose. Dirty Nikes on her feet. Bandage on her left hand. When the bluish, flickering light from the room's TV gave way to darkness I called it a night. I needed to talk to Ching.

The stocky Korean leaned back in his chair, lidded eyes focused on mine. "Joe, you maybe got something, maybe not. Working girl come to you, tell you story. You follow man, go places might be okay, might not." He clasped his hands together, hands rock-hard and calloused from his martial arts work, and turned to look through the dirty blinds of his office at the clouds battling for space in the bright morning sky.

"We check man's business. Not doing so good. Goes downhill like sushi bar in Harlem. Many debts. But man had half million insurance on wife, we find out. Now wife dead." Ching's shoulders rippled and bunched under his immaculate white suit as he leaned forward again, scowling. "Motive but no opportunity. Husband in St. Louis when wife strangled. Maybe buy hit on wife but all is guessing. Then you see deal going down and see other woman. What it mean, Joe? You got something or you write script for Sunday Night Movie?"

"Let's try my scam, Don," I replied slowly, starting to pace the worn carpeting. "And get a man checking cabs to or from the dead woman's address, or close by, that the missing hooker could've used. Keep an eye on the brunette's room. Let's see what happens."

"We get back to lab today, see what's under fingernails of victim. Skin cream, blood, whatever. Also check out black car from plate through DMV. Things shape up we call you, put your party together. Must have solid for assholes at D.A. office. Okay, Joe?"

I nodded and smiled, turned in my visitor's badge at the duty desk downstairs, and went back to Danzer Security to get some work done. Melissa, my partner, was nursing her sick mother back to health and wouldn't return for three more days. The office seemed empty without her and paperwork was stacking up while I danced around the city with whores and dead bodies and sneaky husbands.

Ching called just before five. "Car man met used by coroner office. Coroner on vacation in Canada, not back for another week. Can't find clerk who check out car yesterday. Look like he did a rabbit, clothes gone, medicine cabinet empty. Live with girl who keep him happy, she gone too."

"And the woman in 110?"

"She still there, not go out. Pizza Hut stop by hour ago. Also techs find blood under victim nails type B negative, make me wonder about lady in 110 blood type. Maybe donate blood from hand where bandage is. Maybe she hooker, maybe old friend man's wife not know about. Or . . ."

"Yeah, Don. Maybes. Let's try my little party. Shake him up. Tip his hand if he's dirty. Just keep a net on the motel lady. You know the place we talked about?"

"Oriental mind like steel trap, Joe. Make bullshit call."

I faked my way past the guy's secretary at his plant, lying like a thief to get through. He came on the line hesitantly, guardedly.

"My friend," I began, "we have some business to transact. It involves your late wife and ten large in used twenties and fifties for me for silence. I think we ought to meet."

There was a long silence on the other end of the wire. Heavy breathing. Then, in a low whisper, "Who the hell are you, asshole?"

"I'm the guy with the comfort of anonymity, pal. Also, bills to pay that your contribution will cover. One contribution only for traveling money. I'm leaving town." If I had the scenario wrong my plan would sink into a deep latrine here. "Nassau is nice this time of the year. Was going with my friend Angie, catch some Blackjack and sunshine, but . . . what the hell, there's bimbos there, too. You reading me, amigo?"

More silence, more breathing, then, "Why do you think I need to pay you anything, you sleazy son-of-a-bitch?"

"Because it buys my one-way ticket. Keeps your pal at the coroner's office from rolling over to save his own ass. So you can skate. Keeps the brunettes sorted out, like the one watching soaps at the motel who looks like your dear departed. You follow or am I going too fast for you?"

A long pause. Time for the hard-sell close. "It's cash or twenty to life in the laundry and exercise yard all day and punking on your knees all night. Your choice." The puke bought it. We'd meet at eleven that night at the shelter house of a nearby park. Very dark. Well treed and shrubbed.

I got there early. In case he got there early. I wore the same Kevlar vest that had saved Ching's life several months earlier on the shore of a small lake up north in the black pit of a night when I'd also almost bought the farm. The sounds of a night bird and a chirping chorus of crickets veiled the distant hum of the city while I waited. He came through the trees, not from the blacktop park road where I had parked. A guilty move. He had a plan. One of his hands held a briefcase, the other was thrust into a dark windbreaker. I stepped out from behind the stone support of the open-walled shelter and spoke his name softly.

"You the guy who called?" His voice didn't waver; it was strong, angry.

"You got him. Bring the money? You bring the money, you win. Without it, you lose." My gun was in my hand, held behind me.

He hesitated, standing stock-still, only his head moving about to survey the night's blackness and the trees around us, seeing no one. Then, after he was convinced I was alone, a blackmailer fearing the risks as he did, the gun came out. It came out fast, faster than I'd thought it would, if he'd be playing that game. The sound split the night air, silencing the other sounds with its thunder, and the muzzle-flash shone brightly as I stepped back behind the protective stone.

In the next few seconds the shouted warnings of Ching and the two other men rang out and the man was spotlighted by their lights from behind the stack of picnic tables and the far half-wall of the open building. As they cuffed him and radioed for their car I walked past and said, "Even with the money you lose."

The rest was easy. The body of his wife was really that of Angie, a surrogate victim. The hooker was well-chosen for her resemblance and her willingness to go to his bedroom where the wife waited. The killer was still in room 110 when they went to take her in. A failing business that half a million in insurance money could save. A coroner's assistant whose signature on the death certificate would earn him a year's pay and who would eventually be found. Nice scam. Rough, desperate scam.

I looked up Nikki. I had to give her the bad news about her friend. And the cops would need her for I.D. downtown.

Helluva business to be in.

THE TELL-TALE HEART

Edgar Allan Poe

True!—nervous—very, very dreadfully nervous I had been and am; but why *will* you say that I am mad? The disease had sharpened my senses—not destroyed—not dulled them. Above all was the sense of hearing acute. I heard all things in the heaven and in the earth. I heard many things in hell. How, then, am I mad? Hearken! and observe how healthily—how calmly I can tell you the whole story.

It is impossible to say how first the idea entered my brain; but once conceived, it haunted me day and night. Object there was none. Passion there was none. I loved the old man. He had never wronged me. He had never given me insult. For his gold I had no desire. I think it was his eye! yes, it was this! One of his eyes resembled that of a vulture—a pale blue eye, with a film over it. Whenever it fell upon me, my blood ran cold; and so by degrees—very gradually—I made up my mind to take the life of the old man, and thus rid myself of the eye for ever.

Now this is the point. You fancy me mad. Madmen know nothing. But you should have seen *me*. You should have seen how wisely I proceeded—with what caution—with what foresight—with what dissimulation I went to work! I was never kinder to the old man than during the whole week before I killed him. And every night, about midnight, I turned the latch of his door and opened it—oh, so gently! And then, when I had made an opening sufficient for my head, I put in a dark lantern, all closed, closed, so that no light shone out, and then I thrust in my head. Oh, you would have laughed to see how cunningly I thrust it in! I moved it slowly—very, very slowly, so that I might not disturb the old man's sleep. It took me an hour to place my whole head within the opening so far that I could see him as he lay upon his bed. Ha!—would a madman have been so wise as this? And then, when my head was well in the room, I undid the lantern cautiously—oh, so cautiously—cautiously (for the hinges creaked)—I undid it just so much that a single thin ray fell upon the vulture eye. And this I did for seven long nights—every night just at midnight—but I found the eye always closed; and so it was impossible to do the work; for it was not the old man who vexed me, but his Evil Eye. And every morning, when the day broke, I went boldly into the chamber, and spoke courageously to him, calling him by name in a hearty tone, and inquiring how he had passed the night. So you see he would have been a very profound old man, indeed, to suspect that every night, just at twelve, I looked in upon him while he slept.

Upon the eighth night I was more than usually cautious in opening the door. A watch's minute hand moves more quickly than did mine. Never before that night, had I *felt* the extent of my own powers—of my sagacity. I could scarcely contain my feelings of triumph. To think that there I was, opening the door, little by little, and he not even to dream of my secret deeds or thoughts. I fairly chuckled at the idea; and perhaps he heard me; for he moved on the bed suddenly, as if startled. Now you may think that I drew back—but no. His room was as black as pitch with the thick darkness, (for the shutters were close fastened, through fear of robbers), and so I knew that he could not see the opening of the door, and I kept pushing it on steadily, steadily.

I had my head in, and was about to open the lantern, when my thumb slipped upon the tin fastening, and the old man sprang up in the bed, crying out—"Who's there?"

I kept quite still and said nothing. For a whole hour I did not move a muscle, and in the mean time I did not hear him lie down. He was still sitting up in the bed, listening;—just as I have done, night after night, hearkening to the death watches in the wall.

Presently I heard a slight groan, and I knew it was the groan of mortal terror. It was not a groan of pain or of grief—oh, no!—it was the low stifled sound that arises from the bottom of the soul when overcharged with awe. I knew the sound well. Many a night, just at midnight, when all the world slept, it has welled up from my own bosom, deepening, with its dreadful echo, the terrors that distracted me. I say I knew it well. I knew what the old man felt, and pitied him, although I chuckled at heart. I knew that he had been lying awake ever since the first slight noise, when he had turned in the bed. His fears had been ever since growing upon him. He had been trying to fancy them causeless, but could not. He had been saying to himself—"It is nothing but the wind in the chimney—it is only a mouse crossing the floor," or "it is merely a cricket which has made a single chirp." Yes, he had been trying to comfort himself with these suppositions: but he had found all in vain. *All in vain;* because Death, in approaching him, had stalked with his black shadow before him, and enveloped the victim. And it was the mournful influence of the unperceived shadow that caused him to feel—although he neither saw nor heard—to *feel* the presence of my head within the room.

When I had waited a long time, very patiently, without hearing him lie down, I resolved to open a little—a very, very little crevice in the lantern. So I opened it—you cannot imagine how stealthily, stealthily—until, at length, a single dim ray, like the thread of the spider, shot from out the crevice and fell upon the vulture eye.

It was open—wide, wide open—and I grew furious as I gazed upon it. I saw it with perfect distinctness—all a dull blue, with a hideous veil over it that chilled the very marrow in my bones; but I could see nothing else of the old man's face or person: for I had directed the ray as if by instinct, precisely upon the damned spot.

And now have I not told you that what you mistake for madness is but over acuteness of the senses?—now, I say, there came to my ears a low, dull, quick sound, such as a watch makes when enveloped in cotton. I knew *that* sound well, too. It was the beating of the old man's heart. It increased my fury, as the beating of a drum stimulates the soldier into courage.

But even yet I refrained and kept still. I scarcely breathed. I held the lantern motionless. I tried how steadily I could maintain the ray upon the eye. Meantime the hellish tattoo of the heart increased. It grew quicker and quicker, and louder and louder every instant. The old man's terror *must* have been extreme! It grew louder, I say, louder every moment!—do you mark me well? I have told you that I am nervous: so I am. And now at the dead hour of the night, amid the dreadful silence of that old house, so strange a noise as this excited me to uncontrollable terror. Yet, for some minutes longer I refrained and stood still. But the beating grew louder, louder! I thought the heart must burst. And now a new anxiety seized me—the sound would be heard by a neighbor! The old man's hour had come! With a loud yell, I threw open the lantern and leaped into the room. He shrieked once—once only. In an instant I dragged him to the floor, and pulled the heavy bed over him. I then smiled gaily, to find the deed so far done. But, for many minutes, the heart beat on with a muffled sound. This, however, did not vex me; it would not be heard through the wall. At length it ceased. The old man was dead. I removed the bed and examined the corpse. Yes, he was stone, stone dead. I placed my hand upon the heart and held it there many minutes. There was no pulsation. He was stone dead. His eye would trouble me no more.

If still you think me mad, you will think so no longer when I describe the wise precautions I took for the concealment of the body. The night waned, and I worked hastily, but in silence. First of all I dismembered the corpse. I cut off the head and the arms and the legs.

I then took up three planks from the flooring of the chamber, and deposited all between the scantlings. I then replaced the boards so cleverly, so cunningly, that no human eye—not even *his*—could have detected any thing wrong. There was nothing to wash out—no stain of any kind—no blood-spot whatever. I had been too wary for that. A tub had caught all—ha! ha!

When I had made an end of these labors, it was four o'clock—still dark as midnight. As the bell sounded the hour, there came a knocking at the street door. I went down to open it with a light heart,—for what had I *now* to fear? There entered three men, who introduced themselves, with perfect suavity, as officers of the police. A shriek had been heard by a neighbor during the night; suspicion of foul play had been aroused; information had been lodged at the police office, and they (the officers) had been deputed to search the premises.

I smiled,—for *what* had I to fear? I bade the gentlemen welcome. The shriek, I said, was my own in a dream. The old man, I mentioned, was absent in the country. I took my visitors all over the house. I bade them search—search *well*. I led them, at length, to *his* chamber. I showed them his treasures, secure, undisturbed. In the enthusiasm of my confidence, I brought chairs into the room, and desired them *here* to rest from their fatigues, while I myself, in the wild audacity of my perfect triumph, placed my own seat upon the very spot beneath which reposed the corpse of the victim.

The officers were satisfied. My *manner* had convinced them. I was singularly at ease. They sat, and while I answered cheerily, they chatted of familiar things. But, ere long, I felt myself getting pale and wished them gone. My head ached, and I fancied a ringing in my ears: but still they sat and still chatted. The ringing became more distinct:—it continued and became more distinct: I talked more freely to get rid of the feeling: but it continued and gained definitiveness—until, at length, I found that the noise was *not* within my ears.

No doubt I now grew *very* pale;—but I talked more fluently, and with a heightened voice. Yet the sound increased—and what could I do? It was *a low, dull, quick sound—much such a sound as a watch makes when enveloped in cotton.* I gasped for breath—and yet the officers heard it not. I talked more quickly—more vehemently; but the noise steadily increased. I arose and argued about trifles, in a high key and with violent gesticulations; but the noise steadily increased. Why *would* they not be gone? I paced the floor to and fro with heavy strides, as if excited to fury by the observations of the men—but the noise steadily increased. Oh God! what *could* I do? I foamed—I raved—I swore! I swung the chair upon which I had been sitting, and grated it upon the boards, but the noise arose over all and continually increased. It grew louder—louder—*louder!* And still the men chatted pleasantly, and smiled. Was it possible they heard not? Almighty God!—no, no! They heard!—they suspected!—they *knew!* —they were making a mockery of my horror!—this I thought, and this I think. But anything was better than this agony! Anything was more tolerable than this derision! I could bear those hypocritical

smiles no longer! I felt that I must scream or die!—and now—again!
—hark! louder! louder! louder! *louder!*—

"Villains!" I shrieked, "dissemble no more! I admit the deed!—tear up the planks!—here, here!—it is the beating of his hideous heart!"

TERROR'S NIGHT

I. R. AUSTIN

Hamilton was just rinsing off his supper dishes when the bell on the wall jangled sharply. He counted the rings. Two short, one long; it was his station. In two strides he was across the cabin and had picked up the receiver.

"Tolmie Peak lookout," he said.

"Longmire calling. That you, Hamilton?"

He laughed. "Now who else'd be up here on this forsaken peak?"

"Thought it might be Farrell. He oughta be there."

"He's not coming tonight, is he?"

"Yeah, with your supplies. He picked them up in Carbon River and was heading for Pete's to get the horses. We tried to get him at Pete's. Listen, Hamilton, there's a killer up there—"

"You're telling me," cut in Hamilton. "I've seen him!"

"Tonight?"

"No, but he's roaming these woods since Saturday."

"Who'n the hell—"

"The cat," said Hamilton. "A nice big black mountain cat. I haven't had my face outside the station after dark since I saw him."

"Not the cat, Hamilton. McCloney's up there."

Hamilton let out a low whistle. "When did he get out?"

"When—or how—we don't know. We just know he turned up in Carbon River tonight. Somebody called us. Said McCloney's been there all evening drinking and shooting off his mouth as how he's gunning for Farrell. Then somebody let out that Farrell's over there packing in your supplies tonight, and McCloney lit out faster'n rabbit—carrying a gun."

A cold shiver ran up Hamilton's spine. "What time did Farrell leave?"

"We don't know. Nobody answers at Pete's. Either they're both out loading the horses or maybe Pete's coming up with Farrell."

"McCloney's not the kind to jump two men. One unarmed man is more his game. You think I ought to start down?"

"No, with the cat loose and McCloney skunking around with a rifle, you'd better stick close to the station. We'll try Pete's again."

Hamilton hung the receiver up thoughtfully. He lifted his rifle from the hook where it hung on the wall, propped it carefully against the door. Then he snapped off the light that lit the second story cabin room which served as kitchen and bedroom, and peered out through the glass that completely circled the upper half of the lookout station.

The blackness made him dizzy. He could hardly make out the railing that ran around the outside catwalk. On a bright night he could see a good part of the trail that wound up the rocky climb from Eunice Lake. It was the only trail a horse could take that last mile up, but there were numerous foot trails, dangerous and slippery, but navigable if a man knew the territory. Tonight, when even the stars were hidden behind layers of grey, rolling clouds, a man could cover the whole distance from Eunice on the open switchbacks without the slightest fear of detection until he hit the open space at the top, that two hundred feet of rocky, shale-covered ground. It was on this area that Hamilton concentrated. Dark as it was, he counted on spotting any sign of movement. Ten minutes passed and the night was still quiet.

Hamilton stretched out on his cot. He would have liked to read, but he knew better than to turn the light on. A man outlined in yellow glass would make easy pickings for a rifle. McCloney might be hunting Farrell, but he certainly hadn't forgotten Hamilton's part in his arrest two years ago.

It had been Hamilton who had first stumbled upon the carcass of the buck, shot between the eyes, but it had been Farrell, veteran of the woods and familiar with the mountain terrain, who had been assigned to the job of tracking down the killer. Forty miles of woods and mountains is no place to go looking for a man who shoots between the eyes unless you know every inch of that territory, know where a horse can climb, know which passes are clear of snow, know the destination of each of those winding switchbacks, the tricky mountain streams, know where you'll turn a corner and face a sheer drop, and most important, know the likely haunts of a lone hunter out for illegal game. But it hadn't taken him long to track down McCloney and his cabin, hidden away up almost to the foot of the Edmunds Glacier—the cabin which served as a cache for nearly a hundred skins, dried, tanned and ready to sell in Canada. The three-day trip from the cabin back to Ranger's headquarters must have been tough. No one ever got the whole story. All they knew was that Farrell turned up in Longmire with a bullet still lodged in his right shoulder, grim but still captor.

Hamilton looked at his watch. Nine o'clock. If Farrell had picked up the supplies at the general store, six would have been the latest. Allow an hour to drive to Pete's, a half hour to load. An hour and a half was plenty of time to make the mountain trail of three miles to the lookout. Hamilton was getting fidgety lying there in the dark. Once he thought he heard something. He waited. It was quiet. He thought, *by this time they ought to be at least to Eunice.* He moved across the room and noiselessly slid back the bolt. Cautiously he stepped out onto the catwalk. The night was still.

Suddenly he gripped the railing and listened hard. He heard the echoes. One shot about a mile down, he estimated. It was hard to tell with the echoes still sounding. Why just one shot? Because Farrell wasn't carrying a gun?

It took Hamilton half a second to clear his mind, and another half to spin back into the cabin for his coat, gun, and flashlight. Halfway down the wooden steps he stopped, swung back up and reentered the cabin. He lifted the receiver from its hook and listened. The line was dead. Hamilton's eyes narrowed and his lips were set. McCloney was not only out there shooting down a man in the dark, but he had made sure no help would get through to Longmire by phone. This time Hamilton took the steps three at a time. Rob was itching nervously around in his stall. Hamilton swung his saddle on the big horse and backed him out.

Rob knew the trail down even in pitch darkness. He picked his way warily, stepping over the loose stones and feeling his way close to the inside. Hamilton held his rifle in position with one hand, and with the other hand the flashlight, ready to break the darkness. He knew the horse would sense the cat before he was dangerously near. The light might keep the cat away if it surprised him. The woods were ominously still, as if all the gentler animals had cleared the stage for the black killer. It was only the cat that Hamilton was worried about. McCloney would probably beat it back to Carbon River and head for Canada.

There was a dankness about the woods. It smelled of decaying leaves and dirty snow. Even in late June there were still patches here and there dotting the mountainside with its dingy white. Hamilton sat stiffly, not daring to relax his watch for even a moment. Somewhere along the path or halfway down the side lay a dark, inert figure. He had to spot it. It might be anyplace between here and Eunice Lake.

The cat would smell blood. A wounded man made easy prey. Hamilton shivered at the picture in his mind. He had to find Farrell soon.

Suddenly Rob stopped. He shied to the right, dangerously near space. Hamilton could see nothing. He turned the light on and flashed it into the woods. There was the frightened whinny of another horse, and Rob answered. Then the fast, muffled beats of hoofs on leaves and a horse appeared from the woods. Hamilton recognized the black mare. It was one of Pete's. Not a pack horse, but one of his best riders. She was breathing hard, but came to a stand when he grabbed her reins. Whatever had frightened her wasn't close now, or she wouldn't have stopped running. Probably the shot had set her off. He whipped the reins around in back and they started on.

Half a mile later the mare began to pull. They slowed, and Hamilton swung the light down to the right. It was a sheer drop. The path ahead was clear, and the woods revealed nothing but a hopeless tangle of underbrush. The mare was pulling hard on the reins, so he let her go and swung off Rob. There was something in the woods, but the mare went no farther than the edge. She whinnied softly as Hamilton waded into the brush. Not far in, he saw a flattened piece of ground where something had lain. A trail of broken branches led farther into the woods. Hamilton was jumpy. The forest seemed to be closing in. There was a crashing behind him. He whirled, and the flashlight shattered against a tree.

"Damn mare," he muttered. "This is a hell of a place to be without a light." There was no use looking farther. He turned and began to feel his way back. He hadn't come in far, he estimated, a hundred yards maybe.

He was close to the horses when it happened. His foot came down on something soft. It rolled as he stepped harder. For a moment he stopped breathing and thinking, then he forced himself to reach down. He felt sick as he ran his hand over the body. It seemed to be one piece. The hand was warm.

"Farrell?"

The man moaned.

"Farrell, it's me, Hamilton. Can you talk?" He heard Farrell catch a breath. "Can I lift you? Where did he get you?"

The figure moaned again. The speech was thick.

"I can't hear you, Farrell. Where are you bleeding? I lost my light."

The wounded man was trying to say something. "Bro—broken," he whispered.

Hamilton quickly felt the leg. It seemed all right, but the body was bent at a strange angle from the hip.

"I heard a shot," said Hamilton.

"Ca—cat," the whisper died out and the form was again limp.

"The cat!" breathed Hamilton. Then it hadn't been McCloney shooting. The mare must have thrown Farrell a good thirty yards. *The shot?* he asked himself. *Farrell must have shot at the cat before the mare bolted.*

He had to get him out of there. But how, with a broken hip, he asked himself. What a tumble! It's a wonder his neck wasn't broken. He only hoped the shot had scared the cat to a safe distance. There was certainly no danger in the near vicinity now, or the mare wouldn't have come barging in after him. But Hamilton hadn't forgotten McCloney. He whistled for Rob. The big horse came sidling up and stood still while Hamilton lifted the limp figure onto the saddle.

There was no question of which way to go. Pete's was over two miles as compared to less than a mile back to the lookout, but there was nothing at the station to cope with a broken hip. Pete at least had a car. They had to go on.

Hamilton was nervous on the mare. He didn't like the way she skittered. She was a rider, not a mountain horse, and not used to the smell of wild animal or the tricky trails of the switchbacks. Rob was setting an easy pace, jogging along easily in the dark, his limp cargo rising and falling with the gait. Rob was as surefooted as a mountain goat, but still he took it slow. Minutes seemed like hours. It was only five minutes to Eunice, but to Hamilton it seemed endless till they rounded the last bend and came upon the little lake. It looked like a smooth, flat table in the dark. They skirted only a corner of the open section, but Hamilton didn't breathe until they were again into the woods. With only the cat to worry about, the woods seemed evil, but with the threat of McCloney again, their enfolding darkness seemed like a protecting cloak.

Just exactly when Hamilton became aware of the uneasiness of the horses, he wasn't sure. It was gradual. But now even Rob was acting strangely. Once he stopped and turned his black nose in towards the woods. He sniffed, then as if to warn Hamilton, he turned his head back and whinnied. There was no doubt in Hamilton's mind. The cat was near.

Hamilton raised his rifle, his finger locked over the trigger. The horses were moving, but they snorted noisily. Hamilton kept his eyes glued to the shadowy wall of trees—waiting. His arm was steady, but the blood pounded in his throat.

It happened in a split second. A long form hurtling through the air ahead. Hamilton shot just as Rob screamed and reared. The cat fell back and Rob regained his footing. At first Hamilton thought he'd hit the horse. The cat was crouching now, ready to spring again. Hamilton fired once more. The mare bolted and he grabbed the pommel of the saddle and hung on.

They covered a mile in what seemed a few short minutes. Rob was no longer in sight. *He must be hurt,* thought Hamilton, or he'd never travel at that speed. The mare began to slow after another mile, because the pine needles had turned to rocks and leaves as the path neared the bottom. The great form of Rob was again visible picking his way over the logs on the marshy end of Mowich Lake. The light was on in Pete's cabin, and Hamilton breathed a prayer of relief.

The door swung open as they came into the clearing. Pete stood outlined in the light, squinting at the arrivals. Hamilton tried to call their usual "Hallo," but his throat was too dry. He swung off the mare and came into the arc of light.

"What the hell happened, Hamilton?" asked Pete.

"It's Farrell," he answered. "Help me get him off."

"Farrell! You're out of your mind! Farrell's inside sleeping. We've spent the evening looking for this damn mare and my best saddle." Pete stepped off the porch and grabbed the reins of the big horse, swinging him around into the light. "Your line's dead. Been trying to call all—It's McCloney! Hamilton, you've got McCloney here!"

Hamilton sat down on the steps. He wanted to laugh, but no sound came forth.

Thaxton's Call

Jack Dolphin

Moore jammed his foot down on the accelerator and glanced over at Thaxton studying the map. Thaxton's face remained impassive. Moore wondered what it would take to break through this annoying front. Here they were in a stolen Crown Vicky with the remains of one "Jocko" Menna stashed in the trunk, and Thaxton sat there so cool it was making Moore shiver.

And the way he'd done Menna, with the *garotte*, like a real old-timer. Spooky shit, man.

Moore much preferred the impersonal two in the back of the head, but the idea had been to keep it clean, leave no sign of what had happened. Mr. Costa had been very clear on that point. Jocko was to simply disappear.

And Thaxton never broke a sweat, even when they hauled Menna's 300-pound carcass out to the car and folded it up in the trunk.

"Left at the light," Thaxton said.

Moore took the turn a shade too fast, but Thaxton seemed not to notice.

"Look, we gotta get rid of this car," Moore reminded him.

"No rush," Thaxton replied. "Be a couple hours at least before it hits the hot sheet. Gives us plenty time."

Since his look of exasperation was ignored, Moore turned back to face the road just in time to notice the backed up traffic from a red light. He stood on the brake and the big Ford skidded to a halt, inches from the back of a delivery van. Moore craned his neck, trying to look past the van.

"Damn things shouldn't be allowed on the road," he muttered. "Can't see shit past 'em."

"Relax," said Thaxton without looking up.

The van lumbered forward, then its left blinker flashed. Moore swung the wheel right, tromped on the gas and shot a triumphant grin in Thaxton's direction.

Thaxton glanced up at the road ahead and spoke sharply.

"Watch it!"

Moore returned his attention to the road and hit the brake again. This time he barely avoided a front-end crawl up the kiester of a dawdling Pontiac.

"C'mon, c'mon," he chanted softly. The Pontiac started to gather speed, then abruptly the brake lights flashed. The woman at the wheel looked around, as if searching for an address. Moore's hand darted for the horn button, but Thaxton grabbed his wrist in mid-move.

"Kid, either you cool out or I take the wheel."

"Yeah, well, we wouldn't be doing any driving at all if you'd listened to me in the first place," Moore complained, pulling his hand free. "It'd be done and we'd be back at Rudy's right now, throwin' back cool frosties like big dogs."

"Why would you want to go someplace where a dozen guys, who know you but maybe don't like you, can make up their own version of when you got there and how long you stayed?" Thaxton asked. "Be better to go someplace where nobody knows you and people have better things to do than pay attention to you."

"What are you saying? You don't think the guys at Rudy's would stand up?"

Thaxton looked back at the map. "Bear left here and then up onto the highway."

Moore moved the big car over a lane and shook his head back and forth like he was trying to break free of a depressing thought.

"Look, I don't get it," Moore said. "I say stop, you say go. I say black, you say white. You difficult by nature or what?"

Thaxton glanced at Moore, then began folding the map.

Moore went on. "You still haven't told me why my idea is no good. How come? That's what I keep asking myself. Why don't he make with a reason, I say, and my gut's telling me that it's cause you got no reason, what you got is an attitude."

With that, Moore sat back a little and stretched his arms out in an exaggerated driving posture. He felt good now he'd told the legendary Thaxton to stick it in his ear. This was the guy they whispered about, the goddamn ice king, harder and colder and sharper and meaner than anybody else. Supposedly. And Moore had actually looked forward to working with the guy, figuring he'd learn something. So, he'd volunteered. Volun-fucking-teered! All the other guys in the crew ducking their heads and wishing they were in Hawaii or even in stir or some of them actually wishing they were at home with the wives they hadn't had a civil word with in years. Because Thaxton was supposed to be a very scary cat. But Moore wasn't scared. He was psyched. So, he raised his hand and for what? To end up driving around all day with some relic from the old school with an overdeveloped sense of importance. If there was one thing that really pushed Moore's buttons, it was being shoved off like some dumb kid.

"We're supposed to be working together." Moore snarled. "It ain't like I'm some geek citizen. I been involved in my share of jobs, y'know. I done some stuff'd curl your teeth. *And* I been inside."

Thaxton's turn to shake his head. He was going to have to explain it to the kid. Pain in the ass, but apparently that was the only way they were ever gonna get past this crap. Thaxton wondered whatever happened to the days when guys did what they were told and kept their mouths shut. Now, everybody wanted to know everything. Like in the movies—what's my motivation?

So, Thaxton spoke. "You've been *inside?* Am I supposed to be impressed? Why is it that people constantly confuse failures with experience?"

Moore started to say something, but Thaxton just kept talking, calmly, quietly.

"All that tells me is your judgment isn't sound. You don't think like a pro, you don't act like a pro. You seem to think you're dangerous cause you're tough, but that's not the case. If you are dangerous, it's cause you're stupid."

The kid's shoulders hunched.

Time to lighten up, thought Thaxton. Snap him back then play him out. Thaxton had been doing it so long, it was second nature.

"See, you toss Jocko off the San Pedro docks, two things are gonna happen. First, you're gonna be seen. Too many people down there. And second, old Jocko may go out with the morning fleet, so to speak, but what if he comes floating back at sundown? Not to mention the play it'd get in the papers if he comes back in some fisherman's net—dumped out on the dock with the day's catch."

Moore saw it in his mind and had to stifle a laugh.

"This way's much better. We give him the heave off one of the mountain roads, he rolls down an arroyo—by the time anybody finds him, the coyotes and buzzards have chewed on him so long, they'll bury what's left in a Baggie."

Moore thought about it.

"Okay, but what if somebody sees us out here?"

"So what? They see a couple guys in three-piece suits in a big car, they figure us for big shots headin' to Vegas. Beats gettin' spotted wandering around the waterfront with a rolled up blanket."

Moore wasn't completely convinced but he didn't say so. Instead he peered through the window at a slow-moving Volvo that was taking forever to pass the eighteen-wheeler in the slow lane.

"What the hell are you doing?" he growled in the Volvo's direction. "Looking for a place to pitch a tent?"

Then after a moment he turned to Thaxton. "But outta the state? That just gets us in deeper shit. Interstate transport of a stiff or some damn thing. That's federal."

Thaxton played his ace. "Exactly! Now you got two police forces involved, along with a government agency. So nothing gets done cause they spend all their time withholding evidence from one another and beefing over who gets their picture in the paper. Meanwhile, we're up in Tahoe at one of the last truly great whorehouses in America getting our bellropes pulled. We wait a few weeks, soak up some rays, head back to La-La land and collect on some long green."

Moore's scowl faded and a lazy grin spread across his face. He eased up on the gas a bit and settled back into his king-of-the-road pose again.

"Yeah?"

"Yeah!" Thaxton opened the map again. "This exit then a right."

"Sure." Moore thought about things for a minute. Maybe the old guy had something after all. Then, he said, "What if somebody makes the car?"

"Big deal. Between where we drop Jocko and where we go after, there's a guy in a little garage that's already expecting this Ford. He'll have it wearing a new color and new numbers inside of a couple hours. Meanwhile we head north in a mace that we ditch in any Tahoe parking lot we want. Then we hit a Caddy dealer and grab a new Eldorado, like we just won big at the tables."

Moore was impressed. So, the old guy was actually gonna live up to his rep.

Thaxton glanced at the kid from the corner of his eyes. Too much mouth and that made Thaxton nervous, but maybe he wasn't a total moron. At least he realized the plan was sound once he heard it. Costa had asked him to check the kid out and up till now he hadn't been too impressed. He had, in fact, been toying with the idea of chucking the kid down the same canyon he was gonna use for Menna. Costa knew this was a possibility. It was part of what he used Thaxton for, checking out up-and-coming talent. If you made it past Thaxton, you had the goods. If you didn't, well, there were plenty of guys waiting for an opening in Costa's crew. Either way, it was Thaxton's call.

But Thaxton saw something in the kid that he liked. He definitely had balls; Thaxton couldn't remember the last time anybody's talked to him like this kid had. Still, he had a lot to learn.

"I'll tell you something, kid, you learn to keep a lid on your lip, you could do alright," Thaxton said.

"Well, it's just I like to know what's what, that's all."

"Sure. But what you have to learn is that guys who ask questions make other people nervous. People like a guy who keeps quiet, watches carefully, and learns from what he sees. Tell you what, you stick with me, I'll show you some stuff. Okay?"

Moore struggled to keep the excitement off his face. He could see it now. Thaxton's pal. Thaxton's right arm. This was even better than he'd hoped. People would treat him different, now.

"Okay, Mr. Thaxton. You got it."

"Fine. Now let's change the subject. You a baseball fan?"

He sat back and closed his eyes as the kid started rambling about the Dodgers' chances in the coming season. What the hell, thought Thaxton, I'll see if I can teach him some stuff. And if he really does turn out to be a joker, well, we gotta drive back this way to get home anyhow.

They Tell
No Tales

Francis Chase, Jr.

The wind, bringing light flurries of snow, whistled down through the scrub pines and whined past taut guy-wires of the windmill that turned the battery-charging gadget George Anderson had rigged up for the storage batteries of his radio transmitter.

Outside the cabin door, George paused with an armload of firewood, staring down the mountain trail to where he thought he had seen a movement, but he knew that his eyes must be playing him tricks. This was only Monday and no one ever came up the steep Summit Peak trail except on Fridays when young Jeff Clapham brought his mail and his week's supplies. All that he could see below him in the dusk was the scraping of the trees on the mountain side under the wind and a faint light or two in the village of Coulee, ten miles away.

He sniffed at the wind. "Snow's a-comin'," he said out loud. In the long, lonely years he had spent in the mountains, he had learned to talk to himself until now all his thinking was done aloud. Then he pushed the door open and dumped the wood into the box back of the big iron stove. He didn't mind the cold himself, but it wouldn't do to have the batteries freeze up. "Got time for another load before I talk to Barrow."

Radio was a miracle the old man would never cease wondering at and, like all his other possessions, he used his amateur operator's license sparingly. "Use a good thing too much," he'd say, "and it ain't good for long."

He lived now for that moment each evening when he turned on the power switch and talked with his radio friend, Steve Barrow in Colon, away down in Panama. He'd tell Barrow all about the ore he'd worked that day, the signs he'd struck up in the headwaters of the creek which looked even better than his big strike. And Barrow would tell him about the ships loaded with diamond shell cocoanuts and alligator hunting deep in green jungles where white orchids grew and tall palms waved in the sun-drenched breeze. It was like living two lives—his own and Barrow's, too.

He dropped the last load of firewood into the box and snapped on the switch. When the tubes were warm and humming and the mike gave back a resonant sound to his whistle, he said: "W2X calling Barrow in Colon, W2X calling Barrow in Colon . . ."

Two miles down the trail, Phil Anderson trotted around in a circle and swung his arms in great arcs to keep his blood circulating. The young man wasn't dressed for the cold, and the sharp wind stabbed through his city clothes like ten thousand pinpoints pricking him at once. Nor did it help his temper to know that his uncle, in the cabin above, was probably roasting his shins next to the roaring blaze. The more he thought about this and the colder his hands and feet and ears got, the blacker became the fury in his heart.

"The old goat's got plenty of dough to spend on radios and tubes and such foolishness," he thought bitterly, "but when his own skin —his only living flesh and blood—gets into a scrape where he needs a few dollars to help him out, he turns him down. And him with money a-rotting away in the bank at Coulee!" He shook his fist up at the cabin. The old miser would get his!

In coming from Denver, Phil had cut west at Leadville, avoiding Coulee so that he wouldn't run into anyone who knew him. Then he had doubled back around the foot of Summit Peak and taken the trail four miles out of town. During the afternoon, he had cut a stout cudgel from the branch of a fallen pine tree. When it was dark, he would sneak into the cabin, strike down the old man with a single, telling blow and then disappear without touching a thing— not even the money he knew the old man kept on hand to pay for supplies.

When Jeff Clapham came on Friday with the groceries, he would find the old man dead. They'd figure he'd just fallen over dead, him being so old, and maybe struck his head on the table or floor in falling. Afterwards, they'd call him in Denver and tell him about his uncle and that all his uncle's money was rightfully his, him being the only kin and the old man not being the type to make a will.

It was dark when he crept up to the cabin. Through the window he could see the old man talking and laughing into his mike like a crazy man. He estimated the distance between the door and where the old man sat and noticed that the old man's back was directly towards the door. Phil hefted the club experimentally. Then, he pushed the door open, leaped across the narrow floor and brought the cudgel down on the old man's head with a sickening thud.

George Anderson sat upright in his chair for a long moment. Then he slid lifelessly to the floor and it didn't take a second look for Phil to know that he was now the sole and undisputed heir to the old man's fortune.

He didn't touch a thing. He moved over by the stove and warmed his hands near its redhot surface. As soon as he was thawed out, he would start back to Denver. His eyes fell longingly on the old man's sheepskin coat, but he didn't dare take it. The wind howled gloomily about the cabin, driving the sleet in heavy gusts against the window-panes and over the slanting roof. It was a regular blizzard and the warm crackling of the fire was an invitation to drowse. After all, he had four days. This was only Monday and Clapham didn't come till Friday. . . .

He lay down on the bunk and coolly went over the whole business. Now that he was warm, it was easy to think and he knew it was silly—downright dangerous—to start out in the dead of night in a blizzard. No one ever came up the Summit Peak trail in good weather and it was a cinch no one would come up on a night like this. He'd get a good night's sleep and start out at daybreak. He could hardly keep his eyes open. He mustn't forget to throw the cudgel on the fire before he left in the morning. Then he was dreaming of the horses running at Hialeah Park and himself, standing there at the rail. . . .

Ernie Beale, the marshal of Coulee, snapped his radio onto the shortwave band, lighted his pipe and settled back in bed to listen to the late war news from Europe. He caught the end of the English news broadcast from DJD in Berlin, and when they started talking in German, he twisted the dial, looking for London. That was when the amateur caught his ear.

". . . Listeners in Coulee, Colorado. Please send a doctor to Summit Peak to see George Anderson. When I talked with him a few minutes ago, he suddenly stopped talking. All I heard was a dull thud and then sounds too faint to distinguish. He is an old man and lives alone. Please rush a doctor. This is Steve Barrow in Colon calling listeners in or near Coulee. . . ."

The marshal called Dr. Jordan on the phone and then Jeff Clapham, because Jeff knew the trail like a book. Fifteen minutes later, the trio was pushing its way up the trail with the sleet and the wind driving in their faces.

Phil Anderson was having the strangest dream. He had put all his money on a sure thing in the seventh race at Hialeah and the horse had come in. But as he pushed his tickets across the pari-mutuel window to be cashed, the clerk snapped a pair of handcuffs on his wrists. He was trying to free himself when he awoke covered with perspiration. Still half asleep, he recognized the marshal and Dr. Jordan and Jeff. He knew he was still dreaming because Jeff wasn't due until Friday and the marshal and Dr. Jordan weren't due at all. But the handcuffs were very real, and struggle as he did, he couldn't shake them off.

TILL DEATH DO US PART

DANA MCGUIRE

The gang at the Chesapeake Boat Club thought I was nuts when I said I was going to take Nancy sailing in the bay. The storm was heading our way fast. They said we were crazy to venture out in it.

Crazy I was, all right! Like a fox!

I laughed at the poor dopes. There wasn't a one of the crowd who could handle a sailboat as well as I, and I had my own reasons for taking Nancy on that little trip.

I said to them, "So, all right! Let it blow! My wife and I go sailing every Sunday, don't we?"

I can see Hal Wallis now, camera in hand—he must sleep with

the damn thing—standing on the pier, his face red from arguing with me to change my mind.

"Look, Jim," he was saying. "There's going to be a bad blow."

Hal was a club member on Sundays and a photographer on the *Times* the other seven days of the week. He would have married Nancy himself, three years ago, if I hadn't happened along and swept her off her feet.

I was fresh out of M. I. Tech, easy on the eyes, and big, like I am now. But, Hal—he'll always be a skinny punk with a camera. Sounds as if I don't like him? Well I don't—I never did! If it weren't for Hal Wallis. . . .

But Hal wasn't the reason I took Nancy sailing that Sunday. Not that shutter hound. Nancy's luscious sister, Helen, was the real reason.

Helen was modeling in New York. She was only twenty, but she was a sweet dream. Dress Lana Turner in a shoulder length bob of soft, red-gold hair, poke a dimple in the left side of her face, and there you have a rough draft of Helen Miller. Of course, Nancy didn't know how I felt toward Helen. But then, neither did Helen, for that matter. It was just one of those things.

But Hal was still sounding off about the storm. I said, "So what?" and helped Nancy into the boat. "We aren't going to let a little wind spoil our afternoon, are we, Nancy?"

Nancy laughed and shook her blonde head, which was partly covered by a brightly colored scarf she'd tied under her chin.

"Mama goes where papa goes," she said.

Hal got real pleading. "Look here, Nancy," he said. "Can't you do something with this dope?" Meaning me. "Feel how chilly the air is getting."

"And see how black the clouds are." I laughed, pointing, and jumped into the boat. "Goin' to be a Nor'easter, boy."

But still Hal wasn't satisfied. "Be sensible, Nancy!" he argued.

Nancy laughed and called up to him, "If Jim has his heart set on going, I'd better go along, too. Jim's a big sissy, you know. He's never learned to swim. I might have to rescue him!"

"Okay, you hard headed lugs," Hal gave in, "If you gotta go, you gotta go. But I want a picture for posterity!" He raised his camera and pointed it at Nancy.

"This ought to make headlines," he said loudly.

Nancy laughed and made a face. "Make it a good one, Hal. I want to look pretty on the front page."

"That's right," I added with a show of enthusiasm, and cast off the line. "Wave good-bye to the gang."

Hal caught Nancy just as she waved gaily and said something to me. So I waved and smiled and said something to her. Then I ran up the sail, which caught the wind and billowed out with a flutter, and the boat headed out into the bay.

"Poor Hal," Nancy said loudly from the bow, because the wind was blowing so hard. "He seemed so upset."

"Yeah," I said, seeing a mental picture of the punk and his camera in front of me. "Hal's been upset for three years, now."

Nancy lifted an eyebrow and said, "You've never liked him, have you?"

"Sure I like him," I lied. "Hal's all right. He's a good photographer."

Nancy tilted her head to one side, like she always did when she wanted to be coy and said with a silly giggle, "Why . . . Jim! I do believe you're jealous!"

"Don't be idiotic," I said. She made me so mad with that crack, I wanted to knock her overboard right then and there.

Next thing, she was hollering at me to turn back. I shouted at her to come in to the midship and lend some weight to port. It was raining hard as the devil and the bay was washing in over the gunwales.

I got her to brace her feet to starboard and press down with both elbows on the port gunwale. The wind had ripped the scarf from around her head and her wet hair lay flat and sticky looking across her face. She was scared plenty—and so was I.

Nancy kept begging me to turn back, and finally she cried out, "If it's Hal you're thinking of . . ."

I burst out laughing. "Don't pat yourself on the back." I lit in to her. "It isn't Hal—it's Helen!"

She threw a hand up to her face and cried, "My *sister!*"

I said, "Don't act so dramatic. Didn't you know?" I knew she didn't know, but I wanted to make it sound as if I'd been open about it, all along. It hurt her plenty. Her face took on a hang-dog expression and when she spoke, it was as if she had to drag the words out of her mouth.

"How long has it been going on?"

I said, "Ever since Helen visited us last month."

She asked if Helen loved me, and I said she would—in time.

"She's only a child," Nancy said. She was on her knees, then, holding on to both sides of the rail.

"But how she is growing!" I said, and let the sheet start to slip through my fingers.

Nancy started to spring at me, screaming at me to let Helen alone.

"I'll let her alone!" I shouted, and let go the sheet. The boom swung around and struck her, knocking her into the water. She screamed once, when she fell, and quickly disappeared. I watched aft for her to come up—but she didn't. The boom had knocked her unconscious.

Well, the first act was over, and beautifully done.

Now for Act Two. . . .

Hal Wallis, swinging his camera and looking scared to death, was the first person I saw when I brought the boat in and made her fast alongside the landing.

Hal kept shouting, "Where's Nancy? Where's Nancy?" I thought he was going to jump off the pier into the water.

I put on a blank expression and acted like I was all broken up. I wanted it to look good. I wanted all the blame for Nancy's disappearance.

Somebody in the crowd—I don't remember who—helped me out of the boat. Everybody was talking at once. I started to totter, pretending I was too weak to stand alone. Somebody saw me and put his arm around my waist.

Hal was standing there. I caught a glimpse of his face. It was white as a sheet and he was good and mad. Hal charged at me like a wild bull, shaking me by the shoulders and shouting, "What happened? Where's Nancy?"

I shook my head and said she was gone, surprised as hell at the emotion in my voice.

"I tried to save her," I said, bowing my head and letting my knees buckle, like I was going to collapse.

Somebody caught hold of me and said I was all in and they'd better get me to the club house. I closed my eyes and doubled up and they carried me into the club and laid me out on a lounge. Somebody threw a blanket over me and everybody crowded around. I nearly suffocated. But everything was turning out just the way I wanted it to.

I heard Hal shouting at them to stand back and give me air, so I cracked my eyes open a little and saw him coming through with a glass of brandy in his hand. Hal knelt down beside me and raised my head a bit, touching the glass to my lips.

"Here, drink this," he said.

I groaned and opened my eyes. Time to start my act. Besides, I needed that drink.

I got the brandy down without any trouble at all—naturally. Then I guessed it was about time for me to start explaining things. I'd gotten them all pretty well teed up, by then—especially Hal.

I caught hold of his arm very dramatically with both hands, and sobbed, "Why didn't I listen to you?" The old voice sounded like I was really having a time of it.

I thought Hal was going to cry. "How did it happen?" he asked. I believe he really pitied me.

"The storm struck us broadside," I began, taking my time, because I wanted to keep up the shocked appearance I had managed to display so far. I even panted a little. "Nancy was sitting in the bow. I shouted at her to take over the tiller while I hauled in the sail, and we'd ride out the storm. As she started aft, the wind shifted suddenly. The boom swung around and struck her. She went over the side. I couldn't go after her, I couldn't help her, because I can't swim—you all know that! I threw over the life ring, but it didn't reach her. She was carried away. I saw her disappear." I let the word "disappear" trail off into a broken sob.

After that recital, I relaxed and waited for somebody to say something. There was plenty of talking going on, all right, but I couldn't make out what was being said. So I cracked my eyes open just wide enough to catch their reactions. What a sight!

Everybody had turned away and voices were humming all at once. Hal was on his knees beside me, the empty glass in his hand, staring across the room at something that wasn't there.

I was feeling good. I had committed the perfect crime. Nancy was gone and I was shouldering all of the blame—openly. Even Hal was sympathetic. I gave myself a mental pat on the back.

Then all of a sudden a terrible thought struck me, almost rolling me off the lounge. In my eagerness to let them know how much of a hero I'd been, I had forgotten to get rid of the life ring! The thought of the thing still in the boat, almost paralyzed me. I'd have to get back there and get it, somehow, later on. In the meantime, I prayed that no one had noticed it.

After awhile, Hal drove me home and helped me into bed. He acted pretty decently about it, too. But this time, it was I who was sitting on pins and needles. It had gotten dark outside, and I wanted Hal to leave so I could get back to the boat. Hal made a cup of hot tea and brought it in and set it down on the bed table beside me.

"Anything else you want?" he asked. "Anything I can get you?"

I said no, and thanked him. The only thing he could do for me was leave. I turned my head. Hal was looking at a picture of Nancy, smiling up at him from behind a glass frame on the bed table.

"You know," he said, turning to me suddenly. "I feel damned sorry for you—for her sake."

I smiled like a bosom friend. "Thanks, Hal," I said. "You've been swell."

Hal said, "See you later," turned and walked away.

I allowed Hal plenty of time to get out of the neighborhood, before I got up and started to dress. I'd have to get down to the boat landing—fast. If anyone had seen the life ring in the boat, after my having said I'd thrown it to Nancy while she was struggling in the water, my goose was cooked. It was a fifty-fifty chance, and I had to take it. I told myself that maybe in all the excitement no one had paid any attention to what was in the boat.

The next thing was to get out of the house without being seen. I had to take a chance on that, too; and on the telephone ringing while I was gone, or somebody coming to the door. My car was in front of the house, where Hal had left it, so I decided to go out the back door, come up the driveway, and make a dash for the car. There was no one on the street, and if the neighbors heard me drive off—well, I just had to risk it and think up some sort of an alibi, if they did.

About a quarter of a mile from the club, I slowed the car down and turned off the highway onto an unused side road through the woods. The road came to a dead end facing the bay. At the end of the road, I turned the car around so that I would be all set to scoot out of there after I got back. Then I climbed out and started walking up the beach.

I could hear conversation coming from the club and I guessed the gang was eating, so I wasn't expecting to run across anybody on the landing. On the other hand, the storm that afternoon had turned the air chilly, and the water was still a bit rough.

Keeping well in the shadows, I crept along the beach until I reached the landing. Then I laid down on the sand and listened. I didn't hear anything but the water splashing against the piling, and the pier looked empty. I guessed the coast was clear, so I got up and ducked down to the water's edge.

Taking off my shoes and socks, I started to wade out between the piling under the pier. The boat was bobbing up and down in the water, right where I'd left her. At sight of the little craft, a wave of excitement swept over me. I thought of Nancy, out there in the bay —or, worse still. Suppose she had washed up and was there under the landing with me? My teeth began chattering like a clacker box.

I caught hold of the rail to steady the boat, and waded aft to the tiller. I stretched out my hand and felt the life ring on the after thwart. My fingers trembled like mad as I unfastened it. Then I started to make my way back, stumbling, to the beach. I didn't stop to put on my shoes and socks, but grabbed them up in one hand, while I held on to the ring with the other, and made a beeline back to the car.

Reaching home, I stopped in front of the house, put on my shoes and socks and scooted up the driveway to the back door. I didn't stop until I was safely in the bedroom, where I flopped, panting, into a chair, shaking like a leaf and wet through. But I had the life ring, and no one had seen me.

In a couple of days, I would throw it back into the bay. That would be just the right amount of time it would ordinarily have remained in the water before being washed ashore—from where we were.

I hid the thing inside the mattress on the studio couch in my den, then went to bed.

The next couple of days I spent running to the telephone and answering the door. Friends of Nancy's and mine. Some called; some came around and wept a little; others just sat. They all said the same thing—"You poor guy!" "Tough, Jim!" "If there's anything I can do. . . ." And so on.

Everyone seemed more concerned over me then they were over Nancy—just how I wanted them to feel. But I wished they'd get out of there and leave me alone. I was jumpy as the devil. Of course, everybody attributed that to a natural state of affairs. But the truth was, I was scared—scared plenty. I had killed my wife.

Everywhere I went in the house, I could feel that Nancy was somewhere near. Whenever the floors creaked, or the curtains blew. Whenever there was music, whenever the wind was sighing in the trees.

That afternoon Hal dropped around for a few minutes with a friend of his, Ed Fenton of the homicide squad. But there was nothing unusual in that. Fenton had often been a guest in my house before. Hal and Ed were good friends and often worked together. I went over the whole thing again, for Ed's benefit. But I didn't mind. I guess I'd told the story about that Sunday afternoon a hundred times—since it happened. I knew it by heart now.

We talked about the newspaper's account of Nancy's disappearance. Made the front page, all right, just like Hal said it would—picture and all. I guess my face must have flushed, because Hal called me a poor man and Ed patted me on the back sympathetically trying to cheer me up.

We had a drink and they left. Then I went into the den and took the life ring out of the mattress on the studio couch. After it got dark, I was going to carry it up the beach, a mile or so from the club, and heave it over into the bay. The tide would do the rest, and that would cinch it. Nancy's body would wash ashore, too, I guessed. But I hoped I had gone far enough in the bay for the undertow to carry her body out to sea.

At seven o'clock, the door bell rang. It was Hal. I invited him in, surprised at his sudden return.

"Later," he excused himself. "Get your hat. We're going to the morgue."

The morgue! "Nancy?" I asked in a low, tense voice.

Hal nodded. "Yeah. She washed up late this afternoon. You've got to come down and identify her."

My mouth dried up and I swallowed hard, but I managed to say okay, and went for my hat.

We didn't talk much on the way. But when we reached the morgue and got out of the car, my knees were shaking.

"In here," Hal said.

I had never been inside a morgue before. Everything was white and still as death. Still as death. That was a good one!

Hal led me down a passageway between rows of slabs holding bodies covered in white. I remember the clacking sound our heels made on the bare floor, and how damp and chilly the room was. I remember seeing Ed Fenton and another man I recognized as Doctor Quigley, the city coroner, standing beside one of the slabs at the far end of the room. I knew what was under that white cover. And I wasn't going to like seeing it.

Hal introduced me to Doctor Quigley; and when I turned to speak to Fenton, I was trembling all over. Ed was holding a brown envelope in his hand. Doctor Quigley drew back the cover.

"Is this your wife, Mr. Casslin?"

I swallowed hard. "Yes," I said, and turned away. Nancy wasn't . . . pretty anymore.

Quigley covered her over. I looked at Hal. Ed was handing him the brown envelope. Quigley coughed and began putting on his coat. Hal opened the envelope and took out a couple of pictures, holding one up in front of me so that I could see it.

"Recognize it?" he asked. It was the one he had taken that Sunday afternoon on the landing, just before Nancy and I shoved off. She was waving and smiling.

I swallowed hard, stalling for time. "Yeah," I said, slowly. I'd have to be cagey and not commit myself. "Yeah, I've seen it before. That's the one in the papers."

Hal said, "Good!" and stepped up close to me. He was mad. "Now maybe you'll tell me what you've done with the life ring!"

That was like a slap in the face. "The life ring?" I stammered, trying to pull the words out of my mouth. "I . . . I don't know, Hal," I said weakly.

"You must have gone back to the pier Sunday night and gotten it," Hal said. "It was gone when I got there."

I shook my head. Hal looked like he was going to strike me.

"Jim, you've lied about this all the way through." His voice sounded all chopped up. "You killed her! I don't know why, but you did. I've known it from the beginning, but I've had to wait for . . . this!" He pointed to the bulky thing under the cover.

Doctor Quigley coughed again. You could hear it echo around the room.

"When did you find out?" I asked Hal. I had to know. It was all over, anyway, and in a way, I was glad.

"In the club," Hal said. "When you slipped up about throwing Nancy the life ring." He held the second picture up in front of me.

"This one you won't recognize," he said grimly.

I looked at it. They were helping me out of the boat. My head was bowed.

"See the ring there, on the back seat?" Hal touched the spot with the tip of his index finger.

"Yeah," I said after a time, feeling like all the blood had rushed out of my head. "I see it."

Ed Fenton said, "You'd better come along with me, Casslin."

I nodded. Hal was putting the pictures back into the envelope. He said, "When are you guys going to get smart and stop making mistakes?"

I must have laughed. Anyhow, I wasn't trembling anymore.

"Never, I guess. It's guys like me that keep people like you in jobs!"

THE TIME IS NOW!

DOROTHY DUNN

It was an ordinary cocktail lounge in an ordinary hotel. There was a penthouse, I discovered later, and an odd woman that I discovered right away.

I was sitting at a table near the bar, waiting for Gary Winstock, and anyone who waits for Gary can build up quite an edge. But his lateness was never his fault. You knew that and kept waiting; Gary was worth it. And he always arrived eventually. There was never the feeling that he was going to forget or skip a date. So I could look around and relax, with the sure knowledge that he'd come.

I noticed Sally Porter immediately and my interest was held. I have a bad habit of watching people I've never seen before and trying to place them in a category. It's amazing how much can be learned about strangers just by imagination, observation and plain rude listening.

She came in shortly after I did and made straight for the bar, settling herself on one of the uncomfortable high stools. The bartender knew her as did the waiters and a portly gentleman on the next stool with black, shiny hair. She lived here, I decided.

I checked her clothes, as women do who are curious about each other. Expensive, but rumpled. The grey suit nipped the waist like nothing under a hundred dollars, but it was certainly ready for the cleaner. Not that it matters, I thought. The dark man, or any other man, wouldn't notice the wrinkles. She had a figure that would have glamorized an old flour sack.

After a few minutes, though, I knew she wasn't making any effort to be glamorous. She had something on her mind under that beautiful crown of auburn hair. I gave the hair a flash thought and checked the color off as natural. Then I went back to picking up the shreds of conversation that I could hear when she turned her head to one side toward the dark man she called Benny.

"Honestly, Benny, you've got to fire that piano player. What he does to my song styling is a sin. Surely you know he's doing it on purpose!"

Benny's broad hand dropped to her back and moved in a motion that was more like a massage than a caress.

"Take it easy, kid. I hate to see you like this."

She jerked one shoulder and reached for her highball, draining the glass. Then she sagged a few inches toward the dark man who had kind eyes and a therapeutic hand.

"I wish you'd fire him, Benny. After all, I'm your drawing card. The people come to hear Sally Porter sing. They do come just to hear Sally, don't they?"

"Sure, baby, they used to. And we'll get you back there one of these days."

"But last night! Did you hear what he did to my song last night? I just won't have it!"

Benny drained his glass and signaled for more. He looked tired as he faced her.

"Last night, kid? *You haven't sung for three weeks.* But we'll get you back."

She gave her head an impatient flounce and attacked the new glass with dangerous gusto. That one's going to hit you, Sally, I thought. You're not giving them time—you're trying to drown your anger with fire instead of water.

She and Benny had their heads turned away from me now. They were listening to a story the bartender was telling, and I couldn't hear enough to keep interested.

I ordered my second martini and snuggled down to a few cozy thoughts of my own about Gary Winstock. I wished he would show up soon. The poor dear so often had his plans interrupted. One never knew what the next demand was going to be on the time of Dr. Winstock. But it didn't matter. There was always the moment ahead when he'd come in, flushed and bright-eyed, eager to begin enjoying himself.

When I looked back at the bar, Sally Porter wasn't there. Her coat was draped over the high-backed stool and her red-tipped cigarette was smoldering on the edge of the ashtray. Another highball—the third or fourth—was waiting for her.

Benny ran his hand through his thick, dark hair. He seemed troubled. I wondered if he were married to Sally and worried about her excessive drinking. Probably not. He must be a band leader, interested in her professionally. Sally hadn't sung for three weeks, but, in her alcoholic haze, she thought she had sung just last night. There was something eerie about that.

The bartender was leaning on the bar and I could see his lips, now that Sally wasn't there.

"It's a shame, Benny. A cryin' shame she has to be that nuts about the guy. Goofiest thing I ever heard of!"

"She may come out of it," Benny said.

So that was it. Emotional upheaval, drinking to forget, and another singer left at the starting gate.

She came back then, not weaving, but walking very, very straight. I noticed her eyes and they looked sad, pitifully tortured. Then I remembered something Gary once had told me about marijuana smokers. They lose their sense of time. The few minutes it takes to walk across a room can seem like hours. I wondered if the drug could keep a person from projecting forward into time. Poor Sally seemed to have lost three weeks somewhere.

She was restless, a roaming drinker. She emptied her glass, asked Benny for a nickel and walked over to the phone booth. She came back with the nickel still in her hand. "Not there," she said, and Benny patted her arm solicitously.

The waiter brought me a message from Gary with the next martini. He'd be along in thirty minutes.

That called for a new face. I headed for the powder room on the other side of the lobby. If I didn't get to be a doctor's wife so I could spend the rest of my days waiting for him, it wouldn't be my fault.

She was sitting at the dressing table when I came out of the other room after washing my hands. Sally Porter, whom I knew so much about. She said, "This is a crummy place, isn't it?"

I nodded and straightened the seams of my hose, a little ashamed of having eavesdropped, of having tried to strip away the film and find out what was beneath the surface of a perfect stranger. Even your friends are entitled to their private lives. We were alone in the room. I knew too much about Sally Porter and she knew nothing about me. It wasn't fair.

She fumbled through her purse, then asked me if I had a match. That cut off an easy exit.

Close up, in the light, her face looked ravaged. The planes of beauty were there, and her hair *was* natural, but mental strain had pulled at the skin until it looked patchy. Dark mantles of sleepless nights lay under her miserable eyes. But her lips still smiled and her voice still held spirit. With an easy mind, she'd have been a bundle of fire, unpredictable, and as quick as lightning.

"I'm going to kill that man!" she said, blowing out a hiss of smoke and tossing her shoulders.

I gave a little laugh. Girls in the powder room are often going to "kill that man."

"Don't be too hard on him," I said, gathering up my purse. I turned to leave.

She caught my arm and I felt suddenly trapped. This wasn't going to be nice.

"I mean it. I'm not kidding. I'm going to smoke this cigarette and then I'm going to take the elevator up to the penthouse and kill my husband. I've been planning it all evening. If Rand Porter thinks he can leave me for that blonde witch, he's crazy. I'd kill him before I'd let him go! It's awful to love a man so much! He makes me furious!"

She sank down in the desk chair again and began to cry. She'd had much too much to drink, and I loathed this maudlin stage. I wanted to get out fast, back to my martini and thoughts of Gary.

But she was swaying on the chair and the lighted end of the cigarette was resting on the skirt of the rumpled grey suit. I took it out of her hand and crushed it in the ashtray.

"Rand is leaving me tomorrow," she said in a jerky voice, looking up through tear-soaked lashes. "He left me a note last night saying: 'Forgive me, but this is the only way.' Then he went off and slept somewhere else. I called him this morning at his office and he's coming back tonight to talk to me for the last time. I'm trying to get myself ready to go up."

It served me right, I thought. I'd read lips and strained my ears to find out what made other people tick. Now I was getting the whole sordid mess dumped into my lap by a jealous woman in her cups.

"How about a dash of cold water?" I suggested. "It'll make you feel better."

"It doesn't matter. I know I look terrible, but that doesn't matter, either. I'm going to kill him when I go up! His note said: 'Forgive me, but this is the only way.' I'd rather have him die! Going off with her isn't the only way. I can't forgive him a thing like that. I just can't!"

The look in her eyes, the purpose in her clenched hands, scared the heart out of me. Tragedies happen this way.

"I'll push him," she muttered to the wall. "Just a little push and he'll never leave me. He didn't even have the courage to tell me. He had to write that silly note. It spoiled my singing last night completely."

Last night? I thought. Honey, you haven't sung in three weeks! Out loud, I said, "You've got to get hold of yourself. Things may look a lot better tomorrow."

She stiffened. "There'll never be a tomorrow!"

Then she walked into the inner room and I could hear water running in the basin, and the splash of it on her face. I shuddered, realizing that she had revealed her plan without knowing she had. I've never drawn an alcoholic blank myself, but I know it can happen. She must have started drinking long before I started counting her highballs downstairs.

I left her. It's dangerous to meddle with the problems of strangers. She had friends here. She'd probably go right back to Benny and have another drink. He'd take care of her.

But halfway down the stairs I remembered her eyes. She was getting herself steeled to go up to the penthouse and push her faithless husband off the top of the building. So she had said. The little fool might really do it! I pictured a man leaning on a low balustrade above the city. Smoking and waiting. Hating the last interview with his volatile and jealous wife. I could see her pushing him, without giving any warning.

It was a hideous picture. She might clutch at him as he lost his balance, and go hurtling down with him. Or she might kill herself afterward. She'd said, "There'll never be a tomorrow!"

I couldn't stand it. There were people on the sidewalk to consider. Chances were, Sally was just talking nonsense. But she had put me in the horrible position of knowing too much. If I didn't do anything to prevent a possible tragedy, I'd feel somehow responsible if it happened.

A phone call would let me out. I could do that much and my conscience would be clear. I could tell Mr. Porter that his wife was coming up in a state bordering on frenzy.

I walked over to the desk, to the smiling clerk. I didn't know the room number and hated to do it this way. But I could make it seem casual and still give the alarm.

"Will you ring Rand Porter for me, please."

The smile dropped away from the clerk's lips, leaving them rounded in astonishment.

"I'm sorry if you're a friend of his and don't know about it, madam. But Mr. Porter is dead. He jumped from the top floor of this building just three weeks ago."

To the Point

Hugh B. Cave

It was the maid, Miss Myrtle, who found the body.

Whenever she served salt fish and akee, her two aged employers insisted upon having wild susumber with it. And the only place on the property where susumber grew was the deep gully behind the house.

Miss Myrtle could not understand why the two old men were so fond of what she would have called gully beans. Or for that matter even akee, which was the fruit of a tree and tasted like scrambled eggs. Most Jamaicans liked both, of course, but Mr. Duncan Macdonald was a Scot and Mr. Henry Lawson an American. They had worked together for years, however, on the same big sugar estate. Now they were widowers, retired, who had bought this old mountain house in which to spend their remaining years together.

On discovering the body in the gully, Miss Myrtle ran back with the awful news and found Mr. Lawson idly tossing darts on the veranda. He was a great one for darts. When the two men played skittles they took turns trouncing each other, but no other man in the parish threw a straighter dart than Mr. Lawson.

When she babbled the news, Mr. Lawson sank into a chair and

stared at her as though in a state of shock. "Are you *certain?*" he finally whispered.

Miss Myrtle began to cry.

Henry Lawson pushed himself to his feet and went slowly down the veranda steps, followed by his little black mongrel, Soot. He went to the gully and looked at the body of his friend. Then he trudged the mile and a quarter to the village police station and returned with Corporal Roberts and Constable Quint in their Land Rover. Roberts and Quint examined the body with care.

"Whoever killed Macdonald must have been a very strong person," the corporal said. "It isn't easy to break a man's neck with one's hands. Not even an old man's neck. Are you sure the motive was robbery, Mr. Lawson?"

"He always carried his wallet in his hip pocket," Henry said. "It's not there now, as you can see. He must have come here to pick susumber, thinking Miss Myrtle might forget or wouldn't have the time."

"And someone came along—someone who lives around here and was passing through," the corporal said. "Someone with strong hands. Well, Mr. Lawson, we'll do our best to find him, but it won't be easy. As you can see, he hasn't left a clue."

The corporal and constable carried Duncan Macdonald to the house and departed with a statement, leaving Henry Lawson to sit alone on the veranda. While he thought, his fingers mechanically plucked pigeon-fat seeds from his trouser legs. The wild grass known as pigeon-fat was especially abundant in the gully, and with the autumn rains the plump, sticky seeds clung to anything that brushed against them.

While Henry worked on one leg, his little black dog nibbled at the other, curling her upper lip back as she gently tugged the seeds loose with her teeth. This was not an attempt to be helpful. Like most bush dogs, she liked the taste of them.

When the nibbling at his leg caught Henry's attention, he stopped his own seed-picking to frown at the dog. Thoughtfully, then, he stood up and called to Miss Myrtle that he was going to the village.

It was a Saturday, with enough moonlight to brighten the dirt road and make a flashlight unnecessary. With the black dog at his heels, Henry went straight to the only village shop that had a bar. On Saturday evenings the bar was always crowded with peasant farmers.

The place fell silent as Henry entered. By now the whole village knew of the murder, of course, and the men in the bar must have thought he had come from his house of death to drown his sorrow in Red Stripe or Appleton.

If so, they were mistaken. After a single drink of rum, which he sipped slowly to make it last, Henry spoke to his dog and went through to the skittles room at the rear. There another dozen men stood or sat about, watching a game.

Henry looked on in silence while the jukebox hammered out a Jamaican reggae tune and the little black dog explored the room.

After a while, in deference to Henry's grief, someone turned the jukebox down to a whisper and the talk dribbled to silence.

So unnatural was this kind of quiet on a Saturday night that when the black dog crawled under a stool to nibble at a man's trouser leg, and the man lurched to his feet, the crash of the stool was a thunderclap.

The game stopped.

Every eye in the room turned to the man, the dog, and the overturned stool.

He was a huge man. His name was Belford, and he lived alone because no woman would put up with his brute strength and violent temper. He made his living, it was said, by stealing and selling what honest farmers planted. No man called him friend, and when he savagely kicked the dog away from his leg there were mutterings.

The dog, unhurt, picked herself up and darted to Henry, who had risen from his stool and was gazing without expression at Belford's twisted face.

"Come, Soot," said Henry quietly. "We can go home now."

Henry walked homeward without stopping at the police station. He knew what he knew but was aware, too, that the police would insist on hard evidence. A dog was not evidence. Nor was the lingering smell of pigeon-fat seeds on a man's trouser legs.

Alone on the road, Henry walked slowly and listened for footsteps behind him, but was fairly certain there would be none so soon. After kicking the dog, Belford would not be stupid enough to follow him from the shop and kill him on the road.

It was nine o'clock when Henry reached home, and ten—very late for her—when Miss Myrtle finished serving his evening meal and departed.

Henry sent the black dog with her. The moon had disappeared behind a mass of clouds, and the night was dark as pitch.

Henry blew out the lamps. With the house in total darkness, he went to the far end of the veranda and sat.

It was almost midnight before he heard a sound of heavy breathing in the deep gloom at the foot of the veranda steps.

Henry moved his right hand slightly, then leaned forward a little on his chair and became motionless again.

The old wooden steps creaked. A man-shaped lump of darkness materialized at the end of the veranda, where only night had been before.

In Henry's left hand a flashlight clicked softly. A beam of light fastened on Belford's face.

"So you've come to kill me, too," Henry said. "Because you know I know."

The big man raised a hand, and there was another soft click. Like a snake's tongue, a knife blade flashed out from his enormous fist. No doubt he had expected to find an old man asleep in bed, but the sneer on his face said he liked this even better. As he moved forward on his huge bare feet, his left arm shot out to block any attempt Henry might make to get past him and escape.

Henry stood up. Except for a half dozen darts arrayed on the table beside him, he was unarmed. But he was an accomplished man with darts.

So expert was he, in fact, that when he had thrown only four of the six, he was able to march his whimpering captive to the police station, simply by threatening to use the remaining two darts if he had to.

TURNABOUT

COLBY QUINN

The filling station was only a hundred feet ahead when she felt headlights blooming on the road behind her, turned and saw the car slow down. He might be slowing for the filling station, but maybe not just for that. And she wanted a ride badly.

It would be hell to be stuck on a swamp road at night. Paved highway, but the shoulders were mucky and soft, and from three feet on either side of the road began the swamps, with their slimy water, their thickly sprouting trees dripping with moss, that harsh, incessant croaking of bullfrogs. Ugh!

"Want a ride, sister?"

She looked the gray V-eight sedan over carefully and looked intently at the man's face, which was about all she could see as he leaned over toward the window on her side. He was young, honest-looking; handsome even. He looked all right.

He laughed. "I don't blame you for being careful, getting picked up by a man at night. But you can trust me."

She smiled. "Thanks. I'll take a chance."

He opened the door for her. She settled down beside him, pulling her skirt neatly over her knees.

"We need gas." He pulled in at the filling station. She glanced at the gas gauge, which showed almost empty. But that meant, she knew, still a little gas in the tank. Probably enough for a few miles.

Her companion got out, ordered the single attendant on duty to fill the tank, and departed toward the wash room.

Lois leaned out, glancing nervously around. She asked softly of the gas man: "Are there any cops around here handy?"

The fellow grinned familiarly. "Nope, lady, not one in miles. Don't worry, the law against hitch-hikers doesn't work this time of night. I saw you thumb the ride, but don't worry about me."

"Well . . ." Lois sat back, her heart pounding. "Thanks."

Two hours later they were still traveling together. She could have got away from him before now, if she'd really wanted to. They'd stopped at one more filling station, but he hadn't left the car, and she didn't either. A painful sort of fascination kept her.

He hadn't asked her much. "Where you going, sister?"

"Atlanta." Carefully looking him over as she answered. He didn't seem to be paying much attention to her.

"Long ways off. Well, here's part of your trip." He didn't say how much. She didn't ask.

"Live in Atlanta."

She hesitated. "N-not exactly. My husband just got a job there, and I'm going to join him. He doesn't know I'm on my way."

Instantly she regretted having said that her husband wasn't expecting her. Why, she wasn't sure. If she was in any danger, that wouldn't make any difference. She examined this man again, furtively. You read so much about attacks and murders committed either by hitch-hikers or their benefactors. And certainly she didn't trust this man, despite his looks.

Once she stared intently at a passing motorcycle and he watched her curiously. He said understandingly:

"You don't have to tell me any more than you want to. But I can assure you there aren't any cops along this road tonight."

"I—I was just wondering," she said weakly.

Neither made any more mention of cops, and after another hour, he said matter-of-factly, "I can't drive all night. And there's a place about three miles from here, according to the map, with good tourist cabins. Cheaper than hotels; anyway we don't hit any towns soon, and if we did there wouldn't be a hotel, the size they make towns here. I'll get you a cabin if you want. What do you say?"

Lois drew a deep breath, considering. She was afraid of this man, yet she wanted to stick with him. They'd go on in the morning.

"All right. Thanks."

The young man reported to her, after consulting the proprietor of the cabins:

"They've only one left, but it has two rooms, if that's okay by you."

"All right." Her heart jumped. He'd be right in the next room. A man she'd only met tonight. But she had to take a chance now. She couldn't back out.

Inside her room, Lois set the little suede zipper bag on the one chair and opened it. She drew out closely folded pajamas and then peeled out of her dress. She sat on the edge of the bed and took off her shoes, her stockings, apprehensively watching the curtained doorway. For there was no door between the rooms. Slowly she reached for one shoulder strap of her slip, let it slide down her arm.

It was then that the curtain rustled and her companion stepped casually into the room.

"Pardon me," he said, but his eyes were bright on her thinly clad form, from bare feet to shoulders.

"What do you want?" she asked tensely, one hand going instinctively to her breast.

"Just to say good night." He was still fully dressed. He must have been waiting for her. . . . "And to tell you I'm only going to Mobile. But I'd like to help you get on to where you're going."

Gradually he advanced into the room toward her. Lois stood up and retreated almost to the wall.

"You would?" Her heart was pounding heavily again. And what

surprised her, almost frightened her, was that it wasn't entirely from fear. She was thinking with a hard cool thought that the best thing she could do was stick with this man. Lead him along, until . . .

She had to get along with him now.

She knew he wasn't just big-hearted. And neither was she. Her eyes narrowed as he approached her. "You'd better stay there," she whispered.

He smiled, his eyes still stabbing brightly at her. "I said I wanted to help you."

"You don't need to come any closer to do that."

"I like you, baby. That's why I'm willing to help you." He took another step.

When he took hold of her arm, Lois didn't scream. She couldn't do that . . . but he'd pay for this!

"Let me alone!" she whispered fiercely. But she didn't twist away from him. His arms enclosed her stiff, unyielding figure and pressed her while he kissed her mouth, her face, her throat. Shivers crawled over her skin, and abruptly she began pushing at his chest and face, trying to get away. She knew now she couldn't go through with it, no matter for what advantage.

But she'd let him go too far. He held her, one arm low around her waist. With the other hand he finally captured her two wrists and held them while he kissed her again. He worked her arms down between their bodies and locked them there quickly as he held her tight with both arms.

She moaned, suffering the roughness of his mouth, bruising her lips, parting them. Soft, tender curves were forced savagely against his chest until she could hardly move. When she tried to thresh her legs, he held her back to the wall. . . .

Lois was crying presently, her face in her hands, and he was bending over her, urging:

"Listen, baby, don't take it that way. I like you, see? And I'll help you along."

Fury and humiliation almost choked her, but she managed to lift her face to his and smile. She kissed him, tasting it bitterly. "Thanks." Her eyes still didn't meet his.

He seemed relieved. "That's the way to act. I thought you would."

"Good night."

"Okay, baby. I'll get out."

He did.

As he disappeared through the doorway, she called, "Oh!"

When he reappeared, she was standing close beside the doorway with the water pitcher from the table, poised.

She brought it down with an awkward cross-arm swing that took him across the temple. He stumbled, sank to his knees, clawing blindly with his arms and groaning, and she hit him again, this time squarely on top of the head. He folded with his face against the floor.

"Damn you!" she cursed him in a whisper, bending over him. She felt his pulse. It still beat strongly, so she was not a murderer.

She searched his pockets, found the car keys in a license folder; looked at the license briefly and got to her feet.

Lois smiled as she completed dressing and packed the zipper bag.

Outside, she got into the car, found the handbag in the glove compartment, and made up her face practically in the dark. A minute later she was speeding down the road.

With daylight, she stopped at the first place she could find a phone, called the police in the last large town she had stopped.

"I want to speak to Lieutenant Moore. He's not—Well, I'd like to leave a message. This is Lois Wharton. I reported my car stolen last night, and I want to report I've recovered it. I started out hitchhiking for Atlanta, and I must have got a head start on the thief, because he came along and gave me a ride! What? Oh . . . I was scared of him, and I couldn't get to a phone or find a policeman. So I stayed along with him and finally hit him over the head. If he's still there, you'll find him in a tourist cabin at . . ."

Two Must Die!

Ric Hasse

Apparently Sergeant Jaeger was handling this case. Jaeger is Lieutenant Beauchamp's right hand, especially on burglary cases. You see, I know all about the cops in this town. I make it my business to know.

Beauchamp has charge of all the burglary and armed robbery cases, but he's usually too lazy to get out of that nice padded leather chair he has down at headquarters. He gets the homicide cases, too, but there aren't many killings in this town. A nice, clean town, this. I like it. A nice clean town with dumb cops.

Each case is just like every other one to these cops, and they handle them all with exactly the same worthless routine.

Take these four I was riding with. Sergeant Jaeger was a big man, fat and untidy, and right now he was giving me the silent treatment. He came up to my room with his crew and got me out of bed. He told me they wanted me down at headquarters, and said nothing more. I'd washed, brushed my teeth, and put on my dark brown suit that I wear to work. I didn't want to get my new sharkskin mussed up, in case Jaeger got rough on the way downtown.

They took me down to a squad car, and still none of them made a sound. I didn't say anything either, but inside I was laughing. These guys! Thinking they could get anywhere with these corny tactics.

I glanced at Jaeger's sagging, weather-beaten face. He was looking disinterestedly out of the squad car window, and his only motion was when his fat lips shifted the position of the sodden cigar stub he held between his teeth.

I turned my head to the detective on the other side of me on the back seat. His name was Niblack, and he was slouched down, with his head thrown back and his eyes closed. He looked asleep, but I knew he wasn't.

The driver was just a driver, in a police uniform, but the young man beside me was a new one on me. He was wearing a neat blue suit, and from the alert way he carried his head and the way he stared around him, his eyes bright with interest, I figured him for one of the new rookies recently added to the force.

Bright, ambitious youngsters, these rookies. The police Department gives them six weeks of schooling, as if these cops could teach anyone, then circulates them around through the different squads.

I decided to have a little fun, so I asked, "Why don't you guys find someone else to play games with? I wasn't near the Elite Loan Company last night."

I knew what Sergeant Jaeger would say before he opened his mouth. "How'd you know we wanted you for the Elite Loan job?" he would ask.

Jaeger turned his head toward me and looked as though he were surprised that I was still there. He took the cigar stub out of his mouth and said, "What makes you think we want you for the Elite Loan job?" I was fairly close, anyway.

The rookie saved the day. He twisted his alert head around and snapped, quickly, "How did you know the Elite Loan safe was cracked?" Ah, he had me trapped!

I chuckled. "I saw it in the morning paper."

"How, Sanford?" the rookie demanded.

"My landlady always puts the paper on the chair inside my door." I chuckled again. "I saw it on my way to the bathroom."

The rookie opened his mouth to say something else, but Sergeant Jaeger said, "There was a morning paper in his room, Holt. You should learn to keep your eyes open." The rookie's shoulders drooped.

The squad car pulled into the curb, and Jaeger leaned forward. I looked out. We were in front of a third-rate hotel.

"Look, Jaeger," I demanded. "What is this? What are you trying to pull here? You've no right to take me anywhere but police headquarters."

"Tell it to your lawyer," Jaeger said.

He pushed me out, and the detective, Niblack, took my elbow and guided me into the hotel lobby, with Jaeger and the rookie following behind.

The clerk at the desk looked like he was ready to duck as we paraded across the murky little lobby, past the red cigarette machine and up the dimly lighted stairway. We went up two flights and three doors down a dirty, disinfectant-smelling hallway. A wizened little character carrying a black leather case was coming out of the room.

Lieutenant Beauchamp was standing with his back to the room, his hands clasped behind him.

Jaeger said, "Here he is, Lieutenant," and walked over to a chair and sat down. The rookie closed the door and stood stiffly in front of it. Detective Niblack walked into the bathroom, and I could hear him running himself a drink of water from the faucet. Beauchamp just stood there.

"You can't get away with this kind of stuff, Beauchamp," I said finally. "If anyone in town so much as opens a can of beans that don't belong to him, you guys blame it on me."

Lieutenant Beauchamp turned around slowly. He was thin and hard, a granite slab of a man with deep-set eyes that told you nothing. "That's what you get, Sanford, for being the best cracksman in this part of the country," he said.

"Who, me?" I tried to sound confident, but I was beginning to get nervous. "Why I can't open a jammed window by myself."

Beauchamp made no comment. He walked over to the bed, and I noticed for the first time the long, sheet-covered lump lying on it. Beauchamp said, "Come over here, Sanford."

I wiped a shaking hand across my mouth and went over. I stood on the other side of the bed, and I couldn't take my eyes off that sheet. Beauchamp grabbed a corner of the white cloth and threw it back.

The man was big and young, with coal-black hair. His head was thrown back unnaturally, his mouth hung open, and his bulging eyes stared unseeingly at the ceiling. His shirtfront was a bloody mess.

Beauchamp flipped the sheet back over the body, and said, "Know him, Sanford?"

I shook my head, and Beauchamp nodded a signal to Niblack. The detective went to the door, opened it, and motioned to someone in the hall outside.

A fat little guy in a white shirt, with a black tie, came in. He looked scared.

Beauchamp said, "This the man?" and the little guy in the bow tie looked at me and said, "Yes, sir. That's him."

I recognized him. He was the bartender in a joint a couple of blocks down the street. I had been in the place last night.

"Well, Sanford?" Beauchamp said. "What were you fighting with Hammond about?"

"Who is Hammond?" I asked. I was trying desperately to figure this thing out.

"The guy on the bed, that you don't know," Beauchamp said sarcastically. "This bartender says you were in his joint with Hammond last night."

"Yeah," I said. "Yeah, that's right. I met the guy in there, but I didn't know what his name was. I just called him Nick."

Beauchamp turned to the bartender and asked, "Did he meet Hammond in your bar?"

The fat little man put a hand up to his bow tie and tugged at it nervously. "I wouldn't want to swear to it, sir," he said. "But I think they came in together. At least, the first time I noticed them, they were together."

Beauchamp turned his deep, piercing eyes back to me. "What was the fight about?"

"I don't know what you mean," I struggled. "I didn't fight with the guy."

"Tell it again," Beauchamp told the bartender.

"These two guys were back in the corner booth," the bartender said. "It was maybe a half hour before closing. I heard them scuffling back there, and looked back. They went out of the booth and this guy here was swinging at the Hammond guy. Hammond swung back, and this guy went down on the floor. I grabbed my club from back of the bar and went back there and told them it was closing time and they'd have to leave. They didn't argue with me. They just went on out together. That's all I know, sir."

Beauchamp looked at me with the question written plainly on his face.

I remembered last night all right. I'd been in the back booth and this young fellow sat down across from me and started talking. We were drinking the same brand of beer; I think that's how he picked me to jaw to.

I had a half hour to kill before I went out on this job, so I didn't mind a little company. I discussed the qualities of the different brands of beer with this big black-haired joker, then we switched to baseball, and from that to boxing.

Then this guy, who said his name was Nick, laughed and said, "Boxing! Brother, a man who uses his fists don't stand a chance against anyone who really knows how to fight. Here, look at this."

He pulled a scabbarded knife from under his coat and handed it across the table to me. It was a pretty fancy weapon, fairly short, with a shiny black handle.

"I took this away from a Storm Troop officer," Nick boasted. "I broke his arm when he tried to knife me. Here, let me show you how I did it."

He insisted that I get out of the booth so he could demonstrate, so I did. I made a half-hearted pass at him with the knife, its blade still in the scabbard, and—bam! Nick hit my wrist with the back of one hand, caught my elbow with the other, hooked a heel behind my ankles, and I was sprawling on the floor.

By the time I'd regained my feet, this little fat bartender had puffed his way back, and told us we'd have to get out.

I told it to Beauchamp like that; just the way it happened. One side of Beauchamp's thin lips lifted into a half smile. From Beauchamp, that's the same as having someone else laugh in your face. He walked over to the dresser and fumbled through some papers and cards, then walked back and held a little bit of worn pasteboard up in front of my eyes.

There was a date on it, 3/5/42, and there was a name, NICHOLAS HAMMOND, and the notation, 4-F.

"If you'd just met Hammond," he returned to me, in a tired, matter-of-fact voice, "Why did you come up here with him last night?"

"I didn't come up here," I protested. "I couldn't get rid of the guy, so I walked to the hotel with him. I told him good-night in the lobby, and that's as far as I came."

Beauchamp nodded to Niblack again, and this time the detective brought back a bald-headed man with sleepy eyes.

"Tell it again," Beauchamp told him, and the bald-headed man said, "I've already told it to you twice."

"Just one more time," Lieutenant Beauchamp said patiently.

"Okay," the bald-headed man said. "I'm on the desk downstairs last night. Hammond comes in with this guy here," he nodded in my direction. "They walk across to the stairway, and Hammond starts up first. Then this guy here says, 'What the hell you got to be sore about?'"

Beauchamp prompted, "Then what?"

"Then the switchboard buzzes, and I turn around to answer it. Behind me I hear a noise that sounds to me like somebody gettin' smacked on the kisser. When I look around again, they've both gone on upstairs."

255

"I didn't go upstairs," I said in a voice that sounded too loud, even to me. "I walked across to the stairway with him, because the cigarette machine is there, and I needed some butts."

Beauchamp just looked at me.

"I said good-night to Nick, and he said, 'Nuts to you,' so I said that about getting sore—just kidding him. The noise the desk clerk heard was me pulling the lever on the cigarette machine. Here, look."

I don't know what I expected it to prove, but I dug into my coat pocket and came out with a pack of the mentholated cigarettes I always smoke. Then, too late, I remembered that this wasn't the pack I'd gotten from the machine. I'd taken these from the glove compartment of my car.

The sleepy night clerk looked at the cigarettes in my hand, then raised his eyes to my face. "Mister," he said, "that cigarette machine in the lobby don't carry that brand, and never did."

"Thanks," Beauchamp said softly. "You can go on to bed now."

The night clerk went out, and Beauchamp turned to study my face. "That the same suit you were wearing last night?" he asked, and I nodded dumbly. He was staring at my cuffs, and I looked down at them. There were three brown buttons on the left sleeve, but only two on the right.

Lieutenant Beauchamp shook something from a little manila envelope into the palm of his hand. It was a button.

"Where did you get that," I choked, desperately.

Beauchamp didn't answer me, but from behind me, Sergeant Jaeger's voice said, "It was clenched in Hammond's fist."

"He—he must have pulled it off when he was playing around in the bar."

"Yeah," Jaeger said in a monotone. "And then carried it around in his fist for two hours. He was probably a button collector."

Beauchamp picked up a knife from the dresser, dangling it from a tag tied around the haft. It was a fancy knife, with a round disk at the hilt and a swastika carved on it. Its blade was stained now, and the black, shiny handle was dusty with a fine white powder that made the fingerprints on it stand out clear, even across the room.

"This the knife you were talking about?" Beauchamp asked. "The one you saw outside of this room, but no one else did?"

I didn't say anything. I wanted to scream, but my voice was glued in my throat, strangling me.

"The fingerprints aren't Hammond's," Beauchamp said. "We haven't checked it with yours yet. You want to make any bets?"

I couldn't say anything, so Beauchamp kept talking.

"You fought with him in the bar at eleven-thirty," he said. "And you fought with him on the stairway at midnight. Now, all we want to know, Sanford, is what you did up here between twelve and two-thirty. The coroner says he was alive at twelve-thirty, and probably knocked off somewhere between then and two-thirty. Why don't you be a good boy and tell us all about it."

"At one o'clock I was thirty blocks from here," I blurted desperately. "I was just cutting through the floor to the Elite Loan office. It took me until three-thirty to bypass the alarm system and crack the box there."

Beauchamp smiled his laugh-in-the-face smile again. "You, Sanford? You couldn't open a jammed window without help. Remember? No, Sanford, after all those safe jobs you've been getting away with, we're glad to pin you, all right. But it's not going to be any little five or ten year trip for you. You're going all the way; all the way to the end of the line!"

"I tell you, I pulled the Elite Loan job," I screamed it at him.

Behind me, Sergeant Jaeger said, "We've got the guy who pulled that job, Sanford. A pete man from Chicago. We picked him up a couple of blocks from the Elite Loan. His tools on him and everything. He hasn't admitted it yet, but the boys have him down in the basement at headquarters. He'll confess to it all right."

"I'm the one that pulled that job," I insisted. The blood was pounding in my ears, and I had to make them believe me. "I mailed the stuff I got from the safe. I mailed the gloves I wore, and all my tools. I always have packages all addressed and stamped and ready to mail, before I go on a job. That's why you never get anything on me. I dropped the packages in the mail collection box at Illinois and Thirty-fourth Streets, just four blocks from the Elite Loan.

"They're addressed to J. Fordham at General Delivery, Chicago. I was going to drive to Chicago, pick up the money and mail my tools back to General Delivery here. The packages will prove that I'm the one that pulled that job! I couldn't have killed Hammond!"

I stopped babbling, and stared at them. They were all grouped in front of me now, and they were all grinning. Sergeant Jaeger, Niblack, the rookie, even Lieutenant Beauchamp—all of them grinning at me.

"That'll prove it, all right, Sanford," Beauchamp said.

From behind me, a familiar voice said, "Hey, Lieutenant. I gotta sneeze. Is it all right if I come up for air now?"

I turned around slowly. The body had moved. It was sitting up in the middle of the bed, and there was a big grin under the black hair.

"Hi, Sanford," he said. "You and I will have to have another beer together sometime. Say, about ten years from now. I should be at least a detective sergeant by then, shouldn't I, Lieutenant?"

Lieutenant Beauchamp looked at him and said, "Maybe, rookie, maybe. If you use your head."

Untimely Visitor

John Bender

Twice, while he sat there waiting in the richly appointed cabin, the phone rang, but neither time was it Lona calling.

The first inquiry came from the Naysons, the rich, young Hollywood couple down at the other end of the court: could the major make it for cocktails? Which he could not, of course, considering the possibility of Lona's arrival or call. He didn't dare chance going over for the drink, however much he could have used a bracer or two right then.

The second time the telephone summoned him out of the wing chair by the window, he listened to the chilly voice of the resident manager: would the major be good enough to stop over at the office cabin sometime during the following morning?—the matter of the rent. Probably slipped the major's mind, what?

"Quite," the major said, "quite," more worried now than bored with the wasted evening.

He went back to the wing chair and smoked two cigarettes and, for keeping him waiting, cursed Lona Mainwaring in his recently adopted accent. He stumbled slightly on some of the word formations, particularly when the dropped *g* of current English fashion interfered with the more prevalent Anglo-Saxon terms he employed. But on the whole it was a satisfactory performance for a man who had been no closer to the land of his purported birth than his imagination took him.

Why hadn't she called, at least?

Usually, she was punctual. Like most women who engage in infidelity, the major knew, she had learned she damned well better be if she expected to enjoy the privileges of one life and the favors of another.

But more important to the major, Lona Mainwaring was wealthy. And he had counted on the money.

It was not much, he thought, and this annoyed him further. For a woman of Lona's means, his month's rent of three hundred dollars was nothing. She had told him last week—quite airily, he recalled —not to worry about it, and he had proceeded not to, after a suitable, admirably managed suggestion that he would repay the— ah—loan, you know, directly his next bank draft reached him. He did not, of course, intimate that he had not the least idea of which draft or what bank. Instead, he had dismissed finances from his mind and from Lona's with another admirably managed but by no means reserved suggestion. . . .

The major rose, crushed a cigarette in the tray and paced the luxuriously carpeted cabin. He was a tall man, not thin but finely made, and his attraction to women—of which he was not the least bit unaware—lay in the smoothly silken movements of his well-tended body, the excellent head and shoulder carriage. He could well have been the former English officer he claimed.

Perhaps he had been too careful, too glib in his technique. Perhaps she thought he did not really need the money, though she had advanced him enough. No, he had dropped the hint too often. Lona was not stupid. She was a bored and lovely young matron, but she was not stupid.

It was impossible for him to think that her interest in him had ceased. In that respect, *he* was not stupid.

Her husband? Had that unfortunate lost interest in his money-making long enough to assume the stature of a husband and exert a closer scrutiny on Lona's time and interest? The major hardly thought so. He and Lona had been more than discreet. Their first meeting in the cocktail lounge in town, where Lona waited while George Mainwaring busied himself at a board meeting of his bank, had been the only public association. From that first time, Lona had come here, to the cabin court which she had herself suggested the major take, and both would swear that not a soul knew of their clandestine meetings.

Damn, the major thought, why doesn't she call?

He poked at the logs burning in the fireplace, consoling himself with the thought that she was on her way over here even now, that she had decided to come after all. He imagined the brushing, finger-tip tap on the door, his quickly opening up and her sweeping entrance, the gown a silver flame caressing her lovely body, her dark eyes radiant with excitement. Beneath the mink cloak, her shoulders would be bare, her throat a velvet-smooth column for that exquisite head; and her lips would caress his name briefly before he found them with his own. . . .

He felt warmer, for which he thanked not the fire but his own imagination, and for a little while the glow persisted. But, finally, the room remaining still and empty, his annoyance reimposed itself. He stood above the phone, coiling and uncoiling the wire about his fine hands.

Abruptly he decided; he dialed and waited.

"Mainwaring residence," a woman said.

His keen ear detected the unnatural voice. "Mrs. Mainwaring, please," he told the maid.

"I'm sorry, sir, but she is not receiving any calls. Whom shall I say called?"

"Never mind, thank you."

So she *was* home!

Something was wrong. He felt it with the instinctiveness that had kept him alive professionally for these many years in a career where intuition counted for more than daring. Carefully he put down the phone, his face tight, his head canted to one side. He considered Lona Mainwaring for some moments. She had been a more than pleasant interlude. Fire, cruelty, selfish strength—a girl to stir a man's blood. A companion he might wish to meet under other circumstances. But the circumstances were not that flexible. They were what he had planned them to be, and his critical mind told him that the sooner he got on with this business the better.

With just the faintest trace of regret, he said aloud, "Good-bye, my dear. Good-bye."

He had them in his pocket when he mounted the long flight of stone steps that led to the stately, baronial estate on the city's edge. Going through the formal garden, past the pool, the major tapped the pinseal wallet that bulged his jacket slightly and hoped it did not mar the appearance of an otherwise impeccable cut. He did not carry letters; the collection of papers in his wallet were scrawled notes mostly, and of sufficient legibility to prove their authorship.

Lona Mainwaring, he had observed, was not stupid, and it had taken quite a variety of ingenious suggestions on the major's part to get her to write them. Several notes to tradespeople—directions to leave milk or eggs or butter, instructions to have the major's shirts starched so, his coat sleeves pressed without creases. Lona had suspected nothing when he had asked her to write these notes for him, at one time or another, and probably did not even now suspect their exceptional suggestiveness.

As a blackmailer the major had no affection for letters, with their sometimes incoherent text—though he had one charmingly naive gift note which he had not solicited in the least; it had come with the gold ring Lona had given him and which he wore now. The type of notes he carried, he had learned, effectively suggested not a mere dalliance to a suddenly enlightened husband but a more thorough relationship. A tender love-nest in which the errant lady had concerned herself with the most minute details. . . .

He had no qualms about revealing Lona's other life, nor about the price which would buy his evidence and silence. Five thousand seemed a fair enough sum, to keep the notes out of the hands of several unscrupulous gossip columnists who could do a masterful job of persuasion with this kind of evidence.

Yes, the major thought, pushing the doorbell, five thousand would not bother George Mainwaring too greatly.

"Yes," said the man who opened the door.

The major blinked. "Mr. Mainwaring?" he asked with some surprise. He had expected the maid, or possibly a footman.

"I've dismissed the servants," George Mainwaring said, sensing the hesitancy. He was a tall man in a faded smoking jacket, and old, much older than the major had imagined. The vitality of the man had been sapped beyond belief; his face was gray, lined and weary. He looked almost ill. No wonder Lona had gambled in other fields!

"I've come to see you about your wife."

"Yes, of course." The door swung wide, admitting him. "Come in, sir."

They went through the long hall, past the winding staircase to a main living room, where the older man indicated a chair. From a massive, carved sideboard he produced a decanter of brandy, measured drinks for them both, offered the glass.

"Now," Mainwaring said, his face showing the effect of the liquor. "Now, sir!" He nodded at an open door off to one side which led apparently to a library or den. "Lona is in the other room. Shall I—"

"There's no need to call her." The major smiled. "My—ah—business is with you. Perhaps I should acquaint you with myself," he began, warming to his introductory speech. "I am Major—" He broke off at the look in the other's eyes, the sudden leaping life in them.

"The major!" Mainwaring said. He raised his voice. "Lona, Lona, darling! The major's here! He's come to see you!"

Clutching the major's sleeve he said, "This is a surprise, sir! A most welcome surprise! Come, we must join Lona, by all means!"

Not quite persuaded by this sudden welcome, the major nonetheless allowed himself to be led into the smaller room. He looked for Lona, but did not see her—not at first, at any rate. Not until after a startled moment, when he looked down—

"My Lord!"

She was lying on the rug, her hands claw-like, already constricted, an ugly stain below her chest . . .

"A surprise indeed, sir!" Mainwaring croaked. "I thought you were the police, in answer to my call. But you're not, are you? You're the major. Her major!"

And he brought up the gun. "Good-bye, sir!"

A Valentine from Teacher

Jim Knapp

It was late January and the city was frozen solid. Christmas was long forgotten but spring was still a million miles away. The Rock River lay still and snow-covered as I stared sourly at it from my office window. The distant winter sun diffused by shapeless clouds left the stark downtown landscape dreary and shadowless.

Darlene Anderson came into my office carrying two styrofoam cups of coffee. She handed one to me and sipped from the other as she propped one plump cheek of her bottom on the corner of my desk and said, "Irma's here. She's waiting in my office."

I grunted.

Dangling her high-heeled shoe from her toes Darlene said, "There's no use being a poop about this, you know. You already agreed to talk to her."

"Only as a favor to you," I argued. "It was a weak moment. This just isn't the kind of thing I get involved in. You shouldn't have asked me."

"Fine," she snapped. "Don't see her! Don't put yourself out. Don't do me any favors. I'll tell her to leave." She stood up and silently slammed the cup down on my desk, sloshing coffee across the polished wood.

I grinned and nodded at her crumpled cup. "Woulda been better if that was a ceramic mug. Styrofoam just isn't much good for slamming."

It was her turn to grunt.

Darlene manages the insurance agency for me. She's good at it, and in the five years she's been with me she has never asked a favor nor has she made any unreasonable demands. I began to feel guilty.

"Darlene, I'm sorry. You don't deserve this crap. Brief me again and then bring her in."

Irma Traplin was Darlene's former teacher and a current friend.

She was having some kind of problem with her seventy-nine-year-old father.

"Look, Lee, I'm not asking you to make any commitments. Just listen to what she has to say. If you can help her, fine. If you can't, you can't. But at this point she's just . . . lost."

Christ! What was I getting into. Ineffectual old-maid school teacher that couldn't handle a senile old man. I have little patience with people who are unwilling to tackle their own problems. I know —it's a shortcoming. I should be more tolerant. Lee Skinner, hard-ass.

She was about what I expected. Teacherish. Thick horn-rimmed bifocals magnified myopic brown eyes. A gray wool suit hid the shape of her body, but she appeared trim and she was tall—five eight or nine. Her dark brown hair was piled unfashionably on top of her head. She had to be in her mid- to late forties, but her skin was smooth and tight and the lines in her face served to accent handsome features. She moved with youthful ease, almost athletically. When she spoke she looked straight at me and her voice was husky. "I'm so sorry to trouble you, Mr. Skinner, but Darlene insisted that I talk to you."

"Mrs. Traplin, let me clear the air. Darlene has told me a little about your problem. I'll be more than happy to hear you out, but in all probability I won't be able to help you. You need to understand that I'm not an attorney and I'm not a shrink and I'm not a private detective."

She looked at me, disappointed, beseeching. "Darlene said that you . . . sometimes . . . took shortcuts . . . if you felt an injustice was being done to someone. True?"

"Yeah. True, I guess."

"Why?"

Teachers. The good ones will force you to think and to justify the things you do. Irma Traplin was, no doubt, a good one. I can be a hothead. Sometimes my anger flares like a roman candle. But I don't go off half-cocked. I don't jump into things without knowing where I'll land. At least, not often. So, her question didn't catch me flat-footed. I had pondered the "why" of it many times.

"From time to time, Irma, I see something so outrageously unfair that it incenses me to the point of taking some action to set it right. I'm not looking for money or recognition. Life's been good to me. I try to pay back a little. Besides, I'm intolerant. To me it's like fixing a squeak. I wish I was different."

After she finished telling her story it took a while to sort out, but it boiled down to this: her father was giving away his money—to his cleaning lady.

Her father, George Kincade, had run a very successful restaurant and bar. Kincade's Steak House had been an institution in Rockford for more than thirty years. A place where you got full value for your dollar. Steaks guaranteed tender and drinks with a generous shot of alcohol served in an atmosphere of old wood and brass and leather. It was a rare occasion if George Kincade himself failed to stop at your table and ask about the food and service. When George was ready to retire neither Irma nor her brother, Rolland, were interested in taking over the business. They had seen too much of long hours, frustrations with employees, problems with difficult customers.

George Kincade had been a hard-nosed businessman and a good money manager. With his savings and the money from the sale of the restaurant he retired with more than half a million dollars. He had lived the good life with Goldie, his wife of nearly forty years until she passed away six months ago.

After Goldie died George changed. He would have nothing to do with Irma or her brother or any of his three grandchildren.

"He became infatuated—almost obsessed—with the cleaning lady. He talks of nothing else. I think he wants to marry her. For crying out loud, she's younger than me," Irma said, her voice rising. "I hate it because she's such a loser. She's had three failed marriages. Her kids are obnoxious . . . probably on dope. That's not fair. I don't know that. But she can't even clean well. The house is filthy. And he thinks she's *wonderful*. Mother would die. She'd just die."

I could understand her frustration, but hell, he was, after all, a grown man. "How is his mind? Is he still with it?"

"That's what's so infuriating," she said. "He's just like he's always been but he just can't see this woman for what she is. She's obviously after his money. Mr. Skinner, I love my father, even though he's not a very lovable man. He's usually overbearing and disagreeable. Except for the family, not many people even like him, except for his customers. Why would a forty-year-old woman spend all her time with an odious, seventy-nine-year-old man if she wasn't after his money?" I could think of no reason.

She told me how she had tried to reason with her father to no avail. She had asked George's own friends to talk to him. He paid no attention to what they said. She had talked to his attorney. Unless George could be declared incompetent, there was nothing anyone could do. Being stupid and being incompetent are not the same thing.

"I'm sorry, Irma, but it *is* his life and his money. Shouldn't he be able to spend both the way he wants?"

"I sound like a selfish money grubber don't I? Believe me, I don't really care about the money, Lee. I just don't want her to get it. I would rather it go to the church or the homeless. I keep thinking about Mother. What would she think? After all those years. He's giving Mother's personal things to that woman. Oh, what's the use. I'm sorry I took up your time. It was kind of you to listen."

Lonely old men and their cleaning ladies. It's not all that unusual. A guy's wife dies and for the first time in forty years the horny old fart is free to get back in the game. Only problem is, the field is pretty narrow . . . except for the women with dollar signs in their eyes. The desperate. The lonely. It was disgusting and it was sad and it was nothing I wanted to get involved in.

As much as I didn't want to be involved, there was a pain in her eyes that I couldn't ignore. "Irma, I sympathize with your situation. I really do. But I don't know what you expect me to do about it. You don't expect me to beat up or bump off the cleaning lady, do you?"

"Of course not!" she said, obviously shocked. "I don't know what I expected. Maybe I'm wrong about the woman. I can't bring myself to talk to her and Rolland refuses. Oh, I don't know, I shouldn't have come here."

I wanted to tell her that I was sorry that I couldn't help. In fact I was preparing to do just that when I caught sight of Darleen's hopeful face peering through the open door from her office. I heard myself say instead, "Maybe I can poke around a little. See what happens."

Irma told me that Lilly Stivitch worked mornings at Perrine's Diner and had a few cleaning jobs in the afternoons. It was a place to start.

Perrine's was just off Main Street on the south edge of town, only a few blocks from George Kincade's home of thirty years. The area had deteriorated over the years, but George had stubbornly refused to let his home fall to the level of its neighbors.

It was almost one-thirty the next day when I parked my Cherokee in the snow-packed lot next to the diner. A beefy woman of about sixty was behind the counter. There were a dozen stools along the counter. A narrow aisle separated the stools from a row of booths along the front looking out on the street.

A grizzled guy, somewhere between fifty and five hundred, wearing a red-checked flannel shirt and bib overalls, sat at the counter. He looked settled in. His coat was folded on the stool next to him. On the counter in front of him was coffee, cigarettes, lighter, and an ashtray overflowing with at least a half-pack of butts. I picked a stool two slots away from him.

"Sign says breakfast anytime," I said. "What's good?"

"Everything's good, handsome," said the hefty woman.

"Hey, not often anybody calls me that," I said with my most winning smile, hoping to set her up for some talk.

"Yeah. Well, don't let it go to your head. All my paying customers are handsome to me. Even old Leo there." She nodded at Bib Overalls. "You can see my standards aren't all that high." She wiped the counter in front of me and asked, "What'll it be?"

"Ham and eggs. Eggs up and runny. Black coffee."

While she was working the grill I said to her back, "I was hoping to catch Lilly Stivitch. Understand she works here?"

"Yeah."

"She around?"

"Works mornings."

I knew that, but it's all just part of "poking around."

Then old Leo dealt himself in. "Gertie here, she don't talk much about her help. Real close-mouthed, Gertie is."

"Don't need to talk much with you around Leo. You talk enough for about four people. Just never say nuthin'."

Turned out she was right about that. "Why are you looking for Lilly?" Leo asked, lighting a fresh Marlboro from the butt of his last one. "You lookin' for a crumby waitress or a crumby cleaning woman?" He started laughing at his own joke but the laughter deteriorated into a coughing spasm. He stared accusingly at the cancer stick in his yellowed fingers, then shrugged.

"Actually, I *was* looking for a cleaning lady," I improvised. "Mine quit and I heard about Lilly and thought I would look her up."

Leo had stopped hacking and said, "Well, you're in luck. She ain't here. I hear she's a terrible housekeeper. A real loser, she is."

Gertie put my order in front of me and said, "Look who's talking."

" 'Sides," Leo continued as if she hadn't spoken, "Lilly says she ain't gonna be cleaning nothing much longer. She's got some dumb old shit on the line and she's gonna marry a half a million bucks, she is. She says she don't care how disgustin' it is to have him grabbin' at her; it still ain't as bad as scrubbin' toilets."

"You talk too much," Gertie muttered at him.

"Maybe so," Leo said, "but I always tell the truth, me and ol' honest Abe share that. We even have the same birthday, we do. Did you know that, Gertie?"

Gertie grunted but didn't look up.

The breakfast was good. Gertie had made gravy from ham or bacon drippings and served it over a mound of crispy fried potatoes along with the ham and eggs. Heart attack on a plate.

As I was mopping up the last of the yoke with a piece of toast I said to Gertie, "You're a great cook. You interested in a job?" Since I wasn't actually looking for a cleaning lady I don't know what I would have done if she said yes.

"Hell, the truth be told, I'm not interested in working at all. But the last thing I want to do is clean somebody else's house."

If I was looking for the honest intentions and feelings of Lilly Stivitch I had found what I was looking for. She was a gold digger and the old man was a fool. It wasn't what Irma Traplin wanted to hear but that was the bald truth of it. Unfortunately, there will always be fools and there will always be gold diggers and there wasn't a hell of a lot I could do about either. I crunched back across the hard-packed snow in the parking lot following puffs of my breath and headed back to the office.

I had nearly forgotten the whole incident when a few weeks later on an icy Saturday afternoon the phone rang. It was Valentine's Day. I had a fire going in the fireplace and a kettle of hunters' stew simmered over the open flames. A bottle of Gallo Hearty Burgundy waited on the counter next to a loaf of sourdough bread and I was set to settle in for the evening with the latest Clancy novel and a very mellow blues tape. Clancy writes good books, but he's a poor substitute for a cuddly valentine of your own. One makes do the best one can.

The phone call interrupted my daily workout. I was in the middle of the third set of bench presses in a bedroom converted to an exercise gym. Sweat was flowing freely and I was looking forward to guilt-free eating and drinking.

It was Darleen. "Irma Traplin has been arrested and charged with murder. Somebody killed Lilly Stivitch and they think it was Irma."

"Was it?" I asked.

"Not funny. She needs your help."

Darleen was waiting in the lobby of the Public Safety Building when I pushed through the door. Irma was being held without bond, and the police wouldn't let us talk to her, but we learned why she had been arrested. Sometime between seven and nine P.M. on

Friday evening someone had entered Lilly Stivitch's apartment and fired three bullets into her chest. There was a rather amateurish attempt of trashing the apartment to make it look like a robbery. However, since there were no signs of forced entry nor of a struggle, the police said it was likely that Lilly had known the killer and admitted him or her to the apartment. The only other possibility was that party or parties unknown had knocked on the door and forced their way in at gun point with the motive of robbery. But, since Lilly was a part-time waitress, part-time cleaning lady, it was unlikely that she would be a target for armed robbery. She lived in a modest, if not downright dingy, apartment in a deteriorating building in an unsafe and undesirable part of the city. Not a prime candidate for money or anything fencible.

George Kincade, distraught over Lilly's death, learned that Irma had been talking to his friends, and his attorney, and anyone else who would listen, trying to stop the old man from marrying Lilly. The police interviewed everyone involved and were able to put together a pretty good circumstantial case. They even managed to find someone that swore Irma had tearfully said, after consuming a couple of glasses of wine, that she wished Lilly Stivitch was dead. Irma remembered the conversation and claimed that she had said she wished Lilly had never been born. Unfortunately, Irma's only alibi at the time of death was her sworn statement that she was at home grading papers.

It was almost ten o'clock when I got home, too late to reheat the refrigerated stew. The coals in the fireplace were red-edged ashes. I carried a can of Coors to the patio doors and drank it as I looked into the winter night. City lights cut through the darkness. The wind blew dusty swirls of snow across the frozen surface of the river. I pitched the empty beer can into the wastebasket and went to bed.

Because of Darleen's faith in her former teacher, I wished that there was something I could do to help. But what could I do? Round up fifteen or twenty witnesses to swear that they hadn't seen Irma in Lilly's decaying neighborhood? They could even testify under oath that they didn't see Irma murder Lilly Stivitch. How do you prove something didn't happen?

They held Irma for three days and ended up releasing her for lack of evidence. The murder weapon could not be found. There were no unidentified fingerprints anywhere in the apartment. Not one witness could be found that had seen Irma or anyone else in the neighborhood that night.

Though there wasn't enough evidence to bring Irma to trial, there was enough supposition to drive away many of her friends. Her father, convinced of Irma's guilt, would have absolutely nothing to do with her. There were even rumors that her teaching contract would not be renewed the next year. Irma's reputation was worth about as much as monkey bars at an old-folks home. The case stayed on the books as "unsolved," though little effort was made to solve it since the police were convinced of Irma's guilt.

The old man had found a new cleaning woman that "could clean *and* was one hell of a cook" and it appeared his obsession was taking a new direction. Irma was considering moving to California. To escape. Forget.

That's the way it would have ended, I guess, if I hadn't got a hankering for ham and eggs and some of Gertie's special gravy over fried potatoes. It had warmed up and the snow in the gravel parking lot had turned to mush. I pushed my way into the old diner and claimed my same stool. Leo was not, however, in the same spot. He was behind the counter frying eggs. A cigarette dangled from his lips. Looking at Leo killed my appetite. "Where's Gertie?" I asked.

He turned and studied me for a moment before recognition struck. "Ham and eggs. Eggs up and runny. Right?" The grin in his weatherbeaten face revealed crooked yellow teeth. "I never forget a face, I don't."

"Right. But today, just coffee." As he filled my cup I asked, "Where's Gertie? Thought she might have found a cleaning woman for me."

"You're lookin' at the new proprietor," Leo said, waving a spatula in one hand and a Marlboro in the other. Ashes dropped onto the grill and melted into the grease. A new twist on Cajun blackened? "Bought out ol' Gertie, I did."

"Congratulations," I said, wondering how long he could keep the place going.

"Yep. Paid one dollar for the joint, lock, stock, and barrel. Kind of a birthday present, it was. Ol' Gertie walks right up to me on my birthday and says she wants to get out of the business. Has another deal workin' and before long she'll be in tall clover. One damn dollar! Opportunity only knocks once, you know, and I for damn sure had figured it missed me altogether until this happened."

In spite of his dirty overalls and craggy, grizzled face and disgusting teeth, I had to like the guy. But I didn't have to eat his food. I left.

I was almost asleep, somewhere in that drifting, no-man's land between sleep and consciousness, thinking about missed meals of hunters' stew and fried potatoes and gravy, when it hit me. Suddenly I knew who had killed Lilly Stivitch. And why. And it wasn't Irma Traplin.

Lilly Stivitch had been murdered on February thirteenth, the day before Valentine's Day. The day before that, Leo's and Abraham Lincoln's birthday, February twelfth, Gertie had signed the diner over to Leo. Like maybe she wouldn't need it anymore. Like maybe she knew Lilly Stivitch was going to die and Lilly's cleaning job with the pot of gold at the end would be available. If Gertie wasn't George Kincade's new cleaning woman I would eat one of Leo's personally cooked breakfasts.

The next day was cold and clear. Some snow had melted, revealing patches of ice on the river's surface. Irma confirmed that her father's new cleaning woman was named Gertrude. Gertie was apparently upgrading her image.

But, what good was this knowledge? There were no witnesses to testify that they saw Gertie, or anyone else, in the neighborhood that night. There was still no physical evidence. It would be no easier to prove that Gertie killed Lilly than it would to prove that Irma hadn't. If I told the police of my suspicions it was doubtful that they would do anything. I had seen nothing. I knew nothing. I was merely speculating, and it didn't make much difference how sure I was of my theory, the police had to have hard evidence to make an arrest, or even obtain a search warrant for that matter.

One thing worked in my favor, however. I wasn't restricted by the law like the police were. I didn't have to say "Captain May I?" before making a move like the police did. I didn't have to give the criminal more rights than the victim. If I could find a way to expose her, legal or illegal, I would do it.

I considered the possibilities. The only thing that would definitely tie her to the murder was the gun that killed Lilly. If she still had the gun. And if I could find it. And if I could figure a way to point the police in the right direction. A bagful of ifs.

If she still had the gun I knew I could figure out some way to make sure the police would find it and do a ballistics match against the bullet that killed Lilly Stivitch. If she didn't still have it there were other possibilities.

When there are too many variables the process of logic calls for you to make an assumption and then proceed to eliminate the possibilities. Best to assume she still had the gun. If that failed, go to plan two.

I checked my watch. Twelve thirty-five A.M. No time like the present to get started. I pulled on jeans, a navy pea coat, navy watch cap, and waterproof Timberline leather boots. I stuck a cellular phone in the coat pocket and a small crow bar in my belt and drove to Gertie's neighborhood and parked several blocks from her home.

Standing next to a large pine in her front yard I punched her number into the phone. I was close enough to the house to hear it ringing inside. After a half dozen rings a light came on. Then a groggy voice said, "Hello." The message of that one word was more like "This damn well better be good."

"I don't want to alarm you," I said, "but this is your neighbor from across the street and I thought I saw a prowler in your yard." Leaving the line open so she couldn't call out I stuck the phone back in my pocket and went to the rear of the house and started prying on a window with the crow bar, making as much noise as I could and hoping I wouldn't really wake up a neighbor.

The light in that room came on and I ducked below the window just as a bullet exploded through the glass, showering me with fragments. I retreated to a tree twenty feet from the house and dialed 911. "Somebody's firing shots from a home at 505 Federal Street. When you check it out, I suggest you do a ballistics comparison with the bullet that killed Lilly Stivitch." I broke the connection and just to keep the excitement high I threw a hard-packed snowball through the next-door neighbor's window. As I ran back to my car the icy wind cut through my clothing, reminding me how good it felt to be alive.

The winter moon bathed the bedroom in silvery light. I slept like a baby. A happy, peaceful baby.

It was Saturday again, a few days after Gertie was arrested for the murder of Lilly Stivitch, and it was still cold. I had put away a pot of coffee and finished reading the newspaper and the only thing on my agenda for the day was a hard workout and a long run. Since I wasn't expecting company the doorbell startled me.

It took a few ticks to figure out who it was. Her hair was down and flowed below her shoulders. The glasses were gone and the face that had been so serious before was now smiling. She looked anything but "teacherish." She had on a long cloth coat but shapely purple spandex legs showed below its hem.

"I don't know how you did it," she said, huskily, as she shrugged out of the coat and set a shopping bag on the kitchen table, "and I don't even want to know. All I care about is that it's over. Dad is speaking to me and while he isn't admitting anything it's pretty obvious he feels a little foolish about his recent behavior." She laughed. "The news stories finally made him face the truth. I'm trying not to scream 'I told you so,' but it's hard."

Her perfect body looked like it had been sculpted from purple marble. "I'm here to thank you," she said, pulling a bottle of dark red wine, a chunk of cheese, and a loaf of French bread from the shopping bag. "Darleen told me you wouldn't take any money." She moved close and wrapped firm purple arms around my neck. "I thought maybe we could think of some other way for me to repay you."

I didn't get in my long run that day. But that was okay. The workout I got was harder than the one I had planned. Later that evening I took the stew out of the freezer and heated it in the fireplace. Valentine's Day came in March that year and I never even thought about Tom Clancy.

THE WHITE SQUARE

EVERETT M. WEBBER

It was a raw, cloudy day—coming dark, and Dirk expected to find his uncle cooking supper, or eating it. But the little windows of the house showed no light as he stopped the buckboard. Then Dirk saw his Uncle Mac down below the corral working on the earthen dam of his pond. He had evidently heard the buckboard for he straightened slowly, one hand at the small of his back, the other still holding the shovel.

Dirk's heart beat a little fast with a mixture of apprehension, excitement and something a little like fear. There was also a tinge of shame mingled with his feeling at being here begging again. But none of that must show.

He waved at the old man, clambered down and swiftly unhooked the horse. Easing the collar a bit and roughing the wet hair under it, he tied the animal to the porch post. And then, seeing that his uncle wasn't coming up to greet him, he walked down toward the pond, careful to close the gates behind him. Bluffly, above the croaking of frogs and the blatting of sheep, he exclaimed, "Hello, there, Uncle Mac! You look younger every time I see you!"

And, as he clambered the grassed-over dam and shook hands with the old man, he saw that his uncle knew he was here again for money.

Sweating, old Mac said, "Well, I don't feel any younger, lad. . . . Guess I've done about enough here. Just fixing the dam a little against the rain. We'll go to the house. Throw your horse in the corral and feed 'im an' we'll eat supper. You're in money trouble again?"

The words graveled Dirk, but they gave him a sort of relief, too, at having the reason for his trip brought up. "Well, not exactly trouble," he said, "but I am needing another loan."

Old Mac grunted dourly, squinting at the heavens as the wind became suddenly dank. And then, before they reached the house, a fine drizzle set in.

"You'll bear in mind," he stated as Dirk presently untied the horse to lead him to the corral, "you haven't paid the other four loans. And like I've told you over and over, I can't let you have any more till I'm paid. But you're welcome to stay the night, or longer."

It was only gradually, after supper, that Dirk brought the matter up again. It was sprinkling rather steadily, now, and as old Mac opened the door to let the extra heat from the fire go outside, the buckboard glistened in the lamp light, and the bare earth of the yard shined wetly. A night hawk zipped past the door and away.

"The fact is," Dirk said as casually as he could, "I've had tough luck at cards, and I promised to pay up in a hurry. Five hundred would hold them off."

Old Mac turned from the doorway and stared at Dirk who still sat at the table, and Dirk saw that his little eyes were troubled as he shook his grizzling head.

Dirk swallowed the black anger that rose within him, and then the entire story was tumbling from his lips and he couldn't hold it back: How he had had to beg like a dog to get a few days' grace to drive the sixty miles over here, across wild prairie, to try to raise a little cash. How, if he didn't get it, he wouldn't dare go back for fear of his very life, and how the men he owed would hog up his land, the well he had dug, and the few cows he still had left.

But still his uncle shook his head. "I can't do it, Dirk. I'm an old man. I can't work forever."

"You could live with me. You could sell out and get away from this God-forsaken place."

"And come to a place where someone else is owner, a place you'll gamble away any day? And this isn't so God-forsaken. It's only four miles from town. I've got friends. It's not that I want to hurt your feelings, nor—"

"But like you say," Dirk reasoned desperately, "all you've got will be mine some day."

"I couldn't live in another man's house, and that's what'll happen if I keep giving—"

With a sudden angry oath, Dirk came out of his chair, jerking at the revolver in the waistband under his coat. The old man stood paralyzed a second, there by the door, and in that second Dirk was upon him, firing almost in his face. Old Mac tottered to a chair, collapsed across the back of it, and then sprawled to the floor with it half upon him. He didn't move after that, but a few drops of blood trickled down onto the wide, clean boards.

Dirk stood there, staring down at him, his heart thundering furiously. And then, half aloud, he panted, "The pennypinching old varmint—it serves him right."

He put the gun back into his waistband and stood listening, lest there might have been someone who heard, or saw, the shooting. When there seemed to be no one, he quickly closed the door. The shades were already drawn. At the fireplace, he worked out the right hand corner stone of the hearth and thrust his hand into the hole.

A short, sharp cry burst from his lips. It was empty. Frantically he leaned low to peer into it, and then he brought up a slip of paper. The red printing at the top said, "Bank of Boiling Springs." And under that: "Deposit Receipt." Dirk stared with blurring eyes at the firm, pale writing under that: "Silver, $670. Currency, $15,665. Gold, $1,445." It added up to $17,780.

Dirk licked his dry lips. The slip was dated a scant two weeks before. He put it back into the hole and replaced the stone and rose.

"The dirty old varmint!" he growled. His heart was slowing now, and he forced himself to steadiness as he rose. "Banking it—now I can't touch a dime." The anger somehow restored him.

But it was his. He was old Mac's only kin. It was all his. And this little ranch, which he could sell for good cash. He wouldn't go back home. Let them take his few cattle and his shack. Why, with cash like this, what couldn't he do! He would go to some city—maybe Denver or San Francisco. Liquor—women in fine clothes—new cars —good horses. . . . Set himself up in a nice saloon in a good part of town. Buy railroad stock and run his money up. . . .

His enthusiasm suddenly cooled. First, he must get the money. And he must avoid getting himself into trouble for what he had done. Maybe it would be best to get on back home and wait to be advised that old Mac had tossed in his chips. On the other hand, it was known there that he had come here—and, besides, that infernal buckboard would leave tracks clear across the country the way it was sprinkling.

Dirk began sweating as he stood in the middle of the floor, racking his brains for a notion of what to do. First off, he guessed he should get rid of the gun. And after that, drive to town and report that he had come to see his Uncle Mac, and found him murdered. Maybe they would suspect him, but what could they prove? Nothing. All they could do, after the funeral, was to hand him the money.

He reached for his dusty old hat and jumper and put them on. The drilled well, six inches in diameter and two hundred feet deep, would be a fine place for the pistol, and in the pitch blackness of the yard Dirk found the little well shed. He raised the cover and dropped the gun in and heard it scrape and bang the casing several times before it struck the water.

The rain was coming harder, now, already soaking him through at knee and shoulder as he headed for the corral. Stooping low, he could faintly see his hammerheaded old horse against the skyline. His eyes were getting used to the dark. He caught the animal by the mane and led him up by the barn and brought the harness out and threw it on. The leather was wet and slick as he fastened the buckles.

It was as he reached under for the belly band that he heard the pound of hoofs and then the rattle of a buggy, and for an instant he leaned there, paralyzed. Whoever it was would be coming here, for no one else lived down this way. Suddenly he grabbed the belly-band and buckled it and caught the bit ring. Let them come. Give him three more minutes, and let them come—

He led the horse out of the corral and flung himself upon its back and rode him swiftly to the yard and slid down. In a second, he had backed him into the shafts and was fastening them. He hooked a tug, then, with the sound of the horse and buggy coming closer, and ran around to hook the other, and as he undid the lines from the hame he could see the moving blackness of the rig coming at him. Swiftly he clambered to the seat.

The rig pulled up. A man said, "Hello, there. That ain't you, is it, Mac?"

Dirk knew the voice. Old man Vanderwet. Then some other man said, "Mac?"

Dirk got a good grip on his voice. "It's me," he said. "Dirk Callen. Uncle—Uncle Mac—has been killed—"

Vanderwet exclaimed, "I told you! I told you something was wrong!" And as the two men piled out of the rig, he added, "Every Friday night for twenty years we've played checkers, and when he didn't show up tonight—I—I knew something must be wrong, so I brought the doctor—"

Startled, Dirk kept quiet as he stepped from hub to porch. He had forgotten it was Friday. Maybe, in the excitement of their talk, his uncle had forgotten it, too.

The rain beat down with sudden fury as he shoved the door open and let the yellow light flood out. That was fine. It would smooth out the tracks he had made, getting the horse up here from the barn. He led the way in and stood silently as Vanderwet moved ponderously behind him. Vanderwet looked at the body for a long time, face shaken and pale and his grey mustaches trembling a little now and then. The doctor, a little man in baggy clothes whom Dirk did not know, knelt by old Mac and took his wrist.

And, in surprise, he exclaimed, "Why, he's only just been shot!"

Dirk tensed. "He—he's dead, isn't he?"

"There's no doubt of it."

"I heard the shot," Dirk explained. "I drove up just before you got here. I wasn't quite to the gate when I thought I heard a gun, and when I came inside, this is what I saw."

The doctor said, "Somebody evidently ate supper with Mac."

"They must have taken out the back way," Dirk declared, "when they heard me."

"But why?" Vanderwet exclaimed. "Why would anybody—"

* * *

He fixed a long, searching look on Dirk, his little grey eyes peering out above bustles of grey flesh, his brows glistening a little with drops of mist. Dirk forced himself to keep a steady countenance.

"You weren't by any chance the one who ate here?" the old man asked, and his look moved to Dirk's shirt front and back up to his eyes.

In spite of himself, Dirk glanced down and saw the streak of egg yoke down his belly. He felt sweat break upon his body. "I . . . I didn't mean to mention it," he said, "but—well, I was starved when I came in. Uncle Mac was dead. Past help. They had left a little stuff, he and whoever ate with him, and, being hungry, I bolted it down, and started for you."

Vanderwet nodded. "Then you—you must have got here, say, ten minutes ago? Fifteen, maybe?"

"Maybe fifteen."

Vanderwet said, "How long has Mac been dead, Doc?"

The doctor shrugged. "Who can say? Five minutes—ten minutes —maybe a quarter of an hour. Not longer."

"I told you I heard the shot!" Dirk exclaimed. With an effort he toned his voice down. "I heard it."

Vanderwet sighed heavily and picked up the lamp. "I'll hold the light for you to turn around, Doc. Have John and them bring out the very best coffin—that all right, Dirk?"

"Sure." Dirk was getting a little dizzy with relief. "Sure. The best."

"We'll lay him out an' shave him while you're gone," Vanderwet added. He led the way onto the porch and stood there a second and then he whirled on Dirk, drawing a gun from his armpit. He cocked it, holding it unwaveringly on Dirk's middle.

"I would enjoy shooting you," he said, as Dirk backed toward the table in the room. "I hope you move one more step." He came in with the lamp, squinting his left eye against it. "Find his pistol, Doc, and tie his hands behind him . . . and don't get between me and him."

Dirk tried to speak as the doctor moved behind him and felt over his body for a gun, but no words would come. He calculated his chances for a break. They were nil. Then it came to him that he must brazen it out. Old Vanderwet was merely suspicious and trying to stampede him into talking.

"All right. Find my gun," he said. "Since I never owned one of the things, I'd like to see it."

The doctor's hands moved quickly and expertly over him a second time, and finally the man grunted, "Well, there's no gun, that's sure."

"Tie him!" Vanderwet exclaimed. "Out of his own mouth, gun or not, he stands convicted. There's a rawhide lace on the nail behind you, Doc. Put your hands behind you, Callan."

Dirk obeyed before the cold, hungry mouth of the pistol. His sweat had dried. "But—you see I have no gun—" he croaked, his mouth growing dry.

"I'll see something else before snow flies. A hanging."

Dirk felt the rawhide bite into his wrists, and the doctor's warm breath blowing upon his hands.

Then Vanderwet backed onto the porch again, the lamp throwing heavy angles of shadow into the room. "Come out!" he ordered. "Doc, pick up that poker and if he tries anything, brain him."

Something in the man's manner, in his voice, struck an icier terror into Dirk than he had ever felt before. His knees wobbled as he moved out onto the porch, and it was hard for him to breathe. But he would think of something yet. He would admit nothing to them.

"You've been here fifteen minutes, you say, and it's been raining upwards of an hour. The ground is muddy, the road full of puddles." Vanderwet took a deep breath, pointing. "And yet—"

At first, Dirk thought he was pointing at the buckboard, and he stared at it, dripping and shining, but he could see nothing wrong. And the horse, standing dejectedly, looked all right.

"Look under it," Vanderwet grunted, and the doctor gave a sudden cry of understanding. "Take a look under the buckboard, Callan."

Dirk looked. The ground there hadn't been rained on. It was dry and white. A white square of it, in the lamp light, the size of a gallows floor.

WHITEMAIL

Joyce Kilmer

Spike Ritchie and I worked together on the *Daily News* from 1904 to 1907, and I always liked him. He was bright, hard-working, companionable and—I thought—perfectly straight. The other day he told me about a pretty crooked deal he was mixed up in. In fact, he told me that he was an unrepentant blackmailer and traitor. And I like him more than I ever did before.

When I got back to New York last week I looked over the pictures I had bought in Turkey and decided that I had the material for some Sunday stories. So I went around to the *News* office. The elevator man didn't know me—he had been on the job only two years—but he knew Spike.

"Mr. Ritchie is assistant Sunday editor now," he said. "But I don't think you'll find him in his office. Today's Thursday, so I guess he's in the composing room."

I made him let me off at the composing room and went in. There was Spike, telling the foreman that Matty had a glass arm, and making up the fashion page. He had grown much balder, but otherwise he had changed very little since I saw him six years before. He was the same little stoop-shouldered fellow, with the same rat-tail mustache, and apparently the same cigar butt fixed in the corner of his mouth. Also, I discovered in a few minutes, he had the same alcoholic breath.

"Hello, John!" he said. "Wait till I fix this up and I'll go out with you."

Soon we were comfortably seated at a table in Jimmy's bar. Jimmy, I was absurdly pleased to notice, remembered me and put a few drops of syrup in my Irish as if I were still a daily visitor. Spike looked at my pictures and told me to go ahead with the stories. Then—of course—we both grew reminiscent, and after the third drink and a little lunch came his confession. That is, if you'd call it a confession. . . . "You're not the only globe trotter," he said, lighting for the fourth time his amorphous cigar butt. "I went abroad two summers ago."

I expressed interest—without much enthusiasm, for I wanted to talk about Turkey.

"Yes," he said, "I had a little money saved up—I wasn't married then—and I was feeling pretty rotten, so I decided to knock off for a while. I traveled around the Continent for a few weeks and then I went to London. I wanted to see something of the country, so I bought a knapsack and made a leisurely walking tour of the Midland counties. The result of that walking tour was a mighty queer experience. And, in spite of the fact that you are bursting with the desire to tell me how you matched pennies with the Sultan and chucked the harem under its chin, I am now going to take up some minutes of the *News's* time in telling you about that experience. It has never been used as a news story, and it never will. But the villain—unless you call me the villain—is dead now, and I guess it wouldn't do any harm if you fixed it up with different names and made a fiction story out of it. Then if you sell it you can split with me fifty-fifty."

"Go ahead," I said.

"Well [began Spike], I struck a little bit of a market town called Ashbourne that I liked pretty well. So I got a room at an inn entertainingly called *The Green Man and Black's Head* and settled down for a week's stay. There were very few other guests, so the proprietor and I got rather friendly. Of course, like all Englishmen, he was surprised that I didn't know his cousin who was on a ranch in Texas and his nephew who was manager of a grocery store in Milwaukee.

"'There's one of your fellow countrymen I can't say that I care for,' he said one evening. 'There was a Mr. James Rodney who came here from New York City, and we all wish we'd never seen him, sir. Perhaps you know him—he's a tall, thin gentleman with a sort of a mole over his right eye. He told us that he owned a big flour mill, but I don't know as he told the truth. Do you know a man of that name?'

"I told him that I had never before heard of James Rodney, and by asking a few questions I heard a story that was unpleasant though not particularly strange. Two summers before, an American calling himself James Rodney had come to Ashbourne and stopped with Mrs. Clarke, the widow of the old vicar. She had very little money, and made a living by taking lodgers. He was on his way up north, and he had a two hours' wait between trains in Ashbourne. He took a walk through the town, stopped to get a drink of water at Mrs. Clarke's house, found that she took lodgers, and by that night he had given up all idea of going north. He said that he liked

Ashbourne and the Clarke cottage but, said the innkeeper, 'what really attracted him was Mary Clarke. She was an amazingly pretty girl in those days, sir; in fact, she is still, though she's had a hard time.'

"It did not take Rodney long to make Mrs. Clarke and Mary believe that he was a person of some importance in New York. He seemed to have plenty of money, his manners were those of a gentleman, and he became popular in local society. In fact, everyone was pleased when, after a tempestuous courtship, Mary and he were married in the beautiful old parish church.

"Mary thought that her husband would take her to America at once, but he said that he would prefer to see a little more of Europe. So they went to Switzerland for a couple of weeks and then returned to Mrs. Clarke's cottage. Rodney had received a cable from New York, he said. He must go back to his mill for a little while. It was an urgent matter—he must get the boat sailing from Liverpool on the very next day. He would send a letter by every mail and within a month he would come back for his wife and her mother.

"Of course you have guessed what happened. James Rodney, or whatever his real name was, never came back. He did not write and, what is more important, he did not send any money. Letters sent to James Rodney, the Rodney Flour and Grain Company, 13 West 98th Street, New York City, U.S.A., were returned. His name did not appear on the passenger list of the steamer on which he said he intended to sail. For a while Mrs. Clarke and Mary thought that he had met with some fatal accident, but after a friend of theirs, visiting America, had found that no such concern as the Rodney Flour and Grain Company had ever existed and that there were no mills on 98th Street, they knew that they had been cruelly deceived. In the course of time Mary had a baby, a very nice baby. It was a little boy, as pretty as Mary herself and resembling her strikingly. In only one respect he resembled his father—there was a small but unmistakable mole over his right eye.

"This story interested me very much, and I took the liberty of calling on Mrs. Clarke the next day, on the pretense of looking for lodgings. Indeed, it became more than a pretext, for Mrs. Clarke was such a charming old gentlewoman and the cottage and Mary—it was hard for me to call her Mrs. Rodney—so attractive that I took a room and stayed for three weeks.

"Of course I got from them all that they knew about the mysterious James Rodney, and that was little more than the innkeeper had told me. But just before I left Mrs. Rodney gave me a little kodak picture of her husband and herself, taken by her mother on the porch of the cottage.

"I went back to America with a fixed determination to find this Rodney person, smash his face, and make him send every cent that he possessed back to Ashbourne. You see, I knew the suffering that his little game had inflicted on Mary and her mother and I was pretty angry about it. I confess I didn't have much hope of finding the fellow, but I was going to make a good try at it, anyway. Well, I didn't have to try very hard. I never was much good at this suspense business, so I'll spring my sensation on you right away. James Rodney was Andrew Judd. Yes—don't spill your whisky—Andrew Judd, president of the Judd Iron Works, philanthropist and reformer.

"Two days after I got back, Boss Ridder sent me out to interview Judd for the Sunday edition. Judd had just invented a very fancy sort of model tenement with a gymnasium and swimming tank on every floor. In order to understand just what improvements were needed in the housing of the poor he had spent two days in a tenement house on the lower East Side, and was very eager to talk about it. As soon as I saw him I recognized him, and you can readily understand that my first desire was for a large encouraging draught of the beverage known as whisky. And, by the way, ring that bell, will you? Jimmy, two more of the same.

"Well, of course I thought right away just what you thought—here is one scoop of a story! In spite of the fact that we were running this page interview in the Sunday, the *News* had no particular friendship for Judd. In fact, we were going to oppose him in the Fall, when he was going to run for Mayor.

"I had all the facts and there was plenty of time to get the story in next morning's paper. All I had to do was to flash that little kodak picture (which I always carried with me) on Judd, tell him what I knew of his little European jaunt and let him throw me out of the office. Then back to the *News*, to grab all the space I wanted for the biggest sensation that the paper ever had. Think what a story like that would mean to me, an absolutely exclusive story with a picture to prove it! I saw myself getting a whopping bonus and a regular job to boot. Then, too, you know that I'm not talking sentiment when I say that I was—have always been—loyal to the *News*. You were long enough in the game to find out what a newspaperman's loyalty is—how his first idea when anything big happens is always to hammer it out on his machine and get it in before the first edition goes to press.

"But I had sense enough to hold on to myself for a while. I shook hands with Judd—I guess I stared pretty hard at that mole over his right eye—and I went ahead with the interview as had been arranged. Judd was feeling expansive that day, and he really knew how to talk. He gave me a great little story, full of human interest, and with a lot of new stuff in it, but all the while I was listening to him I was thinking harder than I ever thought before. There were three different plans in my mind—I couldn't, to save my life, think just what I ought to do. After a while Judd felt that he'd given me all I needed and he stopped talking.

" 'Mr. Judd,' I said, almost involuntarily, 'when were you married?'

" 'Why, my dear boy, I don't see what that has to do with what we've been talking about; but I was married five years ago. In St. Marmaduke's Church, of which I am junior warden, if you wish the full particulars. My wife was Miss Emily Lindsay, and here is a picture of her.'

"He took from his desk a framed photograph of a very lovely woman with a little girl on her lap.

" 'I see,' I said vaguely. 'And when was it that you went abroad?'

" 'Well, I really don't think that the public will be interested in matters like this,' he said, 'but I have been abroad several times. Two years ago I spent the summer in England, and then made a somewhat extensive tour of Germany. But I think that I must ask you to excuse me now. I've given you all you need, have I not? Oh, yes!' he added. 'I suppose you will want a picture of me. I think I have some in my desk drawer. I'll look and see.'

" 'No,' I said, in a voice which seemed strange to me. 'I've got a picture already.'

"His back was turned to me, and he was rummaging in his desk. 'But I'm afraid that's been used before. I think I can find some new ones for you.'

" 'This picture has never been used before,' I said. 'It was taken two years ago in Ashbourne.'

"At the word 'Ashbourne' he turned suddenly and looked at the little square of gray cardboard in my hands. Then he grew very white and stood perfectly still.

"For a minute neither of us spoke.

"Then, with a self-control for which I could not help admiring him, he pushed his chair to the desk, sat down, turned his back to me and wrote.

"I heard the rip of torn paper. He whirled his chair and stretched out his hands to me. In his left hand was an oblong of green paper with his name written in the lower right-hand corner. His right hand was empty.

"'Here is a blank check, which I have signed,' he said. 'Give me the photograph, please.'

"I admit I hesitated for a moment. I am not so devoted to my job that I would hate an independent fortune. But I didn't hesitate long.

"It was a ridiculously theatrical thing to do, but I took the check, tore it into four pieces, and dropped them on the blotter on his desk.

"'To hell with your check!' I said, in a quiet conversational tone of voice. 'You'll need that money when you start defending yourself against the charge of bigamy.'

"Judd deliberately lit a cigar and sat looking at me.

"'So, you've got an interesting item for tomorrow's paper, have you?' he said. 'But what's the idea? Just what do you gain by attacking me? That little picture is interesting, but it proves absolutely nothing.'

"I rose to go. 'In the first place,' I said, with my hand on the doorknob, 'I know the girl whom you illegally married two years ago, and the *News* will bring her over here—with her child. We will gain two things—we will be purveyors of a very interesting story and we will bring punishment on a damned hypocrite.'

"He was perfectly calm. 'I see your first point,' he answered reflectively. 'You can publish a very sensational story—there is no doubt of that. But I doubt very much your ability to substantiate your charge, and I fail to see why you are so bitterly enraged at me. There must be some motive. . . . I think I see. Yes, I think I see. But what earthly good will it do the young woman to drag her name into this scandal? You cannot carry out your amiable design of ruining me without also ruining two women.'

"'All right,' I said, 'I'll tell you what I'll do. You've got to square yourself, and I'll keep quiet about this business.'

"'Just what do you mean by "square myself"?' he said.

"'James Rodney must die.'

"'My God!' he exclaimed. 'Do you want me to kill myself?'

"'You must kill James Rodney,' I said. 'See here, Mary Clarke has never heard of Andrew Judd. What you've got to do is write her a letter signing your own name, saying that James Rodney was Tom Smith, or John Jones, or anything you like. Anyway, you must say that he was a friend of yours and that he is dead. Say that he confessed to you on his deathbed that he had married and deserted a girl named Mary Clarke in Ashbourne, England, and that he asked you to notify her of his death and to send her all his money.'

" 'I'll do it,' he said. 'I'll do it this afternoon. I'll send her ten thousand dollars—fifty thousand dollars—all the money you say.'

" 'You certainly will do it today,' I said, 'for I'm going to stick around and watch you do it. You will write the letter at my dictation and I will mail it myself. But as to the money that you are sending, you've got the wrong idea. You will send Miss Clarke enough money to buy that little cottage so that they won't have to earn the rent by taking lodgers and enough to pay for a trip abroad for her and her mother. They need a little holiday after the trouble you got them into. Then you must add enough to send your son through school and through the university. I guess we'll put it at twenty thousand dollars—that's letting you off pretty cheap, and I don't want to burden them with a lot of your dirty money.'

" 'I suppose you know,' Mr. Judd said to me, 'that what you are doing is blackmail.'

" 'Today,' I answered, 'I am, in suppressing this story, breaking the commandment of the newspaper business—violating a code of ethics which you could not possibly understand. I am a traitor to the *News* and to my profession. And after that I don't mind a little blackmail.' "

Jimmy had taken away our empty glasses and was ostentatiously wiping the table with a gray napkin. Spike looked at his watch and got up to go. As we walked down the street I turned to him and said: "But didn't Mary What-you-may-call-her ever get wise? When Judd died last year she must have seen his picture in some English paper and known that he was the fellow that fooled her. I should think she'd sue his estate and get good money."

"Sure she got wise," said Spike. "But she wouldn't start anything now. She's perfectly comfortable, I guess."

"What is she doing?" I asked.

"Why," said Spike, lighting his cigar butt for the ninth time, "she's married to the assistant Sunday editor of the *Daily News.*"

Whose Turn Is It?

C. J. Henderson

Paul stared at the window, watching the snow and the night crowd up against the glass. His fingers dug into the sheet under his palms, tearing to grip the mattress as if a firm hold in his hand might give him one on his situation. Sweat slid down the back of his neck, across his forehead, down his sides, freely from any pore with water left to give.

"Jeez o'man," he thought to himself, the cords beginning to chaff, "How could she do it? How did she even know? I thought for sure —there was no way. No way. No Way."

Paul's mind went back to earlier in the evening. It had been one of their perfect dates. One of the few things New York can be good for is supplying breath-taking backdrops for romance. Paul and Sally had just walked—from Times Square, where they'd arranged to meet after work,.over to the waterfront up to Lincoln Center—it had been the nicest evening they had spent together in a long time —none of the usual tension hanging between them.

Of course, it wasn't as if they fought all the time—Paul was always quick to point out that he and Sally rarely had shouting matches, or guilt bickers—to most of their friends they were "that perfect couple." But none of that explained what had happened in the park.

They had eaten at that little Jamacian cafe on Broadway—the one with the bizarrely colored rattan chairs—the one they'd always wanted to stop at but never had. His mind raced through the steps they'd taken after that. Which of them, he tried to remember, suggested the walk in the park. Which one? Was it him or her? Did she suggest Central Park? Did she?

"Are you all right, dear?" Her voice came from the bathroom, a hint of sarcasm in her lilt. "Are you . . . comfy?"

He winced, the terror creeping through his brain making him nearly frantic. Quietly, for the first time ever fearing to let her hear him move, he strained against his bonds, making sure he really was tied too tightly to move.

"Sweetheart," her voice laughed, "I can't wait to see your face when you see the surprise I have for you."

He shut his eyes involuntarily in a shudder of anticipation.

"I'll bet you can't guess what it is."

Black images of dangerous objects, some blunt, some sharp, all in Sally's hands, swam in his brain. If the wad of silken underwear tied in his mouth wasn't perfectly positioned to strangle all sound, his screams would have shattered the windows.

Grasping at his nerve, Paul chased back his fears, trying to somehow get his thoughts ordered. He got himself back to the restaurant and then struggled over their conversation to try and find who had suggested the park. He could see their meals come again, could smell her scampi, taste the pepper in his cream sauce—the wine finished, dessert tray in view, picked over, coffees lingered over, drained, brown rings drying, bill discreetly slipped between them in the chic Manhattan nonassumption of recipient. Laughing, standing, up and walking, out the door, down the street, turning the corner . . .

"Let's walk through the park; it's not too late."

Him! He had said it.

"Oh, and it's snowing. That would be so nice."

And she had agreed. But he had done it. He had said the park. Not her. Him. Damn. Damn. Damndamndamndamndamn. Maybe it . . .

No.

She'd steered their route. He remembered now. When they'd stepped out of the restaurant. She pointed them toward the east, toward the park. It had been her! Oh, god—it had been her.

It all started falling into place. Yes, he'd set up a date, but she had picked ending up at Lincoln Center, right across from Central Park. He'd suggested the restaurant, but she had put them in the direction of the park when they'd left. Then, he'd seen the tops of the snowbound trees and been maneuvered into his line.

"Let's walk through the park; it's not too late."

She knew she could count on him to want to walk through the park. She knew he'd say what he did. She knew. Oh, god . . . what's she going to do to me? Just because of two stinking dates.

Dorrie had started working at the same firm he did only a month previous—a New Yorker for only two weeks. It hadn't taken Paul long to spot her. She was a lot like Sally, physically, same legs, same thick, down-the-back hair, thin, nicely drawn smile, green eyes—but not so clever, so hard, so searching, so smugly in charge.

It had been nice, his date with Dorrie. Like with Sally, only back at the beginning, before they had grown used to each other, before the boredom with each other's jokes and ideas and goals had set in, before the games had started. They had talked for a long time, he hearing about why she had come to the city, she listening to his dreams—plans that sounded big and fresh and reasonable being reflected back at him by her newness and enthusiasm. And then the sex.

Dorrie had proved no stranger to double occupancy. They had taken a room in a midtown hotel to avoid their respective roommates, to cut themselves off from phones and doorbells, television and the evening mail, to be alone with each other and a bed and hours of darkness—new bodies against each other, old tricks and tired habits suddenly as inventive as if they were high school kids. Sweat had pasted them together, the freshness of their love dragging heights out of them both had forgotten. It had been wonderful.

They met again on the weekend, going to a movie, eating Italian, back to "their place." Their manners were so different that even their second time together seemed exciting. Paul had been transformed, made younger, walking straighter, acting happier about most everything.

Even his life with Sally seemed better. He found himself talking to her, feeling good about his little affair, and the way it was helping his main relationship. He and Sally had been in a rut for such a long time. They had exhausted each other as things of interest months earlier—maybe a year earlier. Everything between them had become pretty much routine, which is, of course, where the games had come from.

It had been his idea at first; stockings, garters, full costumes, and the restraints of hemp and plastic, nylon, tape, leather, metal. Poles to keep the back straight, to separate legs—cuffs to bind, belts to discomfort, masks to hide faces from each other, to build suspense, terror, anticipation. But Sally had taken to it all easily, especially since she got her turns, too. In fact, it was her inventiveness that had kept them together.

Sally had introduced the reality twists, the moments where safety had seemingly gone out the window. She was a good actress, and she loved proving it to Paul. Not that he hadn't caught on to them quickly, enjoyed planning them as much as she did. Sally had still never equaled the time he'd let her see the metal rods heating on the stove and then masked her—told her it was time she was marked as his—and then touched her repeatedly with ice. She'd truly believed he'd burned her from neck to ankle. But tonight was no act. Things hadn't been set up to terrify him. When they'd gone into the park, found Dorrie, that had been no act.

Dorrie was dead. Face unmarked, only a few drops of blood reaching that high. The work had been abdominal; gutting strokes laying her open—insides spread in every direction. They had stumbled across her by accident—but it hadn't been one—going to the top of the rock outcropping Paul loved so much for its view. There they had found her, eyes frozen in pitiful desperation, birds pulling away bits of her punctured organs, their frozen leakage worming through the new falling snow.

The horror of it had sent them stumbling down the rock face, running away through the darkened park. They agreed they did not want to be involved. Who wanted to be hounded by reporters, grilled by police, possibly be the killer's next victim? Or, as Paul realized, connected to the corpse as a recent lover? No—let's just get out of here, forget all about this. Let's go home—come on, we'll just go home and, get "comfy," okay? Whose turn is it, anyway?

Idiot, he thought. Idiot. Whose turn is it? Whose turn? What a chump. What an asshole. She'd set him up—she knew whose turn it was. She knew everything.

The realization had hit him then.

She *knew!* She knew about Dorrie. She had to. Coincidences like this just don't happen. Oh god, oh god please, pleasepleaseplease—oh Christ, oh shit, oh man—

Paul pulled at his restraints in earnest, praying for the slightest slack to generate hope for escape. How had she gotten Dorrie to the park? She had to have killed her there—the blood, the freshness—god, she must have done it just before their date. The storm would have kept people out of the park, certainly off the mount. . . .

Mounting desperation doubled Paul's strength, the bed's headboard bouncing off the wall behind, banging with repeated fierceness. He no longer cared if she heard; what did it matter? She was going to kill him anyway. Panic knotted his muscles as he strained. He pulled this way then that way, harder, harder, all thought gone, erased by fear and the need for release, knowing that just another ounce of pressure, just another few seconds would do it, would free him, would . . .

"Paul?"

He froze. The clammy stain of sweat soaking the sheets chilled him. She had heard him.

"Paul, are you all right?"

She was coming. This was it. He could feel her moving, feel the air parting around her, knew she was reaching to push the door open.

"Oh, silly me. You can't talk with your mouth full."

He buried his tearing eyes in the pillow.

"A mouth full of panties keeps you pretty quiet, doesn't it?"

She entered the bedroom. Ready.

"Keeps all those lies inside where they belong, not running around free getting you into trouble."

Paul braced himself, steeled himself. He had to look, had to see what was coming. He couldn't die and not even see the stroke—

"I guess you know what comes next, lover."

He opened his eyes, blinking at the unending tears, trying to see. He could turn his head far enough toward the mirror to catch sight of Sally moving toward the bed, toward him—of the look in her eye, knife in her hand. Ashamed, he buried his face again. The pain came quickly, nerves letting him know she'd started slicing.

He screamed into Sally's underwear until he fainted, which really wasn't very long at all.

Sally poured the second cup of coffee, leaving enough room for the milk to come. Placing it on the table in front of Paul, across from hers, she said,

"Here you go, nice and hot."

Paul took the cup without making a response, holding it in both hands as if it were the only warm thing in their apartment. Sally laughed.

"Oh, come on. It's daytime. Playland's closed. Stop sulking."

She put a hand on his shoulder, but he shrugged it away.

"What's the matter, dear? Don't like being the scared one for once?"

"Scared?" He put the cup down awkwardly, slopping coffee out of one side. "Scared? I was more than scared. Goddamned plenty more than scared!"

Sally grinned widely with satisfaction.

"Of who? Little me?"

"Will you stop kidding? Who else do you think I was scared of?"

His voice fell into whisper. "You murdered someone! What the hell are we going to do about that, for god's sake?!"

Sitting down across from Paul, Sally arranged a serious look on her face and told him.

"We're going to do what we've always done. Have fun." Going past the questions welling up in her mate, she continued. "All of this was your idea. I'm not saying I didn't see your point and get involved as deeply as you wanted me to, but you started it—so let me ask a few questions.

"Number one . . . isn't the point of these little games of ours to scare the hell out of each other? Isn't the idea to push each other to the edge so that the sex that follows is the best we've ever had?"

Paul nodded, avoiding her eyes.

"Number two . . . after I untied you, after you saw you weren't cut to shreds, that the blade you'd felt had just been a credit card, the running blood just water from a sponge, was or was not that the best sex we ever had?"

"Yes, yes—but . . ."

"No 'buts,' Paul. We play games or we don't."

"But you killed someone."

"You fucked her, I killed her. I could have killed you."

Sally put her arms around Paul's neck. He grabbed for her involuntarily, pulling her around the edge of the table and onto his lap.

"I didn't, though," she told him. "I just wanted to be yours. So some little slut from Kansas dies. So what? As long as it keeps us together."

Paul agreed. He kissed Sally then, wanting her as much as the first time they'd made love, wanting her as much as life. He knew he would never turn her in to the police. As they slid to the floor, kicking chairs out of their way, they tore each other's clothing away, attacking each other with a passion they had no idea they still possessed.

"We'll always be together," he told her.

And he meant it. The police might put her in jail. Probably only some mental hospital. But Paul, Paul could do better than that. He could think of much better things than that. After all, it was his turn next.

The Witch's Way

Joseph Shallit

"Cross yourself," Valentino Loreto said to Antonio Lopez, the chief of police. "Cross yourself, for here comes the witch."

"Better that you should not speak such foolishness," Antonio said. "Only children and fools believe such stories."

"Then I am a fool, for it is too late to call me a child by forty years," Valentino said. "Nevertheless, better that you should cross yourself. It is good protection."

"Be still and do not frighten the old man," Antonio said.

Into the doorway, passing beneath the sign reading, Chief of Police, Municipality of Tompon, Leyte, walked Vicente Honorio, leaning on his cane. He wore a brown hempen shirt, blue, cotton American trousers and a brown crust of dirt on his bare feet. He had a large, hooked nose unsuited for his flat face, and a smile that was lost in a jungle of wrinkles.

"I am ashamed that I must trouble you," he said to Antonio.

"It is no trouble, old man," Antonio said. "Sit in this chair."

"I would not come if my rice were not taken," Vicente said, sitting down softly so as not to disturb the chair unduly. "I do not care so much for the fish."

"Tell me what is your trouble," Antonio said.

"My rice," Vicente said. "Three sacks stood on a shelf close to my cooking pots. Late in the night I am sleeping. I hear a noise as of someone walking on the bamboo ladder. 'Who is it?' I say. 'Go to sleep, old man; it is a dream,' a man's voice tells me. Therefore I go to sleep again. When I wake in the morning, I have only two sacks of rice. And of the twelve fish which I myself brought from my fish trap yesterday, I have only two small ones. I do not care so much for the fish, for the sea runs plentiful these days. But two sacks of rice will not last until the next harvest."

* * *

"Why do you weep, old man?" Vallentino Loreto burst out. "Can you not send out your accursed pig to get more rice for you?"

The smile went away from Vicente's face. "It is not an accursed pig," he said meekly. "It is a pig like any other pig."

"Does not your pig run through the roads at night, frightening good people with his golden teeth and causing them to lose their wits?" Valentino demanded.

"It is not true," Vicente said tremblingly. "I know that many people say this of my pig, but it is not true. My pig does not have golden teeth. It is a pig like any other pig, and I keep it in its pen at night."

"And is it not true," said Valentino, half rising from his chair, "that you transform yourself into a large black bird and fly through the night, crying *woc-woc*, bringing trouble to men's homes?"

"It is not true, not true!" Vicente said, almost weeping. He turned a sorrowful face to Antonio. "Ay, all the people say these things of me, but they are not true. My pig is like other pigs. I am a man like other men. But since the time, many years ago, that Tomas Escuadra's little son died of the dysentery as I was walking past his house, people have spoken these evil things of me."

"Do not mind them," Antonio said kindly. "And you, Sergeant Loreto, do not trouble this old man who seeks only to find the rice which has left him."

"Yes," said Vicente. "I do not care so much for the fish, for I believe it stinks already."

"I wish to help you, old man," Antonio said, "but it is very difficult. In every home in Leyte one can find sacks of rice like yours. Is there any one you have a sentiment upon as having taken your rice?"

"Yes," Vicente said promptly. "It is one of my three neighbors: Juanito Repulda, Julio Ontimaro or Salvador Campos."

"You speak quickly, old man," Antonio said. "Why do you name these three only?"

Vicente leaned forward, and his wrinkles twisted as he pondered. "I think about this in the morning," he said. "You know where my hut is, at the end of Juan Luna Street, at the edge of the rice fields. The thief could not go through the fields because they are too wet now. He must go through Juan Luna Street. If one walks from my hut, one passes the huts of my three neighbors, and then one comes to a muddy place. There is rain in the evening yesterday, and it makes the mud smooth. Early this morning I go there to look. There are no foot marks in it."

"You are wise, old man," Antonio said softly. "If you were younger I would make of you a policeman and give you the place of Sergeant Valentino Loreto."

"Very good," said Valentino. "And I shall take the old man's wings and fly at night and cry *woc-woc*."

"Go, old man," Antonio said. "We shall try to find your rice."

Vicente rose. "You are very kind," he said. "You will receive many blessings for my rice." He followed his cane out through the doorway.

Valentino stood up and gave a snort like a carabao. "That accursed witch! It is some new evil he is trying to make this way. If he wishes to find his rice, he can do it himself. Why does he not make himself into a bird tonight and cry *woc-woc* in the windows of his neighbors? They would give up their rice soon enough for fear of having their wits destroyed."

Antonio took a report form from his desk drawer and began to write.

"Oy!" said Valentino. "You are not going to make serious business of this witch's story?"

"A crime is a crime," Antonio said, "and will be so entered in the monthly report."

"You are too kind to a witch," Valentino said.

"I am not kind," Antonio said. "I think of myself only. Look at this report I must send to the provincial provost marshal this month: Crimes reported—seven. Crimes solved—none. The provost marshal will not like that."

"Oy, but you are making it only worse, for now you will have eight crimes reported."

"Yes, Valentino, but this crime will be solved."

Valentino stared at him. "How will you do that?" he asked respectfully.

"Do you not know that you have already suggested the way?"

That night, at half an hour before midnight, Antonio and Valentino left the police office and walked through the dark streets of Tompon. They went past the hemp warehouse, past the Chinese bakery, past the market shed where the clean-up boys were making music with pans and bottles, past the seamstress' place, past the Liberation Café where a few old men still sat, drinking tuba, past the chapel and into Juan Luna Street.

"Good that there is no moon," Antonio said.

"Yes, for even the moon would laugh to see us doing a witch's business," said Valentino.

The street, of packed dirt and gravel, became softer as they went on, softer and grassier, for few persons came this way. On both sides of the street the low rice fields lay beneath a blanket of water, resting from the harvest.

"Oy!" Valentino exclaimed. "The mud!"

They had come upon the muddy spot Vicente had told them about.

"This is for carabao to walk in, not men," Valentino said.

"Hold your breath and you will not drown," Antonio said, walking after him.

They cleared the muddy spot and continued to walk. And now on their left appeared the nipa-palm hut of Juanito Repulda, standing on bamboo stilts at the side of the road.

"Here we must be very quiet," Antonio whispered. "We must go as a bird goes."

"Then better that a bird were doing this and not I," Valentino said.

They walked to the window. It was covered by a thick bamboo and nipa screen, to keep out the injurious night air.

"Now bend," Antonio whispered, "so that I can put my knees on your shoulders and be lifted to the window."

Valentino looked at Antonio's thick shoulders and thick, round belly. "My wife will have a husband with a broken back tonight," he whispered.

Valentino stooped. Antonio put his hands against the side of the hut and put his knees on Valentino's shoulders. Valentino rose with a quiver and a grunt, and Antonio slid upward against the rustling nipa leaves. He put his mouth to the edge of the screen.

"*Woc-woc*," Antonio said softly.

"Oy, speak louder and be done with it," Valentino said. "I cannot suffer this burden all night."

"*Woc-woc!*" Antonio cried. He flapped his arms like a bird against the screen.

There was a sudden cry within, and then a voice began to mutter.

"*Woc-woc!*" Antonio cried. "*Woc-woc!*"

The voice became louder. It was saying, "Jesús-Maria-Josip! Jesús-Maria-Josip!"

"*Woc-woc!*" Antonio cried, louder still.

"Jesús-Maria-Josip!" persisted the voice inside. "Jesús-Maria-Josip!"

"Oiga, come down!" Valentino exclaimed. He stooped, and Antonio slid down along the hut to the ground. "It is a terrible sin," Valentino said, "to be speaking a witch's cry against these holy words. A great harm will come."

"Jesús-Maria-Josip!" said the voice inside the hut.

"Oy, let us go quickly," Valentino said. He leaped to the road and ran a few paces.

Antonio came slowly after him. "Do not run, imbecile," he said. "There are no devils here."

Valentino waited for his chief to come beside him, and said, "Oy, it is foolishness for a chief of police to play the witch."

"It is no harm," Antonio said. "Perhaps in this way I can frighten a man into confessing his crime."

"Surely there are other ways to catch a thief."

"If I am dealing with men who believe in witches, I use the witch's way."

"Better that the crime never be solved than to catch a thief in this unholy way."

"I sign the monthly report," Antonio said, "and I shall sign for the sin."

Now they came to the hut of Julio Ontimaro. "Once more give me your back," Antonio said.

"My wife will say to me, 'Go, you are a bent old man,'" Valentino said.

He stooped and raised Antonio to the tightly screened window.

"Woc-woc!" cried Antonio. "Woc-woc!" He pressed his ear against the screen. "Listen, Valentino," he whispered. "Do you hear the noise?"

There was a whirring, grinding sound inside.

"Woc-woc!" Antonio cried. Then he stopped. "I think we have found a thief," he whispered. "He is grinding his stolen rice in the dark. Lower me, Valentino."

Valentino let him down, and they moved quietly to the bamboo ladder leading to the doorway. Antonio went up the ladder. Valentino stooped beneath the hut where he could hear the sound coming through the bamboo lattice floor.

Antonio rattled the door. It was unfastened. He pushed it slightly open. The sound of grinding continued. He took a match box from his pocket and struck a match. He held it inside the door. "Oy!" he said.

"Yes, I know," said Valentino. "It is no rice grinder."

Antonio came slowly down the ladder. "I have never heard such snoring," he said.

"I can smell the tuba from here," Valentino said. "He has drunk so much, a regiment of devils could not wake him."

"If you knew it was not a rice grinder, why did you not tell me?" Antonio demanded.

"I do not interfere in a witch's work," Valentino said with haughtiness.

When they came to the hut of Salvador Campos, Antonio said, "Well, then, this is the last time you must raise me. Perhaps you will cease weeping."

"It is no matter now," Valentino said. "I have become a carabao with a hump. I shall hire myself to farmers and drag the plow."

He stooped and hoisted Antonio to the window. "*Woc-woc!*" Antonio cried. "*Woc-woc!*" He grasped the corner of the overhanging roof, and pressed his mouth to the edge of the screen. "*Woc-woc!*"

"Who is it?" a sleepy voice groaned within.

"*Woc-woc!*" Antonio cried, striking his shoulder against the screen.

There was a sudden sound of ripping leaves. The corner of the roof moved in Antonio's hand. "Oy!" he cried, his body shifting away from the building. He grabbed for another hold on the edge of the roof. There was a rending and a thrashing, and Antonio came tumbling down, and the corner of the roof crumbled down upon him.

"Thieves! Thieves!" the voice cried inside the hut.

Valentino dragged his chief to his feet. "Run!" he shouted.

"Let us tell him—" Antonio began.

"Thieves! Go or I shall kill you!" the voice cried.

"Oy, let us run!" Valentino shouted. With one leap he was on the road, and his feet went pounding away into the darkness. Antonio tried to think of what to say to the occupants of the house. Then he heard a click as of a rifle bolt.

He heaved his fat body to the road and ran after Valentino.

"Thieves!" the voice cried after him. Then his ears were shattered by a great explosion. He kept running, not knowing whether he still had all his limbs, not knowing whether the wetness that clothed him was sweat or blood. He kept running miraculously until he came to the mud hole. There, in the darkness, he almost stumbled over the body of Valentino.

"Oy, Valentino, you are wounded!" he cried.

"No," said Valentino with a sour voice. "I am resting. And you, old fighting-cock, I see that you also are not hurt."

"Of that I do not know," Antonio said, gasping. "It is too dark to see."

The next day Antonio sat at his desk with all the records for his monthly report spread out before him. The number of policemen on duty. The number of arrests made. The number of crimes reported. The number of crimes solved. The number of illegal firearms confiscated. . . .

"Oy," said Antonio. "Here we shall have something to say. Valentino, we have discovered a case of illegal possession of firearms, have we not? Go to the home of Salvador Campos and confiscate the shotgun."

"Yes, sir," said Valentino. "But I think—" He took a sheaf of papers out of his desk and looked through them one by one. "Yes. Salvador Campos was given a permit to have a shotgun eight months ago."

"Oy!" said Antonio.

A little while later, Valentino exclaimed, "Oy, here comes the witch! But do not cross yourself, for you are his brother."

Vicente Honoria pushed his stooped body into the doorway and tapped the floor with his cane.

"Come, sit in this chair," Antonio said to the old man.

"I am ashamed that I must trouble you again," Vicente said.

"It is nothing," said Antonio.

Vicente sat down by Antonio's desk, and his smile ran away among his wrinkles. "What I must tell you is that I do not wish you to search for my rice because it has been returned to me."

"Oy!" said Antonio. "Valentino, hear what this old man has to tell us. You say that your rice—"

"Has been returned. I am ashamed that I troubled you yesterday."

"It is no trouble, old man. Some thief's heart troubled him and he returned your rice? Is that not so?"

"Oy," said Vicente, "it is a foolish thing. You will laugh at me if I tell it."

"No, no, old man," Antonio said. "Only tell it. Who was the thief?"

"Julio Ontimaro."

"Julio Ontimaro!" Antonio exclaimed.

"The one who slept," said Valentino.

"He heard my call even in his drunken sleep," Antonio said. "But speak, old man. How was it that he returned your rice?"

"It is in this way," Vicente said. "I go to his hut this morning and I say, 'Julio, return to me my sack of rice, or I shall tell the police you are a thief.' Julio becomes angry and he says, 'You are crazy, old man. Why do you say I have stolen your rice?' I take him outside and show him a trail of rice grains going to his door. I say to him, 'There is a hole in the sack of rice you take from my hut. This is the sign of your guilt.' Then Julio begins to weep, and he says, 'Do not tell the police. I shall return your sack of rice and another also.' 'No,' I say. 'Give me only what is mine.' And so he does, carrying the rice to my hut. Now I wish that you do not put him in prison, because he has returned my rice. I do not care about the fish."

Antonio put his hand on his thigh and sat up straight and stared at Vicente. "Old man," he said angrily, "why did you not tell me yesterday about the trail of rice grains?"

Vicente shook his head. "Oy, but it is not there yesterday. I place the rice along the road to Julio's hut in the darkness of this morning."

Valentino began to laugh.

Antonio struck his desk. "Be quiet, you foolish Filipino!" He turned again to Vicente. "You say you placed a trail of rice to Julio's hut? How, then, did you know that he was the thief? Tell me that, old man."

"At that time I do not know," Vicente said. "I place a trail of rice to the hut of Juanito Repulda and Salvador Campos also, and this morning I accuse each one, but Julio is the only one who returns my rice. That is how I know he is the thief."

When Vicente departed, Antonio picked up his pen and dipped it in the ink bottle.

"What are you going to write now?" Valentino said.

"A crime solved is a crime solved," said Antonio, "and will be so entered in the monthly report."

Notes

Notes